To my darling Z,
A bouquet of *forget-me-nots*,
white lilies and *violets*.
Yours, indefinitely.

The Unlikely Pursuit of Mary Bennet

LINDZ McLEOD

carina
press®

Recycling programs
for this product may
not exist in your area.

ISBN-13: 978-1-335-92826-9

The Unlikely Pursuit of Mary Bennet

Copyright © 2025 by Lindz McLeod

Carina Press
22 Adelaide St. West, 41st Floor
Toronto, Ontario M5H 4E3, Canada
www.Harlequin.com

Printed in U.S.A.

Acknowledgments

I must first thank my incredible agent, Laura Zats at Headwater Literary Management, who gave me the courage to fling myself wholeheartedly into romance—it must be difficult to be so constantly correct, but you bear this heavy burden with grace and fortitude.

I would also like to thank my fantastic editor at Harlequin, Stephanie Doig, for being the first one to fall in love with Charlotte and Mary, as well as the amazing team at Atom—especially Alice and Olivia—for getting so giddy with me about flowers.

To my friends who constantly begged for more chapters, as well as my social media acquaintances who shipped these silly, tender idiots from the start, thank you for being a ravenous horde eager for all the sapphic crumbs. Your enthusiasm has meant the absolute world to me.

And last—but never least—my wonderful fiancée, Z, who inspires the entire rosy spectrum of love every day. This book was (yet another) love letter to you, sweetheart. I may never understand why you're so suspicious of owls in plurality, but I promise never to be in cahoots with them.

Floriography—the language of flowers—was used to communicate secretly between friends or lovers in a time when society's oppressive nature did not allow certain desires to be discussed openly.

This bud of love, by summer's ripening breath,
May prove a beauteous flower when next we meet.
—William Shakespeare, *Romeo and Juliet* (1595), act 2, sc. 2, l. 118

Chapter One

After procuring several fervent assurances that his wife would apologize sincerely and deeply for his absence from Rosings that evening, Mr Collins reluctantly died.

Charlotte sat by the bed for a few minutes, watching his reddened cheeks grow ashen and pale in the light of dawn. He had been a decent husband, by all accounts—never knowingly unkind, ready to please and be pleased by everybody, and his loyalty never in question. All in all, her four-year marriage had been more pleasant than she had expected, and yet less satisfying than she had hoped. Her fingers pressed into the cover of the leather-bound Bible she'd been reading—Mr Collins' second-favourite, the first being a gift from Lady Catherine de Bourgh which never left his private study at the front of the house—leaving five temporary starbursts, then she leaned over and tucked it under his limp arm.

Swallowing down a lump in her throat, Charlotte rose and regarded the body with consternation. First, she would need to send Bessie to tell the undertaker, but then what ought she do? Though she was one-and-thirty, Charlotte's experience of managing death so far had been limited to Mr Collins' parishioners, since both her own parents were still alive and the rest of her relatives in good health. She owned a black dress, which she'd previously worn only to visit bereaved families with Mr Collins, but a single dress would not do. She would be required to mourn in black for a year and a half before she could wear even the slightest hint of colour, and even then she would be limited to dull purples and greys. She considered her range of dresses, none of which she was particularly attached to apart from a lovely blue silk which her mother had presented to her as a special post-wedding gift. Dyeing two dresses would surely be enough.

No, two would not do—Lady Catherine would expect Charlotte to present in a particular way at Rosings, and would not be slow to chide her inferior if she saw any reason to do so. Charlotte's fingers twitched into fists upon the realisation that even the very smallest of comforts was to be denied her. The blue silk would have to be dyed too. Mr Collins had always paid her an especial compliment when she'd worn it, though the scant pleasure of his attentions in that respect had usually been accompanied by the pain of knowing that she would be expected to join him later in the marital bed.

The maid and the cook were hovering anxiously in the dim hallway outside the door when Charlotte emerged. "Bessie," she said to the maid, "pray run down to the village with several of my dresses and ask them to dye them black. Take the blue silk, as well as any two others. I must have something decent to mourn in."

"Oh, ma'am," Bessie said, her lip wobbling. "I am dreadful sorry. I'd hope he would soon regain—"

"You'll need to tell the undertaker too," Charlotte interrupted. A great wave of aching hollowness threatened to overcome her. There was so much to be done, and focusing on the tasks ahead made her feel steadier. "Have his woman come at the earliest opportunity to help us wash Mr Collins and lay him out. And Mrs Waites, would you please fetch me a pair of scissors and a locket? There ought to be one in a drawer in my room."

They did as they were bid, Bessie disappearing out of the back door with a clatter, and the cook vanishing into the kitchen. Charlotte stepped back into the room and closed the door. The room, which had seemed so normal to her in the many hours she'd sat there tending to her dying husband, now smelled unbearably stale. She crossed to the window and flung it open. Then, thinking of Bessie's return and how it might look, pulled it demurely half closed. A cool breeze crept in, making her shiver, bringing with it the scent of the garden. *Nothing like the smell of wet roses*, her husband had used to say, though he'd never cared much for any of the other flowers beyond the ability to show them off at length to visitors. It must have rained in the night, though she scarcely remembered anything but Mr Collins' wheezing, labored breaths, his muttered prayers, and her own helpless anxiety. Perhaps she should have opened a window before, and let the smell of wet roses guide him into the arms of God.

The cook returned in short order with both items and, after muttering some further words of consolation, left Charlotte alone. Bending over the body, she cut a small lock of dark hair—the curl that had forever hovered over Mr Collins' left ear and which impishly grew back no matter how she had trimmed it—and placed it in the locket. The pendant seemed much heavier than it had previously, the metal harshly cold against her palm, so she slipped it back into the drawer instead of putting it on. Making her way along the corridor, she knelt and rummaged amongst the cabinets in the dining room, finally finding a box of black china, which had come with the house for just such a purpose and which she'd never had occasion to use before. She unpacked the crockery quickly, laying it out on the dining room table. It was a little dusty, despite its box, but Mrs Waites would take care of such things. Charlotte picked up a plate from the usual set which adorned the dining table—a rather ugly, silver-edged set which Lady Catherine had purchased as a wedding gift without consulting either bride or groom on their preferences—and began to pack it away, the ache in her chest growing. Even the very crockery must mourn Mr Collins' departure.

Finding herself exhausted after her night's vigil, Charlotte retired to a small chamber at the back of the house, which had been her preferred abode except for those nights where her husband had been sick or had requested the pleasure of her company with an ardor which had never outgrown an original awkwardness. Despite these not infrequent requests, her marriage had not been blessed with children, so at least there were no young hearts to break with the news.

Wrapping a grey shawl around her shoulders, Charlotte sat down at an old-fashioned oak desk which had once belonged to the great estate at Rosings, and which Lady Catherine had seen fit to bequeath unto them. Mr Collins' parents were long dead and he had no relations she knew well bar the Bennets. Picking up her quill, she began a quick letter to Longbourne to inform them of the sad occasion, but halted, a sudden realisation sending a shiver down her spine; with Mr Collins dead, another distant male relative of the Bennets would now inherit the Longbourne estate. The future she and Mr Collins had imagined together—and all the financial security that came with it—had been snuffed out the moment her husband had ceased to draw breath.

Pale sunshine crept into the room, as if anxious not to disturb her, though the air grew no warmer. After she had finished her first letter, she took a fresh piece of paper and, with a less-steady hand than before, wrote:

Dearest Lizzie,
Mr Collins passed away last night after a short illness. I am
thankful to report that he did not suffer much. I know that your

son is still young, but I miss you terribly and it is so quiet here.
I wondered if you might visit, if only for a short time.

For the first time, tears blurred her vision, threatening to spill onto the page. Charlotte added a few words and signed her name, hoping this would do. Though she longed to see Lizzie, in truth she would have even welcomed Mrs Bennet's absurd dramatics at such a time. She had few friends, and those she did have were scattered widely over England. Her parents were miles away in Hertfordshire, her aunt comfortably settled in London. Loneliness made her chest ache, and she cried a little, feeling guilty that her thoughts were all for herself rather than poor Mr Collins.

Overnight, her situation had become precarious. In all truthfulness, it was now barely more or less so than before she married. Lady Catherine would surely wish to install a new parson as soon as possible, and the man would expect the post to come furnished with the parsonage; a home she had adored for the last four years. Charlotte would have to return to her parents' home, Lucas Lodge, and either content herself with widowhood or be continuously on the prowl for a new match. She dabbed at her cheeks with a handkerchief and picked up a new piece of parchment. This third and final note she wrote to Lady Catherine to inform her of the sad news.

Charlotte left the addressed letters on the small table in the hallway near the front door. The maid would collect them upon her return, but for the moment Charlotte could do no more. She slept fitfully in the back room for an hour or so, dreaming of nothing, until the maid shook her awake with a cup of tea. "Did you deliver the message to Rosings?" she murmured. Mr Collins would have been proud of her attention to her proper duty, though had he been present at the writing of the letters, he probably would have insisted on Lady Catherine being rightfully first.

"Yes ma'am." Bessie's pale blue eyes were ringed with red. "They're all very sorry for you, ma'am, and Lady Catherine desires that you visit as soon as possible. Oh, and the under- taker says he'll send his woman to you this afternoon. Would you like Mrs Waites to make you a plate?"

Charlotte couldn't face eating at that moment. Instead, she fell into another sleep and this time a dream, whereupon her legs were bound fast with tangled, knotted vines as thick as men's fingers. When she cried out in alarm, strange flowers burst from the ground and grew teeth, sinking their fangs into the vines winding around her legs and nibbling her free.

Charlotte ate alone, staring down the table at the empty chair which had been Mr Collins' particular favourite. She had not been back into the room which held the body since cutting the lock of his hair. She picked up another piece of toast and buttered it liberally, then cracked the top off a soft-boiled egg, spooning the soft yolk into her mouth without really tasting it. She might not have much appetite, but she would need her strength for what was next; a visit to Rosings. A March breeze, sharp but not cruel, rustled the leaves in the trees overhanging the road, allowing them neither peace nor quiet. Wearing her sole black dress—and hoping that the others were being dyed promptly in the village—Charlotte ventured on foot to Ros- ings around eleven on the clock, where Lady Catherine of- fered blunt condolences over tea, fruitcake, and lemon biscuits.

The great lady held court in her favoured sunroom. It was a palatial space only sparsely furnished compared to the rest of the house, yet the sum of the furniture was worth several times Mr Collins' annual income. The sideboard here had come from India, and Charlotte had heard the story of its voyage so many times she could recite it from memory. The fire was lit in the grate and burned away merrily, though the room was so large that Charlotte did not feel the comfort of its heat at all. Lady

Catherine sat in a high, straight-backed blue chair with gilded edges, which always reminded Charlotte of a throne illustrated in one of her childhood fairy tales, and stared sternly out of the window as the servants withdrew.

In contrast her daughter, Anne, the heiress of Rosings, offered Charlotte a warm, compassionate smile, though she looked pale and wan as ever. The spring-green gown she wore did not help matters, but Charlotte knew Anne well enough to distinguish between one of her mild headaches and the first rumbles of a week-long retreat into her sickbed. Such frailty might have put many men off their marriage suits, though when such a large estate was in question, many still would overlook it. Charlotte had often wondered why Anne did not have more suitors, though it would benefit her not to marry at all since any husband would take full control of her entire fortune. Anne had never expressed any particular disappointment over not marrying her cousin, Mr Darcy, and besides, she surely knew that any suitor she had would have to undergo a rigorous and unending series of interrogations from her formidable mother, an action no one with a heart would knowingly inflict on someone they purported to love.

"It would have honoured Mr Collins very much to know that his great benefactress could spare the time to attend his burial," Charlotte said, desirous of getting the request out of the way quickly. Lady Catherine did not like to feel fooled in any respect, whether intentional or not. "I realise the request may be a little unorthodox, since women do not usually...but then again you are no ordinary woman, and my husband thought so very highly of you." Archimedes might have claimed a lever could move anything on earth, but flattery could be applied to the same place for the same result and required less machinery besides.

"As well he might," Lady Catherine said, before catching her daughter's eye and sighing openly. "Yes, I will attend. I am due in London the week after next, and then in Rome, but I…" She frowned down at her half-empty teacup. "I will grant that Mr Collins was a good man. Always so attentive. If only more were like him, the world would be a better place." She gestured to Charlotte to take more fruitcake, which she did obediently. It really was very good.

"Indeed," Anne piped up, her eyes bright with sympathy. She resembled Lady Catherine in some ways—the arch of her brow, the jut of her chin—but she had not her mother's bullish temperament. Had not Lady Catherine been present on most occasions they'd met, Charlotte suspected she and Anne might have been rather good friends. "A very sweet man. You must miss him dreadfully."

Charlotte nodded gravely. *Do I miss him?* she wondered. *Certainly the house is quiet without him, and I am sorry that he died. Perhaps the shock of the loss has affected me more than I—*

"I am to be away for at least four months, and Anne will be lonely," Lady Catherine added, interrupting her thoughts. "You must come to tea twice a week at least and keep each other company. Anne simply cannot abide being lonely."

Anne raised her eyebrow at this declaration of feelings she had neither shared nor claimed, though she did not dare contradict her mother outright. Despite herself, Charlotte had to bite back a smile. "I am sure she will miss you a great deal."

"Of course she will." Lady Catherine sniffed, and sipped her tea again. She patted her high nest of white hair, before touching the necklace of emeralds which matched her dress perfectly. "I myself understand only too well what it is to lose a husband. It does rather try one's patience, does it not, Mrs Collins?"

Oh, Charlotte thought with some surprise, her amusement fading. *I am still Mrs Collins.* The idea of being referred to as such for the rest of her life made her stomach sink. He had left his mark in every way, and she could never escape it.

"As such, I am willing to put off arranging a new parson until my return," Lady Catherine said, reaching for another biscuit, and not waiting for Charlotte to answer her prior question. "There will be several clergymen passing through in order to attend some lecture or other in London, and they will take on such duties as they can in the meantime." She paused, staring down at Charlotte with sharp eyes. "You are a sensible woman, Mrs Collins. I dare say you will take stock of your situation by the time I return."

She means marry or leave, or ideally both, Charlotte thought. *It took me years to land one husband. How can I possibly find another in such a short space of time?* There was nothing for it; she would have to move home to her parents and likely die a spinster. After four years of marriage, she would end up right back where she'd started—a burden on her parents. Though none of this had been her fault, and knowing she could not be blamed for any of it, Charlotte nevertheless felt the sharp sting of humiliation amidst the dull ache of grief. She picked up her cup and downed the still-scalding tea, focusing on the pain of it to stop from dissolving into tears in the middle of the handsome Rosings sunroom. "Of course, Lady Catherine. I shall do my very best."

"Mother, please," Anne pleaded. "The poor man only died this morning. It is far too soon for Charlotte to have to consider such—"

"Every day dawns afresh," Lady Catherine said calmly, and reached for yet another lemon biscuit.

Chapter Two

On returning to the parsonage, Charlotte waved away Mrs Waites' offer of more tea—she was already full enough to feel queasy—and sat for a time in her parlor, staring out of the window. Thick, fluffy white clouds scudded over the sky as if late for a ball. Bessie had said the undertaker's woman was due to come this afternoon to help them prepare Mr Collins for laying out, though she had not specified a time. The clock on the mantel struck twelve, then one, and still no sign of any visitor emerged.

Sighing, Charlotte got up and paced the room, unable to remain still for too long. The room, though mainly her domain, was full of memories which crowded into her mind unbidden. On Lizzie's first visit to Hunsford, not long after Charlotte and Mr Collins had first been married, Mr Collins had taken care to show off every article of furniture in the house to their guest. Every angle and aspect of the doors and windows had been commented on and praised to the highest degree, and their guest invited to offer her own compliments. Charlotte had been able to tell from Lizzie's fixed expression that her friend did not quite know what to make of this performance—that Lizzie perhaps even thought the act put on to spite her, since she had first turned Mr Collins down and had therefore rejected the possession of all that she now beheld.

Charlotte, however, had known her husband too well to suspect anything of the sort. He had been a very predictable man, not prone to sudden outbursts of temper or sullenness and his vanity, whilst conspicuous, was limited to his surroundings and not his own person. He had not been arrogant as some men were, nor vain about his looks. He simply took pride in their parsonage and in his situation, and could not imagine that anyone might do otherwise; a rather endearing flaw that Charlotte had identified from the first, and had known she could tolerate quite easily for the next few decades.

The memory of Lizzie's countenance—her playful smile, rather than the pitying expression she'd sometimes worn when she thought no one could not see—warmed Charlotte's heart. Lizzie would soon receive her letter and would surely visit, at least for a week or two, and would offer good counsel. Marriage had softened Mrs Darcy's tongue, though never her wits, and motherhood seemed to agree with her though she had once or twice complained about sleepless, colicky nights. On the rare occasions she had visited over the last few years, Charlotte had found it harder and harder to part from her friend. The silly old girlhood tenderness came back in full force each time she saw Lizzie's smile and smelt her familiar perfume.

Charlotte paused in the doorway of her small parlor. Though this room faced onto the back of the house with only a limited view of the garden, here she'd spent many happy days in solitary contentment, reading and sewing and creating floral arrangements. It contained two comfortable green armchairs and a brown couch which could seat three comfortably, a side table which had once decorated the smallest breakfast parlor at Rosings and was in truth far too big and ornate for the room, and an infrequently used pianoforte. Though a set of shelves inhabited one corner of the room, there were fewer books than she would have liked, divided by bright pink and purple geraniums in small, equally colourful pots. Beside the shelves, a large parlor palm sat in a pot on the floor, offering the room a much-needed splash of green. A visiting foreign dignitary had brought it to Lady Catherine a year ago, proclaiming the plant's symbolic meaning as a bringer of good fortune. Lady Catherine, apparently secure in her fortune, had gifted it to Charlotte on the Collinses' next visit, complaining that the plant did not look neat enough for her rooms. Charlotte had gratefully accepted, but couldn't help feeling sorry for all the Rosings plants, who had been excessively pruned and were never allowed to grow according to their own desires.

Instead of entering the parlor, Charlotte sidled back down the hallway to Mr Collins' preferred room at the front of the house, which overlooked the road, and pushed the door open before really thinking about what she was doing. For a moment she had expected to see her husband sitting there at the desk, surrounded by many papers, a cup of now-cold tea beside him. With a jolt, she realised the room was empty, and that its previous occupant would never again pace back and forth, ruminating out loud. He would never sigh, or laugh, or read a favoured passage from the Bible.

He would never let another cup of tea go cold.

Charlotte pressed a hand to her mouth. The finality of the moment shocked her. One day he had been there, and the next, gone. She would pass too, in time, as would everyone she knew and loved. What a strange experience, to be alive. *And yet*, said a mean little voice at the back of her mind, *could you even have argued yourself to be so alive in the first place? You have achieved nothing of note. He may have only been a simple parson but at least he pursued his vocation and interests with great eagerness.*

Charlotte frowned, her eyes falling upon the shelves which lined one wall of Mr Collins' room. Most of these were religious texts or lectures, but several were books of science which had been gifted by visitors. A passing scientist had once explained Archimedes' lever to her, which seemed sensible enough, and then followed it up with some story about a crown which she had not quite understood so well. She cast a look of longing at the books. It was not considered appropriate for a woman of her class to desire any vocation beyond being a wife, though she had often yearned to understand even a little of the great rules and laws which governed the world. However, Mr Collins had politely but firmly steered her away from such things. Now, she hesitated on the threshold of the room. Mr Collins would never know. Even so—

Bessie's voice called along the hallway, making her jump. "The undertaker's woman is here, ma'am."

"A moment, please." Charlotte smoothed her skirts down and hustled towards the kitchen, where a thin woman waited, empty-handed, flanked on either side by the maid and the cook. "Mrs Waites, please make a pot of tea. Would, um—" she stumbled uncertainly, realising she had no idea what the visitor's name was, "would you like some tea?"

"No, thank you, Mrs Collins. I've got several more people to lay out today." The woman's cheeks were reddened by the cold, and she was clad in a dark brown dress that had seen far better days. A thick brown shawl hung over her arm. "A nasty sickness over in the village," she added.

"Oh, how dreadful." The fact did not make her feel connected with the world at large. Instead, she only felt more isolated, and aware that without Mr Collins to keep her abreast of the goings-on of the parish, she was quite at a loss to know who went where.

Mrs Waites held out her hands. "I can take your shawl, Mrs Peasley. I'll keep it warm by the fire until you're done."

Charlotte cast a grateful eye at the cook, who responded by grinning behind Mrs Peasley's back. Mrs Waites, with her cloud of grey hair and her permanently affixed white apron, had come with the house and was as much a fixture of it as any of the furniture or garden paths. Charlotte would be sorry to leave Mrs Waites' cooking behind when she left; the woman could do things to a chicken that stopped only just short of witchcraft. The cook would fare well with any reasonable parson, particularly one who enjoyed his meals—and she had never met one who did not—and Bessie was a good girl who performed her duties in a timely manner. Charlotte needn't worry about their futures, for their positions were more fixed than her own.

That afternoon, Mrs Peasley and Bessie helped Charlotte to wash Mr Collins' body before they wrapped it in a wool shroud. The act took longer than Charlotte had imagined, and was conducted in a hushed silence. Bessie, pale-faced and wide-eyed, was clearly as new at this as Charlotte was, but Mrs Peasely directed them deftly, and was much stronger than she looked. By the time they'd finished, the undertaker's boys had arrived, carrying a temporary wooden casket, and helped them move the body into it. Word got around quickly, and before the afternoon was out, several parishioners had already come to pay their respects.

Once the house was empty again, Charlotte sat down to write yet more letters, including one to her parents, informing them of the sad news and reassuring them that she was well. *Please do not trouble yourselves to visit me here*, she wrote, *for I will see you soon enough.* They would understand what she meant, and would be kind enough to welcome her back without fuss. Not everyone had such an easy family. Afterwards, Charlotte ate dinner, though she was too exhausted to manage more than half a plateful of Mrs Waites' excellent ham with buttered peas, and retired to bed early to dutifully read a few Bible passages by candlelight.

The following days passed in a blur, with more parishioners turning up to share stories and pay respects. Mr Collins was buried hurriedly on a Wednesday when a passing clergyman acquiesced to give a liturgy the dead man would no doubt have found lacking. Worse, the clergyman mispronounced the dead man's name several times as "Mr Colin", causing Lady Catherine to glower so ominously that the clergyman stuttered over far more of the ending than he had of the beginning. As the mourners dispersed, Charlotte laid a bouquet of hand-picked flowers on the grave. She'd taken particular care over this, and had chosen dark crimson roses on a bed of green foliage, with strands of ivy woven in; flowers of mourning, interspersed with the symbol of wedded love.

Gardening had been one of Mr Collins' particular passions when they'd first married, but as Charlotte's skills surpassed his own, he had soon allowed her entire control of it. Visitors often exclaimed over the beautiful rosebushes, the unusual quantity of bright blooms and startling pinks and oranges amongst the geranium beds, and even the shrubbery, where the Collinses could boast of having American flowering trees like the Carolina silverbell—Lady Catherine had been generous enough to gift them two, after deciding the layout her own gardener had planned was too crowded. A low fence separated the parsonage garden from the lane, where the occasional carriage rumbled past, and Rosings could be viewed directly through a gap in the trees. Indeed, Mr Collins had spent many a happy hour simply standing in this spot on the path, gazing out at the handsome building where his benefactress lived.

Her late husband, Charlotte suspected, had only really enjoyed the garden insofar as it afforded him the opportunity to entertain visitors and point out the proximity of Rosings. While he had enjoyed the sight and smell of the flowers—and always could be relied upon to remark on the industriousness of the honeybee, as well as the flowers themselves in bloom under the light of God's sun—as his parish grew, he had neither the time nor the patience to spend hours in the garden. Likewise, he had never been interested at all in the meanings of flowers, a subject which had interested his wife very much. Invariably he got them wrong—comically so—and on more than one occasion Charlotte had to repress laughter upon receiving a badly-tied bouquet. His last attempt, given on their most recent anniversary, had consisted of milkweed and geraniums, which represented indifference and folly respectively. He had meant well, she reflected, and did that not count for a great deal? Many men would not have bothered to give flowers at all, had they even remembered such gestures were possible. Still, the attempts had always left her feeling amused, embarrassed, and a little strange.

That morning, Mrs Waites informed her that the local butcher had died, and his three grown sons were now squabbling over the rightful inheritance of the business. Charlotte simply nodded, though she privately thought that Lady Catherine would not consider it below her station to swoop in and arrange the outcome to her satisfaction. In the event that she had already departed for London, perhaps Anne would take charge in the meantime, though she did not have her mother's desire to get involved in every little aspect of village life. As if hearing her thoughts, a messenger arrived from Rosings, inviting Charlotte to tea with Anne that very afternoon.

Without her overbearing mother present, Anne de Bourgh was a much livelier soul. She pressed Charlotte to take more scones, more fresh strawberry jam, and could hardly bear if Charlotte's cup were half empty for more than a moment. "It is such a shame," said she, "that we did not become more acquainted during your time here. Is there no way you could stay?"

"I have little choice in the matter, I'm afraid. Without Mr Collins, I have no real ties to the area. I must return to my parents."

"I am sure they will be very happy to see you, of course." Anne picked up her cup, then set it back down again. "There are so few women around here with whom I have had any real friendship. I do not care for balls, as you know, for they trouble my head so." She picked up her cup again. "If you were to find a husband, as my mother suggests, would that not solve all your problems?"

Charlotte almost choked on a scone. Anne may have seemed quiet and sickly in Lady Catherine's shadow, but she had certainly inherited her mother's forthrightness. "I confess I—" She hesitated, hardly knowing what to say. "I do not know who might introduce me to such a man as may want me."

"Why, I could do so! I know many suitable gentlemen. And you are so kind, so amiable, my dear Mrs Collins, that I cannot think of a single man of my acquaintance who would not be delighted to have your company."

It was on the tip of Charlotte's tongue to say no, to declare herself in mourning for life. Yet she hesitated. That answer could be given, but perhaps it would close a door through which a handsome stranger might otherwise have stepped. There could be no harm in allowing Anne to introduce her to one or two men, though it wasn't as if they were likely to be interested in her in return, and the whole situation might very quickly become humiliating. Still, she could not very well turn down an offer of help from the heiress of Rosings. Not directly, anyway. "Very well," she said, forcing a smile. "Though I beg you not to go to any trouble for me."

"Nonsense," Anne declared. "I shall find you the perfect man, and you shall stay right here in Kent." She sat back and with a look very reminiscent of a satisfied cat, gestured imperiously for more tea.

Chapter Three

My dearest friend,
I cannot say how sorry I am to hear this news. My own heart breaks to think of you suffering. How I wish I were there to comfort you in some small way.

Unfortunately, my son has taken ill. We do not think it very serious, but Darcy is hesitant to travel given his condition and I am loath to leave either behind to come alone. Therefore I invite you to Pemberley for as long as you please, though I fully understand if you wish to remain home to mourn.

The next portion of the letter looked like it had been written in a different ink, as if added as a hasty afterthought. *I wonder if you might consider inviting my sister Mary to stay? She is on her way to Meryton from Canterbury, where she lives with one of our aunts, and will no doubt pass through Kent.*

Here, Lizzie had written something and then scratched it out. If Charlotte had to guess, it was probably something uncharitable that her dear friend had pronounced impetuously and then thought better of it. It was nice to see that some things did not change. She smiled, despite the yawn of disappointment widening in her chest. Mary had been the sister she knew least, and from what she remembered, the middle Bennet had been an awkward, plain girl who played the pianoforte well but often could not be induced to stop. The more Charlotte thought about Mary, the more she built up a picture in her mind. Had not Mary been the most devout of that family, always preaching something or other in the background? The thought of having someone around who might be entreated to ramble piously at length struck Charlotte as a strange kind of succour she was unlikely to get anywhere else.

A female companion would be a deep comfort, she decided, and wrote back to Lizzie to say as much.

The carriage arrived in the late afternoon, and the young woman who emerged, waving away the driver's help to descend into the road, was somehow not at all as Charlotte remembered and yet quite the same; once a solemn girl of nineteen or so, Mary was now a cheerful woman of four-and-twenty. Unlike Lizzie, who was all softness—a perfect English rose in full flower, Charlotte had often thought—the younger Bennet possessed a thinner nose and a wider mouth, though the sisters shared the same fine, dark eyes. Mary offered her condolences immediately, embracing Charlotte as though they had been much closer friends in their youth. Grey clouds had been massing all morning, and Charlotte's welcome was cut short as they both hurried inside to escape the first fat drops of rain. It wasn't long until it turned into a veritable torrent, and Charlotte found herself distracted thinking of her poor flowers, and hoping they survived the deluge. She couldn't very well abandon her newly-arrived guest merely to defend the garden from the opening of the heavens; Mary would think her quite mad.

Charlotte studied her guest's profile while she removed her travelling cloak, revealing a pretty, though sober, green dress which brought out the tiny golden flecks in her brown eyes. Lizzie had never had such flecks, Charlotte was certain, and she could not stop a blush at the memory of staring into Lizzie's eyes as her friend talked with lively animation. Leading Mary down the hallway to a guest room at the back of the parsonage, separate from her own only by a single wall, Charlotte fought the urge to wring her hands. The bed was decent, though the iron-wrought frame was really too big for the room, and the writing desk was weathered and creaky. The walls were painted a dull yellow, like the petals of a buttercup on a gloomy day such as today. At least it was clean. She had never worried so much about the comfort of Mr Collins' visitors, but she supposed her concern was simply borne of the fact that she had not had visitors of her own for a long time. "It is not much, but I hope it will do," she said, wondering what the younger Bennet had grown accustomed to now that she was out of her parents' house.

"Oh, this will be perfectly suited to my needs," Mary declared, while Bessie dragged in the first of her suitcases. "Do not trouble yourself," she directed at the maid, "I will fetch the other myself."

The maid gaped for a moment before closing her mouth with an audible snap. "Yes, ma'am." Her eyes flicked to Charlotte, who gave a half shrug. If her guest wanted to carry her own luggage, who was she to judge?

"Thank you, Bessie. Please tell Mrs Waites that we'd like tea first, and dinner shortly afterwards." The maid disappeared, and Mary followed her into the hall, only to return a moment later with a bulging suitcase. It must be full of dresses, Charlotte thought, suddenly a touch envious. London was the height of fashion, and Mary no doubt attended many balls and met many interesting people. "Do take a moment to get yourself settled," she offered. "My parlor is just down the hall on your left."

She left her guest for a moment and retreated into her parlor, which had been tidied and thoroughly cleaned just the day before. The rain battered against the windows, the wind groaning like a sick man, but the fire had been built up beautifully and the flames crackled with a warm, welcoming glow. Looking around at the parlor, Charlotte could not help compare it to those few London houses she had visited with Mr Collins on their extremely infrequent excursions to the city, and found it lacking in elegance. She wrung her hands, wondering what could possibly be done now to improve the place, and was only interrupted in her spiral of uncertainty by the entrance of her guest. "How cosy," Mary said, without the slightest hint of insincerity. "As much as I adore being outdoors, I do so love a rainy day and a warm fire, do you not?"

"I do," Charlotte agreed, her anxiety fading a little.

Mr Collins would have immediately launched into some long ramble about the angle of the room's walls, or the particular situation of the windows, but she did not wish to repeat his words. Instead, she stayed silent and watched Mary move around the room, exclaiming over the mantel—it was truly a pretty one—and the small collection of potted flowers on the shelves. "Why, these are beautiful," Mary said, cocking her head and leaning closer to sniff some of the geraniums. "And this?" Her fingers brushed the fronds of the parlor palm which sat in the corner. "It has grown so tall. I've rarely seen one this high. Why, it is almost to my shoulder."

Flattered, Charlotte blushed. "I confess I do like to garden."

"Really? Lizzie did not mention any such thing. Though I supposed it was not foremost on her mind when she wrote me. I myself am—" She hesitated, as Bessie appeared carrying a tea tray, and the next couple of minutes were taken up with settling themselves into the two armchairs which sat opposite each other nearest the fire, and taking tea.

Charlotte encouraged Mary to try a lemon biscuit, which were Mrs Waites' particular recipe, encouragement that her guest needed very little of to indulge. Though she was curious as to what Mary had been about to say earlier, Charlotte could not think of a polite way to recall the conversation, and was casting about for a similar topic when Mary spoke.

"Have you lately spoken to my sister?" Mary inquired. "I confess I do not write her as much as I ought to."

"Yes, Lizzie and I correspond frequently." Charlotte smiled. "She offered to visit, of course, after she heard the news, but I would not tear her away from Pemberley, and her son is far too young to make such a long trip in any case, even if he were not ill." A twinge, deep in her chest, reminded her that she was not telling the entire truth. "I really am very grateful that you came. You were in Canterbury, I believe?"

"Indeed. We have a distant aunt with whom I have been staying for almost three years, though I confess she is so rarely there that it quite feels as if I am mistress of the house myself. I am often in London too, though I find the society there rather stifling." A flash of discomfort crossed Mary's face, though it was gone so soon that Charlotte thought she might have imagined it. "In Canterbury, one may move around a little more freely, though it is still a very constrained freedom compared to America, from what I have heard."

"To which balls did you lately attend?" Charlotte asked, remembering the bulging suitcases.

"Oh, none which would please my family, I am certain."

She blinked, unsure what to say to that. "Oh, I—"

"I do not care for the kind of balls that Lydia and Kitty once wept over," Mary continued, picking up another biscuit. "I prefer to attend lectures and the occasional salon for those interested in the natural world. Botany is a particular passion of mine." She chewed, thoughtfully, eyeing Charlotte over her teacup. "Though I prefer to see a flower in full bloom, shivering in the breeze, rather than pressed lifelessly into a book."

"I see." Charlotte was not quite sure how to take this remark. Certainly the parlor held potted plants, which Mary had praised, but her own attempts at flower-drying were sitting on the side table in full view. "I suppose while I think it best that flowers are as God intended, growing outside, that it is also nice to preserve some for...for..." She indicated the side table. "Those are for my mother when I see her next."

"Your parents are coming to visit?"

"No, no. I will have to return to Lucas Lodge. The parsonage was Mr Collins', and without him, I am at best a burdensome lodger. I must quit the place before the next parson is appointed, for no one will want to take up the post without all the benefits it entails."

"That is indeed a shame," Mary said, and seemed on the verge of adding more when Bessie announced that dinner would be served shortly.

They made their way to the dining room. Charlotte seated herself without thinking, then froze. The seat opposite hers was the head of the table, where Mr Collins had always sat. It would be strange to see another in his place, though she was quickly reconciling herself to the fact when, instead of seating herself in the most obvious place, Mary selected the chair on Charlotte's right, close enough for their knees to touch. Mrs Waites brought out a dinner of fish in a creamy sauce, accompanied by potatoes and carrots liberally brushed with butter and dill. The smell made Charlotte's stomach rumble. She offered her guest red wine, which was gladly accepted, and Mrs Waites poured two glasses for them. That was another thing which was different now—Mr Collins had only ever drunk a small sherry on special occasions and could not be induced to try anything else. She had rather missed sharing a bottle of wine with someone; it was less about the taste of the wine itself than the experience, the equality of it, the discussion of vintage and year and associated memories which might result therein.

The moment Mrs Waites left the room, Mary leaned closer. "I do think it a shame that you are being forced out, though I understand the reasoning. Women are so often boats buffeted by the tides of men, are they not? With no oars to paddle ourselves."

Charlotte had expected to receive some pious, lengthy lecturing on morality at best, philosophical rambling at worst, and found herself a little peeved that neither was the case. "Once upon a time, you would have quoted me a Bible verse about moving aside to make room for others. I did not expect you to have matured so."

"And I expected to find you a weeping widow," Mary retorted. "Yet here we are, both rather surprised."

Flushing, Charlotte stared down at her plate. Humiliation trickled through her chest. *You've barely cried for him*, the cruel little voice inside reminded her. *Was your husband so undeserving of your tears? Are you so cold and bad-mannered as all that?* "I'm sorry." She cleared her throat. "I did not mean to offend you."

Mary, however, merely threw back her head and laughed. "Dear Charlotte, were you always so serious? While I recall your tempering influence on Lizzie, I did think you possessed a little more good humour."

Charlotte forced a smile. Humour had been in short supply in the Collins household. God, Mr Collins had always claimed, did not have a sense of humour. Charlotte had privately thought if that were so, perhaps God had not yet seen her husband without clothes on.

"I apologize for my callousness. I have been too merry when you are so lately—" Mary pressed her lips together, looking ashamed. "Perhaps your grief is too great and private to be on display to a relative stranger."

"I do not think you a stranger. Though I admit we were never friends."

Mary picked up her fork and speared a potato. "Upon consideration, that does not surprise me. I have not the exuberance of Lydia, nor Jane's easy ways. I believe I used to be rather vain, too. No, do not mistake me," she corrected, seeing Charlotte's surprised expression, "for I was certainly never the beauty of the family. In fact, if you had asked my mother to rank the looks of all five of her daughters, I believe I would have come sixth."

Despite herself, Charlotte snorted, and was immediately mortified at the undignified sound.

"I seek knowledge as much as I ever did," her guest continued, "but as a child I rather thought understanding would come from the accumulation of facts and figures. As an adult, one discovers the more you know, the less you know."

"Yes," Charlotte agreed. "One's self is often a mystery, is it not?" She should be weeping still at the mention of grief. She should feel something akin to agony; her husband was only recently dead, after all. *Is there something wrong with me?* she wondered, and not for the first time.

After dinner, they moved back into the parlor. "I have been admiring your pianoforte," Mary offered, glancing at the instrument in question.

"A wedding gift from Lady Catherine. My husband liked to hear me play sometimes." Charlotte hesitated. "You used to play very well, I recall."

"I play, but I do not know if I would call it well." Still, she sat at the piano, playing competently but mechanically. Her left hand bore an ink-stain, smudged up to her wrist, which Charlotte could not help noticing. Halfway through a third song Mary stopped, fingers hovering above the keys, and began to play something quite different. A soft, haunting melody—a lover's song, Charlotte thought, puzzled. "Which piece is that?"

"Oh, some small thing I composed. It is nothing, really. I cannot make sense of it."

"May I?" Charlotte gestured at the bench. Mary moved over to make space, though not much. The faint, distracting scent of violets drifted through the air. She played the melody back but drew out a note here and there, shortening another, until it sounded less like a stuttering stream and more like a great river flowing. "There, perhaps? Though I do not presume to change your—"

"How did you do that?" Mary's gaze followed her fingers, like a hawk hunting five vulnerable mice.

"My teacher once told me that music ought to be thought of as a conversation. See how the melody," she played it again with her right hand, and reached over to play a couple of lower chords as accompaniment, "works alongside the rhythm. To and fro. Not a battle but a parley."

"Well," Mary said, hands folded in her lap. "There is my problem, then, since I find conversations more like battles than truces." She smiled without humour. "My opinions on philosophy, politics, and the sciences are many and varied. They make me quite unsuitable for marriage in the usual circles."

And the unusual circles? Charlotte's hands stilled on the keys. "I thought he might have chosen you, once upon a time."

Silence. No need to clarify who *he* was.

"I rather thought he might have, too," Mary mused, shifting in her seat. Her knee touched Charlotte's, though she made no attempt to move away. "Though I'm very glad he did not, in the end."

"Why?"

She blinked, evidently puzzled by the question. "Well… Did not you love him?" Charlotte stiffened. Mary stammered, a faint blush rising in her cheeks. "That is to say, I had believed you to be—"

She sighed. If it were Lizzie, she might have made a rebuking remark about practicalities. If it had been another friend she might have simply smiled and nodded, yet there was something about Mary's blunt air which compelled her to be honest. "I suppose I loved him in my way," she murmured, "and he loved me in his. You must understand, not all marriages can be like Jane and Bingley, or Lizzie and Darcy. Most are just…" She searched for a charitable word. "Companionship at best. It is sensible to hope for as much, lest worse happen." The room had grown dim by now; she should light another candle lest her guest think her unwelcoming. The heat of Mary's leg, now pressed against her own, felt as if it were scalding her.

"Did you never feel passion towards a suitor?" Mary questioned.

Ugly shame curled in her stomach, forcing her up and out of the seat. "Never towards a suitor. Not that I had any." *Though your sister was quite another matter.* The wicked little voice which had wanted her to steal some of the books from Mr Collin's room made a reappearance when it was least wanted. This would not do. She had banished that particular longing a long time ago. "Tis a great lacking in my character as a woman, I think, though I dare say it has made me an amiable wife."

She had in fact long convinced herself that such a lack of ardor was a strength, rather than a weakness. She might not be capable of passion, but she was steady and reliable, and besides, did not the very definition of passion suggest a sputtering flame which might one day be extinguished with the slightest gust of wind or falling raindrop? Was it not better, therefore, to remain cool and composed, able to weather any storm?

Rising, Mary regarded her steadily. Charlotte was suddenly very aware that they were standing only a foot apart. "I see nothing lacking in your character. Nor have I ever."

Panic rippled through her guts, though she had no idea why. The compliment was benign enough. "You are too kind."

Mary closed the lid of the pianoforte. "Might I ask—"

"I confess I find myself quite tired," Charlotte said, forcing a smile. Her stomach clenched. Had there been something in Mary's praise—something untoward in her tone? Surely not. "I do not wish to leave you alone but I fear I must retire for the evening."

"Of course." In the flickering light of the one remaining candle, Mary's eyes were forested hollows. She nodded politely. "Do not trouble yourself on my account."

Chapter Four

Dear Charlotte,

I am so sorry to hear of your husband's passing. I suppose you must be terribly upset. Emily has suggested that you visit, or that perhaps we ought to send one or two of the children to you for a while to busy you. James is learning to play the violin, and makes the most interesting noises with the instrument. Do let me know when is suitable and how many you can house.

Your brother,

John

Charlotte woke the next day and spent a few minutes contemplating the pale ceiling before she rose and dressed. Light rain pattered against the window in the parlor and though the grey clouds outside were still numerous, none of them hung as heavily as they had the day before. "The weather may yet clear up in the afternoon," she offered over breakfast, watching Mary butter a piece of toast with exacting precision. "You said you liked flowers, and my garden—while of course only modest—is something I am rather proud of."

The strangeness of the night before had vanished, much to Charlotte's relief. Her guest declared that she did not mind a little light rain in the slightest and therefore they shortly found themselves stepping outside into the misted drizzle of the parsonage garden. As they strolled along serpentine paths and ivy-covered walkways, Charlotte pointed out flower-beds of varying arduousness while Mary asked insightful questions about the specimens therein, as well as Charlotte's particular favourites. She was gratified to be asked her opinion, and even more gratified to find that Mary waited to hear it with interest. Mr Collins had sometimes asked her opinion, but often he had interjected with his own preferences before she could get a word in edgewise. "I admit I have a fondness for foxgloves," said she, "but larkspurs have such a bold colour, have they not? The blue is such a deep and clean shade, stopping just short of purple. And the simple daffodil is not treated with as much reverence as it ought, for it is inextricably associated with the turn of winter season into spring. Perhaps people forget that it exists during the rest of the year. But it is such a lovely flower, and the shape is both unusual and pleasing to the eye."

"Daffodils represent new beginnings, do they not?" Mary murmured, leaning down to touch one. "The end to cold, dark days. It is a floral herald, trumpeting of better days to come."

"Precisely!" Charlotte clapped her hands. Though the air was cold and the wet grass underfoot was beginning to soak into her shoes, she felt a warm glow of contentment. It had been such a long time since she'd felt she had a friend with whom she could simply talk, without being reminded that she must keep up a particular appearance. Mary chattered with similar enthusiasm, exclaiming over every new turn and view, and was in positive raptures over the Carolina silverbell trees which marked the boundary between the parsonage garden and the meadow beyond.

As they rounded the corner of the walk, the conversation turned to Mary's correspondence with people in her field of interest. "The late Ellen Hutchins, who was a most marvelous botanist, did me the great honour of replying to several of my amateur queries," Mary declared. "She had this most unusual way of writing. Down one page entirely," she demonstrated, pretending to write on a piece of parchment, "and then she would turn it sideways and begin again, often writing over her own words in the centre. A cross-hatch, she called it. Quite marvelous to see someone so unfettered by custom. It is a great shame she died so young—a mere nine-and-twenty."

"How awful." Charlotte's stomach swooped unpleasantly as she was reminded once more that mortality was ever-present.

"Death is a part of life." Mary shrugged. "The cycle begins anew, with little changes wrought here and there to improve upon what came before. I think it rather beautiful, in a way. Look," she added, pointing, not noticing Charlotte's frown. "Holly. I believe they say it provides defense and domestic happiness." Stooping, she broke off a sprig and handed it to Charlotte, her fingers lingering. "There. Now you may have fortune and felicity, whatever that may mean to you." She still had not removed her fingers from Charlotte's palm. "Tell me, what would it mean to you? Truly?"

Their gazes met. For a single, heart-stopping moment, Charlotte was on the verge of saying something very stupid about Mary's fine, dark eyes. Her breath hitched. A bird fluttered in the branches above, jolting her from her reverie. With flushed cheeks, she murmured a thanks, and turned back towards the house, chattering away with a calm she did not at all feel.

Charlotte was deeply relieved when Mrs Waites delivered a deliciously distracting luncheon, causing her guest to exclaim over the sweetness of the tomatoes, the sharpness of the local cheeses, and the rich, savoury sauce in the generous slice of cold pigeon pie. Charlotte took the opportunity to ask about Mary's favourite dishes, promising to have the cook provide some later in the week. Before long, the conversation turned to memories of happy times at Longbourne, which helped Charlotte to relax. Mary repeated some of her earlier news about Jane and Bingley, who of course were as happy together as springtime lambs, as well as her good opinion of Kitty's husband. Lydia's man she refused to speak of entirely, and Charlotte did not press the issue, sensing there was more to the story than she'd heard.

That afternoon, she and Mary read side by side on the couch. Nose-deep in a novel Mary had brought, warmed by the crackling fire and a fresh pot of hot tea, Charlotte found herself sublimely content. The realization brought with it a fresh wave of alarm, shattering her fragile peace. In order to cast off her weakness, she must first acknowledge it. Repressing a sigh, she stared into the flickering flames. Whenever Lizzie had walked into a room, a trail of humming, satisfied bees had taken up residence in Charlotte's chest. The hive was long-empty, of course, but the memory of buzzing remained. The younger Bennet was not a bee person in the slightest. If anything, she resembled a falcon with a scythe-sharp mouth and dark, keen eyes searching out every detail. How much had she overheard in those younger days? How much had she catalogued, unnoticed?

Mary shifted, moving sideways an inch so that her elbow grazed Charlotte's arm. Charlotte stiffened, sucking in a breath. A thrill shivered up her forearm, trailed across her collarbone, and wrapped cool fingers around her throat. Guilt and shame bubbled in her stomach; no touch of Mr Collins had ever produced anything like such an effect. Charlotte shifted away from Mary on the pretext of pouring more tea, and reclined against the opposite arm of the couch, far from temptation.

On the following day, an invitation for lunch arrived from Rosings, written in Anne's neat script. Charlotte replied quickly, asking if it would be acceptable to bring her guest along, which obliged Bessie to run over with the note and then run back with the confirmation that Anne would be delighted to welcome any friend of Charlotte's. She was pleased to be able to introduce one of her own friends to Anne, and relieved at having another distraction. Mary, who admitted she had only ever heard of Rosings described by Mr Collins and her sister—apparently in quite different terms, though she would not elaborate on that proclamation—enjoyed the short walk over to the house. Charlotte felt as if she was seeing the great estate for the first time through fresh eyes, and was able to provide all manner of detail about the number of rooms and servants contained within the handsome house. "Though I suspect you may be more interested in the gardens and grounds," Charlotte teased, noticing Mary's eyes drawn to the shrubbery which lined the fine, wide walkway leading to the front of the building. "There is a beautiful pond over the left, situated just past the diamond-shaped lawn. A little further on, one may walk through a series of archways over which honeysuckle has grown—that is my favourite part, for I do so love an archway. The gardener recently introduced some rhododendron bushes near the vegetable garden in the grounds behind the building, though I have heard Lady Catherine complaining that they are not as pleasing to the eye as she had been led to believe. I fear that, unless the bushes learn to stand in line, tall and straight as soldiers, the flowers may soon come to an untimely demise."

Mary raised her eyebrow. "I hardly believe you do not live here yourself, with such intimate knowledge of the place." Her white gloves, Charlotte noticed, were embroidered at the wrist with tiny green flowers, which matched the floral neckline of the pretty pink dress she was wearing.

"Mr Collins was a keen enthusiast of all things Rosings." Charlotte bit her lip, her stomach sinking. She had hardly thought about him in these last days, but had that not been the purpose of Mary's visit? It was not wrong to enjoy a little company, after all. "I dare say he had every room catalogued and memorized."

Expecting only Anne de Bourgh as host, Charlotte was therefore surprised when two gentlemen rose from their positions at the table and bowed. The taller of the two was introduced as Sir Gordon, a gentleman in his fifties with a large nose and a kind countenance, dressed in a red jacket so fine that even Lady Catherine would not have been able to find fault with it. The shorter man with curly brown hair was introduced as Mr Innes, a great friend of the family, who could have been no more than five-and-thirty. He bowed low and smiled, his face pleasant and open. Charlotte was glad she had decided to wear her black silk dress which, although no longer a beautiful larkspur-blue, was still the nicest gown she owned by far.

They sat down to luncheon at a table piled high with cake, scones, cold cuts, and cheese. Sir Gordon engaged Anne in a long conversation about people whom Charlotte had never heard of, while Mr Innes, dressed in a fine gold-buttoned coat and black breeches, fixed Charlotte with a charming smile. "I believe Anne said your late husband was a clergyman? I heard the de Bourghs held him in very high regard."

"Thank you." She did not like the way Mary hid a smirk behind her teacup. Mr Collins had been, on occasion, prone to a certain kind of pompous foolishness, but he had done his best with the gifts God had given him. The whole world could not be blessed with exceptional wit or beauty, or they should grow dull, common traits indeed. Irritation bloomed with her guest, followed quickly by resentment. While Charlotte had endured four years of marriage, Mary had apparently been gallivanting around Canterbury practically by herself, and had enjoyed the kind of freedom and liberty that Charlotte had never known.

"He was a cousin of mine," Mary offered. "Heir to my father's estate too."

The resentment grew a little stronger. Charlotte did not need reminding that she had failed to produce any heirs of her own. She could see the wheels turning in handsome Mr Innes' head—no husband or estate, likely no children, a boring old woman of one-and-thirty—and prepared for him to turn his attention to Mary instead. Though not a traditional beauty, the middle Miss Bennet was well-mannered and well-dressed. The thought of Mr Innes charming Mary, and she in turn plying him with that dry wit which had so lately cheered Charlotte, produced an unexpected spike of a different emotion. Was she truly jealous? Mary's attention had been so focused on her and her alone since her guest had arrived, which had felt like a welcome change. The resentment in her stomach cooled, turning into embarrassment. Charlotte had so often been cast aside in favour of others that she was surprised she was even still capable of feeling such a thing. It was natural, though, that a flower starved of sunlight would therefore do everything in its power to grow towards that source. She could acknowledge her feelings to herself without blame, though she would not behave impolitely in company.

"Is that so?" Mr Innes said, as Anne laughed at Sir Gordon's jest. "And I suppose you two have been very great friends since childhood?"

Charlotte and Mary exchanged amused looks, and Charlotte felt the last lingering sting of resentment subside. "No, sir," Mary said, helping herself to a scone. "I confess that I was not honoured with such a wondrous thing as Charlotte's friendship in my younger years. It was my older sisters who were her particular friends. You may know Elizabeth now as Mrs Darcy."

"Why so I do." He studied Mary's face more closely. "What a fool you must think me—I should have seen the resemblance from the start. Your sister is a fine woman. In fact, I should not expect to meet finer anywhere. She has turned Darcy into quite a pleasant fellow, something Bingley could never do." Charlotte was warmed to hear such praise of her friend, and Mary's bright eyes showed that she felt the compliment most keenly.

As the plates emptied of delicacies and the forks were finally laid to rest, they moved into the sunroom. Charlotte had long since noticed that while Mr Innes was courteous to Mary, he paid herself particular attention. At first, she had been convinced she'd imagined it, but as the servants passed around small glasses of sherry, Mr Innes took the seat next to Charlotte on the chaise and questioned her politely about her time in Kent. Had she enjoyed it? What were her favourite pastimes? Had she participated in her husband's vocation in some way? These questions might have been used to engage any gentleman or lady, but his attention, though pleasant, was singularly focused. Though Sir Gordon had directed several questions to Mary and she had answered, Mary's gaze always returned to Charlotte and her face conveyed an odd, inscrutable look. Charlotte felt rather like a beetle on her back, squirming under a glass under so much notice. It was difficult to concentrate on ensuring her answers were long enough to be satisfactory. Though Mr Innes smelled pleasant enough—soap and bergamot, if Charlotte was any judge—she could not help noticing that Mary's faint scent of violets was always there, and found herself searching for the scent in every breath.

"And where did you meet Mr and Mrs Darcy last, Mr Innes?" Charlotte asked, keen to divert the conversation and some of the attention away from herself.

As Mr Innes launched into a long description of the latest ball and who had attended, Charlotte nodded along politely, falling into old habits. She did not miss the way Anne's head cocked towards them, as if listening for faint music, nor her faint smile. Likewise, it was impossible for Charlotte to ignore the way Mary's eyes kept flickering to a spot of bare skin just above her clavicle, and the strange thrill which prickled in her chest every time their eyes met.

Back in the parsonage, Mary loosened her bonnet and shook out her dark hair. "Would you not like to marry again?"

"I do not know." Charlotte had grown somewhat used to Mary's questions, which fired like bullets without the usual noisy warning. "I did not really wish to marry in the first place. But you know it is the done thing, and I was already seven-and-twenty. What man would have had me, if Mr Collins had not—" *If I had not thrown myself at him after Lizzie rejected him,* she thought grimly. *A desperate act and one I am not proud of, though I doubt he ever realised.* "I hope you are not talking of Mr Innes," she added. "For I do not think his interest indicated anything other than decent civility."

The lie hung between them like thick fog. Mary paused with one glove off, examining her like a specimen to discover what secrets lay within. The thought of being pinned down and studied at length sent a shiver through her, though it was not entirely unpleasurable. To Lizzie, Charlotte had always been a stolid, supportive companion. To Jane, another gentle soul. To her husband, she had been a pleasant wife, an eager listener for all his lectures, yet the thought of marrying another man, to sit in silence day by day and merely listen, rather than be asked to speak her mind—as odd as it felt to voice such blunt truths—was intolerable. Mr Collins knew less of her in four years than Mary had learned in a few days, simply by asking.

"Your friend thinks herself an excellent matchmaker, I suspect." Mary dropped her gloves onto the table and busied herself with a loose button on her dress.

"I dare say she does, but she will not succeed with me. Love must be more than chess, moving two pieces into the same square and hoping for a spark." She surprised herself with her own vehemence. She would have answered quite differently five years ago—perhaps even five weeks ago. *Why do I say love when I mean marriage?* she wondered. *And why do I resist when Anne knows my situation only too well?* A husband, particularly a wealthy one, would save her from having to return home to Lucas Lodge. Yet the thought prompted a slow, aching feeling in her stomach. It was foolish to want something else, something more from life.

Wasn't it?

"You do not strike me as one who has ever thought of love as a game." Mary's voice was airy and green as new leaves, but Charlotte heard at once that it concealed some far earthier thing, rooted in a deep, dark place.

"Can you read me so well?"

"Well enough, perhaps." Mary hesitated, shooting Charlotte a coy look from under her lashes. "With a little more time I might read you further still."

"You talk in such a strange way," Charlotte mused. "One normally expects people to say one thing and mean quite another, but you say one thing and mean the same."

Genuine amusement flitted across Mary's face; a beam of sunlight, chasing lithe shadows. "And which approach do you prefer?"

"You tell me," Charlotte retorted, and was rewarded with a grin.

Chapter Five

Darling Charlotte!
I am quite beside myself at the news of your husband's passing.
What little I knew of my brow-in-law assured me that he was a
kind and decent man (although the comparison to John's wretch
of a wife must surely improve anyone else's impression). I expect
you'll return to live at Lucas Lodge with Mama and Papa, but
there is always a room, however small, here for you at Belmont.
With all the sisterly love a mere quill can convey,
Maria

The next morning dawned clear and bright. Yolk-yellow sunshine dribbled in through the gap in the curtains, kissing Charlotte awake. She stretched and yawned, still in the clutches of a half-forgotten dream, before rising, washing, and dressing in yet another black dress. Regarding herself in the looking-glass, Charlotte sighed. Black made her look paler than usual, like an awful, strict governess. Still, wearing such a stark colour did afford her temporary respite from the endless business of courting. Apart from the de Bourghs, who were incorrigible, few others would dare mention even the possibility to a woman in mourning clothes.

When Charlotte opened the bedroom door, she was greeted by the welcome golden-brown smell of baking wafting in from the kitchen. Inhaling deeply, she ambled down the hallway to the parlor to find the fire lit, but the room empty. Puzzled, Charlotte stepped back into the hallway, wondering whether Mary's claim to be an early riser had been only a jest, and was almost bowled over by Bessie, who came rushing along the corridor armed with a loaded tea tray. "Begging your pardon, ma'am," the maid said. "Miss Bennet is in the dining room."

Mary was indeed in the dining room, and stood poring over a large book, muttering something unintelligible. None of the chairs had been pulled out, suggesting that she had yet to settle herself. Papers covered half the table, though they were covered in strange-looking diagrams and scribbled notes. Charlotte shivered; the room held a chill, as if the fire had only been recently lit. "Good morning."

"Oh, good morning." Mary beamed, and Charlotte was amused to find that her guest's inky fingers had left a smudge high on her left cheekbone. "Pardon me, I did not realise the hour." She gathered the papers, shuffling the papers into a neat pile. "At home I often forget to break my fast until lunchtime. It is a terrible habit."

"Some say books do feed the soul as well as food," Charlotte offered, keen to make her guest feel at home.

"That is very true."

Bessie put the tray down and, after shooting her mistress a strange glance, busied herself with pouring tea. "What were you reading?" Charlotte asked. She picked up the nearest paper, fully intending to hand it over, but the image caught her eye; a foxglove, drawn as if cut open to show the inside of the plant in every respect, with tiny labels on each separate part. "Does this relate to the scientific salons you talked of?"

Bessie clanked out of the room, closing the door behind her. "I am afraid I quite offended your maid," Mary said apologetically, without answering the question. "I asked to build up the fire myself this morning."

"I am sure that Bessie would never be offended by such a thing. Relieved, perhaps, that you sought to do one of her duties for her. Do you make a habit of attending to fires, Miss Bennet?" She slid into a chair and raised an eyebrow, but couldn't help a smirk escaping.

"In fact I do," Mary said, all seriousness, and took the seat next to Charlotte. "It is one of my many eccentricities, but I believe that ladies ought to know how to do essential tasks within the home. Why, if your maid could not attend you in the wintertime, would you build the fire yourself or simply freeze to death?"

"Of course I would build a fire. It cannot be so hard to do."

"It is not, of course, but the way a fire is constructed makes all the difference. Why, you cannot simply throw a log or two in and expect them to instantly set ablaze." She sipped her tea, dark eyes glittering in the light. "You must construct a nest of smaller twigs first, with some piece of cloth tucked inside that will ignite easily, causing the rest to fall in line. It is a dance of sorts, with one small flicker of movement leading inexorably to the next."

Charlotte had the feeling that Mary was talking about something else, though what she could not possibly guess. Perhaps it was an allusion to science, which her clever salon friends would understand. Feeling rather stupid, Charlotte poured more tea for both of them, and savored the sweet aroma. "You make it sound poetic, rather than a maid's thankless daily task."

"It can be both." Mary shrugged. "And to answer your earlier question, an acquaintance of mine is currently travelling through Austria. She has met several learned mineralogists, who are extremely knowledgeable about aspects of the natural world, and has made some interesting discoveries. I never understood this fascination with stones and cliffs. A plant at least can be grown, can be tended to, can surprise you with some secret unfolding where you did not expect one. A rock simply is." She pulled a slightly silly face, though Charlotte sensed real discomfort behind the expression.

"I must agree with you there. A flower is much more beguiling." Charlotte's stomach rumbled. "I am afraid that I cannot wait until lunchtime as you do. Would you like something to eat?"

"Yes, thank you." As Charlotte stood up, intending to ring the small bell for the kitchen, Mary put a hand on her arm. Her fingers were warm, despite the chill, and sent a shiver of a different nature down Charlotte's spine. "No, do not trouble yourself. I have another book in my suitcase which may interest you. I shall fetch it and then inform your wonderful cook that we are in need of something delectable."

The second Mary had left the room, Charlotte leaned across the table and dragged the sheaf of papers towards herself. Flicking through them, she saw diagrams of plants and flowers she recognised—bluebells, honeysuckle, the common daisy—as well as those she did not. The words were all new to her; most were in Latin, underlined, with additional notes added in a scrawled hand. Towards the end of the pile, her fingers stuttered over several papers different from all the rest. One was a letter addressed to Mary, which began *my most beloved friend* in cramped, spidery handwriting. Charlotte blanched and moved on quickly, hoping to bypass seeing any more. Yet the fourth page, which comprised the last section of the letter, was a drawing of a young lady in the full flower of womanhood, reposing nude on a chaise.

Charlotte sucked in a gasp as voices murmured at the end of the hallway. This friend had drawn someone in a wanton and licentious manner, and thought nothing of including the drawing in her letter to Mary. *Or*, the ugly little voice in Charlotte's head suggested, *this friend drew herself unclothed and thought Mary might like to look at her. Perhaps you are not the only one who appre-*

ciates the female form in such a manner. The name scribbled underneath was almost unintelligible—Anne, perhaps, or Anna? Charlotte could hardly make it out, and her eyes kept sliding back to the woman in the picture. Dark-haired, with narrow eyes and a strong, thin nose. Unarguably an attractive face, to say nothing of the body, which was soft and curvaceous in all the—

Charlotte shoved the papers back across the table and clamped her hands down on the arm of the chair. It was perfectly natural to appreciate womanly beauty, she reminded herself. Were not women generally referred to as the fairer sex? It did not signify anything other than the fact that Mary's friends were scientists and artists both, who likely saw the human body as no more than another diagram to be labelled. It was Charlotte who was the weak one, she who saw the flesh as something to be desired and touched, instead of some lofty artistic ideal.

Mary bustled back into the room holding a book, and Charlotte did her best to focus on the explanation of the title, which seemed rather long and ponderous. She was saved by Bessie, who brought in a tray of buns still warm from the oven, spiced with caraway seeds, along with a pot of strawberry jam which was Charlotte's particular favourite. Mrs Waites' baking was uncommonly good, far better than any of the village shops, and Charlotte was proud to be able to offer something so delicious to her guest, who no doubt had a much more refined palate. As Mary cut her first bun in half and reached for the jam, the firelight caught her face. Charlotte smiled.

"What is it?" Mary asked, looking down at her dress, evidently wondering if she'd already spilled something.

"I should have warned you earlier. You have a little ink on your cheek."

Mary's hand drifted towards the right side of her face. "I am forever getting ink and charcoal and stains on every part of me. I know not how I manage it. Where is the mark, please?"

"On the left. A little higher. Yes, just there." Charlotte

watched as Mary rubbed a wet thumb along her cheekbone vigorously, removing the ink-stain. Somehow, the sight made her feel hungrier than ever before. Her fingers twitched around the sides of the teacup. *Do not think about the drawing*, she warned herself. *And certainly don't ask about it, for goodness' sake. She'll think you nothing more than a prying busybody.*

"Is it gone now?"

Charlotte forced a smile. "Entirely."

Over breakfast, Mary announced her intention to continue on to Longbourne the following week, and extended the offer to accompany her. Charlotte declined politely. Most people she knew would have simply smiled and changed the subject, but Mary was not like most people. "You would be most welcome, I am certain," she pressed. "Even my mother likes you, and she does not like anybody much."

"I am sure I would be. Your family have always been so kind. But I could not visit Meryton without seeing my parents, and I know full well they would encourage me to remain with them, and to send for my things here." She sighed. "I know that returning to Hertfordshire is my fate, and I cannot avoid it, but I would postpone it a little longer if I could."

"Then I shall return much sooner than I had planned," Mary announced, "and stay with you again if you should like it."

"I would like it very much," Charlotte agreed, warmth flooding her chest. She'd assumed Mary would leave and that their paths would simply diverge as they had once done. The idea that Mary would want to return earlier from a trip just to spend time with her was a flattering one.

"And what's more, I propose a scheme. You ought to come to Canterbury with me for a week or two."

Charlotte blinked. "Oh, I couldn't possibly intrude on your—"

"You certainly could. After all, am I not your honoured guest? Would you not be mine in turn?"

What else was Charlotte going to do—count down the hours

here until she had to return to Lucas Lodge, with nothing but an occasional lunch at Rosings to keep her entertained? The thought was a pathetic, lonely one. "Well… I suppose it might be nice to have a change."

"We shall have a grand time," Mary promised. "I shall even attend a ball if you so desire, on one condition." She held up a single finger. "You must attend a salon with me."

Charlotte's jaw dropped. "I—I do not think I would be good company at such an event," she stammered. "I fear I am too much of a country mouse to amuse your clever friends. I have not read widely, nor do I understand most of the studies you speak of, so I have nothing of note to contribute."

"I shall leave some books with you and when I return, we shall discuss them at length. No, no," Mary said, and waggled the same finger when Charlotte opened her mouth to protest, "I have every faith in your ability to comprehend the smallest of details and the largest of ideas, Charlotte Lucas."

Collins, Charlotte mentally corrected, but didn't say out loud. She'd missed the sound of her old name, and to some extent, her old life; though it had been underlaid with anxiety amid the constant pressure to find a suitable match, she'd had friends in Jane and Lizzy, and had enjoyed dancing at the balls thrown at various Hertfordshire houses. Mary made her feel as though anything were possible, as though the book of her life was opening up to a new chapter, rather than closing on a bitter-sweet ending.

"Very well," said she, unable to repress a smile. "An adventure to Canterbury sounds rather grand."

After breakfast, they took a walk around the garden, where Mary begged a little time to sit and sketch a clump of lark-spurs. She seated herself on the small green bench which rested against the eastern wall of the parsonage, and unrolled a black cloth from which she plucked a piece of charcoal. Charlotte seated herself beside Mary and occupied herself with some embroidery, though she had not the least interest in what she was doing. As the hour passed, the time between stitches grew longer and longer, until the embroidery lay forgotten in her lap and her eyes were riveted on Mary's drawing. Her guest was a clever artist and had captured the nature of the tall plant, the way it bent in the slight breeze, the way the small flowers clustered together as if cold.

Mary rummaged around amongst pieces of charcoal and pencils, and added a slash of vivid blue to each flower, before turning the parchment towards Charlotte for inspection. "What say you?"

"It is beautiful work, but where are your labels?"

Mary blinked, puzzled, before realization dawned. "Oh, this isn't a diagram. This is a present for you. You said you admired their bold colour, did you not? I know foxgloves are your particular favourite," she smiled apologetically, "but I could not do the colour justice for I have no red left. So I hope this will do."

She offered the drawing and Charlotte took it with unexpectedly shaky fingers. "You are too kind," she murmured, feeling quite overcome. *She remembered what you said,* the little voice in her mind said. *She was listening and she cared enough to remember.* "I shall have it framed."

Mary blushed. "If you like it so much, I shall draw another upon my return."

"Have you ever drawn people?" The question came out of Charlotte's mouth before she'd considered the implications, and instantly she wished she could take it back. The drawing from Mary's letter came vividly to mind—the curves, the full lips, the legs stretched out languidly. Who on earth was Anne and what was her relationship to Mary? The question burned inside Charlotte but she would have sooner gone to the stocks than asked directly.

"I have indeed." Mary opened her mouth as if to add something, studied Charlotte for a moment, and closed it again. "I hope this may not scandalize you, but occasionally our salons provide a suitable model for artists. Often it is a young woman, though men do volunteer. They sit in the middle of the room, sometimes clothed, sometimes nude, while we sit about in a rough circle and draw as best we can. Women have such interesting bodies, do they not?"

Charlotte bit down the immediate impulse to disagree. Why bother, when Mary had already espoused the opinion so clearly? It was a question, not a trap. *Or is it?* she wondered. Maybe the drawing included with the letter had simply been an artistic endeavour after all. "Yes," she said, slowly. "I quite agree. And though I married a parson, you may not find me as prudish as to think people are clothed every moment of the day."

Mary's eyebrows raised a fraction, but she offered no comment. Her dark eyes roved over Charlotte's face as if calculating and cataloguing every detail. Charlotte forced herself to look away, counting the bright heads of the foxgloves in an attempt to stave off the blushes she knew full well were shading her cheeks. "You may know this already, but in a bouquet, larkspur indicates humour and lightheartedness, or possibly an ardent bond of love."

"I did not know." Mary's voice had lowered to a purr. "And what of the foxglove?"

"That all depends on the colour of the flower and the intention of the giver, really, but it can range from secrets and riddles to insecurity and immortality."

"That's a rather broad range of interpretations. When putting together such a bouquet, how can one be sure that one's meaning is received in the spirit one intended it?"

Charlotte frowned. "I supposed you can only do your best and hope that the receiver is…well, receptive."

"Hmm. Flowers bring much more risk than I had previously thought." Mary's mouth was perfectly serious, but her eyes crinkled with amusement.

"Indeed, you shall have to tread carefully if you draw me another," Charlotte said, getting up and brushing off her dress. "Shall we take some tea?"

The parlor was warm and stuffy after the refreshing air of the garden. Charlotte seated herself on the brown couch, fully expecting Mary to occupy one of the armchairs, and was surprised when Mary sat down next to her and began to sketch a rudimentary oval, which quickly turned into a face. Shooting quick glances at Charlotte, Mary's hand moved over the parchment in short, sharp strokes. An ear emerged, then two, then the curly, fair tendrils which hung down at the sides of Charlotte's face, framing it in the usual fashion.

"This was my mistake," said Charlotte, laughing, and putting a hand up to shield her face. "I did not intend to suggest by my question that you actually draw me. I was merely asking if you had done so in the past."

"But you have such a pleasant face," Mary countered, rubbing her cheek absent-mindedly, transferring a charcoal stain. "It would be a shame not to draw it."

Charlotte winced. She'd expected better from her guest than such a blatant, fanciful lie. She knew full well she was not attractive in the way that ladies ought to be, and though Mr Collins had taken great pains to compliment almost everything else— her embroidering, her pretty manners, and so forth, the sort of trivial accomplishments that every young lady was supposed to possess as a matter of course—he had never once called her beautiful, or even hinted at it, though he had once conceded that her hair was exceedingly soft. She hadn't minded this lack too much. He was, after all, a man of God, and was therefore more preoccupied with the quality of a soul rather than the body housing it.

Still.

The drawing now had Charlotte's wide eyes, her dark brows, her stubby nose. Mary squinted at Charlotte again, evidently considering some aspect, before the charcoal touched parchment again. Unable to bear this scrutiny, Charlotte reached out, tipping Mary's chin with her left hand. "You have a little something on your cheek." She licked the pad of her right thumb. Mary's eyes widened as Charlotte brushed her thumb over the charcoal mark again and again, until it was entirely erased. "There."

She hesitated. They were too close. Mary's breath was hot on her palm, her pink lips slightly parted, the smell of violets tickling Charlotte's nose. Mary's dark eyes were gleaming with something and Charlotte knew she ought to drop her hands, ought to move away or say something to break the strange tension of the moment, but in truth no one had ever looked at her like that before. If she had to name the expression, it would be something very close to hunger.

Like desire.

Do you really think that anyone could see beauty in plain old Charlotte Lucas? the little voice asked. *Even your husband did not think you so. You put away that sort of girlish foolishness a long time ago; do not seek to resurrect it now.*

Charlotte pulled away like she had been scalded. Mary lifted her hands as if to catch Charlotte's retreating ones, but Charlotte shifted backwards on the couch, hearing one of the floorboards in the hallway creak. A moment later Bessie entered, bearing a tea tray and two thick slices of rum cake. After the maid had left, Mary sought to take up her drawing again. Charlotte entreated her not to do so, a plea which was reluctantly agreed to, and instead guided the conversation towards Mary's travel plans for the following day. She would miss the company, and had already grown rather fond of her guest, but the danger of saying or doing something very stupid increased every moment.

A few days and some distance would put everything right again, Charlotte decided, and all would be as it once was.

Chapter Six

Dearest daughter,

Our deepest condolences for your loss—Mr Collins was, we believe, a good husband to you these past few years.

Though we have taken heart that one of the Miss Bennets has kept our dear Charlotte company in this time of tragedy.

We strongly encourage you to return to Hertfordshire as soon as you please so that we may comfort you too.

With fondest regards,

Mama and Papa

Charlotte's parents often wrote their letters to her together. One sentence in a looping hand, the words leaning backwards as if facing a heavy gale, was both preceded and followed by a smaller, less neat hand, though the words were far more upright, as if they'd taken brief shelter from the storm. Charlotte folded the letter up with a heavy sigh. She would reply later, though her own letter would not reach them until after they'd heard of Mary's arrival at Longbourne. They might even visit the Bennets, and then Mary could put them quite at ease about how well their daughter was faring.

Mary had departed so early the next morning that, by the

time Charlotte had awoken, her guest was already gone, though she had left the bulk of her luggage in the spare room, so that her journey to Meryton was made a little easier. Seeing the rumpled bedsheets through the open doorway and a scarf casually strewn over the headboard had given Charlotte a pleasant feeling in the pit of her stomach which she had refused to examine further.

Less than an hour after she had breakfasted that morning, and halfway through said pile of letters, Charlotte received a lunch invitation from Rosings. She'd never been able to work out how Lady Catherine had known everything that went on in the parsonage—even news Mr Collins hadn't yet had the opportunity to convey to his benefactress—and apparently Anne was using the same gambit, whatever that might be. After casting suspicious glances at both Bessie and Mrs Waites, who were shelling peas together at the kitchen table in companionable silence, Charlotte set off for Rosings.

She had hoped to have a quiet, brief luncheon with Anne and afterwards spend some time in solitude in the parsonage garden putting her thoughts in order, and was therefore surprised to find an even larger party than before in attendance. Anne introduced Charlotte to Mr Humphries, Mr Fitzherbert, and Lord Barrington, and added with an arch smile that of course Charlotte already knew Mr Innes.

"Of course," Charlotte said, and was gratified when Mr Innes bowed deeply, his wide smile showing every evidence of being pleased to see her again.

"Sir George has left on business," Mr Innes informed Charlotte, as they seated themselves at the long table in the great hall, "and has promised me he will return in a week or two with his wife. She is a very kind soul. I am sure you would like her very much, Mrs Collins."

"I am sure that I would." Charlotte hesitated. "But I am to

go to Canterbury with Miss Bennet next week. I fear I shall miss their visit entirely."

"Why, that is a shame indeed," said he. "But no matter, we are all often in London and I believe you have an aunt there, do you not? How often do you—"

Before Charlotte could answer, Mr Humphries let out a great guffaw which drew the interest of everyone at the table. "No, do not repeat the jest," he scolded Mr Fitzherbert, when the latter began to explain their conversation, "for it is only funny to those who have visited that particular region of France."

"Which region do you speak of?" Anne inquired, and the conversation swiftly turned from recollections of pleasant holidays to matters of French politics.

Charlotte knew enough to follow, but not to make any particular opinion of her own felt, and so remained quiet, observing the rest of the party. Mr Humphries had a rebuttal for every point, though his companions did not seem to mind too hard. Charlotte thought that if one had to spend more than an hour in the presence of a man whose every comment was intended to disparage one's own, even if he had been espousing a similar view only moments before, she would go quite mad. Anne presided over the table with the air of a queen whose mind was on other, more distant matters, and more than once Charlotte caught her staring out of the window at the fluffy white clouds beyond.

"I say, that is a very pretty dress, Mrs Collins," Mr Humphries said unexpectedly, his eyes sliding down Charlotte's curves.

Surprised, Charlotte could not quell a blush. "Thank you."

Mr Innes cleared his throat. "Did Mrs Darcy help you pick it out?"

"No, I'm afraid she did not." Charlotte repressed a smile. Lizzie had never been the type to fuss over a dress; everything she'd worn had always suited her well, though it frequently lacked in adornments or embellishments. Mary had quite a different style, and Charlotte had noticed the inclusion of small details on her outfits which, although subtle, were evidently the consequence of some care. "It was not always black, I must admit. I rather miss the colour it once was."

"Mrs Collins' husband passed away recently," Anne added, shooting Mr Humphries an odd, inscrutable glance.

"Well," said Mr Humphries, leaning over the table a little and lowering his voice, "sometimes things which begin one way often end up another entirely, and much for the better. Is that not so, Mrs Collins?"

"It may be so, sir." Charlotte fumbled with her fork. Was he flirting with her or was this some jest at her expense? "Anne is wearing a very pretty dress today too, I see," she said, keen to divert the attention onto a far more deserving party.

It was true—Anne's dress was the colour of a pale summer morning, with all the promise of brilliance ahead. "I quite agree. Why, I saw the very same colour when I was sailing along the coast last year," Lord Barrington said, stroking his whiskers. "My father had business in Germany, you see, and when I took over the management of the country estates I quite—"

As Lord Barrington talked of his latest journey and boasted of all the places he had been, punctuated by the occasional contradiction by Mr Humphries, Charlotte's eyes also drifted towards the window. Questions plagued her mind: had Mary already arrived in Longbourne? Could she make herself comfortable at home, or had she been away too long? How long had Mr Bennet coped with his middle daughter's arrival before he retreated to his study? Was Mrs Bennet already in hysterics about some trivial matter, declaiming her poor nerves? And might the marriage-minded mama seek to introduce Mary to some eligible suitors during her swift visit? Now that all four of her other daughters were settled, surely it could not be long before Mrs Bennet's thoughts—never far from matrimony at the best of times—turned to her final unwed daughter?

The idea sent an unpleasant shiver down Charlotte's back. She had rather enjoyed getting to know Mary, and the invitation to Canterbury had even ignited some small hope that she might occasionally escape Lucas Lodge for a change of scenery. If Mary married a gentleman who lived in Canterbury, it would still afford Charlotte the same freedom, but something about the notion irked her. She could not imagine Mary wed, nor a brood of little ones around her feet. Her friend—for that was what they were now, she was sure, after sharing so many confidences—was a kind soul, but a clever and impatient one. Mary would not like to be tied to a home and hearth, unable to attend her beloved salons with any regularity. Even the idea of Mary married to a benevolent man who encouraged her hobbies was an unwelcome thought.

"You are rather quiet today, Mrs Collins." Mr Innes offered a smile, breaking Charlotte out of her ruminations. "Where is your charming guest? Do not tell me she is unwell."

"No." Charlotte smiled back. "She is gone to her family in Meryton and upon her return we shall set off for Canterbury."

Mr Humphries let out another one of his loud guffaws, which drowned out whatever Mr Innes said next. Before he could repeat himself, Mr Fitzherbert leaned across the table and drew Mr Innes into a discussion about land taxes from which he could not easily extract himself. Charlotte spooned spiced carrot soup into her mouth and helped herself to another warm roll. The fare at Rosings was always excellent, but in her opinion nothing could compare to Mrs Waites' tremendous creations.

Back at the parsonage, Charlotte wandered into the kitchen to tell Mrs Waites as much. After all, an artist deserved compliments on their work, and the time in which she could convey such frequent praise was quickly running out.

"You're very welcome, ma'am." Mrs Waites wiped floury hands on her even more floury apron, managing to somehow transfer white smears from the latter to the former. "I wondered if I might ask you…well, in truth, I wondered if you knew what was to happen after you leave for good? Whether you know who our next employer will be?"

The question was a reasonable one, but it reminded Charlotte again that her time residing in the parsonage was fast running out. The clock on the kitchen mantel sounded less like a tick than a distant cannon shot. "Lady Catherine will appoint someone to the position when she returns from her travels. I would be surprised if she has not already settled the matter in her mind, regardless of whether or not the new man has agreed to it yet."

"I rather feel for him, whomever he might be," Mrs Waites murmured, and they shared a smile.

"In any case, neither you nor Bessie need to worry. I will ensure that Lady Catherine hears my glowing recommendation for both of you."

"Thank you, ma'am." Mrs Waites wobbled a curtsey, and wiped her floury hands—now floury arms—on her apron again. "I suspect Bessie's young man will make a move sooner rather than later, but that should make no difference to her working here awhile longer. Unless they do not sell the butcher's shop."

Charlotte's face must have betrayed her confusion, because Mrs Waites quickly added, "You did know that her beau is the butcher's second son, did you not?"

"Yes, of course," Charlotte said, not following at all.

Mrs Waites turned towards the stove and lifted the lid. Steam rose into the air, curling like a beckoning finger. Inside, a brown mass bubbled and roiled, an occasional carrot disturbing the surface like a small orange kraken. "After the butcher died, the eldest wanted to sell the place. He has no stomach for the business. But the second son, a good lad who has always had his eye on our Bessie, wanted to take it over. He'd make a good job of it too. Was there in all weathers, helping his father, while the other one gallivanted about hunting and what-not, though he was oft too drunk to sit a horse."

Charlotte wondered just how drunk one had to be to fail at sitting on top of a horse, but Mrs Waites's stern expression forbade her from further questioning. "Ah," Charlotte said, putting it all together. "And if this boy kept the shop, then Bessie would be expected to help him out with the customers and such once they were married."

"Precisely, ma'am."

"I would be happy to see her married well," Charlotte mused. Though the women under her employ had to work for a living—and work hard they did, from dawn until dusk—at least they had the freedom to go where they wished and marry whom they wished, without any reference to particular society or standing. She was surprised to find herself a little envious of Bessie's situation. "And what of you, Mrs Waites?"

Only a few weeks prior, Bessie had, with a wicked grin, informed Charlotte that the new grocer's ears turned bright pink every time Mrs Waites stepped inside to buy vegetables. Charlotte had been waiting for the perfect opportunity to tease the cook about it. The lid of the saucepan slipped through the cook's fingers and clanged down onto the rim. "What about me?"

"Would you ever marry again?"

Mrs Waites eyed her. "That depends on who's asking." Charlotte hesitated, but the cook added, a pink tinge to her cheeks, "Or what you've heard. Would you remarry, ma'am? I know you weren't—" She broke off, her cheeks flushing more darkly.

Wasn't what? Charlotte wondered. *Happy? Was it so obvious to everyone but my husband?*

"That's not to say..." Mrs Waites bit her lip. "It's not my place to comment on such things."

Charlotte sighed. Over the years, she and Mrs Waites had developed the kind of friendship she could never have imagined with any of her parents' staff, but here in Kent, isolated, friendless, and unaccustomed to being the lady of the house, Charlotte had leaned heavily on Mrs Waites and in turn the cook had warmed to her, treating her more like a favoured niece than an employer. "No, go on. Speak freely to me."

"It's a delicate subject, I understand." The cook pushed a plate of biscuits towards Charlotte. "Here. A new recipe."

She took one and bit into it; soft and buttery, with a hint of thyme. "Delicious. You constantly outdo yourself, Mrs Waites."

Mrs Waites picked up a biscuit and turned it around in her fingers. "Next month, it will have been five-and-ten years since my husband died, and both my children are full-grown now." One son was married and lived in Sussex, Charlotte knew, and the other had been in the navy but had suffered some sort of accident and had no use of his left arm. "They say not to have favourites amongst your children, but James was the favourite I didn't have. Just as handsome as his brother, and far cleverer, though he had a knack for getting into scrapes and fights. The navy was a good place for him. He lives up in Scotland now. I believe he and his friend are considering sailing around the world next year."

"And he is yet unmarried?"

Mrs Waites put her own biscuit down without so much as taking a bite. "I do not believe James is the marrying type. He and his friend get along very well together." She raised an eyebrow.

Charlotte took another biscuit and chewed thoughtfully. "Plenty of men wait to marry until later in life when they've amassed some wealth or security. A family is not a cheap undertaking, as I understand it."

"Of course, ma'am." Mrs Waites' lip curled for a moment, and Charlotte had the distinct impression the cook was trying not to laugh, though she couldn't think what was funny about a young man trying to make his fortune. "While I have you, I've noticed that there's been an attack on our lettuces."

The subject change was so swift that it took Charlotte a moment to catch up. "And from whom has this attack come?"

"Small beetles. Black and green both. What do you suggest, ma'am?"

Charlotte tapped her chin. "We ought to plant some more basil. There is something they do not like about it... Perhaps the smell is revolting to them? In any case, it should protect our precious lettuces from the beetle army." Mr Collins had hated the scent of basil, and it had been such a long time since Charlotte had been able to enjoy the sweet, delicious leaves. Now it was her turn to smirk. "I am quite sure the grocer would give us one or two plants for free, if you were to ask him prettily."

Mrs Waites purposefully pulled the dish of biscuits out of Charlotte's reach. "Is that so?"

Sensing she was walking on thin ice, Charlotte repressed a laugh and made her excuses to escape the kitchen. Still thinking about basil leaves, and recalling other flavours that she had not savoured since joining her husband in the parsonage, Charlotte headed along the hallway. She slowed next to the door to the spare room, which Bessie had left wide open. The maid had made the bed neatly, and waiting on top of the coverlet were two books and a letter addressed to Charlotte. She picked the letter up and broke the seal, wondering what Mary could possibly have to say.

Chapter Seven

Charlotte,
I do not mean to pressure you into such things, but if you are
curious at all, perhaps these books will prove interesting to you.
Mary

Before the first name, there was a small dot of ink on the page. Charlotte brought the letter closer to her face and squinted at it. Was it simply an errant drop, or had the quill touched the page here, its wielder intending to begin with a different word? Possibly even a *Dear Charlotte*? The thought made her chest feel strange and tight.

As she turned to leave, a scrap of something poking out from a trunk caught her eye. It was the dress Mary had worn to Rosings, the one which had those beautiful little flowers embroidered on the neckline. Charlotte knelt and lifted the trunk's lid, intending to fold the dress more neatly so that it would not crease, and was startled to find her own face staring back at her. The drawing which she had begged Mary to stop had been finished in great detail, with an impressive amount of care. It was unmistakably Charlotte, and yet she looked more alive on paper than ever she had in the looking-glass. She reached for the parchment, her fingers stopping short of the surface. The eyes were animated and lively, and the mouth was bowed in a sweet smile. The neck was slender, arching into bare shoulders, with only a scribble to hint at a dress below. Was this really how Mary saw her? *Certainly not*, argued the little voice, but it was far more subdued than usual. In the face of such evidence, Charlotte had to concede that perhaps Mary, with her odd tastes and strange way of looking at the world, might actually find her beautiful.

The thought made her flush, though it was not the red rash of embarrassment she was so used to, but a sweet pink flutter of pleasure. She traced the line of her chin, her neck, and marvelled at the artist's skill. Her guest must have stayed up all night finishing it, and without the model to work from, evidently had an excellent memory.

Now Charlotte had a conundrum on her hands: fold the dress, and let Mary know that she had been interfering with her possessions, or leave the dress where it was and cause a crease. She bit her lip, thinking the decision over. Mary might well think it had been Bessie's doing as a matter of course, but it felt wrong to lie, even by omission, about such things. She wrung her hands. Really, she had not done anything so wrong, and it was not as if she had meant to go poking around. *And yet this marks the second time you have seen something you ought not to*, the little voice in her mind pointed out. *What is it about this young lady which has turned you into such a sneak? What are you hoping to find amongst her private things?*

Charlotte had no answer to such questions. Pushing down her anxieties, she folded the dress and left the drawing on top. If Mary asked her about it, she would tell the truth. That was all there was to the business, and certainly nothing more.

She spent the rest of the afternoon pruning one of the more errant rosebushes in the garden. That evening, her muscles aching pleasantly, she curled up on the brown couch in the parlor and opened the first of the books. The introduction left her floundering and uncertain, baffled by the scientific terms which the author used as if they were quite commonplace words. After a single page, Charlotte put it aside, a sinking feeling in her stomach. Mary expected far too much if she hoped Charlotte would be able to converse with ease about plants in such a scholarly way. At this rate it would be a miracle if she could even follow a single line of conversation in the salon, never mind formulate a coherent reply to one.

Thankfully, the second book was a far easier read; the diary of a young naturalist called Barton, who had been granted passage on a ship to India and had begun a journal the day before he stepped aboard. Before long, Charlotte lost herself in the descriptions of the creaking mast of the *Rositania*, the rolling white-capped waves, and the marvelous sight of a pod of whales breaching the surface. It was thrilling to experience, especially from the safety of one's armchair, though Charlotte couldn't help a little frisson of jealousy worming its way through her chest. Had she been born a gentleman, all manner of doors would be open to her; even her brother, John, who was not particularly adventurous, had sailed to Italy in his younger days with a friend.

By the time the clock had struck ten in the parlor, Barton had disembarked on an island where new and exotic flowers grew abundantly. Realizing she'd read the same passage about scarlet petals thrice and her eyes were now blurring from fatigue, Charlotte closed the book, covered a deep yawn, and wandered off to bed.

Charlotte woke in the middle of the night and lay still for a moment, wondering what had roused her. The only noise was a faint rasping snore from Mrs Waites, who often slept in the small room just off the kitchen rather than go home where there was no one waiting for her. Outside, an owl hooted twice, much closer to the window than Charlotte expected; perhaps the bird's call had woken her.

She got out of bed, crossed to the window, and pulled the curtains open. The moon hung low and bright, barely skimming the tops of the trees. Charlotte stood there a moment, admiring her garden, which she so rarely did at nighttime. The light cast long, sharp-edged shadows on the grass, and kissed each flower petal with a silver mouth, making the whole scene look like a beautiful fairy tale.

Wrapping a shawl around her shoulders, Charlotte stepped into the hallway. The floorboard creaked under her foot. Mrs Waites' snores hitched, then continued in their usual steady rhythm. She breathed a sigh of relief. If the cook heard her up at such an hour, she'd insist that Charlotte drink her "home remedy"—warm milk infused with lavender, which really was a terrible thing to do to an innocent glass of milk.

She'd had some notion of sitting in the parlor awhile. She would not have need of a fire, for the night was cool rather than cold, but could make do with a candle. Perhaps she might read a little more of the naturalist's diary, which she'd found so diverting, but Charlotte found herself slowing outside the door to the spare room. She'd left it ajar, and no one had been inside since that morning. The urge to return to Mary's room, to throw open the trunk and bury her face in the sweet-scented garments, was overwhelming. *What is wrong with you?* she scolded herself. *You never acted so with Lizzie, and she smelled perfectly nice. Like roses and fresh air, most of the time.* A light, airy scent, completely unlike Mary's ink-stained hands and violet perfume and the faint, bitter smell of old books. Like something precious locked away for a long time.

Feeling exhausted, Charlotte rubbed her eyes and leaned against the wall. Her feelings towards certain women had always been a source of discomfort for her, and it would be stupid to ever speak of them to Mary. At best, it might make her new friend uncomfortable, and at worst might ruin Charlotte's standing in society. She bit her lip, thinking it over.

And yet, Mary attended salons, drew nude models, and by all accounts lived a far more liberal and debonair life than her sisters. If Charlotte were to allude to her feelings in some way, might she find those desires understood? Might Mary even be acquainted with women who felt as Charlotte did? It would be a great relief after all this time, to know that others felt the same way. She had long suspected that it was possible—after all, she was not so special as to be unique in this regard—and if so, then what did that mean? How did other people cope with such things? Did they court like couples did? Dance at balls? Live together in some manner, like a married couple did? She pictured two women kissing, holding hands, discarding their dresses on either side of a large bed. Sharing that same bed.

Oh.

Her mouth was dry, her cheeks flaming hot. Thankful that she was alone, Charlotte crept along the hallway and into the small parlor, where she struck a match and lit the stub of a candle which sat in a brass candlestick. The flame guttered for a moment before righting itself, casting a sphere of light strong enough to read by, provided she sat close enough to feel the heat upon her cheek. She picked up Barton's book, but didn't open it. The idea of two women living together would not leave her mind. *I mean, some do, do they not?* she thought. *For companionship and so forth?*

Charlotte had an elderly aunt on her mother's side who had lived with a long-time female companion until both had died, and no one had found that situation strange. Then again, the ladies had been old, and her aunt had been married twice already. Now that she thought about it, Great-Aunt Ethel had been very fond of Mrs Sudsbury. As a child, she'd thought the friendship sweet, and had hoped to have such friends as would last her whole life long. Now, seeing it through the shade of her new musings, Charlotte wondered whether there had been more than friendship between the two. They'd always chosen seats next to each other at dinner no matter who else was in the party, and their bedrooms had had an adjoining door which she and Maria had often used to escape during games of hide-and-seek as children, and—

Oh.

Charlotte opened the book, then closed it again without looking at it. She had no idea how one broached such subjects. It wasn't as if she could announce her inclinations across the eggs at breakfast and simply hope that Mary took it in stride. Mr Collins had always praised her subtlety and quiet diplomacy, but this was one occasion where a delicate approach might miss the mark entirely. Even if she wrote her sister now, the response would not arrive until after she and Mary had left for Canterbury. Besides, what on earth would she say? *Did the notion ever cross your mind that Great-Aunt Ethel might be bedding Mrs Sudsbury in between our visits?* was not likely to be received with the calm composure which Charlotte required.

Still, it was better than nothing, and once Charlotte had fetched parchment and pen, she scribbled a couple of hasty sentences down. With the letter written, Charlotte breathed a little easier. The answer, though she had no idea whether it would prove helpful or not, would come in time. All she had to do now was be patient.

After breakfast the next morning, Charlotte spent a few hours in the garden. Weeding left her back and arms aching, but gazing upon fresh soil with nary a dandelion in sight left her feeling a sense of accomplishment that none of her schooling had ever managed to produce. If only she could make her fortune by gardening, although even if such an impossible dream should become a reality, her peers would surely consider such an endeavour as sullying not only her hands but her name as a gentlewoman. It would not be worth the cost to her family's status, even if it meant she could contribute to their riches; no amount of money could convince her to humiliate her dear parents.

She took off her gloves and rummaged in the pocket of her skirt for a handkerchief with which to mop her brow, then stretched her hands above her head and then to the side, easing the pain in her back. Mary was due to return the next morning, and Charlotte had thought it might be nice to create a floral wreath as a centerpiece for their dinner. The larkspurs were looking particularly beautiful at the moment, their bold blue blossoms standing out proudly, but larkspurs were not an appropriate flower to choose for such an arrangement; she'd already told Mary that they stood for humour and strong love.

Charlotte cocked her head to the side, considering. If one could send a message in flowers, then why not express one's feelings to oneself that way too? Mary would not know what they signified, after all, and it would be as if Charlotte were writing some message in secret code that only she could read. She hugged herself, delighted by the thought. *It's a childish endeavour,* the little voice inside her head argued, but she ignored it, too excited by the idea. White peonies might do for a start— meaning new beginnings, and a certain bashfulness—and they would look exceedingly pretty when carefully placed around the base of a candlestick. Charlotte had so often been subjected to the pitiful, cruel sight of bunches crammed into a too-small vase, or flowers stuck into holes in a box without being properly trimmed, so that the stalks were uneven and the heads pointed every which way. She shuddered at the memory. No, this wreath would be delicate and carefully laid, like all flowers deserved.

She picked up her basket and wandered down the path until she came to the peonies. Kneeling down, her knees squeaking a protest, she stroked the nearest one, the petals silk-soft under her fingers. Seven or eight would do nicely. The trouble was to find them a decent enough match; a white flower always tended to look a little matrimonial or funereal to Charlotte, and needed something bright to bolster its subtle charms. The bright pink petals of the common corn-cockle would provide that vigor, but corn-cockle stood for overwork and unrelenting struggle—hardly the atmosphere she wished to convey. Cornflowers might do instead, as their pointed blue petals would contrast nicely with the peonies, and they represented hope for the future.

Charlotte stood, sighing. Cornflowers were an obvious choice, so why rebel against the idea? Turning from the peonies, she headed down into the southern part of the garden, just out of sight of her window, where the cornflowers grew. With each step, she became less convinced of her plan, and by the time she'd come within sight of the cornflowers, she'd decided against them entirely. *What is wrong with me today?* she wondered, mopping her brow again. *Picking a simple flower should not be this difficult.* Frowning, she was about to head back into the house when a flash of purple caught her eye.

Of course! She had been breeding pansies for two years now and had managed to achieve a pretty shade of lavender on the outer edge of the petals. Nearer the heart of the blossom, a darker purple surrounded each perfect circle of yellow pollen. Pansies were often used to indicate that the giver was thinking of loved ones lost, but they also might signify a lover's thoughts unspoken. Charlotte hesitated, shocked by her own idea. Still, it wasn't as if she was propositioning Mary. She was simply creating a little outlet for all the confusing thoughts of the past week. Did not a river burst its banks if one dammed the stream? The same could be said of a person. Besides, if Mary did not know what was being said, it couldn't be all that shocking. A person might say appalling or licentious things in Italian, but since Charlotte could not speak the language, she could only appreciate the apparent melody of the words. *Yes*, she decided, pushing down a stab of guilt, *there can be nothing wrong with letting off a little steam. Lord knows I have been under strange pressures of late.*

Besides, it was only flowers. How could one possibly go wrong?

Chapter Eight

Dearest Maria,

Thank you for your kind words. Indeed, I shall have to return to Lucas Lodge soon enough, and though it is not under happy circumstances, Mama and Papa seem eager to have me. Perhaps I will see you at Christmas, if not sooner? How fare your husband and daughter?

Lately, I have been ruminating on some beloved childhood memories. Remember when John played the frog prank on Mrs DeLong? And remember all those glorious weeks we spent at Great-Aunt Ethel's house? This may seem like a strange question, but did you ever think that she and Mrs Sudsbury were rather closer than most?

Your elder—though never your better—sister,

Charlotte

Mary returned late on Tuesday morning, and embraced Charlotte with unexpected vigour before she could so much as close the door behind her guest. The smell of violets tickled Charlotte's nose, her heart quickening as Mary pressed her close. Why was it that only women had ever made her feel such things? Men often smelled pleasant too—though admittedly, often they did not—but no man's scent had ever aroused such a response.

"Lord, but one does forget how trying my mother can be." Mary's voice was muffled, her face pressed into Charlotte's shoulder. She sighed, dramatically. "I was not in the house twenty minutes before I regretted coming at all."

"They say that absence makes the heart grow fonder." *And perhaps there is some truth in the saying,* she thought, *for she was only gone four days and yet I am terribly glad to see her.* She'd almost forgotten how bright Mary's eyes were, the way she held herself, as if expecting the world to deal her a blow she intended to meet with dignity.

"No one who met my mother ever repeated that sentiment." Mary sighed. "Perhaps my heart is too hardened for absence to soften it." She held Charlotte at arm's length and looked her over. "And how have my books been treating you?"

"Very well," Charlotte said, desperate not to disappoint.

"Really?" Mary raised an eyebrow.

"Well," she confessed, "the second, at least. I found the first very difficult. I am afraid I lack the language to comprehend even the smallest part of what the author is saying."

"Good."

This was not the response she had expected. "Good?" she repeated. "Do you not wish to rescind your invitation to the salon? I certainly won't be able to keep up with—"

"My dear friend," Mary said, laying a hand on her arm. Charlotte's heart fluttered. "All of science is knowing a little about one thing and admitting that you know nothing about most of the rest."

"Is it?" Charlotte said, mystified.

"Quite so. Why, if you had told me you were certain of anything after reading one book, I would have known the opposite was true. One must be humble in the face of one's own ignorance, which is so often vast."

"Then perhaps I shall be the best scientist of all," Charlotte said, smiling.

Mary spent all of dinner regaling Charlotte with imperson- ations of a hysterical Mrs Bennet, each funnier than the last, until Charlotte's sides quite ached from laughing. "And then she asked me, why did I not find a nice gentleman in Canter- bury, and whether I wished her to go to her grave with one daughter yet unmarried." Mary rolled her eyes.

"Oh?" Charlotte picked up her wine glass. Mary had brought back a delicious vintage from the Longbourne cellar, and the aromatic bouquet brought back many familiar memories of the raucous household. Kitty and Lydia fighting like wild cats over a bonnet, Lizzie making arch witticisms, Jane chiding her gently for her lack of patience, and Mary in the corner on the pianoforte or reading from an old book.

"I told her that if one shot a grouse in four out of five at- tempts, one would consider that a good afternoon's hunting. Naturally, my father agreed with me. Not that Mother dropped the subject, of course. We returned to it at least two dozen times over the course of my visit."

Charlotte sipped her wine, not sure what to say. Mary had not yet noticed the wreath she'd made earlier, though she found she was rather glad the subject had not come up. It had been bold of her to pick these particular flowers, and it would have been uncomfortable to lie about their meanings. "I am sure she would simply like to see you settled and happy."

"I am happy," Mary declared, lifting her glass. "I have this delightful vintage, I have Mrs Waites' rum cake to look for- ward to, and I have exceedingly pleasant company." She grinned across the table. "What more could a person desire?"

As Bessie cleared away the dinner plates and brought two

great slabs of rum cake in, accompanied by a spiced cream Mrs Waites had recently perfected, Charlotte couldn't help but agree.

The next afternoon, they walked into the village and boarded a coach. Canterbury, being only five or six hours away by coach, was easily made in one attempt though Charlotte had never had reason to visit before.

"I'm afraid I cannot sit for so long in a box that small without my muscles aching for a week afterwards," said Mary apologetically. "If you do not mind, I would prefer to stay overnight at an inn and continue on at dawn. I have in mind just the right one, and I am certain the pigeon pie they serve will impress you."

Charlotte, who knew little of the area, was more than happy to defer to her friend's expertise in the matter, and so it was settled. The sky had been overcast that morning, and while the gathering of white and dove-grey clouds did not hint at rain in their future, it nonetheless precluded the sunny afternoon Charlotte had rather been hoping for. She was not fond of travel at the best of times, but if she had to do so, then she would prefer to while away the hours soaking up the beautiful landscape. The countryside unravelled before them as the coach bumbled along the road and over the small stone bridge which led out of the village. Sturdy oaks stood alone in vivid green fields, their branches still, their leaves barely trembling. Sheep grazed in clumps, one occasionally drifting off from the rest to join another group, mirroring the clouds above. In the distance, the farmland was divided into rough rectangles, each nearly as green as the grass. Soon, the wheat would turn a beautiful golden-brown, and then it would be harvest time.

Mary had set her bag on the seat beside her and rummaged around in it for a while before locating charcoal and parchment. Before she touched the charcoal to paper, she looked up, meeting Charlotte's eyes. "Pardon my impoliteness. I did not ask you last night what you were up to while I was gone."

Charlotte froze. Was Mary hinting that she'd noticed the folded dress? "I did not do much, I confess. I went to lunch at Rosings the day you departed."

There was the slightest of pauses. The charcoal descended again, and again, did not quite meet the parchment. "Ah," Mary said, her tone cool. "And was Mr Innes there?"

"Yes, as well as three other gentlemen of Anne's acquaintance."

"Three? Why, your Miss de Bourgh really is set on marrying you off."

Charlotte adjusted her left glove, then her right. The skin between her shoulder blades prickled. "She has expressed that wish to me openly, and while I think it sweet, I think her unlikely to succeed in her endeavours."

Mary simply nodded, and spent the next few minutes trying to sketch the landscape, before giving it up and turning the paper over. On the other side, clearly visible was a half finished sketch of a nude woman, standing at the edge of a small stream. Charlotte couldn't help staring. She wondered who this was—it did not look like the mysterious Anne from the drawing Charlotte had seen—and whether Mary was also drawing this woman from memory. *Does she know this face as well as mine? Perhaps better? I wonder if there is any way I could convince her to take me to the kind of drawing class she mentioned.* Forcing herself to look back at the fields, though she could not find nearly as much pleasure in them as she had just a moment before, Charlotte leaned her head against the carriage wall and lost herself in thought. The stone road soon turned into a dirt road, and, in half an hour, a small village was visible in the distance. Tiny labourers moved to and fro, no doubt going about their usual business.

"The road is too bumpy to manage anything decent," Mary complained, sighing in exasperation. "One day they shall make the roads between towns as smooth as city streets, but until that time, I fear that I will have to put this away and we shall have to make our own amusements."

As Mary tucked the parchment away, Charlotte found herself relieved. The presence of drawings of nude women, which prior to Miss Bennet's arrival had not featured greatly in Charlotte's life, was already beginning to affect her nerves. Even a brief glimpse of the curve of the waist, the single stroke suggesting crossed thighs, and the slightest smudge indicating what might lie at the apex of that stroke was enough to unsettle her completely. She cast about for some diversion that would take her mind off bodies. Mary shrugged off her light shawl, revealing the pretty, dark green dress below. The colour reminded Charlotte of holly leaves, symbolising peace, goodwill, and the endurance of life. Was it just Charlotte, or was Mary wearing something lower-cut than usual? *For goodness' sake*, she scolded herself. *Do not ogle your friend so.*

She shifted position so that her left leg was not touching Mary's, though this meant she had to keep her heel elevated rather uncomfortably. "One of Mr Collins' visitors had a very droll question he liked to ask everybody, and which might suffice to entertain you for a moment," Charlotte suggested. "If I recall correctly, it was something along the lines of 'how many owls would you have to see before you thought something was wrong?'"

"Before I thought something was wrong?" Mary repeated, thinking it over. "Hmm. I would have to say… Two."

"That is a very small number. What if they were a breeding pair?"

"The problem is that I do not trust owls," Mary declared. "They always look as if they were up to something. No animal by nature innocent should be able to turn its head around so far. Why, what number did you choose?"

"Seven."

"Seven?" she cried. "Seven? No, by God, by seven it would be too late."

She looked so serious that Charlotte had to try very hard not to laugh. "Too late for what?"

"For whatever they were planning," Mary said darkly.

Charlotte dissolved into a fit of giggles, and for the next few minutes, she could not get a sensible word out. "I had no idea," she gasped, "how afraid you were of owls."

"I am not afraid! I am rightfully cautious, and you, my friend, are far too trusting." Mary's smile lit up her whole face, and Charlotte's chest flushed with a pleasurable warmth. "And now you must tell me how your late husband responded, for I knew the man but little and could not possibly guess."

"He said none at all." Charlotte wiped tears of laughter from her eyes. "We tried to make him understand that seeing no owls whatsoever would not be any cause for alarm, or most of England would be running around panicking on a daily basis, but I do not think he quite understood why his guest bothered to ask in the first place."

"It is a capital game, at any rate. What made you think of it?"

"I do not quite know. At the time, it struck me as a rather revealing question, as the person responding so often feels obliged to give their reasons and defend their choice. The answer can tell you quite a lot about a person." Her calf twinged. She was going to have to accept that she would likely spend the entire trip touching Mary in some degree, and she would simply have to cope with it in a normal fashion. She leaned forward, stretching the offending leg in the hope that it would cease complaining.

"Is that so? And what does my answer—"

A sudden jolt threw Charlotte forward. Unbalanced as she already was, a moment later she landed in a heap in Mary's lap. Charlotte tried to right herself and was horrified to find her hands planted high on firm thighs. She looked up, spluttering an apology, only to find Mary's face once again inches from her own. Mary's eyes were so dark as to be almost black, the pupils widened impossibly. Another jolt threw her sideways and her hands slipped, but Mary caught her before she hit the floor. "Goodness," said she, helping Charlotte up. "Perhaps you should sit beside me, lest you start flying about the carriage again."

With flaming cheeks, Charlotte took the seat beside Mary. "You were saying?"

"What? Oh, yes." Mary's voice was perfectly composed, but she looked almost as ruffled as Charlotte felt. "I was merely going to ask you what my answer told you about me."

Charlotte tried to gather her thoughts. The length of Mary's entire body was pressed against her now, and the delicious heat made it rather hard to organise words into any coherent speech. "Well, I have already teased you about your suspicious nature. Perhaps you are the kind of person who sees a pattern before others do, or perhaps you see patterns where there are none." If she hadn't been so discomfited, she might have phrased it differently, and regretted how it came out. "That is to say," she corrected hastily, "you seem to me to be a profound and sensitive person, though you would have me believe otherwise." Charlotte hesitated. This wasn't what she'd meant to say at all, and though Mary's expression had not changed, she sensed a new wariness. "That is to say," she repeated, "that I like your nature very much, though it is not quite like my own. You are right when you say I am too trusting, and I admit I am rather naive at times."

Mary patted Charlotte's hand, her warm fingers lingering. "I like your nature very much too, Charlotte. And you are right." She heaved a sigh, though she did not look away. "I am rather too cynical for my own good sometimes. I would like to be more like you, though without your gullible trust in the dubious goodness of owls." Before Charlotte could press her on that point, she added, "Perhaps you will be the positive influence on me that you were on Lizzie."

"I do not think I was any sort of influence on your sister," Charlotte protested. "She always knew her own mind."

"You mean she was wilful and stubborn. No," Mary waved off Charlotte's second protest, smiling, "I do not consider either a flaw, as some might, if not taken to excess. Though I admit, Lizzie did always seem to be off in her own world, two steps ahead of everyone else. I often thought her too superior to enjoy simple things, and while I admired that quality for a time, I came to see that it was not necessarily the virtue I had once considered it."

The conversation turned, as it often did, to the other Bennet sisters, though Mary once again skirted around the subject of Lydia's husband, and by the time night had begun to fall, Charlotte had been thoroughly apprised of the goings-on of half of Hertfordshire.

"It was all my mother talked about," said she, glumly, "that is, when she wasn't listing off the names of local gentlemen that I might, at the first available opportunity, throw myself at. I'd sooner throw myself under the wheels of their carriages, to be perfectly frank."

Charlotte could well imagine the relentless tirades and guilt-inducing comments Mrs Bennet was capable of, and sought to distract Mary by supplying her own gossip, though her limited circle meant that most of it had come second or third-hand. In the next village—almost big enough to be a town, really—they disembarked outside an inn which overlooked the road. While Charlotte seated herself at a table inside and ordered a slice of the pigeon pie which had come so highly recommended, Mary haggled with the innkeeper. "She will give us a room for the night, but it is the last one she has, so we must share," Mary announced, sliding into a seat opposite. "You do not mind, do you?"

Charlotte half choked on her mouthful of pie. "No, of course not." She cleared her throat. *For goodness' sake, act normally.* "You do not snore, do you?"

"In fact I do. It was a terrible problem for me as a child, and has not improved much in adulthood."

In danger of choking a second time, Charlotte put down her fork. *Who has been close enough to hear her breathe during sleep? Perhaps one of her scientist friends—some learned gentleman with whom she studies the stars or elements. Or perhaps an artist, with long, lustrous hair and a beard to match.* The taste of the pigeon pie, which had been so delicious only moments before, turned bitter on her tongue.

Mary's lips twitched. "Like a great bear, Lydia once told me," she continued. "She slept next door, you know, and said she often lay awake half the night, wondering when the wall between us was going to collapse under the force." She shot Charlotte a sly look. "You may wish to tie yourself to the bed, just in case."

Charlotte was deeply glad she'd already put down her fork, for the insinuation left her hands sweaty and trembling, though she was left with nothing to hide her blushes behind and was unutterably glad when the innkeeper bustled over to say that their room was ready.

The room was nice enough, with walls painted a pretty duck-egg blue, and wide windows lined with dark blue curtains. The bed was a little smaller than the marital bed in which Charlotte had infrequently coupled with Mr Collins, and she heaved a private, frustrated sigh at the thought she had spent all day within inches of Mary and would now have to spend the night in such a way too. *Why fight it?* the little voice in her head suggested. *You have only a short time together in Canterbury and soon enough you will be back in Hertfordshire, alone in a bed until the end of your days.* It was a disturbing thought, but it made a kind of sense. Clearly she was not able to reason her attraction away, so she might as well accept it. Besides, as long as she maintained perfect behavior outwardly, no one need ever know of her silly infatuation; for that was all it was, really, and would surely pass either with more time spent together, or once they were finally apart.

Chapter Nine

Getting into bed with a woman was very different, Charlotte reflected, as she and Mary sat side by side, propped up with pillows. Her companion was engrossed in a book, and the only noise which broke the silence was the soft swish of a turned page. Mr Collins had always made a surprising amount of noise whenever they had shared a bed, hemming and hawing over some passage in his Bible, testing small turns of phrase out loud to see whether they sounded suitable in his next sermon, sniffling and coughing and snorting and—

Charlotte repressed a sigh. Really, sometimes she felt like an awful person. Mr Collins had been a perfectly serviceable husband and a kind man. If she had found him wanting in some areas, well, that was to be expected. And if she had also found him mildly irritating or embarrassing on occasion then, judging by how other women had talked of their own husbands—out of earshot from said husbands—that too was quite normal.

"How do you like it?" Mary leaned over, her dark curls unpinned and lying loose over the shoulders of her white nightgown.

Guiltily, Charlotte flinched. "Pardon?"

"The book." She gestured at the naturalist's diary, lying forgotten in Charlotte's lap. "Does it bore you? Or are you too tired to read? The journey was rather long today."

"You are very kind. No, it does not bore me at all. On the contrary, I find it very interesting. The way Mr Barton describes the place, with particular attention to the sounds and smells, is extremely evocative. I almost feel I were there alongside him." Charlotte touched the book's cover, tracing the name of the author. "I was actually thinking about my late husband."

Mary's smile softened, her eyes becoming more serious. "You do not talk of him often. If you wish to do so, know that I would gladly hear it. It has not been long since he died, and I supposed that…well, grief so often comes in strange forms. One person's mourning process is quite different from another's." She bit her lip. "I apologize again for being so callous in the beginning. I hope that I did not give you the impression that I—well."

She bit her lip again, evidently having trouble choosing the right words. A soft, green tenderness bloomed in Charlotte's heart. Miss Bennet was not the sort to think much before speaking, and taking such obvious effort to do so showed that she really did care about Charlotte's feelings. The room was dim, lit only by a candle on either side of the bed. They'd drawn the curtains, closing themselves off against the night and the world, and the tumult of voices and clank of mugs from the bar below had long turned from a clamour to a soft, oceanic murmur. *We might be the last two people in the world*, Charlotte thought, and the notion sprouted a tiny, bold bud. "May I tell you something in confidence?"

"Of course," Mary said instantly. "I would never divulge your secrets."

"It is simply this: I do not think I grieve him as I ought," Charlotte confessed. "That sounds terrible but it is true."

"Why, who says you ought to grieve him in any particular way?"

She smiled. "You are trying to make me feel better, and I am grateful for your kindness, but I do know the difference between guilt and truth. I never loved him as I ought, and so I cannot grieve him as I ought." She put a hand over her chest, the thin fabric of her own nightgown rustling against her fingers, and felt her heart ache with something she could neither name nor explain. "I worry that I…perhaps I am not a good person if I could not—"

Mary reached for her free hand, and pressed it tightly. "Do not say such things. You are one of the best people I have ever known." Her eyes were fierce and bright, reflecting the candle, and Charlotte could not look away.

"But I—"

"Sometimes," Mary interrupted, "love is like a flower. If the seed is planted too deeply, then it may never see sunlight. If too shallowly, it may be eaten by a passing bird. If the conditions are not conducive, if there is not enough sun or rain or if the soil is not fertile enough, or a hundred other reasons, then the seed will not flourish. That is not the fault of the seed. Sometimes conditions are simply not ripe." She looked as if she were about to add something else, and then hesitated, blushing. "Not that I know much of love, but this I do."

"You may be right," Charlotte conceded.

"I am always right," Mary said, fluttering her eyelashes, making Charlotte laugh. "It makes me the envy of all my friends and the terror of all my enemies. Shall we turn in for the night?"

Charlotte nodded her agreement. Each laid their books aside and blew out their candles. Burrowed down into the sheets, they lay shrouded in absolute darkness, for the hangings of the four-poster blotted out even the tiniest slit of light from the shuttered windows. However, though she was tired from the day's travel, sleep was far from Charlotte's mind. The kind of conversation which had seemed impossible during daylight hours, even with Mary—who seemed to be able to draw intimacies and confidences out of her as easily as pulling a thread—seemed now much closer and, if not necessary, then certainly desirable. She longed to talk and be heard, to explain her heart and in doing so perhaps finally understand herself. Having lived so long to please others, remaining quiet and amiable and bland, had left her hardly able to ascertain what she wanted or what her real opinions might be. The only thing she really felt certain of was that she loved gardening, and in turn, flowers responded well to her careful ministrations. *And much good that will do me,* she thought. *Flowers will not save me from spinsterhood, or land me a husband, or change my destiny. At most, they will give me a little pleasure each day until I inevitably die alone, still a burden to my family.*

"I saw your drawing of me," Charlotte confessed. Mary had been so kind to her, and to lie, even by omission, now seemed wrong. "I did not mean to, I was simply rescuing your dress from being creased. I do hope you are not angry with me."

Mary didn't respond immediately, and the lengthening silence made Charlotte anxious. Instinctively, she reached out and found Mary's hand, warm and rough. Mary's fingers entwined with her own, slotting into place perfectly, and for a single, glorious moment Charlotte allowed herself to imagine that hand upon her hip, pulling her close. She blushed, thankful that she couldn't be seen, for the thoughts must surely be writ large upon her face. These thoughts were impossible to entertain during daylight hours but here in the dark, perhaps one or two silly notions could be permitted.

"I hope you do not mind that I finished the drawing after you asked me to stop." Mary's voice, usually so confident, was softer. More vulnerable. "I just… I thought it ought to be complete."

"Of course I do not mind." Charlotte pitched her own voice low and reassuring, with a hint of amusement. "You made me look quite beautiful. It speaks to your talent as an artist that you were capable of such a thing."

Mary squeezed her fingers. "You are a perfect fool, Charlotte Lucas. I cannot draw anything that is not already there."

Charlotte knew she should let go, but Mary's thumb had begun to draw small circles around her wrist, and the tickling sensation produced a tightness low in her belly that was entirely too pleasant. *How long can one hold a friend's hand without being thought odd?* Yet Mary hadn't let go either. "It must have taken you a long time."

"Indeed. I stayed up all night to do so. In fact, I only slept on the coach to Hertfordshire."

"Now who is the fool?" Charlotte teased, although she couldn't help frowning. "What possessed you to do something like that? And without my face to compare, was it not very difficult?"

"Difficult? Not at all." Mary snorted. "Your face is so familiar to me."

Charlotte blinked, though the darkness was so acute that it hardly made a difference whether her eyes were open or shut. "Really?" Of course, she'd spent a lot of time at Longbourne while growing up, and while she'd noticed Mary, she'd never really spent much time thinking about her. She'd dismissed the middle Bennet sister as dull and preachy, and though Charlotte had always taken pains to be polite, she had never sought Mary out for conversation. *How different things might have been then,* she thought. *How much she has changed, and how little I have.*

"I suppose you know I always admired you. My sisters have their own strengths and weakness, and Lord knows those flaws have got us into some—" Mary halted abruptly. "That is to say, you seemed to me to be the best of us. As kind as Jane, as deep as Lizzie, but with your own cool composure. You were the voice of reason in any argument, and you heard each side with such compassion."

Charlotte had been correct in her earliest surmise, then; Mary had always been watching and quietly cataloguing. Again, she wondered how much Mary had seen, and how much Mary had understood. She fought the sudden urge to pull her hand back. *She was very young then, and not so worldly,* she reassured herself. *Perhaps she did not quite know what she saw, if in truth she saw anything at all.*

"And what about you?" Charlotte asked. "If that was your estimation of your sisters and I, what is your estimation of yourself?"

"Oh, I am an odd duck. I always have been. I retreated into the past as a way of coping with the present, though it did me no favours. I was awkward and blunt and desperate for praise, though deserving none." Mary's thumb stuttered over the soft flesh of Charlotte's wrist. "I may still be blunt, but I would like to think that my other qualities have ameliorated in time. I am, as ever, a work undergoing continual development."

"I like your qualities," Charlotte insisted, and was rewarded with a soft, breathy laugh.

Again, she couldn't help imagining Mary's hand on her waist, gripping tighter; perhaps even Mary's lips, pressing lightly against her cheek. The tightness in her belly rolled lower down, the gentle warmth turning into a low, persistent flame.

"Mmm." Mary yawned, then turned onto her side to face Charlotte, who waited with held breath to see what might be forthcoming. Unfortunately, a snuffling snore was her only response, and Charlotte smiled in the darkness, amused. When she attempted to extricate her hand, Mary only clung on tighter and she was forced to give it up as a lost cause.

It signifies nothing, she told herself. Mary saw her only as another older sister—had she not said as much?—or a new friendship kindled. Still, she couldn't help picturing the drawing of her own face, every line and detail accurate. The drawing she'd seen of the nude woman in the letter to Mary had not so much detail, though perhaps that aspect varied between artists, some preferring a vague outline while some included every wart and wrinkle of their subjects. She'd wanted to ask about that draw-ing too, to admit she'd seen it, but that was quite a different situation altogether, and might have provoked anger, for it had been a private correspondence. In addition to guilt for having pried, some other emotion had been woven into the thread of her feelings; a dark, sour thing, which stung every time she imagined Mary examining the details of the drawing, those warm hands perhaps touching her own lips, caressing her cheek, her neck, wandering lower and lower and—

Charlotte squeezed her eyes shut and took a deep breath. *You are going to go to sleep and not think about drawing or nude women at all,* she told herself firmly. Surprisingly, this did not work. She counted sheep, then cows, then began to list all the flowers she could remember, in alphabetical order. When dawn finally broke, the sun peering in through the thin gap in the curtains, Charlotte found herself both relieved and troubled. The feel-ings she had allowed herself to explore had evidently taken root. She only hoped it would be possible to dig them up later.

Chapter Ten

Dear Mrs Collins,
Mr Collins' death quite disturbed me, for one generally considers the clergy closer to God and therefore less likely to be called away to aid Him, but I suppose, in the end, they are simply men like the rest. Nevertheless, sorrows and prayers for your loss.

While you spend time with our Mary, I hoped you could elaborate on the great felicity of marriage; she may well listen to you, though Lord knows she does not listen to us. Having four girls out of five settled is very agreeable, but having one left over like a spare jar of jam rather ruins the effect. To be a mama to wilful young ladies is to be constantly vexed. Really, no one understands how I suffer.
Sincerely,
Mrs Bennet

When they rose just after dawn, Charlotte felt exceedingly tired both by the brief journey and the lack of sleep the night before. Even the two cups of tea she'd downed at breakfast in lieu of actual food were not enough to keep her awake once they'd set off for Canterbury. The rolling purr of the carriage, gently rocking her from side to side like a babe in arms, did not help matters any. As a result, she was startled to find herself tapped gently on the shoulder—an action which she found detrimental to her attempts at slumber and therefore attempted to escape by burrowing deeper into the soft pillow—and Mary's voice, much closer to her ear than she had expected, murmuring, "Wake up, Charlotte. We shall arrive in a few minutes."

Charlotte sat bolt upright, almost knocking both of them to the floor. Wiping her mouth with the back of her hand, she was disgusted to find that her chin was wet, as was the shoulder of Mary's dress.

"I may snore," Mary remarked, dark eyes glittering with amusement, "but at least I do not drool."

"I must beg your forgiveness," Charlotte said, horrified, her cheeks burning with hot embarrassment.

"No need. It was my own fault for being such a comfortable pillow, was it not?" She leaned in, lowering her voice to a conspiratorial whisper. "Besides, I shall have ample fodder to tease you for the next week, if not the rest of your life."

Charlotte forced a smile. She'd been dreaming something strange; a land of yellow flowers taller than a man. She'd walked amongst the stalks with no fear of harm, though they bent their heads towards her as if whispering their secrets, but she'd had the feeling that something dangerous had lurked in the forest beyond, just out of sight. Discomfited, she stared out of the carriage window. In the dim dawn, she could make out occasional figures passing each other on the streets—a hat tip here, a nod of acquaintance there. It was too dim to see much more, for the clouds overhead were thick and grey, and even with the introduction of lanterns hanging from the ornate metalwork outside every home and townhouse, the sky had not yet broken into true luminosity.

She'd been used to much more darkness in Kent. The parsonage had a sconce on the south wall—Mr Collins had it installed to "provide a guiding light to eternal salvation for those lost", though Charlotte had privately thought it probably only provided a guiding light for those who had wandered too far off the road home from the local tavern. Cities had much more light than small villages and towns; her own village never needed such things. One navigated by the moon or the stars, and when both were absent, one had better find a candle or hope that one's memory was good.

She rubbed her eyes, which felt gritty and sore. "Are we close to your aunt's house?"

"Indeed we are. It is not far now," Mary said, offering Charlotte her shawl, which had fallen to the floor in all the fuss. "I wrote ahead when I was in Longbourne, and the carriage will be waiting for us."

The carriage was indeed waiting when they disembarked the coach outside an inn, two brown horses stamping with impatience. With a couple of murmured words to the eager young footman who bounded forward, Mary helped Charlotte into the carriage. Without thinking, Charlotte took the opportunity to seat herself again next to Mary, though there was now no danger of being thrown bodily out of her seat. Though the carriage was even smaller than the coach, Mary did not seem to mind at all, and a few minutes more brought them into a very fine street. The houses formed two terraced rows, facing each other across the cobblestones, like armies ready to do battle.

"There," Mary said, pointing at the nearest house on the left. "Here we are."

Charlotte admired the tall windows, the elegant, glossy front doors all painted a matching black, and the iron railings outside each house, though she was too tired to linger in the chill air. Mary helped her down from the carriage, waving the young footman aside, and led her up the steps—neatly swept, and flanked on either side by a pair of strange stone creatures with the face and paws of an angry lion, and the long tail of a serpent. The door was opened by a tall man, dressed in a smart black jacket which immediately marked him out as the butler. "Good morning, Miss Bennet," he said, his voice deep and melodious. "Welcome home. Everything is as you requested."

"Thank you, Pitt." Mary hooked her arm into the crook of Charlotte's elbow and led her forward through a dim hallway into a large, open foyer.

The walls were painted a serene green, and the high ceiling decorated with beautifully scalloped cornices just as grand as the Rosings entryway, though Mr Collins would have died much earlier if Charlotte had ever ventured such an opinion. Through a doorway on the left Charlotte caught a glimpse of a blue-wallpapered room she would very much like to investigate. She hesitated but her companion tugged her onwards until they stood directly under the large chandelier, and pointed up towards a large portrait on the right-hand wall of a handsome woman with tawny, brown hair and strikingly green eyes. The subject of the portrait was dressed in a beautiful blue gown and a pink sash. Unusually, she had a dog at her feet and a rifle on her lap. A brace of pheasants, not yet plucked, hung in the background. Through forested trees unlike any Charlotte had ever seen, the great bulky outline of a tall beast—as big as a horse but with mighty, curved antlers quite unlike the pointed antlers English deer wore—was only just visible. Charlotte had seen plenty of portraits in her life, but none had ever featured a woman who so evidently took pleasure in the hunt as men did, nor the scenery, which must be the Americas rather than the English countryside. "Ah!" cried she. "And this must be your aunt Cecily?"

"Indeed. She's rather proud of that portrait." Mary grinned. "It scandalizes most visitors on first arrival though. I am glad to see that it does not unsettle you."

"Quite the contrary," Charlotte protested. "I would like to know much more about her."

"For now it may suffice to know that she is about Lydia's

height, therefore taller than either you or I, and her hair is indeed that most becoming shade of brown. I can assure you that the portrait is a perfect likeness, though it does not fully convey, at least in my opinion, all the wit and wisdom my aunt possesses. Nor does it convey her rather wicked sense of humour. When she first met her husband's family, she fed them all sorts of nonsense. In fact, she had them believing that the Scots hunted wild haggis, which roamed in packs across the highlands, and that you must never offer an Englishman cake, for to do so would cause great offense to his ancestors."

Charlotte couldn't help smiling, though Aunt Cecily sounded rather intimidating. "When is she next due back from America?"

"I do not know." Mary shrugged. "She comes and goes as she pleases, and leaves me at leisure to do the same. It is rather a good arrangement, if I do say so. And not once has she ever harangued me to marry. In fact, quite the opposite. She has some rather liberal views about—" Her gaze flickered towards Charlotte before she cleared her throat. "Well, I shall give you a proper tour later, and answer all your burning questions then too. I suspect you would like to rest a little before lunch."

Charlotte opened her mouth to say that she was entirely well, but her words were swallowed up by a huge yawn. Grinning, Mary tugged Charlotte towards the large staircase, which tapered into a landing before branching off to the left and right. "Come. Your room is next to mine."

Lucas Lodge had been a decent size, but after living in the parsonage for four years, Charlotte had grown used to small means. Constant visits to Rosings had merely served to emphasise all that the Collinses did not have, and Lady Catherine's frequent hand-me-downs had only made the Hunsford parsonage feel even more cramped. This, however, was a large house by her appraisal, and exceptionally well-kept by anyone's standards. The dark wood floors were knotted with black whorls, and the walls were a cream so pale it looked like new milk.

They climbed only one flight before Mary made a sharp turn down the hallway. Charlotte followed, casting curious glances at the paintings which adorned the walls. Here at least there was light enough to see, but Mary seemed keen to ensure her guest was established in a room as soon as possible. Perhaps Charlotte had been asleep for longer than she'd thought. Her cheeks burned again at the memory of waking wet-chinned and hopelessly adrift. Mary had not really seemed to mind, but it was not exactly the graceful image Charlotte would have preferred to portray. She shivered, pulling her shawl tightly around her shoulders. The hallway was not cold, but she had not eaten since yesterday and a distinct coolness had crept into her bones while she'd slept.

"This is your room," Mary said, pausing outside the last door. The handle was brass, polished to such a shine Charlotte could see her own reflection in it. The servants kept the place exceedingly clean—even Lady Catherine could not have found fault here. "I am just next door," Mary added, pointing. "Now, the dining room is on the ground floor, second door on the left. The servants will direct you if you get lost, though I expect you'll manage. Actually," she paused with her fingers on the handle, "perhaps you would like to close your eyes and let me lead you inside. It is not a large surprise, but perhaps you will indulge me?"

Surprised, Charlotte closed her eyes, aware of the rustling of Mary's skirts, the faint violet scent which permeated the air. A warm hand closed around her wrist and a moment later was tugging her forward, ushering her inside. The change in temperature was welcome, and the crackle of a blazing fire on her left provided a clue as to why. "Now," Mary said, and Charlotte could hear the smile in her voice, "open your eyes."

Charlotte obeyed, then gasped. The room was utterly gorgeous; the walls were a pale yellow, the large unshuttered windows letting in pale sunlight. In the magnificent hearth, tongues of orange flame licked along new logs. On either side of the fire sat two winged armchairs, upholstered in sage-green, perched atop a magnificent, forest-green rug. Charlotte could tell at a glance that they were more comfortable than the ones in the parsonage, and couldn't wait to curl up in one to read more of the naturalist's diary. On a small table between the armchairs, a tall white vase held a fresh bouquet of foxgloves in every colour from white to purple to a faded red which Charlotte had never seen before. She crossed the room, all thoughts of thanking her host lost in her excitement, and bent to examine the flowers. "Why, these are delightful!" she cried.

"They are your favourite, I know." Mary smiled, though she shifted her weight from foot to foot as if nervous. "I called in a favour from a friend to obtain that particular shade of red. It is a little unusual, I believe. And you did tell me that they had some meaning, did you not?" She tapped her bottom lip with a single finger. "Secrets and riddles and everlasting life?"

"They can also mean deceit," Charlotte said, still rapturous, "though I hardly think you meant them that way. Do you not think it strange that flowers may mean cruel things as well as kind ones?"

"Not particularly. People use callous words as well as tender words. Why not flowers?"

"It seems unfair to the flower," Charlotte mused. "They're only the messenger, after all." She was startled when Mary giggled, and straightened, remembering herself. "Thank you for such a wonderful gift. It is quite enough to stay in your home, you need not have gone to so much trouble for me. I do hope the favour you called in was not a large one."

Mary waved an airy hand, and Charlotte turned to inspect the rest of the room. A gleaming mahogany desk sat against one wall, a neat pile of parchment accompanied by two small bottles of ink, an array of quills, and a stump of red sealing wax with which to seal letters. A tall wardrobe made of dark wood, matching the floor, stood to attention beside the desk. Under the shuttered window there was a large metal tub, full of steaming hot water. The scent of lavender and mint drifted from it in a very pleasing way, and Charlotte was suddenly very aware of all the dust and dirt of travel clinging to her. Not wanting to rush Mary out of the room, however desperately she wished to bathe, she moved towards the bed; a beautiful four-poster, much nicer than the one they'd stayed in at the inn. The sheets and pillows were a crisp white, and the grey blanket neatly folded over the bottom of the bed was embroidered with tiny blue flowers. Charlotte ran a finger over one experimentally, feeling each petal in turn and then the raised circle of the yellow stitches of the pollen. "This is beautiful," said she. "Did your aunt do this?"

Mary snorted, then tried to cover it with a cough. "No, Aunt Cecily is not the embroidering type. It was her friend, Edith, who did such fine work."

It might just have been the way the firelight flickered, lighting the room with a pretty golden glow, but Charlotte could have sworn Mary was blushing. She would have liked to press the issue, but heavy footsteps could be heard coming along the hallway and the next moment a short, broad footman appeared, carrying Charlotte's trunk. Mary directed him to deposit it next to the bed, where it might be least obtrusive, and the boy did so with a cheerful countenance. He disappeared speedily into the hallway, where Charlotte could hear Pitt directing another footman to bring up Mary's own luggage.

"I thought you would like this room best," Mary said, calling Charlotte's attention back. "I am delighted to be proven correct, as I usually am." She winked at Charlotte before pointing at the tub. "That should be the perfect temperature for you, though if you would like it warmed further, ring the bell. I shall leave you to your *toilette*." She half turned, before turning back. "Are you hungry? You ate not a thing at breakfast."

"A little," Charlotte admitted, though she wanted nothing more than to leap into the bathtub.

Mary nodded. "If you would wait but a moment, one of the maids will bring you a tray. Please do not hesitate to call me or the servants should you require anything. Anything at all. Nothing is an inconvenience if it pleases you."

Charlotte could feel a blush creeping over her cheeks and down her neck. If she didn't know better, she'd think Mary was playing the part of a courteous, dashing swain. "You are too kind."

Mary stepped forward and kissed her lightly on the cheek. "Sleep sweetly, Charlotte. I shall see you in an hour or two."

Mary closed the door behind her, leaving Charlotte frozen in the middle of the room. Once she had regained her ability to breathe, she touched the cheek Mary had kissed with light fingers, tracing the spot where lips had met flesh. This was a new development, and not an unpleasant one, though she would have to be careful not to ruminate over it too long lest new notions took root in her mind which were harder to dig out. Mary was simply more at ease in her own home, as anyone would be, and had in all likelihood slipped into the more formal manners which were to be expected in Canterbury. Charlotte knelt and unlocked her trunk, and busied herself with putting things away in the wardrobe. She sighed over how dowdy her black gowns would look next to Mary's, and wished not for the first time that the mourning period was not so long nor so dreary.

As Mary had promised, a maid appeared in due course, bringing a tray which held a teapot, cheese, fresh bread, and slices of cold ham, alongside a single sugar biscuit in the shape of a star. The maid, a tall, slender sapling of perhaps sixteen or seventeen, poured a cup and left, closing the door behind her. Charlotte ate quickly, only realising just how hungry she had been after she'd tasted the first bite of buttery cheese, before stripping off her petticoats and shift, and submerging herself into the hot water—too hot to be truly comfortable, just the way she liked it—with a lascivious moan that echoed around the room. The soap provided had sprigs of dried lavender running through it, and left her feeling clean and fresh for the first time in days.

After drying off naked in front of the fire, accompanied by a second round of cheese and bread, Charlotte got into her nightgown and then into the bed, groaning with pleasure again. After hours spent sitting upon a hard bench, for no cushioning could disguise a coach seat for what it was, it felt wonderful to sink into downy softness. She could still feel the touch of Mary's lips upon her cheek. Would she be expected to perform the same action? If she did not, would Mary think her rude or boorish? She certainly would not like to offend, and the desire to adhere to the rules of Canterbury society was absolutely nothing to do with the slow warmth in her belly.

She rolled her eyes, aware she was being foolish. No matter. Whatever her real desire, she was not doing any harm with this silly, girlish infatuation—except to herself. *Speaking of girlish infatuations*, she thought, recalling the mention of Aunt Cecily's friend Edith which had made Mary blush so. *I suppose many young women look up to older friends or mentors in such a way. It may signify nothing, and yet, is it possible Mary once had the same kinds of feelings I do?*

She turned on her side, wondering what sort of qualities the mysterious Edith might possess which would make such a deep impression on Miss Bennet, and was asleep in moments.

Chapter Eleven

This island differs only little from the last; where once scarlet flowers grew, now they are pink. Many of my acquaintances and family back home could walk past these bushes a thousand times without noticing the change, and even those who notice would not necessarily care what such a detail might mean. Even the slightest, most subtle alteration may herald some future consequence.

S. *Barton,* Travels of a Young Naturalist

Charlotte awoke to broad sunshine pouring in through the windows. Though her nap had been brief, she felt well rested—if a little groggy—and it took her a moment to remember where she was. She rose, shuffling over to the wardrobe to consider her meagre wardrobe. If they were to attend a ball and a salon, she would need to reserve her silk for such elevated occasions. As much as she would like to look her best every day, she could not very well wander around wearing only the silk for the week or so she intended to spend in Mary's aunt's house. Sighing, she began the process of wriggling out of her nightgown and into various stays and petticoats, before putting on the black muslin and smoothing down her hair to a presentable state. Growing up at Lucas Lodge, Charlotte and her sisters had a lady's maid, though she'd learned to manage quite well without one for four years at the parsonage. She'd half expected Mary's own maid to wake her up and help her dress but, on second thoughts, she couldn't imagine independent Mary allowing anyone to help her any more than was strictly necessary.

Pitt was waiting in the hallway, pretending to inspect a plant pot in the corner, and greeted Charlotte warmly before escorting her down the broad staircase and into the blue wallpapered room she had glimpsed earlier that morning. The grandfather clock in the hall struck eleven when Charlotte entered, the loud noise causing her to flinch in surprise. Mary was already at the breakfast table, wearing a long-sleeved sapphire-coloured dress which made her look as if she had been designed perfectly to fit the room. The table itself was almost as long as the great table in the dining hall at Rosings, and was only laid for two places, making it look rather bare. Even the large centerpiece of white roses and white orchids—both conveying purity and innocence, Charlotte noted, though likely chosen for their look rather than their meanings—did not help matters. Still, the room was beautiful, and airy, with tall eastern-facing windows which let in the morning sunshine most becomingly.

Two footmen stood along the wall in dark livery and black breeches, their hair neatly combed. Pitt pulled out Charlotte's chair, halfway down the table—rather far from her host, she thought, but perhaps one could not help the distance with a table so large—and waited until she was seated before bowing and making his exit.

"Good afternoon," her host beamed, waving a piece of toast liberally spread with jam. She rose and came around the table, kissing Charlotte on the cheek, before retiring to her seat again. "I trust you rested a little?"

At home in the parsonage, Mr Collins had frequently got up early, whether for some particular prayer or parishioner who required his attention, and Charlotte had therefore got into the habit of rising even earlier so that everything was ready for him. It had been a long time since she had slept with such careless abandon, and said so.

Mary smiled. "Well, you shall sleep as much as you like here."

"I shall do no such thing," Charlotte protested. "Would you have me snore away all my hours in an exciting new place?"

Mary took another bite of toast, smirking. "I suppose you are right. In that case, you shall sleep neither too little nor too much."

Charlotte realised she was being teased, though instead of feeling embarrassed, a warmth spread through her chest. Pitt poured her a cup of tea—only a splash of milk, just the way she liked it, making Charlotte wonder whether he had been specifically instructed on something so small. "And how did you fare?"

"I missed my bedfellow, of course, though not the drooling," Mary declared, and Charlotte's warmth turned to embarrassment after all.

Neither footman moved, but held a quick conversation with their eyes which was easy enough to guess. Mary caught it too, and gestured for them to leave. "Out, boys," she commanded. They obeyed, grinning at each other rather than looking rebuked by such an abrupt dismissal. To Charlotte, Mary added, "Do not worry about them. They are silly fish-wives eager for any scrap of gossip, but nothing said or done in this house ever leaves it, on pain of their employment. You may trust me on that point."

"Oh. Why such secrecy?" She hadn't quite meant to voice the thought, but it was out before she could take it back.

Mary's gaze flickered towards the door and then back to Charlotte. "Have not all houses secrets?" Her tone, which had been quite free only a moment before, had become cool and measured. "And this one more than most, though I dare say ours are of a different nature."

She had said *ours*, not *theirs*, Charlotte noted, gulping down the much-needed tea. This secret, whatever it was, must pertain to Mary herself as well. Confused by the conversation, and distracted by her stomach grumbling loudly, Charlotte poured herself more tea before reaching for a slice of lightly-toasted bread. "And when shall you give me this much-lauded tour of the house?"

"Whenever you are ready." Mary's tone had returned to normal, though it retained some slight vestige of coolness. "In fact, I can begin it now while you break your fast properly, if you like. By the way, the jam is most excellent." She pushed a jar towards Charlotte, who likewise spread the jam liberally on a piece of toast and was delighted to find out that Mary was correct—it was delicious and, if she were not mistaken, was a concoction of strawberry and blueberry. Sweet and tart; a match made in heaven.

"I expect you've noticed the wallpaper already," Mary said. "And with all your particular expertise in flowers, you will no doubt recognise these."

"Canterbury Bells," Charlotte said immediately, "and apple blossoms. Though you flatter me with your praise, I do not claim any such expertise."

"Then you shall prove it with my second, more difficult question—what do they mean?"

Charlotte hesitated. "Do you know the answer?"

"Quite the opposite. I have no idea."

She reached for another piece of toast, doing her best to hide a smile. "Then I could tell you any old twaddle and you would not know the difference."

Mary gave her a long, amused look. "Charlotte, the day you tell an outright lie is the day the world ends and the angels blow their trumpets. Go on."

Charlotte smiled, unable to help blushing. "Well, the bells signify *your letter received* and the apple blossoms mean that the giver prefers the receiver above all others. I always thought the latter one of the prettiest meanings in any bouquet. For what more could one ever hope for, than to be someone's chosen first?"

Not that she herself had ever known such felicity; Mr Collins had proposed to Lizzie first, and only by Lizzie's refusal had Charlotte the opportunity to make her own interest known. Before Mr Collins, there had been plenty of balls and dances and young men, but none had ever esteemed her as anything other than a pleasant girl with the same attributes to recommend her as at least four dozen girls in the surrounding area, and nothing at all which would make her stand out as a particular prize. Mary had surely felt the same way, and though she had been rather tight-lipped about any previous suitors, Charlotte was sure that she must have had at least one. She was pretty, after all, with charm and wit enough to intrigue many men and intimidate at least a few, and her family was a good, respectable one. Certainly men often picked far worse brides. The thought distracted her and once again she pictured Mary in church on the arm of some well-dressed gentleman, a veil covering those fine dark eyes, though no matter how she tried, she couldn't picture happiness in the scene.

Pitt passed by the doorway, drawing Mary's eyes. Charlotte sighed. If she had been born a man, then Lucas Lodge would have been her inheritance as the eldest, and she would have been able to pick and choose a wife as she liked, with nary a comment about her bachelor status. Marriage would have been her choice at leisure, and if she had decided never to marry, then the worst she would have endured would have been some good-natured familial teasing and the inheritance passing to the next male heir upon her demise. Even if she'd been born a younger son, she would have been free to take up some employ of her choosing. A position which allowed one to make one's fortune was, in a man, a mark of industriousness to be admired. For a woman, a paid position was a pitiable indication that one had fallen low.

To be a man was to sit astride the mount of society; to be a woman was to be crushed under its heavy hooves.

"You have left me again, and gone off into some dreamland where I cannot follow." Mary poured a little more tea into her cup, then reached for the milk jug.

"Oh, it is very silly of me. I was just thinking that if I were a man, I would be free enough to give flowers to whomever I chose."

Mary bit her lip, her eyes flickering once again to the doorway. "That is not always the case, I'm afraid."

"Well, no," Charlotte admitted. Men of rank were discouraged from falling in love with women of the underclass, though some did anyway. She studied Mary's expression, and realization dawned; Mary's lover might have been a poor man, unable to offer the kind of life she'd been accustomed to, or perhaps her fancy had been taken by one of the footmen—both were handsome, broad-shouldered boys. It would not be the first time a Bennet sister had made a poor choice of match; Mary's unwillingness to discuss Lydia's marriage to George Wickham, together with the impression Charlotte herself had gleaned of the gentleman and the way she had observed him behave towards Lizzie told her enough. Still, she'd thought Mary more sensible than that, even in matters of the heart.

Charlotte gulped down another piece of toast, pushing down a stab of unseemly jealousy, while Mary pointed out the paintings on the walls. These, it turned out, were chiefly by American painters, and featured rather stark landscapes of pines and rushing rivers under pale skies. They were beautiful, and Charlotte praised them aloud, though her host lacked similar ardor.

After she'd swallowed the remainder of her tea, they returned to the foyer, where Charlotte stole another glance at the portrait of Aunt Cecily before following Mary into a large, pretty drawing room which smelled of violets, as if Mary had dabbed her perfume all over this room. Here the black piano-forte gleamed, the polished lid reflecting the scalloped ceiling. Another chandelier, more delicate than the one in the foyer, hung in the middle of the room. Two blue couches faced each other on either side of an elegant mantel above a large hearth, creating a pleasant space in which to sit and converse. "I must warn you that everything is very blue in this house," Mary said, with more gloom than Charlotte would have thought the co-lour warranted. "Aunt Cecily loves it so. Her one concession is the bedrooms, which have escaped the uniformity of the rest. Yours is the prettiest, bar my own."

Arching an eyebrow, Charlotte cast a look at Mary's dress. "It is a colour which flatters you immensely, despite your protests."

Surprising Charlotte, Mary blushed. "Thank you. I do rather like it in a gown, and perhaps in one room, but one gets tired of seeing it everywhere, every day."

"And what colour would you prefer?"

"Green," Mary declared. "A decent, natural green. I'd much rather feel as if I were in a garden than on a ship."

Charlotte couldn't help agreeing, but though the lady of the house was not there to hear these complaints, she felt obliged to say how pretty the room was. "And whom did your aunt marry? I do not recall that you told me."

"Oh, a Mr George Langley—an American gentleman, who did very well for himself after some mines in North Carolina struck gold. His family were not on the British side in the war, though Aunt Cecily seems not to mind such trifling things as that." Mary rolled her eyes, though a smile played around her lips.

"I see. And who do we have here?" Charlotte bent to ex-amine the plants in pots in the corner.

"Mignonette," Mary supplied, coming to stand next to Charlotte. "Aunt Cecily loves the scent. It covers up the terrible smell of the cigars her husband smokes, at least."

"I see why she enjoys it. Though it means meekness, which is a message that I suspect your aunt Cecily does not intend to give her guests." Charlotte inhaled deeply, before rising to her feet. "It's lovely. Is there a touch of it in the perfume you use?" She reached for Mary's wrist and brought it to her nose, pressing it against the pale flesh there. "Yes, it is similar. Yours is a little darker, though. Perhaps they used marjoram or..." she sniffed again, "cloves? Something to undercut the highest notes of the violet. I cannot quite determine—"

Charlotte froze, realising what she was doing must look extremely odd. Mary's lips twitched, though her cheeks were rosy. "Yes? Do go on. I wasn't aware you knew my scent so closely."

"We did spend several days in a carriage together," Charlotte pointed out, dropping Mary's hand. A fat worm of embarrassment crawled down her back, leaving her itchy and burning. "It is to your credit that I recall it so well, for had it been a bad smell, I would have sought to forget it quickly." The jest fell rather flat, but she was too agitated to think of anything wittier.

"Hmm. And your scent is usually rosemary and mint. Am I correct?"

Charlotte nodded. "Mrs Waites insists that Bessie puts a sprig of mint in the water when she washes the clothes. I grew to like it."

Mary stepped closer. "Ah, but since your bath..." She leaned in, dark hair tickling Charlotte's nose, and her breath puffed over the bare flesh of Charlotte's collarbone, sending prickles of a different nature down her spine. "The lavender has quite overpowered it. A shame, really. I shall have our maids do the same as your excellent Mrs Waites suggests."

Instead of pulling back, her hand lingered, fingers skimming over the curve of Charlotte's neck. Charlotte's own fingers twitched, brushing the fabric of Mary's dress. Their eyes met, their noses only inches apart, and she was forcibly reminded of the moment back in the parsonage when she had wiped the charcoal off Mary's cheek. Something had crackled between them in that moment; a tiny flame, which had grown since into a steady, low blaze. Perhaps Mary did not see it, or, if she saw it, perhaps she had failed to recognise Charlotte's affection as something more than mere friendship. The thought washed over her in a cold rush—to be noticed would be bad enough, but to be noticed and rejected, as she no doubt would be, would be a fatal humiliation.

Feeling rather short of breath, Charlotte offered a quick, forced smile and made her escape to the window overlooking the street. That morning, the light had been too dim for her to properly appreciate the elegance of the houses, but now she could see the neat brickwork and black iron railings which guarded every home. Carriages rumbled past, while gentlemen roved in small packs past tittering ladies in elaborately decorated headwear. Focusing on these small details allowed her breathing to calm, and to recognise the stuttering of her heart as the precursor to desire.

Since they had held hands last night in the inn, Mary had acted differently. She brushed against Charlotte more often, or found more reason to touch her; or was that merely Charlotte's imagination? Perhaps Charlotte was simply more aware of Mary now, of every breath and movement. *Was I ever so aware of Mr Collins?* she wondered, though she already knew the answer. In those frequent moments when he had been close to her, she had felt an urge to wriggle free rather than to lean in further. Certainly holding his hand or sniffing his neck had never produced such a low heat in her belly. It was all so very different, and though she told herself that it meant nothing, she couldn't help worrying that it did in fact mean something.

This was a dangerous path to walk. Sooner or later there

might come a moment when she would make a mistake, reveal her true nature, and that might ruin everything. Mary, having grown up with four sisters, was probably so used to feminine affection that she had not even considered it strange. Only Charlotte could be so foolish and touch-starved to consider it anything other than simple friendship. She was probably mortifying herself already, and vowed to keep on her guard against future incidents, though the promise was short-lived when Mary slid warm fingers into Charlotte's own, entwining them and squeezing.

"Come," her host entreated, seemingly unaware of her guest's innermost thoughts. "We have much more to see."

The dark hallway between drawing room and dining room only led down to the kitchen, Mary informed her, and so they crossed the hall and entered the library instead. This room was also blue, albeit a different shade than the drawing room—more a bright cornflower blue, though the walls were so covered with shelves that the effect of the paint was rather spoiled. Charlotte exclaimed over the presence of so many books, and despite the room being only a third of the size of the great library at Rosings, most of these looked as if they had been thumbed through at least in the last century. Mary walked from one end of the room to another, trailing her fingers along the spines and pointing out the ones she'd read which might be of greatest interest, though the titles meant nothing to Charlotte. There was also a large oak desk, spattered with ink, which held a neat stack of books and a fresh candle.

"This is the room where Aunt Cecily talks of business with visitors," Mary said. "She always says that the drawing room makes them too comfortable."

Charlotte blinked. "Does she not wish her visitors to be comfortable?"

"She always says she'd prefer them afraid. I disagree—I think a person who considers himself comfortable might let a little more slip than someone who is on their guard, but what do I know of such things?"

Not quite sure whether Mary was joking or not, Charlotte wandered over to a large curio cabinet. Inside, three shelves groaned under the weight of odd little trinkets and assorted items. "These are the most treasured things Aunt Cecily has brought back from her travels," Mary continued. "See that carved wooden box? She traded one of her prettiest dresses for it."

Charlotte leaned closer and inspected the box. It certainly was beautifully carved, with tiny hares leaping around the rim of the lid. The inlay on top was a delicate, curving pattern which reminded her of tangled roots, and must have taken the carver a considerable time to achieve. "What about this?" she asked, pointing to a long pipe.

"She refuses to elaborate on that one, though she smiles every time she looks at it. My personal suspicion is that she and the rest of her party indulged in some local, herbal delicacy leading to a bacchanalic experience best not discussed in polite company."

"I had no idea such things existed." Charlotte blinked. The local, herbal delicacy, whatever it had been, was surely a long, long way from anything grown in Mrs Waite's vegetable patch.

"I have one myself upstairs, though it is not so large," Mary said, interrupting her thoughts.

"A pipe?"

"A curio cabinet."

"And what treasures have you?"

"I shall show you, though I beg you to lower your expectations. I'm afraid I myself have never indulged in bacchanalian revels."

Charlotte followed Mary out of the library, casting a last glance over her shoulder at the pipe. "What precisely qualifies as bacchanalian?"

"I'm sure the definition varies from one person to the next," Mary said, the back of her neck reddening a little. "Come, there are some wonderful paintings on the second-floor hallway."

The paintings were indeed wonderful. Aunt Cecily evidently had quite the eye for landscapes, particularly those with brilliant sunrises or sunsets, and family portraits hung between each in an alternating fashion. "This is my great-grandmother," Mary said, pointing to an amiable-looking woman dressed in a high collar and pearls, with two children playing at her feet. "And the stern gentleman over there, the one with his boot on the deer's neck, was a favourite of one of the royal cousins, about fifty years ago, though I believe it ended in some sort of scandal. There are a few more paintings at the end of the first-floor hallway, which you did not see last night, as well as a rather lovely bust. Come, I shall show you."

"You have not shown me your own chamber," Charlotte reminded Mary, as they descended the stairs. "Or is it a thorough mess of books, papers, and paint-smudged sheets?" Unbidden, her mind produced an image of Mary in bed, frowning and rumpled, ink-stains reaching all the way down her forearms and vining over the pale flesh of her shoulders and—

She cleared her throat.

"It is not as bad as all that," Mary grumbled, though she was smiling. "Though in truth you are not far off. If you insist upon seeing it, I shall grant you the honour."

Mary's bedroom was painted a delicate pink, in contrast to the strong blue which permeated so much of the rest of the house. Her four-poster was covered in a pink blanket, and before the fireplace lay a plush rug in a similar shade. Apart from the desk—which was as Charlotte had expected, so overrun with books and papers and drawings that there was scarcely an inch on which one could conceivably write a letter—there was not a single chair in the room.

"Why, you have no chairs except the one at your desk," cried Charlotte. "And this is such a pretty place to sit, too."

"Oh. Well… I confess I had the servants move my best chairs into your room." Mary's smile was nervous as she scratched the back of her neck. "I was rather hoping you wouldn't notice. I thought you would be more comfortable that way."

Charlotte swallowed, touched by how thoughtful the action had been. "You are far too kind to me, you know."

"Nonsense, it's just a couple of chairs."

"No." She took Mary's hand, pressing it earnestly. "It is far more than that. You comforted me in my time of need, and you have been such a good listener, and I—" She bit her lip. "Thank you. For everything."

Without thinking, she pulled Mary into an embrace. She felt the body in her arms stiffen, and then relax. "You are very welcome," Mary murmured, her warm breath brushing a sensitive spot under Charlotte's earlobe.

Charlotte gritted her teeth. She had meant the hug as a friendly gesture, but the feel of Mary's body against hers set every nerve alight. "I find myself quite thirsty," said she, detangling herself. "Might it be time for a spot of tea?"

"Why, you fairly read my mind!"

Forcing a smile, Charlotte followed Mary out of the room, really hoping that would never be the case.

Chapter Twelve

Though Mary had been with Charlotte the whole time and had no spare moment to instruct the butler in anything, when Pitt pulled out Charlotte's chair for luncheon, it was next to Mary's at the head of the table. Sitting so close, it was unavoidable that their knees brushed, just as they had that first evening in the parsonage. Charlotte caught the odd glance Mary shot Pitt, though his attention was fixed on the careful adjustment of a candlestick which seemed to Charlotte to be perfectly situated already.

The footmen were nowhere to be seen, and when Charlotte mentioned this, Mary waved a dismissive hand. "Oh, I gave them the day off. They worked hard to get the house back in order, and they deserve a rest."

"That is most kind of you. Many would not even think of such a thing."

"Well," said she, "I was always troubled by the way my mother ran a house. Our servants at Longbourne only had one day off a month and even that was given grudgingly. Now that I am the mistress of this house, I can do as I please."

They enjoyed a light meal of salad, dressed beautifully and featuring cubes of fresh, crisp cucumber littered amongst strips of mange-tout. The meal was a little earlier than Charlotte was used to, though she finished everything on her plate with satisfaction. "Dinner will be three courses at least," Mary warned, "though I have not the slightest idea what Miss Brodie is planning."

Miss Brodie? Charlotte raised an eyebrow. This was a very strange house indeed. Cooks, at least in her experience, tended to be middle-aged and married at least once. *She must be rather young, or perhaps very talented, or both.* "You do not instruct your cook?"

Pitt entered the room and headed straight for the top of the table, collecting Mary's plate and cup. "Heavens, no. I let her do what she pleases, and the result is an excellent one for all parties concerned." Mary smiled. "Thank you, Pitt. So, now that you have had your tour, will you give your opinion?"

"I suppose you already know what I will say. It is a beautiful home and I quite envy you living here." She couldn't help adding, slightly mischievously, "In spite of all the blue."

Mary laughed. "If the constant presence of blue is the price I must pay, then pay it I shall. You are quite right; it is a lovely home. Aunt Cecily has done very well for herself, though she is rarely in the country long enough to appreciate it. And I cannot say I blame her."

"Why so?"

"The Americans are a little more free in some ways," Mary explained. "And I have to say, I quite agree with their thinking. Why, I am a grown woman of four-and-twenty—what need have I for a chaperone? Men do not require them at any age, even when they are little boys, but may gad about as they please. Even married women in England do not have the sort of freedom married women in America do, and I confess it is rather vexing to hear her describe her adventures when I am so confined here."

"Such conditions are intended to protect us from salacious

gossip," Charlotte pointed out, as Pitt slid back into the room like a well-tailored ghost. "Or ardent suitors too keen to press their desires."

"That rather sounds to me as if men should work a little more on keeping themselves in check, rather than women hiding themselves away." Mary smiled. "If only the world were so easily fixed as that. I confess that while I am grateful for Aunt Cecily's kindness which allows me greater liberty than I enjoyed in Meryton, I am still bound by the confines of English society. Had I never heard countless tales of the adventures she has undertaken across the ocean, I might have been content. One does not know what one misses if one is kept ignorant of it."

Charlotte's smile was pained, for she had recently become familiar with the same sentiment. Before she could inquire whether Mary had plans to travel to America, her host smiled back. "Now, I hope you do not mind," Mary continued, "but I must write a few letters this afternoon. I should be finished by dinnertime. If you require any entertainment, I can recommend diversions."

Pitt leaned past Charlotte to remove her plate and now-empty cup. "Please do not trouble yourself on my behalf," said she. "While I shall of course mourn the loss of your company, I admit I am eager to return to Mr Barton's book." Pitt fumbled the saucer—the first time Charlotte had ever seen him do anything without grace—and his eyes flashed towards Mary before he continued out of the room. Charlotte hesitated. *What was all that about?* "He has such a way with words," she continued, seeing that Mary was listening attentively. *Perhaps she did not notice.* "He makes me feel as if I am there beside him."

"Barton was a wonderful storyteller. The world is a far dimmer place without his light."

"Why, you never told me you knew him."

Mary shifted in her seat. "I'm afraid he passed away two years ago. He was a good man, and an adventurous one, and he caught some sort of sweating sickness. He died after a week, though thankfully he had not been awake during most of it."

"I'm so very sorry to hear that." Charlotte bit her lip. This was a blow indeed. She'd grown rather fond of Barton, and hoped Mary might be able to introduce them at the salon.

Mary departed soon afterwards, with a promise to return as quickly as she was able. Charlotte, who despite the tour did not feel able to occupy space in someone else's drawing room while they were not present—at least, not yet—retired to her bedroom. She sat in the armchair, remembering that Mary had given up her own comfort readily to ensure Charlotte's own. The idea suffused her with a warm glow, and it was long minutes before she remembered to even open the book on her lap. Immersing herself once again in Mr Barton's adventure, Charlotte ignored the pang of grief she felt about the author's death, and concentrated on his life. Barton, who had apparently grown up somewhere near the Dorset coast, was not the sort of gentleman to sit idly by while others worked. He had been told off by the captain for getting so involved—the captain apparently preferred a more distinct boundary between the crew and any upper-class passengers—but Barton had taken the scolding with good cheer, and the captain had eventually relented. He had been permitted to assist with navigation, which seemed like very complex work to Charlotte, who had never been aboard anything bigger than a rowboat on a calm lake.

When Barton was not assisting the crew with physical tasks, he was writing notes late into the night on all that he had seen and heard so far: the screech of sea birds, strange winged fish dragged aboard in nets, and the ever-changing colours of the water. *Grey is my least favourite*, he'd written, *for it heralds bad weather*. Charlotte frowned, picturing grey waves rising higher and higher. She shuddered, and was pulled from her reverie by a soft knock upon the door.

Mary poked her head around the door. "Pitt has just told me that dinner will be ready shortly. Would you like to join me downstairs?"

Charlotte blinked, startled. "Have so many hours passed?"

"You must be enjoying that book, then." Mary grinned. "I have been gone almost two and a half hours."

Charlotte rose, rolling her shoulders and finding her neck a little stiff. "Gracious, I must have been entirely engrossed. It is a compelling read."

She followed Mary out of the room and downstairs, feeling her stomach rumble. "I do hope you enjoy dinner," Mary said, as they entered the dining room. "My cook is glad I have a visitor, for I never eat so much or so well by myself. I believe she has gone to a bit of trouble to impress you."

"Impress me?" Charlotte blinked, surprised. *Why would anybody bother to try to impress me?*

Mary did not elaborate, and in a few moments, overseen by Pitt, the footmen brought out a first course of spiced turnip soup, swiftly followed by veal cutlets, liberally buttered new potatoes, and roast asparagus. The accompanying wine was a delicate white, smooth on the palate, with a hint of smoky oak.

"This is simply sumptuous," Charlotte announced. "Why, I cannot remember the last time I had veal so delicious. It quite melts on the tongue."

"You must have eaten well at Rosings, surely? Did you not dine there often?"

"We did," Charlotte conceded, "but unfortunately Lady Catherine does not believe in having a light hand with a cow. I believe she would have served us all blackened slices if she thought she could get away with it. She seemed to prefer her meat done so well the animal was entirely unrecognizable."

"That is a terrible shame indeed." Mary speared a piece of veal and lifted it into the air. Blood pooled on her plate. "I myself prefer it rare. In fact, if the cow has only just stopped moo-ing, that may be a touch too late for me."

Charlotte couldn't repress a chuckle of amusement. "It is exceptional fare," said she, "and you ought to tell your cook so. Why, I was alone often at Hunsford but that never stopped Mrs Waites from creating the most marvelous dishes, or me from enjoying them. One does not have to be in company to savor a good meal."

Mary picked up her wine glass and swirled the contents thoughtfully. "Was Mr Collins gone often?"

Not as much as I would have liked, Charlotte thought, and swallowed a hasty forkful of potato to stop herself from saying it. "Oh, certainly. He liked to go on small visits to the surrounding village, as well as the next few over. On several occasions he was gone for weeks at a time."

"Did you not have any particular friends in Kent?"

Charlotte's stomach clenched. "We hosted people passing through, and met many distinguished guests at Rosings who stayed with the de Bourghs."

Mary studied her. "That is not what I asked."

Charlotte chewed, delaying her response in the hope that her host would move onto a different subject, but the silence merely lengthened. Mary watched her, apparently satisfied to wait until she had an answer. She sighed. "Not really. Anne de Bourgh is very kind, though I would not call us close. And there was not anyone else of my own age or class within walking distance." Her pleasant friendship with Mrs Waites was something that Charlotte's acquaintances would likely find bizarre or gauche; having friendships across class boundaries simply was not done, particularly with one's own servants. Even Mr Collins had been kept unaware of the depth of their camaraderie, for he would have undoubtedly seen it as pity and kindness on Charlotte's part, and would have been unable to comprehend the real value that Mrs Waites contributed. She shrugged. "My job was to be a good wife for my husband, and to allow him to continue his work unimpeded. It hardly mattered what I wanted." *Nor has it ever,* she thought.

"It sounds like rather a lonely life."

Charlotte wasn't quite sure what Mary was getting at. She'd forgotten how these statements could feel rather like judgements. "Perhaps it was. Are you not alone here? Do you ever feel lonely?"

Mary sipped her wine. "I would like to introduce you to a few of my acquaintances while you are here. Miss Highbridge is a particular friend of mine and I believe you shall get on famously."

Miss Highbridge. The name sent a sharp shock through her chest. *Miss Anne Highbridge, perhaps?* She wondered how she would feel if she saw in person the woman from the nude drawing. Would she be able to look her in the eyes? *You told Mary you were not a prude,* the little voice inside reminded her. *I do not believe that I am,* she argued back, *but there is something rather different about seeing a woman's body unclothed before you have even been introduced to the lady in person.*

Hmm, the little voice said. *And it is nothing to do with the fact that Mary might have seen her nude? Also, she did not answer your question.*

Unable to answer that, Charlotte curled her fingers into fists under the table, doing her best to ignore the thrum of discomfort pulsing through her stomach.

"Now, shall we eat a little dessert?" Mary asked.

A little dessert turned out to be a glass of brandy and an enormous slice of rum cake. Charlotte took a large mouthful of the latter, and was astounded by the familiar taste. The cake was sweet without being cloying, and spiced perfectly. "Why, this is just like Mrs Waites'! However did you manage it?"

Mary grinned. "That's because I asked her for the exact

recipe. I wanted you to feel most welcome here. I do hope my cook did it justice."

Charlotte halted mid-chew. In all her life, she could not think of anyone doing anything half so kind and thoughtful for her and, intriguingly, Mary had somehow managed what half the village could not, and obtained a recipe from Mrs Waites' fiercely defended collection. "How on earth did you convince her to give that to you? I would swear God Himself would have to ask for Mrs Waites to even consider sharing. And even then, I believe she would have to think twice."

"I told her it was for you." Mary shrugged, but her eyes watched Charlotte nervously. "I was fully prepared to beg, but she gave it up rather easily after that. Do you like it?"

"Indeed I do. Please give my deepest thanks to Miss Brodie." Charlotte picked up her brandy and sniffed, picking up delicious notes of dried apricot and nutmeg. The first sip sent a pleasurable warmth rolling through her mouth, coasting down her throat. "And how goes your letter-writing?"

"I am afraid I did not finish them all in time." Mary looked tired, though her eyes were still bright and her features animated. "I had more to say than I thought and… Well. Tis no matter. I will finish them tomorrow."

"I would be perfectly happy to amuse myself this evening," Charlotte suggested, afraid that Mary would feel obliged to put off her letters in order to entertain her guest. She sipped the brandy again, feeling the effects already. *Lord, but this is rather strong stuff. Another glass and I will be asleep where I sit.*

"If I am perfectly honest," Mary's voice dropped to a conspiratorial whisper, "I would much rather spend time with you. What say I write one or two, and then come to your chamber?"

"An agreeable compromise." Charlotte shot a sly look over her brandy glass. "Why, you would make a very amiable husband, Miss Bennet."

"You flatter me far too much," Mary laughed, though a

faint flush crept up the side of her neck. Under the table, her knee brushed against Charlotte's once, twice, and then stayed there. "Perhaps I only compromise because I want something, like most husbands."

"Whatever could you want from me?" Continuing the game, Charlotte batted her eyelashes coquettishly, unable to repress a smile.

"Your time and attention, of course. What could be a sweeter reward than that?"

"I've changed my mind. You might be an amiable husband, but anyone who talks with such poetry is surely up to something devilish." Charlotte rose from the table, amused by the way Mary stared up at her in faux-outrage.

"How dare you impugn my character as an upstanding gentleman?"

"Yes, dear. Whatever you say, dear." Charlotte smirked as Mary's outrage turned to indignation, and before her host could splutter a reply, she leaned down and pressed a kiss to Mary's cheek. "I shall see you upstairs, then."

In her chamber, Charlotte allowed herself a single minute's reflection on the way Mary had smiled at her, the way Mary's cheek had felt under her lips, before she turned her attention back to Barton's diary. The fire was bright, the window open and delivering a cool breeze with the dark-edged smells of the night. She was so engrossed in a passage recounting an incident where a dead gull had plummeted onto the deck, sending the crew into a frenzy of superstitious panic, that she startled when the door opened. Mary sidled into the room, holding a decanter and two glasses. "May I join you? I have, of course, brought an offering to tempt you away from your book."

"Yes, of course." Charlotte studied Mary as she settled into the opposite armchair. "Did you know you have ink on your chin? And charcoal on your forehead? And something I cannot name just under your left eye?"

"Oh for goodness' sake." Mary sighed. "You must think me a slovenly wretch indeed. Have you a towel?"

"I think no such thing," Charlotte chided. "Here, let me." She fetched a towel which had been neatly folded next to the empty washbasin, and some water from the pitcher. Dipping the corner of the towel into the water, she took her time gently cleaning Mary's face. Those dark eyes watched her all the while, and although it was a dangerous moment, Charlotte took her time, unlike the first time she had ever done this back at the parsonage.

Her other hand held Mary's chin in place, and she could not help moving very slightly, the fingers stroking infinitesimally. Mary blinked, long and slow, her throat bobbing as she swallowed. It was so strange, Charlotte thought, that when they were together like this, a bubble formed, and they really did feel like the only two people in the world. Jane had once described her marriage to Bingley in a similar way, but that had been a marriage—a love connection sought, established, and built upon—rather than a friendship.

By the time she was finished, she was quite reluctant to let go. "There, now you are quite clean."

"Thank you." Mary's knuckles were white around the arms of the chair, though her voice was calm and collected. "Shall I pour us a glass?"

"What is it?"

"Whisky. Aunt Cecily's preferred Scottish brand, no less. She claims the Americans made a very decent rye whisky, but I personally think the Scots have the right of it."

The spirit proved to be excellent indeed, and soon enough they abandoned the armchairs in favour of sitting side by side on the rug in front of the crackling fire, discussing people they had known in Hertfordshire. "Do you recall Emma Sallow?

Yellow hair, rather tall?" Mary asked. "She was a friend of Jane's in their youth, though I think she turned quite mean-spirited later."

"I think so. Did not she marry a baron?"

"An earl, if the rumours are true."

Charlotte swallowed another mouthful of whisky, savouring the burn. "It just goes to show that kindness is not always rewarded."

"Indeed. In fact, Lydia used to say…" Mary trailed off. A muscle in her jaw jumped, and she raised her glass to her lips, then lowered it without drinking.

Charlotte touched Mary's arm tentatively, and was relieved when Mary smiled at her, eyes softening. "I understand that we all have our secrets, but if you should wish to talk to anyone, I am here."

"I know that you would never tell anyone. It is just…" Mary sighed. "Well, here is the truth. Lydia went off with the militia, and slipped her chaperone one night. She and Wickham ran off together, and they…well, suffice it to say that they did not immediately marry." Charlotte gasped, her mouth flying to her mouth as Mary continued. "Darcy found them and made them undertake the ceremony immediately. I suppose I should not be surprised that Lizzie did not tell you herself. She never told me either. I heard it from Jane, who eventually caved under my questioning."

"Lizzie and Darcy are a very good match." At one time, that sentence would have pained Charlotte, but now it seemed like some faraway dream, lost to the clouds of time. "In his place, I believe she would have done the same thing. She always did have a very strong sense of justice."

Mary gulped down the contents of her glass, and poured another. "Indeed."

"Thank you for confiding in me." The words hardly seemed to do the sentiment justice, for the scandal would have been a huge one and destroyed the family's name and the opportunity of all of the girls to make a match. Lydia had always been headstrong, but to run away at fifteen with a man she barely knew went far beyond the foolishness of youth.

"I trust you, Charlotte." Mary shrugged, as if it were as simple as that. "I would be surprised if you had not already guessed at something similar."

"I had," Charlotte confessed. "Though of course I never would have pried."

Not to her face, anyway, but you are bold enough to go through papers and trunks when it pleases you, the little voice in her head reminded her, causing her stomach to clench unpleasantly.

"I was angry with Lydia for a long time," Mary admitted. "I still am." She tapped her glass absently with a finger, staring into the low flames as they danced. "It's just like her to do something rash and not care a whit about the consequences of her actions for herself or anyone else. She believes that she is the only one who has ever felt passionately about anything and therefore all her actions may be explained away in the name of love." She scoffed. "I do not believe it ever was love, not really. She is too flighty and he too cunning for that. It will be a miracle if they do not separate within five years, or have some other scandal."

Charlotte sipped her drink and waited. Mary was on the verge of saying something, she was certain of it. Mary lay back on the rug, crossing her hands behind her head, and after a moment Charlotte did the same. "You feel passionately about things, too," she prompted.

"Of course I do, but I have been careful to pursue them in secrecy, to keep my family name free from any whiff of impropriety. I would never—" She broke off, turning to face Charlotte, who mimicked her movements. "Have you never thought of what you might do, if you thought nobody would discover it?"

Charlotte bit her lip. "Does not everyone?"

Suddenly Mary's eyes were sharper than they had been. Charlotte wilted under the steady beam of that penetrating gaze. "To whom do you tell your secrets, Charlotte Lucas?"

"To—to no one," she stuttered, "though they are not interesting ones, I am sure."

"I doubt it. I find you quite—" Mary's eyes dropped to Charlotte's lips "—fascinating." Her gaze flickered back up and held Charlotte's own.

The moment stretched out unbearably. Charlotte was acutely aware of her every breath catching, and the placement of her body, so close to Mary's that a single movement could bring them into intimate contact. Was it her imagination or was Mary leaning closer? Or was she? The situation was rapidly getting out of hand. For a moment, she wondered what might happen if she simply leaned in. She might aim for a goodnight kiss on the cheek, and who would mind terribly if her aim—imperiled by the spirits—was a little off? She was shocked to find she was actually considering this as a potential course of action, and even more surprised to find Mary close enough for Charlotte to feel warm breath on her lips.

"Would you say these spirits are strong?" Mary asked.

An odd question, Charlotte thought. Her head was clear enough, though her senses were pleasantly fuzzy and her courage apparently high. "A little."

"You did not answer my earlier question. What would you do if you thought no one would ever find out?"

"I am quite tired," Charlotte said, rolling backwards abruptly, and gaining her feet in a rather ungainly way. "Perhaps it is time for bed." If she had not been looking directly at Mary, she would have missed the strange expression that flickered across her friend's face. As it was, she saw it, but could make no sense of it. "You know, I rather miss the sound of your snoring," she teased, keen to alter the mood.

"Oh, do you, indeed." Mary grinned. "Cannot you hear it well enough through the walls?"

"I am afraid it is not quite loud enough to wake the dead. You shall have to improve upon the volume." She hesitated, the spirits giving her courage to suggest something she ordinarily would not. "Would you stay with me tonight? It was such fun in the inn, though I understand if you desire your own bed. You were away from home for more than a week already."

"Of course." Mary studied her. "And I suppose you were very used to sharing a bed at Hunsford."

"Not as often as you might think," she murmured, and was surprised to find that tears had sprung to her eyes. Mary's arms were around her in an instant and the tension from earlier transformed into a comfortable fire, burning steadily and brightly.

She inhaled the scent of violets, and felt Mary's chest rumble with a chuckle. "Enjoying my scent again?" Charlotte hummed, neither willing to confirm or deny the act. "Let me change," Mary added, disentangling herself, "and I shall return momentarily."

In bed, Charlotte wondered why she had chosen to put herself in such a position again; the first time had not been her choice or fault, and yet she had asked for this torture. Mary, already blinking sleepily, dark hair fanned out across the pillow, reached out and touched her hand. Charlotte allowed their fingers to become entwined—*perfectly friendly*, she told herself, *perfectly normal*—and she faded into unconsciousness with a smile, delighting in the slight pressure of Mary's warm fingers against her own.

Chapter Thirteen

Charlotte could not remember having got out of bed, but somehow she and Mary were lying in front of the fire again, though the rug underneath them was not a rug at all but rather a mat of fresh, green grass. Puzzled, she looked down the length of her body and found that they were wearing matching dresses, dark green with hems and necklines edged in tiny tuberose. She stroked the hem of her dress, awed at the way the flower seemed to bloom as if it were alive. Tuberoses signified dangerous pleasures; the scent was sweet and dark, like candied poison, intoxicating in a way that neither the brandy nor the whisky had been.

"What would you do," Mary asked again, and Charlotte startled, having almost forgotten she was there, though her lips did not move and her voice seemed to come from somewhere distant, "if you thought no one would ever find out?"

This cannot be real, Charlotte thought, her pulse leaping in excitement. *If it is a dream then I may do as I please. No one could possibly hold me accountable for a dream.*

"Anything?" she asked.

"Anything," Mary whispered, her eyes darker than Charlotte had ever seen them, reflecting two small images of herself, pale and brilliant.

She wasn't sure which of them had moved first, but suddenly they were kissing, and all worries about caution and propriety were swiftly overtaken by desire. Mary's hands were on her waist, pulling her closer, in exactly the way she'd tried to stop picturing in the past week. Letting her imagination out to pasture had been a mistake, for now it gamboled free as a colt, escaping her every attempt to rein it back in.

Mary's lips were on her neck, her hands now in Charlotte's hair, tugging at the roots and producing a quiver of longing. Charlotte had never felt such want, such desperate desire, and allowed her own hands to trail down Mary's collarbones, her fingers tracing the pattern on the neckline of the dress, cupping her bosom with all the bravado she'd never felt while awake. Her hands drifted down further and further, finding Mary's knees, pushing up her skirts, rolling until Charlotte was on top of her, rutting wildly, hardly knowing what to do or how to do it, but Mary writhed under her as if she were doing something very right indeed, gasping encouragement with every thrust, until something built inside her like the crest of a great wave and—

Charlotte awoke with an ache between her legs, deep and unsatisfied, and Mary's arm slung across her, body pressed to Charlotte's side. Any attempt to move away was met with resistance and, afraid to wake her friend, she relented and lay still. The blaze of lust still raged inside her, thrumming through her bones. Mumbling something incoherent, Mary tucked her head under Charlotte's chin. Though her heart was pounding and her stomach swooped and stuttered like a wounded bird, Charlotte couldn't help turning the dream over and over in her mind. *That is as close as I will ever get to what I want*, she reminded herself. *Enjoy it while it lasts, and then put it aside.*

Mary blinked awake when the great clock downstairs struck eight. "Why, I have slept so late," she mumbled, and to Charlotte's surprise, did not pull away immediately. "Why did you not wake me?"

"But you were sleeping so deeply," Charlotte protested.

If it had not been for the fact that their bodies were so entwined, Charlotte would have entirely missed the way Mary froze, then made a great show of rolling away to yawn. Charlotte frowned. Had Mary been so groggy that she had mistaken Charlotte for someone else? And if so, who had so lately been sharing her bed that she might confuse things in such a way? Thick skeins of discomfort wound around her chest, pulling tightly.

"Well, I hope I did not trouble you after you so kindly invited me in." Mary turned to face her, and Charlotte's discomfort warmed as she remembered the way Mary had looked and sounded in the dream. Was she a dreadful person, to think about her friend in such a way, when they were so innocently close? Especially a friend who probably saw her as another older sister? *The way she looked at you last night was not very sisterly*, the little voice in her head pointed out, and for once, Charlotte didn't argue with it, though guilt and shame were wound too tightly in her chest to allow the fingers of hope to prise them apart.

"I must return to my letters this morning," Mary continued, "but first, I thought we might have a little breakfast and then a walk in the garden."

The notion shook Charlotte from her reverie. "Wait—you have a garden? Here?"

"Before you get too excited, I must warn you that it is merely shared among the residents of this street. One needs a key to enter, or possess the determination to climb a very high fence in pursuit of flowers."

"I shall temper my expectations but little." Charlotte arched an eyebrow. "Well, what are you waiting for?" she asked teasingly, though in truth she would have happily lain in bed with Mary all day. "Let us go!"

★ ★ ★

After dressing quickly, Charlotte joined Mary in the dining room, where they enjoyed some of Miss Brodie's honeyed oats, adorned with a smattering of fresh berries, before venturing out into the street. Turning the corner, Charlotte saw the tops of trees behind a high iron fence—either very short trees indeed, or the garden had been purposefully sunk in order to provide the residents privacy. The latter proved to be the case, and meant that they had to descend a rather steep set of stairs to enter after Mary unlocked the gates; evidently she had not been joking about needing a key.

"Oh, I forgot to mention—I received a letter this morning from Aunt Cecily," said Mary, helping Charlotte down the last step. "Careful, that one has been cracked a little. We really must get it fixed."

"What did she say?"

"She believes she will return in a month or so. It is a shame you cannot stay to meet her, for she would love you, I am sure."

Charlotte's heart fluttered. *If only I could.* "You are very sweet to say so. It is a shame indeed, but I shall have to return home long before then to pack and prepare for my departure to Meryton." The reality of her situation, which she had managed to almost forget about for the last few days, returned in full force. She followed Mary onto a stone path which wound between two large oak trees. Overhead, the sun shone brightly, and the faint rumble of carriages and voices from the street above seemed half a world away. "Besides," she added brightly, for Mary really did look glum at the thought of her guest leaving, "I am sure you would be sick of me long before the month was over."

"How very dare you suggest any such thing, Charlotte Lucas." Mary poked her in the shoulder. "You are wonderful company and I shall miss you dreadfully."

"Very well, very well," said she, giggling and fending off a further attack of poking as they strolled along the path. "You have made your point. Now, where are the flower-beds? I expect to see marvels here, since they must be agreeable enough to please a whole street of people."

"Oh, then I have grossly misled you. They are pleasant, to be sure, but nothing so pretty as your own garden at Hunsford, which I much prefer."

Charlotte had rather expected Mary to mention Rosings, and was surprised. "Surely the splendor of the De Bourgh estate far outstrips my own modest efforts?"

"In fact, that is why your garden pleased me so. It exists not to impress, not to tantalize with elaborate hedges or expensive imports, but to simply rejoice in all the beauty of nature. There is something unselfconscious about it."

"I feel that way too," Charlotte confessed. "I shall miss my garden most of all. The gardens at Lucas Lodge are beautiful, of course, but they are my mother's style rather than my own, and they tend to be a little..." She bit her lip, struggling to think of the right word.

"Staid? Not that I'm suggesting your parents are at all staid herself," Mary hastened to add. "Your mother in particular was always very warm-hearted, and kind to me."

The path was only just wide enough for two to walk abreast, and Mary's hand had brushed Charlotte's enough that the latter had started to wonder whether she ought to take it as a girlish act of affection, though the more she imagined doing such a thing, the more mortified she became. Charlotte had never been able to manage acting girlish or coy, and she'd certainly never mastered the art of flirting, intentional or otherwise. Before she could get a grip on her stray thoughts, Mary drew her attention to the flower-beds on the left, ringed by an assortment of stones painted white.

"Carnations!" Charlotte exclaimed. "And in so many colours. Why, they are lovely."

"And I suppose you know the meaning of carnations, do you not?"

"Well, that depends on the colour."

Mary looked blank. "Does that make a difference?"

"Oh, certainly." Charlotte ticked the answers off on her fingers. "Red means *my heart aches for you*, white means *sweet love*, and pink means *I'll never forget you*."

"What about yellow?" Mary asked.

"Ah, yellow carnations mean *rejection*. One hopes to never see them in a bouquet, which is rather a shame considering they are pretty enough."

Just beyond the carnations, an elegant fountain had been set into the path, which branched off in three directions. Mary guided Charlotte down the left-hand path, claiming it offered the most sunshine, and the two walked arm-in-arm past tulips, poppies, and peonies, until they reached the end of the garden. A stone bench offered a delightful view of a pond, in which several orange fish were swimming lazily. The bench itself had been warmed by the morning sun, and the scents of flowers and recently cut grass mixed in the air. A bee buzzed somewhere, unseen, and Charlotte sighed with pleasure. "What a lovely spot. You must spend a lot of time here."

"Not as much as I ought," Mary confessed. "I often get so absorbed by my readings that I am not entirely conscious of the hours passing. Pitt does his best to keep me on a reasonable schedule, but if were not for my staff, I would find myself sleeping the day away and eating dinner at two or three in the morning."

"Am I keeping you from your work?"

"Not at all! I did not mean to imply—" Mary sighed, and leaned her head on Charlotte's shoulder. "I'm trying to compliment you, though I must be even more rusty at it than I had thought. What I meant to say is that I am very grateful for your company. The house is beautiful, and I have friends whom I may visit whenever I choose, but, well… I suppose I prefer more intimate friendships to a large party."

"As do I." Charlotte wanted to say more; she wanted to ask if Mary was lonely, if she had always felt lonely, and if there was a possibility that Mary felt a little less alone in Charlotte's company, as she did in Mary's.

Instead, she bit her lip, and said nothing.

Chapter Fourteen

Dear Charlotte,

I hope you received my last letter with my condolences. Maria says that you will soon return to Lucas Lodge, which made us wonder whether we ought to send all the children there for a week or two. After all, whatever will you and Mama and Papa do with your long, empty days? We are quite prepared to do you this kindness.

Do remember that I always favoured you.

Your brother,

John

Upon their return to the house, Miss Brodie sent up fresh scones, accompanied by cherry jam and clotted cream. Charlotte fetched Barton's diary from her room, intending to read a little once she'd eaten her fill, and laid it beside her plate in the dining room. Though the cover of the book was rather nondescript—a pale brown, almost fawn, with the author's name stamped in small gold letters on the front—the butler flinched when he saw it. Yet the next moment Pitt covered his reaction so admirably that Charlotte wondered if she had simply imagined his response.

Puzzled, she spread jam on her scone while Mary complained about the batch of letters she'd received that morning; apparently some new finding had all the mineralogists at her salon ablaze with excitement. "It was the same after Cuvier and Brongniart published *Description Geologique des Environs de Paris*," said she, staring gloomily down at the pile of envelopes at her elbow. "You couldn't get any sense out of them for months. I shall have to do a little reading before I respond to some of these, but—" casting an eye at Barton's diary "—I see you have your own book to occupy you. What say we retire to the drawing room for an hour or two?"

Certain that she wouldn't understand the new scientific discovery even if Mary had explained, and secretly rather glad that her friend had not even bothered to try, Charlotte agreed to the notion with delight, and was once again pleased by the strong smell of mignonette pervading the drawing room. She seated herself on one of the couches. Mary sat next to her rather than on the opposite seat, close enough for their elbows to brush. Had it been anyone else, Charlotte would have minded a great deal, and would have, at the first available opportunity, made her escape to another chair. Here, she felt no such urge. If anything, she wanted to be closer, and so, when Mary shifted, Charlotte inched sideways a little, so that they were elbow to elbow. Repressing a sigh at the thrill which fizzled through her veins at a mere touch, Charlotte opened Barton's diary.

The first third of the book had been taken up with the voyage, but Barton had now landed on a pretty little island and evidently been enthralled with all the flora and fauna he found there; monkeys, lemurs, great trailing vines, and tall trees crowned with leaves as long as the naturalist's forearm. They'd had a warm welcome from the islanders, who held a feast in their honour and presented the captain with a carved trinket box; it sounded very much like the one in Aunt Cecily's study, though Barton had described this one as being encircled with strange, long-legged birds rather than rabbits. He himself had been gifted a wooden statue, carved in the shape of an old man with a beard, which he had received with the tenderest appreciation.

Trading between the crew and the islander took place over several days, and it was plain that Barton did not care a fig for the process, preferring instead to join some of the young native men to learn how they fished and harvested. Every few pages there was some new delight—a drawing of a bird with a voluminous crest, or a description of a broad fish so heavy it took two men to carry back to the main camp. Barton's passion shone through with every word, and Charlotte found herself both pleased and envious of his innocent joy, and his ability to travel anywhere he liked at any time without worrying about impropriety. Surely no woman, no matter how rich or connected, would have been allowed to undertake such a journey. And yet, someone always had to be the first to break a rule, did they not, for the rest to come tumbling after?

Mary turned a page, her elbow brushing Charlotte's. A sideways glance confirmed that Mary was intent upon the page, which contained several complicated-looking tables of numbers and unintelligible paragraphs; her forehead was furrowed in concentration, a sight which Mrs Bennet would surely have remarked upon with consternation, had she been present.

Charlotte knew that she herself frowned while she read— though her family had remarked on it with amusement rather than reprimands—and her late husband had thought it sweet to lean over and smooth out the frown with his thumb before returning to his own book. Charlotte had always smiled and thanked Mr Collins, but privately the action had irked her. Did she have to maintain a perfectly smooth face whilst reading, lest it perturb him? Was it not enough that she presented a perfectly pleasant air in company and while alone with him? She had often felt that she had stepped into the role of Wife, a role any worthy woman might have filled for him with little to distinguish her. Why, if Jane or Lizzie or some other Meryton girl had consented to marry him, he would have been just as happy, perhaps even more so. She'd known this only too well, and so had strived to be the most dutiful wife in every way, never to give him trouble or cause him to regret his decision. The result had been achieved, but at what cost?

She glanced up to find dark eyes studying her intently. "I like the way you look when you are deep in thought," said Mary. "I should like to draw you again, if you would permit me to do so. No, wait—" for Charlotte had smoothed out her expression as she had done so many times before, "do not change on my account. Please."

"Well now I wish to smile, and I'm afraid the two expressions cannot exist on my face at the same time. Although, now that you have mentioned a desire, I feel I must mention my own in turn."

"Oh?" A strange expression flashed across Mary's face, as fast as a bird flitting past a window. "What desire is that?"

"I believe at Hunsford you promised that in exchange for accompanying you to the salon later this week, you would accompany me to a ball." Charlotte smiled in what she hoped was her most charming way. "You did promise, did you not?"

"Ah. Yes." Mary sighed. "I suppose I did."

Pitt materialized as if from nowhere, three cards in his hand. "Ma'am, you received three invitations this morning."

Her eyes narrowed. "And why am I only hearing about them now?"

"It must have quite slipped my mind, ma'am."

"Your mind seems lubricated only at inconvenient times," Mary muttered, but took the proffered cards anyway. "Very strange that you should have separated them from my letters."

"You have an unfortunate habit of tripping and throwing said invitations into the fire, ma'am," he said, face politely blank, "which luckily does not often happen with your letters." He tilted his head, looking the very picture of helpfulness. "I thought the presence of Mrs Collins might alleviate your usual clumsiness."

Mary scowled at him. Charlotte watched their interplay with amusement. Mrs Waites had often employed the same kinds of underhanded tactics, though to different ends, and Mary seemed indignant rather than genuinely irritated by the butler's behaviour.

"He thinks I do not go out enough," said she, to Pitt's retreating back as he left the room. "He believes that, left to my own devices, I would be some sort of mad hermit."

"Given what you told me in the garden earlier, it seems as if he might be correct," Charlotte pointed out.

"Do not join forces with him, please. A war on two fronts is not easily won." Mary sighed again. "Look, here are two balls to choose from. The other invitation is merely a luncheon with a friend of my aunt's who is rather lonely in her old age. She will not mind if I put our meeting off for another week or so." She offered the cards to Charlotte. "I shall attend whichever ball you choose."

"I confess I am at a disadvantage here, for I know neither name nor the history of their acquaintance with you." Charlotte held up the cards so that Mary could see them plainly. "However, if you tell me a little about each, then I shall be able to make a sensible decision about which one we ought to attend."

Mary inspected the first card. "Ugh. This one is from Miss Abbott, a friend of Mrs Tremaine's." She pulled a face.

Charlotte had not heard her mention either name before, nor look with such evident disdain. "You do not care for Miss Abbott?"

"Her mind is a vast blue sky and not a single cloud of thought dims its brightness," Mary said, her tone still slightly sulky.

Charlotte snorted. "I see. And what about Mrs Tremaine? Is your opinion of her any better?"

"I..." Mary trailed off, which was odd given how freely she had spoken of Miss Abbott's faults just a moment before. "In that lady's case the situation is more complicated. She is...how shall I put this? She is ungracious and uses her natural charms in the pursuit of younger quarry. Her husband is a sweet, if gullible, man which makes her behaviour all the worse."

"Oh dear! She sounds dreadful. And the other invitation?"

Mary glanced at the second card. "Ah, this ball is being held by Mr and Mrs Cromley. They are good souls, and though their ball will not be as lavish as Miss Abbott's, who has more money than sense, it will be a very pleasant time."

"I think the choice is clear, though I cannot say I am not a little intrigued by your description of Mrs Tremaine. Surely she cannot be as bad as all that?"

"You are too willing to think the best of everybody, Charlotte. Doubt me if you must, but you shall discover the truth for yourself. She will be at the salon next week, where she does her best to be the reigning monarch of our little republic."

Charlotte frowned. "But a republic needs no monarch."

"Precisely," Mary pronounced, using the same sort of forbidding tone she'd used to describe the great danger presented by a small gathering of owls.

At around six on the clock, they ate a fabulous dinner of pigeon breasts in a rich, velvety sauce, with buttered potatoes and pickled cucumbers to accompany. Charlotte retired to her room to dress in her black silk, her only suitable option, and stared at herself in the looking-glass. She was not beautiful, certainly, but she was clean and presentable, with a cheerful countenance and a pleasant smile.

Mary was waiting downstairs in the hallway when Charlotte descended the stairs. She was wearing a purple gown, lush and dark, which suited her complexion exceedingly. The neckline of the dress was edged in thistles. Charlotte arched an eyebrow. "Interesting choice. Do the flowers represent devotion or suffering?"

"Why not both?" Mary smiled. "I am devoted to your happiness, so I am honour-bound to suffer through a ball."

"Oh." Charlotte's own smile faded. "If you would really rather not go—I mean, I would not wish for you to do anything on my behalf that would cause you pain."

Mary waved a careless hand. "Do not take me so seriously. Besides, a little suffering is healthy, is it not? If God wanted me to stay inside all the time, He would have granted me a snail-shell to carry on my back. On the contrary, I thank you for reminding me that one must step out into the world from time to time and enjoy all it has to offer." She produced a pink carnation. "I felt," said she, blushing, "that you might need a little colour to brighten up your gown. Of course, you cannot change your mourning dress but I thought, well... Here, allow me." She stepped closer, far closer than she needed to be. "This has a hook attached here, so you are in no danger of having your dress punctured by a pin. See?" Mary tucked the pink carnation into the hook and fastened it.

Charlotte watched her fingers work, and swallowed hard. She looked up. Mary was still very close—close enough to see each golden fleck in her dark eyes. Pink carnation, meaning *I will never forget you*. It also meant longing, though she hadn't mentioned. "You remembered."

Mary raised an eyebrow. "It was only this afternoon. Or do you think my memory as bad as all that?"

"No, not at all." She was shy but pleased. "I appreciate your efforts to make me look inviting."

"You need no help with that, I assure you." Her fingers lingered, brushing the petals, her voice dropping to a murmur. "Black rather suits you, although I do look forward to seeing you wearing bright colours again. I recall you once wore a pretty lavender dress to a ball at Netherfield, and I remember thinking how—"

Behind Charlotte, Pitt cleared his throat. Mary straightened, a flash of annoyance crossing her face. "The carriage is outside, ma'am," the butler announced.

"Thank you, Pitt." She extended an arm to Charlotte as Pitt strode ahead of them and opened the front door. "Shall we proceed?"

Chapter Fifteen

My dearest friend,
I think of you often, and with not a little consternation. This
may be partially due to the long hours I have lately spent in the
nursery, though I am delighted to relay that our son is much improved. In truth, I am aware that you and Mary are so very different, and in herding you together without forethought, I may
have created an uncomfortable situation. Perhaps I ought to have
encouraged Jane or even Kitty to visit you. Alas, that a bell cannot be unrung!
Lizzie

The carriage was indeed waiting outside. Mary took the seat
beside Charlotte, ostensibly so she could point out buildings of
interest on the way, though it was difficult for Charlotte to pay attention when Mary's thigh was pressed so firmly against her own.

The journey took just over an hour, though in Mary's company the time flew, and soon enough they were stopping outside a house. The road was busy with carriages stopping every
minute, regurgitating its passengers onto the pavement. It wasn't
necessary to clutch Mary's hand in order to descend the steps,
but Charlotte relished the opportunity to do so anyway.

The Cromleys' house was two-thirds as large as Netherfield, Jane and Bingley's grand house, with short wings on either side. If this was what Mary considered modest in comparison to Miss Abbott, Charlotte was glad indeed that she had selected this ball. The gentlemen were dressed in the dark jackets and tan breeches now so fashionable amongst the *haute ton*, while the ladies peacocked in bright shades of sapphire, ruby, and gold which dazzled the eyes. Charlotte breathed an inward sigh of relief; her black silk dress would not stand out here, but it would not shame her either. She peered through the dim evening at the gardens, though she could see but little; the bright moon was shrouded in thick clouds tonight. "If we can escape later," Mary murmured, taking her arm, "then I shall show you Mr Cromley's prize roses. Prized by him, of course, although Mr Mellor has bested him in the annual competition for the last eight years."

"I would like that very much," Charlotte whispered back, and they ascended the steps, smiling at each other.

Inside, servants dressed in fine livery stood to attention, while the cheerful crowd bustled in and out of a stately room. Charlotte saw at once why Mary preferred such a ball to something stuffier and more formal; the atmosphere was one of charming amiability rather than the haughty judgement which tended to overshadow any Rosings event. A string quartet in the corner played a lively tune, and the dancers whirled and spun in perfect time. The air smelled of a hundred different perfumes, though Mary's violet scent seemed to Charlotte to be the most pleasing.

"Ah, there are our hosts," said Mary, jerking her chin to indicate a handsome couple at the other end of the hall. "I shall introduce you in good time. Let us fetch some punch first, and then—oh, there is Delia!"

The young woman who came towards them was perhaps seven-and-twenty, dark, with a broad nose and uncommonly pretty green eyes which sparkled with animation. Charlotte compared the girl to the drawing she'd seen in Mary's letters, but even a cursory recall proved that this girl was a different person entirely. Perhaps she was the artist, or perhaps this was another one of Mary's intimate friends. *And just how intimate is she with her friends?* the little voice asked. *Even if it were possible, would you simply be one amongst many? How could you ever hope to compare to all these beautiful women?*

"Miss Highbridge," Mary said, beaming, "I am delighted to present you with my good friend, Mrs Collins."

Charlotte couldn't help blinking in surprise at the introduction; she had forgotten that Mary only referred to her married name amongst company. "Why, Mrs Collins, it is a pleasure indeed!" cried Miss Highbridge. Her dress matched her eyes, the late-summer sheen of dry bracken, and her slender waist was encircled with a pine-coloured ribbon. "Miss Bennet has told me so much about you."

"Has she?" Charlotte couldn't help wondering what had been said. The look which passed between Mary and Miss Highbridge spoke louder than words, though in a language which Charlotte could not decipher. "All bad, I suppose," she teased.

Miss Highbridge feigned surprise. "On the contrary, she could not praise you enough. Why, she holds you in great esteem indeed."

"Enough, Delia," Mary murmured, a pink flushing creeping up her neck. "I have only just arrived and already you are embarrassing me."

"There is nothing embarrassing about a truthful compliment," said she, cheerfully ignoring her friend's scowl. "And how long are you in town, Mrs Collins?"

"I assume Mrs Tremaine isn't here tonight?" Mary asked, changing the subject before Charlotte could answer.

"Oh, I do hope not." Miss Highbridge snorted. "We are safe for an evening at least, although I believe she has petitioned to chair the next salon meeting."

"I had already volunteered to do so," Mary said, a muscle in her jaw jumping.

"Pfft. Tell that to Mrs Tremaine."

"I would give quite a lot to never say anything to Mrs Tremaine ever again," Mary muttered, causing Miss Highbridge to snort again. "Hark, a ship sails near."

Charlotte frowned, baffled by this sudden statement, but the meaning was made clear in a moment. A young man was heading through the crowd towards them, his eyes intent upon Mary. "Good evening, Miss Bennet," said he.

"Good evening, Mr Hillinghead."

"Would you care to dance?"

"I am afraid I must abstain for the moment, sir," she said politely and the young man's smile turned rueful. He gave a jerky bow before marching away back to his fellows, who slapped him on the back with comradely good cheer.

"One of that group try to win you over every time." Miss Highbridge shook her head. "One must admire their determination, at least."

"That is one of the many reasons why I would never encourage their suits," Mary declared. "A young man must learn from his mistakes, and not keep making the same ones over and over. Besides, none of them wish to dance with me for the pleasure of my company, but only to be the one to break me first, like some sort of wild horse. It is but a game to them. It will not be long before Mr Hillinghead realises that a far better companion awaits him." She nodded towards a girl on the fringes of a large group, gathered near the punch bowl, who was watching the young man with longing writ large across her face. "Miss St Clair has been quite in love with him for two years, and he is a fool not to notice it sooner, perhaps because he is too busy making sport with his fellow fools."

"Well, we do not always recognise what is right in front of us," Miss Highbridge said archly.

Mary shot her another warning glare. "Would you like a glass of punch, Charlotte? It is quite warm in here and my throat is terribly dry."

Charlotte agreed, but before either could move, a man in a captain's uniform stepped into their path, who Miss Highbridge introduced as Mr Harold. "He is married to my cousin Abigail," she said, smiling at him before turning. "You know Miss Bennet, of course, and this is Miss Bennet's friend, Mrs Collins, who is in town for the week."

"It is a pleasure to meet you." Mr Harold bowed. His waistcoat was a warm cream colour, his black boots polished to such a sheen that they reflected the movements of the crowd above. "Do you dance, Mrs Collins?"

"I do."

"Then perhaps you would gratify me with a dance?" He held out his hand.

Now? Charlotte thought, dismayed, though she forced a polite smile and took the offered hand. Mary's expression flashed something, though Charlotte could not tell what, as Mr Harold led her onto the dance floor. The band struck up a song she knew, for which she was grateful, and they began to dance in two long lines. "I have only just arrived at the ball," said he, bowing. "My dear lady wife is unable to accompany me tonight, though she insisted I come. And what about yourself?"

"I am only visiting from Kent," she explained, as they circled each other.

"I adore Kent! I am there often, visiting a dear cousin. Which part of the country?"

"My late husband was the parson at Hunsford, across from the de Bourgh estate, Rosings. Perhaps you know it?"

"Know it?" cried he. "Why I spent two summers there as a young man. I was great friends with Mr Fitzwilliam Darcy in my youth—we came up together at Cambridge, you see. I don't suppose you're acquainted with him?"

"Indeed I am, sir," said Charlotte, smiling, "for he married my best friend."

A little further questioning proved that Mr Harold knew Lady Catherine too—of course he did, Charlotte thought ruefully, for even in another city she could neither escape the shadow of the Darcys nor the keen eye of the de Bourghs—and this provided several minutes of diverting conversation.

"I was hunting with Sir George the other day, and I…" Mr Harold gave her a queer look. "Why, you would not be the Mrs Collins he spoke of, would you?"

"I cannot say for certain that I am the woman in question, though I am Mrs Collins," Charlotte confessed. *Why on earth would Sir George be talking of me?*

He laughed, as if she'd said something funny. "You are every bit as modest and charming as he claimed, Mrs Collins. And Mr Innes was most keen to impress upon me his good opinion too. Why, he said that—"

"Oh, you know Mr Innes as well?" Charlotte swallowed. Of all places, she'd expected Canterbury to be free of such reminders: that she must return soon, that people would expect her to try to land another husband before settling into her status as an burdensome widow, that Canterbury was but a dream and she must soon wake to the realities of life alone in a place where Mary did not live.

"Indeed I do. He is a fine fellow, do you not agree?"

"I think him very fine indeed," Charlotte agreed, and then, concerned about how such a statement might be perceived, added, "He was most kind to me when we met, which was not long after my late husband's passing."

Mr Harold could not have failed to notice that Charlotte's black dress was a mourning one, but the reminder was helpful, just in case he mistook her cheerfulness for some particular attention to what Mr Innes had said. He began to talk of his own wife in lively terms, but Charlotte's attention was caught by Mary whispering with Miss Highbridge in a dim corner. Charlotte couldn't help her eyes drifting to that corner with each spin, and as a result floundered in the dance, too distracted to keep up with Mr Harold's conversation. Her stomach ached with something sour and green; perhaps she had overeaten at dinner.

Mary leaned in and whispered something in Miss Highbridge's ear, causing them both to break out into giggles, and then they both sidled out of the room and disappeared from view. Mr Harold insisted on a second dance, and though Charlotte found his company pleasant, the strange feeling in her stomach grew and grew. After the second dance ended, Charlotte made polite excuses to Mr Harold, and edged into the hallway. No one here was paying her any attention, and the group of young men talking in loud voices at the end of the corridor provided perfect cover. Charlotte inched forward until she caught the sound of Mary's voice on the balcony outside. She peered around the corner as much as she dared, and caught a flash of Mary's dark purple dress.

The two friends were speaking in hushed whispers. "I never saw you act so, my dear Mary," Miss Highbridge declared. "Why, you sound entirely in love. Will you confess it?"

"I will do no such thing." Mary sounded amused, though a little chagrined. "You must cease larking about, Delia. This is serious."

"Whatever will Anne say?"

A slight hesitation, marked by a moment of silence. "What Anne says is no longer any business of mine. And what I feel is no longer any business of hers, either."

"Ah! So you do not deny your feelings?"

A rustle of skirts. Mary's voice sounded again, slightly further away, as if she'd walked a few paces in the opposite direction. "How long have we known each other? Seven years?"

"It will be eight in the springtime," Miss Highbridge corrected.

"Ah, yes. Always looking forward, never backwards. And how often have you known me to be—" Mary's voice dropped so that the last few words were lost in the tumult of the young men's voices. Charlotte frowned, wishing they'd hush up.

"In truth? Just the once. Apart from now." The tease was evident though the speaker's face could not be seen from Charlotte's current position.

"So you know that I do not say such things lightly."

"I do not believe you have said anything at all, lightly or otherwise. You have always been the bolder of the two of us. What halts you now from speaking your heart?" Mary murmured something which Charlotte could not hear, and Miss Highbridge laughed. "You may glare at me as much as you like, Mary, but it will not change matters."

This is lover's talk, is it not? Charlotte knew she should leave, lest she be discovered eavesdropping, but it was extremely difficult to pull herself away. So she'd been correct, at least a little, regarding the mysterious Anne. Evidently that lady's opinion had meant a great deal to Mary once upon a time, even if something had happened in order to change that situation. Had Mary wanted Anne? Had Anne wanted Mary? Had one of them denied the suit, or had they both entered into it willingly? The ache in Charlotte's stomach soured further. Her throat was as dry as old bone, and she headed for the table which held several large punch bowls. *A drink will put me right.* An elderly gentleman with white whiskers offered to pour a glass for her and she gratefully accepted, sipping the spiced drink with relief. It was strong—far stronger than she was used to, but it helped calm her racing thoughts. No matter what had happened in the past with Anne, Mary was evidently interested in Miss Highbridge now, and with good reason. The young lady was beautiful, charming, witty…everything, in short, that Charlotte was not.

The punch curdled in her stomach.

Chapter Sixteen

Before she could do much more than thank the elderly gentleman for his courteousness, the Cromleys approached. "We have not been introduced," Mrs Cromley said, and then added, "Oh, Miss Bennet! I wondered where you had got to."

Mary had appeared at Charlotte's elbow, smiling widely. "That is my fault entirely. This is my dear friend Mrs Collins, who is visiting me from Kent." Unlike many others Charlotte knew, Mary did not add anything about Mr Collins, or Rosings, or the de Bourghs, but merely allowed her to exist on her own. She rather appreciated the gesture, even if Mary was not aware she was doing it.

"Any friend of our Miss Bennet is welcome any time," Mrs Cromley said, patting Charlotte on the arm.

"And how do you like Canterbury, Mrs Collins?" Mr Cromley asked.

"It is beautiful. And you have a beautiful home," she added, keen to impress upon her hosts that she was having a good time. "I hear you grow exceedingly pretty roses, Mr Cromley?"

"That I do!" cried he. "Though I am always bested by our Mr Mellor, unfortunately. Still, I think my roses the prettiest, as one ought to when one has tended to their growth so long and laboured over their upkeep."

"Much like children." Mrs Cromley arched an eyebrow.

"Oh, no, nothing like that," said he, earnestly. "For I never put a sack over our children's heads when the frost crept in."

She rolled her eyes at him good-naturedly, and he grinned back at her. Charlotte turned to Mary, and was surprised to see her watching the Cromleys with a slightly wistful expression.

"Come on," Mary whispered, while someone called Mr Cromley's name and distracted the couple. "I shall take you to the garden now. Unless you wish to dance again?"

Charlotte shook her head, and followed Mary outside. The gardens were dark and empty, with only a few stragglers lingering at the entrance of the house. The candlelight inside stretched golden fingers out to the hedges but fell short, so that by the time they reached the rosebushes, Charlotte was obliged to stop for a moment and close her eyes to adjust to the darkness. They had wandered off the path a little, and the grass underfoot was spongy and soft. "I admit this was not one of my better schemes," Mary said regretfully. "I ought to have brought a candle, or we ought to have arrived earlier when there was still light."

"It was a sweet thought, nonetheless." Charlotte felt Mary's hand brush hers, and the fingers entwine with her own. To be standing here in the dark, in a beautiful garden, holding hands—was this not what lovers did? Did they not sneak off together? She wondered what Miss Highbridge would think if she saw them now, and reflexively tightened her grip. Mary responded with a squeeze of her own, and as Charlotte's eyes adjusted to the gloom, she was able to perceive the myriad shades of roses. An occasional shaft of moonlight lent the scene a magical air, like that from a fairy tale.

"Pink roses?" Charlotte guessed, leaning over to inspect the nearest bush more easily. Though the night was dark, the air was warm, and she had hardly any need of the shawl slung over her shoulders. The sound of the string quartet inside was only just audible, adding to the strange, dreamlike quality of the moment. "And yellow?"

"You have sharp eyes. I suppose that roses, like carnations, have different meanings with each of their colours?"

"Indeed. Let me see…pink means *grace and joy*. Yellow stands for *friendship*. Red, of course, is *love* but also *respect*. There are more too, for a rose is more than just its colour."

Mary's fingers twitched. "What do you mean?"

"Well, a single rose can mean *I love you*, whereas a rose plucked of all its thorns can mean *it was love at first sight*."

"Charlotte," Mary said, and her voice was not the charming tone she'd used with the Cromleys, nor the amused way she'd spoken to Miss Highbridge, but something lower, rougher, rawer. She turned to face Charlotte, her face a mask of shadows and silhouettes. "If we had a pair of scissors right now, which would—"

Light flashed across the gardens, throwing them into relief. Charlotte let go of Mary's hand instantly, stepping back to put appropriate distance between them. Raucous shouts echoed as the group of young men stumbled past, each carrying a lamp, heading for the bottom of the lawn where a tall hedge seemed to mark the end of the estate.

Mary smoothed down her dress, though it was not ruffled, and stared up at the sky for a moment. "Would you like to go back inside? We could find you another dance partner."

She's probably keen to get back to Miss Highbridge, Charlotte thought, and gritted her teeth. *She was probably about to ask which rose she should cut for her dear Delia*. "Yes, of course."

Her suspicions were correct, for Miss Highbridge found them quickly once back inside, and while Charlotte acquiesced to dance with two men, neither Mary nor Miss Highbridge seemed to want to do anything but sit and chat with each other.

In fairness, they included Charlotte too, but she was so aware of every glance and word that passed between them that sitting in their company felt like agony rather than a pleasant evening.

In the carriage, on the way home, Charlotte responded to each of Mary's questions with polite, but abrupt answers. After the third, Mary studied her, frowning. "Are you well?"

"Yes, quite well. Perhaps a little tired." She needed to get away, to sit alone and put her thoughts in order, to sift through the chaos and identify what was really bothering her. Good manners would see her through for now. "And did you have an agreeable time? You did not dance even once."

"I am not a terribly good dancer," Mary said. She seemed about to add something else, but instead stared out of the window at the darkened sky before glancing back at Charlotte. "Besides, you looked rather cosy with Mr Harold, and those other gentlemen. Far be it from me to keep you from enjoying yourself." Her fingers drummed her knee for a moment before stilling.

Charlotte blinked. "During my first dance with Mr Harold, we discovered we had a friend in common, so I do not think his asking a second time was anything other than an excuse to talk a little more, and to dance with a safe partner in his wife's absence. The others were merely being polite, I am sure."

"You and Mr Harold have a mutual acquaintance?"

"He knows Mr Darcy well, and the de Bourghs somewhat," Charlotte added, and then, though she felt some strange anxiety about mentioning the topic, "and he also seems to be acquainted with both Sir George and Mr Innes, whom you met at Rosings."

"Oh, Mr Innes." Mary bit her lip. "I see."

Charlotte desperately wanted to retort, though she knew not precisely what she wanted to say: that she had no interest in Mr Innes, or that Mr Innes' potential interest in her signified nothing, or that she was surprised Mary had even noticed what Charlotte was doing since she had spent most of her time paying attention to Miss Highbridge, or—

Charlotte was jealous. Stomach-churningly, green-bitter, truly jealous. The notion knocked the breath out of her, and she pressed a hand to her chest, struggling to draw air. The small prickles of jealousy she had felt before were mere grass snakes compared to this dragon. And why ought she be jealous, really? It was unfathomable, unless—

Unless she was beginning to fall in love.

"What is the matter?" Mary was beside her in a moment. "Are you ill?"

"No," she choked. The carriage was already so small, and Mary was right there, the smell of violets tickling her nose again, overwhelming her senses. "Just a momentary dizziness. It will pass."

"Here," Mary said, and took Charlotte's hand, pressing two warm fingers against the flesh of her wrist. "Why, your heart is beating so quickly. Shall I ask the coachman to halt a moment, so you can get some fresh air?"

"No need." She closed her eyes, against the urge to weep. "Miss Highbridge seems pleasant. Have you known her long?"

"Seven years," Mary said.

"I would like to know her better," Charlotte said, keen to smooth over her strange fit of pique. "Any friend of yours must be worth knowing."

"You flatter me. Besides, you are my dear friend, and you are worth knowing. I was eager for her to make your acquaintance as much as for you to make hers." Mary's fingers were still pressing against Charlotte's pulse. "There, your heart is slowing down a little, though it is still far too quick for my liking. What can I do for you?"

"Nothing," Charlotte assured her. "The punch was a little strong for my tastes is all."

"Those infernal boys! They likely spiked it. I knew they were up to no good."

"Do not worry," Charlotte said, opening her eyes. The jealousy simmering in her stomach cooled a little when she saw the look on Mary's face: concerned, compassionate, caring. "I simply need to rest and I will be right as rain."

"I shall put you to bed the moment we get home," Mary promised, and Charlotte laughed.

"Will you stay with me again?"

Mary blinked. "Do you want me to?"

She nodded, feeling a blush creep up her neck and invade her cheeks.

"Then I would be delighted to." Mary pulled her closer, wrapping an arm around Charlotte's shoulders. "Just close your eyes and rest for now."

True to her word, Mary stayed in Charlotte's bed again that night, and made such a fuss of her with cold compresses and iced drinks that Charlotte began to feel rather guilty for allowing herself to be so spoiled when nothing was wrong. *It hardly signifies*, she told herself, *for in a week or so I will be gone from her life forever. At least I may allow myself the tiniest shred of comfort now.* Their conversation was quiet and limited, lest Charlotte's "dizziness" become worse, but Mary never stopped watching her, which forced Charlotte to act more amiable than she felt. It was unfair, really, to play pretend in such a way with Mary, who had done nothing wrong, and had no idea of the way Charlotte felt. In truth, Charlotte herself had not even understood the depth of her feelings until that moment in the carriage, and the idea had shaken her to her very foundations.

Once the candle had been blown out and Mary's breathing had evened, Charlotte turned on her side, facing away. She had so rarely been jealous in her life that she had mistaken the first inklings for something else—envy, perhaps, of a freedom to experience things that were so beyond her ken, and of an unruffled attitude which refused to conform to the rules of society in the way that most people did. Maybe it was both envy and jealousy, all tied into one unpickable knot. The only thing she was certain of was that her infatuation with Mary was not the silly, girlish crush she had once thought it, but something far more serious. *The bud has begun to bloom*, she mused, pursing her lips. *And it is entirely my fault for not snipping it off in the first place.*

And yet, despite the horrible way her jealousy had stung, it was somehow tempered by the ecstasy of every touch, every look, every smile. If this was love, then Charlotte had never felt it before—had never even come close—and no wonder people went mad in pursuit of love, did ridiculous things, made elaborate and desperate speeches to convince another of their desires, their needs, their hearts. She drifted off into a troubled, though thankfully dreamless, sleep, and awoke to the gentle touch of Mary's hand on her shoulder.

"Good morning." Mary looked tired, though her eyes were still bright. She was still in her nightgown, and there was a streak of charcoal on the left side of her chin. "How are you feeling?"

Charlotte sat up, and Mary immediately leaned over to help prop a pillow behind her back. "I am quite well, thank you," she said, smiling. "I promise I have not become an invalid overnight."

"I'm glad to hear it." Mary rubbed her eyes, then covered a yawn.

"Have you been awake long?"

"Unfortunately, yes. I am afraid I did not finish all my correspondence yesterday. I had much more to say than I thought, and… Well. Tis no matter. I shall finish it all today and then we shall have the rest of the evening to ourselves, and tomorrow too. Would you mind terribly if I left you alone for breakfast?"

"Of course not! Do not worry about me. I would relish the chance to get a little more reading done."

"You are a dear. I promise to make it up to you later."

Charlotte arched an eyebrow. "In what way?"

She'd meant it as a joke, but it came out sounding unexpectedly sultry. Mary's eyebrows rose until they were practically in her hairline. "Why, in any way you want." She grinned. "I shall be entirely at your disposal around, say, two on the clock?"

After a solitary breakfast of eggs and ham, accompanied by hot buttered toast, Charlotte spent the morning in the drawing room. By now, she had only a quarter of Barton's diary; the naturalist had visited several more islands over the last pages, and his journey seemed to be drawing to an end. Though the mentions of his *dear P*—Penny, perhaps? Peggy? Prudence?—were infrequent, Charlotte could not help the sense that P, whoever she was, was always on Barton's mind. Whether he was describing some new iridescent beetle or the gift of the hollow wooden statue which the islanders had bestowed on him or a trick the crew had taught the ship's cat, he did so in the manner of one imparting a much treasured story. No detail was too unimportant to include, and yet he never rambled or lost the thread of his tale; it was quite a remarkable feat.

Charlotte halted at the second-to-last chapter, and hesitated before putting the book down on the couch. She wanted to finish the book and find out whether Barton married his dear P upon his return, but at the same time she was loath to finish the book. There was something so final about a last page, an ending confirmed, particularly when she already knew that the man in question had passed away. Delaying the ending felt like a way of keeping him alive a little longer.

Instead she got up and wandered over to the window, staring out at the sky. The day was warm but grey, the breeze which ruffled the curtains as tepid as a yawn. There was no clock in the room, so she could only make a cursory guess at the time. She did not wish to disturb Mary, for it could only have been an hour or so since they parted, so she ought to amuse herself in other ways for a while longer.

Charlotte had only just descended the stairs into the foyer when Pitt greeted her, a letter in his hand. "This arrived for you, ma'am."

"For me?" Puzzled, Charlotte accepted the letter, though her confusion cleared when she saw her sister's handwriting. Mrs Waites must have sent it on the moment it arrived at Hunsford, thinking it a matter of familial importance. "Ah. Thank you, Pitt."

"Shall I bring you tea?" he offered.

"No, thank you."

He nodded and withdrew. Charlotte broke the seal before sitting down on one of the blue-upholstered couches. She wasn't quite sure what she had been expecting from Maria, and braced herself for the answer to her question.

Chapter Seventeen

Dear Charlotte,
Congratulations, sister, it has only taken you one-and-thirty years to notice something plain as day to most. Well done!
Jesting aside, I do hope that you will not hold this fact against Great-Aunt Ethel, for she did as her family bid and married twice to please them, though I do not think it pleased her one whit either time. Here in the north things are not quite so restricted and while I cannot say that these people live without any kind of nuisance directed at them for something they surely cannot control, certainly it is rather an open secret in polite society. I assumed you must have realised that not everyone is happy living as society prescribes, though perhaps your late husband was against such behaviour on principle. Whatever made you think to ask about this?
Your loving Maria

Charlotte re-read the letter to make certain she had not misunderstood, but the words remained the same. So Great-Aunt Ethel had a female lover after all. She'd thought getting an answer to this question might make her feel different—less confused, perhaps—but she was more confused than ever. Folding the letter up again, she sat staring into the flames for a few minutes before getting up and pacing the room. *Why did I even ask?* she wondered, tapping her fingers against the arm of the couch. *What difference does it make to me?* Neither of her parents had ever mentioned it, though Maria had called it an open secret; had Charlotte been the only one who hadn't known? And why would Maria think her so close-minded that she might hold this secret against a long-dead aunt? Besides, Great-Aunt Ethel being in love with a woman in secret changed nothing for the family. It was not even close to the same sort of scandal Lydia had courted by running away publicly with Mr Wickham.

She paused by the window and looked out. A few children were playing together in the street with a hoop and stick, darting this way and that. The sky was clear, with only a couple of fluffy clouds meandering across the blue expanse, and the sun was blindingly bright. Slipping the letter into the pocket of her dress, Charlotte left the room, walking across the foyer and into the library, where she once again admired the full shelves. She read the spines of some, though they sounded rather dull or too complicated for someone like her to understand. The Great-Aunt Ethel question continued to bother her immensely; if everyone had known and everyone had accepted it, might they accept the same thing about Charlotte? After all, that had been thirty years ago. Times had changed, surely for the better. Although perhaps Ethel had been the exception to the rule— after all, she'd had enough money to live on even without her companion's income supplementing their lifestyle.

Money is the key, she thought glumly, *and unfortunately it is money I do not have. Having a fortune of one's own permits a host of choices not permitted for the poor, and keeps the wagging tongues of society silent.*

Sighing, she checked the time. It was only a quarter past one, and Mary had said she would likely be finished around two on the clock. Though the day was lovely, she did not know where Mary kept the key to the garden, or she might have gone there instead. She ought to have asked this morning, rather than bother Mary now when she was no doubt in the middle of important correspondence. *Hmm,* she thought. *How might I occupy myself for another forty-five minutes?* Hovering in the doorway of the library, Charlotte spied the dark hallway leading down to the kitchen, and a sudden idea dawned.

She descended the few stairs leading to the kitchen and emerged into a large room, stone-bricked and swelteringly hot. A slender youth in an apron was rolling out dough with practiced strokes, and looked up, panicked, at Charlotte's appearance. "I am looking for Miss Brodie," said she, gazing around with interest. Something delicious wafted from a nearby pot; something creamy, laced with—if Charlotte was not mistaken—rosemary and black pepper.

"I—" The youth stood stiffly, flustered. "I... Miss Brodie is out at the moment, ma'am. May I take a message?"

Charlotte's gaze slid down to the apron, adorned with the initials A.B. She saw no other apron in the room, nor had Mary mentioned other kitchen staff. "I just wanted Miss Brodie to know that I appreciated her rum cake very much, and I shall tell my own cook, Mrs Waites, that she did the recipe justice."

The youth's eyes lit up, confirming Charlotte's suspicions. Names were often more difficult than people imagined, and came laden with societal expectations and baggage in every way. A little kindness could go a long way; Maria's letter in her pocket reminded her of that. "Do pardon me if this is a rude question, or an odd one," she said, making sure her tone was gentle, "but...are you Miss Brodie?"

The youth's eyes flickered from side to side, as if looking for an escape. "It's quite all right if you are," Charlotte added hastily.

"I... Yes. I am." Miss Brodie's shoulders relaxed slightly, though she still looked as if she were awaiting a blow or a scream. "Thank you, ma'am. The recipe was a very good one. I would do quite a lot to get my hands on another."

"You and a hundred others," Charlotte joked, and was relieved when Miss Brodie graced her with a small smile. "I apologise, I should not have intruded on your domain."

"Not at all, ma'am. It's not—I mean, they don't often come down here. The guests. Not that Miss Bennet has many of them," Miss Brodie blurted, and then stopped, looking terrified. It was evident that Charlotte had caught her off guard.

"I shall leave you to your marvelous creations. May I ask what is for dinner?"

"Chicken in a creamy white wine sauce, with carrots and green beans. And," Miss Brodie gestured to the pastry under her hands, which were trembling, "an apple pie."

"Gracious, I can hardly wait." Charlotte exchanged a last smile with the timid cook before exiting.

She'd hoped to spend a bit more time in the kitchen, but it was clear that her presence put poor Miss Brodie on edge. She might as well wander around the house a little more—Mary had given her a wonderful tour, but it had been more focused on the paintings and busts, and Charlotte had spied an especially impressive set of antlers set onto the wall on the second-floor hallway Mary had only referred to as "Aunt Cecily's quarters."

Charlotte arrived on the second floor only slightly winded, and proceeded to admire the curved antlers up close. They were not deer, as she'd first thought, or at least were no breed she had ever seen before. Perhaps they belonged to the cervine creature in the background of Cecily's portrait downstairs. A cool draught caught the back of her neck, and she turned to find the door opposite ajar. She bit her lip. Snooping was not ladylike, but then again, a quick peek surely could not hurt. Mary had said that the house contained many secrets—was this one of them? She sidled along the wall and pushed the door open, revealing a room much smaller than she'd expected. It was half the size of the guest room she was staying in, and the furniture was mostly covered with dust sheets. This must be just one of

Cecily's rooms, she supposed, which would be uncovered and cleaned by the servants prior to her arrival. Though all the furniture was covered, several portraits hung uncovered on the walls, and one leaned against a corner of the room.

Charlotte sidled towards the left-hand wall first, which held another portrait of Cecily alone. In this one, Mary's aunt rested against a tree, facing a riverbank. The water was smooth and clear, the bank steep. Cecily was dressed in men's trousers and a smart, dark jacket, her dark hair tumbling loose around her shoulders. Charlotte stared at the painting, trying to picture Mary in the same sort of clothes, and then tried to picture herself in them. She rather liked the idea—certainly it would make gardening easier if one could bend and kneel with impunity.

She turned to the centre wall, upon which hung a portrait of Cecily with her husband. This must have been their wedding portrait, for they were standing side by side looking stiff and formal. It was a far cry from the pictures of Cecily which Charlotte had seen so far. She tilted her head, examining Mr George Langley, who boasted fine bushy whiskers over a short, dark beard. His dark eyes were kind, and either the painter had been very generous or Mr Langley was quite a few years Cecily's junior.

Charlotte turned towards the portrait in the corner and leaned down to take a closer look. She stared, confused, at the portrait of the three people: Cecily, Mr Langley, and another woman. A portrait of three was a little unusual, when it did not contain immediate family, and this woman—with her red hair and blue eyes—was surely no relation of either. The pose was an unusual one too; Cecily's hand rested on the woman's shoulder, and Mr Langley's hand on Cecily's shoulder in turn. It was as if they were all connected somehow, looped like a daisy chain. The woman was surely Edith, the friend Mary had mentioned who'd embroidered the blanket on the guest bedroom.

Charlotte stared at the painting, certain she was not imagining what she was seeing, or what it implied. Cecily had two lovers—her husband, and a woman. Perhaps they were all lovers together, three at a time. Now she understood precisely what had made Mary blush at the mention of Edith, and flush even more deeply at the mention of bacchanalic rituals.

Something burned inside her—knowledge, as yellow-hot as any newborn flame. This was the confirmation she needed, far beyond Maria's passing comment about Great-Aunt Ethel. It was possible for women to like men or other women or both; how had she gone her whole life being so ridiculously unaware of the possibilities? The words swelled up inside her and she found herself dashing along the hallway, down the stairs, and towards Mary's room. The door was closed but Charlotte burst in anyway, hardly knowing what she meant to say, only that she had discovered something glorious and new and—

Pitt's hand was on Mary's shoulder, and hers was on his chest, and they were laughing together, laughing so hard they were weeping, tears in their eyes. Mary turned towards the door, her expression fading into surprise and then horror.

"Oh, I—" Charlotte skidded to a halt, staring at them. "I'm so sorry. I should have knocked. I did not mean to—"

She backed out of the room, cheeks flaming with horrified jealousy; she'd thought at first that Mary's lover must be a lower-class artist or worker, and then she'd suspected it was Miss Delia Highbridge. Never had she considered Pitt, who must be more than twenty years Mary's senior. Charlotte bolted down the hallway to her own room and closed the door behind her. What a fool she had been, and now she had made a fool of other people too. They must have gone to great pains to hide their relationship and—

Quick footsteps sounded in the corridor. Before Charlotte could take more than a couple of steps into the room and spin, ready to meet the reprimand that was surely coming, Mary entered, her cheeks flushed.

Chapter Eighteen

"I'm sorry," Charlotte repeated, before Mary could make excuses. "I did not see anything."

Mary blinked. "Charlotte, there was nothing to see. You mistake me."

Something about the way Mary had looked at Pitt—so intimately, so deeply amused—had scorched through Charlotte's innards. The wound burned, making her feel as if she were about to vomit. The dragon of jealousy, it seemed, had a tongue made of pure fire. "It is none of my business. I—"

"You mistake me," Mary repeated. Her fingers flexed, curling into fists and splaying widely again and again. "And I had thought you understood—well. No matter. Suffice it to say that Pitt is not interested in courting me. Or, for that matter, any other woman. Nor are the footmen. In fact, every servant in this house courts a more..." She cleared her throat. "A secret kind of love."

Charlotte opened her mouth to argue, then closed it again. "Oh."

"Indeed." Mary's eyes were blazing. "My aunt has a particular fondness for those the rest of society considers beneath them. They reside here in safety, for to be caught is death for men. It is the one circumstance in which women have it easier. I thought…well. I thought you might have got the clue from Barton's diary."

"Barton's…" Charlotte trailed off, feeling very foolish. *To my beloved P.* "I'd thought it referred to a young lady."

"It refers to our very own Pitt. And I'm sorry if that offends your delicate sensibilities." There was something under Mary's anger that Charlotte couldn't quite grasp. A hurt, perhaps, though for what reason she could not guess. "I am aware that your marriage to a parson might have convinced you that such things are sinful and wrong but I can assure you, the kind of love that exists between two men or two women is just as pure as—"

A giggle rose in Charlotte's throat, high and shrill and completely unstoppable.

"What on earth are you laughing about?" Mary demanded, flushing with anger.

"I warned you not to take me for such a prude, and yet you did. I already saw—"

"Well, pardon me for not immediately introducing my most secret desires to a clergyman's wife."

"Your most secret…" The laughter had died, replaced by the burning embers of anger, disappointment, and embarrassment.

"Yes, I'm just like them. I should have known you'd had no idea. I was foolish to think that—" She broke off, a muscle jumping wildly in her jaw. "Well."

Mary hadn't been flirting with her; Mary hadn't even thought Charlotte capable of doing so. Charlotte was not even the tiniest ship on Mary's horizon, and yet she had been so open with her affection towards Miss Highbridge at the ball. Had they shared a bed, held hands, just as she and Mary had done? She'd been foolish to think there anything more between them. Charlotte had been so wrong in so many ways that it was mortifying to comprehend them all at once; there was nothing between she and Mary but friendship, and perhaps even less of that than she'd thought.

"I merely misunderstood." The words were a struggle, each one a small agony. "But if we are such good friends as you profess, then why did you not tell me sooner? I would have welcomed Miss Highbridge as your…" Charlotte struggled to find a suitable word, and couldn't help the bitterness that edged the word, "lover. If only you'd told me."

It was a half-truth at best. Certainly she'd have been polite to the girl's face, and squashed down her own feelings more deeply, though she could never have welcomed any lover of Mary's with any real joy.

"Delia?" Now it was Mary's turn to laugh, though the sound was a harsh, bitter one. "We are simply close friends. I assure you, she is no lover of mine and never has been. Whyever would you think that?"

"But you… But I heard her say…" Charlotte trailed off.

Now Mary's eyes were blazing in quite a different way. "You heard her say what?" She took a single step towards Charlotte, and it was as if all the air had suddenly been sucked out of the room.

Charlotte froze like a frightened rabbit. "She called you quite in love, and you did not deny it." Mary continued to stare at her, those dark eyes steady and blazing. "It is nothing," Charlotte added hastily. "I would never repeat anything of the sort to others—that is—" *Stop it*, she scolded herself. *You are ruining everything. Take a breath and say what you mean, for if ever there was a time to be bold, then is it.* "I will keep your confidences, of course," she blurted, and Mary's eyes darkened further.

"I should hope so. I thought we had formed an understanding, Charlotte. I told you that I would never divulge your secrets, and I expect the same in return. My friendship is entirely conditional upon trust and respect."

"As is mine," she snapped. This conversation was going so

badly. *Her friendship, nothing more. You utter fool, Charlotte.* The words stung much more than she was expecting. "Do you think me so callous as to go blabbing all over Hertfordshire? To put good men in danger of being hanged for something so uncontrollable as their hearts?"

"In that case, what on earth is wrong with you?" Mary demanded, her voice rising. "You are acting quite unlike yourself."

"Perhaps you do not know me as well as you thought." It was a foolish thing to say, and clearly untrue, but she was still smarting from *just-friends* and the words were out before she could fully comprehend their consequences.

"Is that so?" Mary took another step towards her, and another. Her voice was raw now, and rasping. Charlotte backed up until she hit the armchair, and still Mary kept coming. "I know much more than you think, Charlotte Lucas. I know that you are unhappy. I know that you have never been happy. I know that you go out of your way to deny yourself happiness even when it is within your grasp. Mr Innes showed you such attention as to make his interest clear—an offer which would solve your problems easily and expeditiously—and yet you demurred. What could possibly be holding you back from such an opportunity? When will you start giving yourself permission to go after what you want, Charlotte? Or do you intend to die alone, satisfied in the knowledge that you lived only to please everyone else around you?"

Mary's chest heaved. Charlotte's heart hammered in her ears. She wanted to declare that Mary was right. She wanted to say, *Mr Innes is a continuation of a road I have already walked down, albeit one with a more pleasant view.* She wanted to scream that regardless, it was not what she wanted, that Mary had awoken some fire in her that refused to go out, that something in her chest had unfurled the very first moment Mary's knee had brushed hers under the table, and that trying to stuff it all back inside her small, withered heart was as impossible as leashing a cloud and bending it to one's will.

"You make it all sound so easy." She sounded choked and indeed, she could barely swallow or breathe, as if something in her chest was trying to clamber up her windpipe and out onto her tongue. The truth; as heavy as a stone, and equally as unlimber.

"Is it not?" Mary took another step towards her and reached for Charlotte's shoulders, her hands fluttering there, her movements hesitant. "I cannot bear to see you look so. I am sorry that I..." She sighed. "My temper often gets the better of me, and my tongue is too blunt. Tell me what ails you, please. I cannot understand this behaviour."

Yet she could not, not with Mary's eyes on her. Humiliation yawned, a black chasm too slow to draw her inside. Mary dipped her head, forced their gazes to meet. "Charlotte? What made you so insistent that I must be with one or the other?" Charlotte bit her lip. Something in Mary's eyes changed. A dawning recognition. "Could it be that..."

Her voice was low, husky, almost like the tone she'd used in the rose garden at the Cromleys' ball. Charlotte desperately wanted to hear it again, but her tongue would not cooperate. *Say you want her*, she shouted at herself. *Say you think of her all the time. For goodness' sake, say something!*

Tentatively, Mary pressed a kiss onto Charlotte's left cheek, then her right. Their noses brushed. It would be the work of a moment for Charlotte to incline her head, to move just so and let their mouths meet.

She could never. She could never. She could never. She could—

To hell with it, she decided, and lunged forward. Women were so often described as the softer sex, all curves and coils, but Mary was sharp angles against her, strong fingers digging hard into her hips, eliciting a pleasurable pain. Charlotte kissed back hard enough to feel teeth clack against her own. A thirst, rather than a hunger. A deep and insatiable thirst, scorching up her thighs and pooling low in her belly, setting her ablaze in places she had never even known coals could abide. Sensations deluged all thought, rendering the world a blank canvas but for the press of Mary's mouth, hot against her own, an even hotter tongue swiping over Charlotte's lower lip.

Charlotte pulled back, panting. Alarm, abrupt and rapacious, overtook her, dousing the flames in her stomach with ice water. This was something beyond the pale, something she had only ever dreamed about doing with any woman. This was all too confusing and new and what if she had ruined her friendship with Mary entirely and Lord but how she wanted to kiss her again and again until the breath had been fairly knocked from them both and—

The sound of footsteps echoed in the passageway. Fighting every part of her body, which yearned to return to the embrace, Charlotte edged backwards, putting several feet of distance between them.

"I'm so sorry. That should never have happened." She put a hand to her chest, her heart aching with every beat. Prior to this moment, she'd thought that to have touched Mary, kissed Mary, even once would have been enough. Now, she knew that she would be thinking about the memory for the rest of her life, and to make matters worse, she had likely ruined a wonderful friendship from a single impulsive action. "I should return to Kent tomorrow. Tonight, perhaps, if there is a coach."

Mary looked as if she were struggling, her cheeks flushed with high colour. "Charlotte, please." Her voice was still low, still rasping, and the sound of it was almost enough to undo Charlotte's control. "Can we talk about this? I think you misunderstand—"

It was a mistake, the little voice screamed. *She's going to tell you it was a mistake. Even if she likes women, why would she ever want to kiss someone like you? It was a moment of weakness on her part, of course, and nothing more. A pity kiss, at best, for you are nothing but pitiable.* "No, please." Her blood thundered, her visions dancing with flashing spots, bright and sparkling, black-red and crinkling like lit paper at the edges. It took all her energy not to faint. "I cannot stay here. I will not. It would not be proper. I am sorry that I…that I did that to you."

Mary stepped forward. "If you wish to leave, I will not stop you. But you must know that I do not wish you to go." She was standing still, not blocking Charlotte's path to the door, not moving. "And you did nothing which I have not been desperately hoping for."

Charlotte gaped at her. "You…what?"

"Listen," Mary said calmly, though her hands were rapidly curling into fists and uncurling as she spoke. "My list of wants is quite simple. I want no further misunderstandings between us. I want you to stay. I want to kiss you again, though I will not do so until you give me leave. If you meant it, then I need to know now. And if this was simply a strange notion on your part, then I am quite prepared to set it aside and never speak of it again. Only you must tell me now which one it shall be."

Charlotte's breath came in shuddering gasps, though true to her word, Mary did not move. Little by little, her vision came back to normal. "I thought I was the only one who had such feelings," she said, tears rolling down her cheeks. The shock of the earlier sight of Mary and Pitt had faded, leaving her weepy with exhaustion. She pressed a hand to her chest, feeling the ache. A lifetime's worth of repression spilling out. "I thought I was quite alone."

"Oh, dear heart," Mary sighed, tugging her into an embrace. "You have never been alone."

Chapter Nineteen

The master gunner has taught the ship's cat to stand upon his hind legs and weave to and fro, while Mr Hawthorn plays a lively tune on the fiddle; indeed, the creature dances better than many in London. It is by such means that we amuse ourselves in the evening, though when the crew have gone to their bunks, exhausted by their day's labour, I often linger to admire the brilliant stars and to muse upon everything I have collected thus far. I could spend a decade devoted entirely to a single beetle, yet I have hundreds of species jarred. Why must men endure so briefly? Is it because we would otherwise take our lives for granted? I pray that I never do.

S. Barton, Travels of a Young Naturalist

Charlotte cried on Mary's shoulder for almost a quarter of an hour, and by the time she'd dried up, she was quite embarrassed by her outburst.

"Come now," Mary said, leading her to the armchair and settling her in gently. "Shall I call for some tea?"

Charlotte nodded and blew her nose hard on her handkerchief. She waited until the tea had arrived. Pitt glanced from one to the other with an air of consternation. "It's all right,

Pitt," Mary said, waving him off, and he left the room, casting only a single backwards glance.

"Here," Mary said, pressing a cup of hot tea into Charlotte's hands. "Drink. You will feel better afterwards."

"I'm fine," Charlotte protested. "Really, I am." Her hands trembled as she lifted the cup, betraying her nerves.

Mary smiled, her eyes full of concern. She reached out slowly, as if Charlotte were a wild animal she was afraid to startle, and brushed a curl of hair back from Charlotte's face. Charlotte flinched before leaning into the touch; why not, after all? The floodgates were open, her secret out. Though, despite Mary's prior declaration, she still could not believe that her friend was not just being nice out of pity.

"It takes time to adjust to a change, whether of the body or mind," Mary murmured, her fingers sliding up into Charlotte's hair and petting her with slow strokes. "I will never press you to say or do anything which makes you uncomfortable, but... do you feel as if you could talk to me about it?"

"Yes, although I do not know what kind of sense I will make." Charlotte put down her cup and moved to sit on the rug beside Mary. They sat side by side, staring into the flames, much as they had only two nights before.

"So," Mary prompted. "How long have you known you had these feelings?"

"I am not sure. I rather think you knew before I did." A more evasive answer than Mary deserved, perhaps, but one which might shield her from close scrutiny, at least for the moment.

Mary made a half shrug, though she did not deny it. Her body had tensed a little. "It was Lizzie, wasn't it?"

So much for shielding. "Yes and no." Charlotte sipped her tea again, trying to get her thoughts in order. "That was the first time I felt something different, that I was sure I ought not to feel for another woman." It struck Charlotte for the first time that Mary might have been feeling jealous at times too, of her own sister. Certainly the Bennet family had never esteemed their middle daughter. "But, to be clear, I was never in love with your sister." This seemed like an important distinction to make.

"Ah." Mary relaxed. "I did always wonder. It played a small part in the discovery of my own feelings—" she shifted a little "—though it wasn't until I confided in Aunt Cecily that I began to see the possibilities of the world in a different light."

"You do appear to have bloomed here."

Mary smiled, picking up her own cup and pouring tea. "Yes, I supposed I have. And so it seems have you."

"On the contrary, I started to bloom the moment you arrived at the parsonage." Charlotte blushed to say such things out loud, but Mary's expression was worth all the blushes in the world.

"Why? What was it that began things?"

"I hardly know, really," said she, thinking back over those first days together. "You came in all grown up, and not at all what I had expected or remembered, and the change quite unnerved me to begin with. Then, the more we spent time together... I do not know, exactly. You made me feel like..." She struggled to find the right words. "A long unwatered plant being offered a drink. Though I tried not to feel such things, or look at you in such ways. In truth, I rather suspected you saw me as just another older sister."

Mary, who had just taken a rather large gulp of tea, promptly choked on it. "Gracious!" she exclaimed, after coughing and spluttering for several seconds. "As a sister!" She descended into another fit of coughing, although this one was punctuated with merry laughter. "I assure you," she said, wiping her streaming eyes, "that I never did such things with my own sisters, nor did I ever see you in that way. I always looked up to you, though I don't think you noticed me then, and I cannot blame you for doing so. No, let me finish—" for Charlotte had opened her mouth to protest "—for I was doing my best to behave well, at least to begin with, and then I found myself growing fonder and fonder of you. I had, I must admit, quite resigned myself to the fact that you were untouchable, though some of your looks and manners gave me several sleepless nights. I thought I was imagining things, and that my feelings of hope were frequently getting the better of my common sense."

"I felt the same," Charlotte admitted.

"We are perfect fools together, are we not?"

Charlotte rested her head on Mary's shoulder. Before long, the memory of the kiss came flooding back. For all its belated joy, it was still edged with anxiety and fear. *Which is perfectly natural*, she told herself. *All those years suppressing my feelings will not simply vanish like morning mist under the heat of the sun.* Her inner voice still warned her about perversities, about giving in to sinful thoughts and desires. Still, the feeling of the kiss overrode all sense. Something which felt so good surely could not really be bad.

"What?" Mary asked, turning to crane down at her.

"Nothing. It is just…" She blushed, her voice dropping to a murmur. "Our kiss."

"What about it?" Mary's voice had dropped too, and the air between them, what little there was, became thick and electric.

Charlotte swallowed hard, and forced herself to look away. It had been one thing to kiss Mary in a blind panic, and quite another to do so soberly. "You were very good."

Mary's eyes crinkled. "Thank you." She put a hand to her chest, stuck her chin in the air, and did her best impression of Mrs Bennet. "Other young ladies in the neighbourhood may be much praised for their needlework but our Mary has added kissing to her impressive list of accomplishments."

Charlotte laughed, though her stomach was churning. She did want to kiss Mary again, so why had she spoiled the moment? Why on earth did she find it so difficult to pursue what she wanted, and so easy to pursue what she did not?

"Come," Mary said, rising to her feet and offering a hand to

Charlotte to help her up. "It is my firm belief that after a good weep one needs to eat a tremendous amount of cake."

She led Charlotte downstairs, chattering all the while, and Charlotte was grateful for the flow of easy conversation. She needed a little time to become accustomed to things, although she had no wish to shut herself away from Mary. If anything, she wanted to cling to Mary, to follow her around, to sit as close as possible. In the drawing room, Charlotte sat first and Mary hesitated, as if waiting for permission to join her. Charlotte patted the seat in encouragement, and Mary acquiesced with a look of relief. The chatter did not stop, however, and soon Charlotte was being drawn into a discussion of the flowers Barton had mentioned in his diary, and whether they bore any resemblance to flowers she was familiar with. She saw now what should have been evident to her before—the way Mary's eyes lingered, the way her companion followed her every word and thought with great attention, the brief displays of affection with a shoulder pat. Charlotte had thought it simply friendship, which in hindsight had been a foolish interpretation. Though her other friends had always been affectionate, none of them would ever have been so frequent or overt about it.

She smiled to herself—Lizzie would have made so much fun of her for being oblivious to a suitor's attentions—but then her smile faded. *Oh no. I hadn't considered Lizzie.* How could Charlotte ever face her friend again, knowing that she'd kissed one of her sisters? Lizzie had never been a particularly staid person, or fond of old traditions when they did not suit, but this was quite a different kettle of fish. One was often more accepting of others' oddities when they did not conflict with the social standing of one's family.

"May I ask a question?"

Mary stiffened slightly. "Yes?"

"Does Lizzie know? About you?"

"Oh, yes. All except Lydia, for I did not trust her to keep it secret from our mother. I suspect even Father knows, though we've never spoken about it directly. He's made several allusions to a boyhood friend that never married, and I am many things but I am not stupid."

"Oh." Charlotte fidgeted for a moment. "And was she— were they…"

"Accepting? Yes. Kitty took a little longer to come around, but even she did, in the end." Mary inched closer, her arm stretching out on the back of the couch. "If you ever wanted to tell them, I know they would not love you any less."

"That is quite a relief," Charlotte admitted, leaning back into Mary's embrace, glad that Mary was giving her plenty of time to get used to touches that actually might mean something. Everything was so new, but the thought that Mary wanted to be close to her, had perhaps even yearned to do so, was undeniably thrilling.

Dinner that evening was the promised chicken in white wine sauce, with apple pie to follow, and a final round of cheese and figs. They retired to the drawing room afterwards, and Charlotte collapsed on the couch next to Mary, rubbing a hand over her full stomach. "Your Miss Brodie is quite the treasure," said she. "And a very sweet girl."

Mary glanced at Charlotte so sharply that at first Charlotte thought she might be angry. "You met her?"

"I did. It was—oh, I never told you. There was a series of events which preceded me bursting into your room. I should have explained already." Charlotte explained the events: the letter from Maria, meeting Miss Brodie in the kitchen, exploring and discovering the portraits of Aunt Cecily, Mr Langley, and Edith.

"Ah, I see." Mary's cheeks pinked. "No wonder you ran in as if your hair was on fire."

"So… Edith?" Charlotte prompted, keen to steer the conversation away from her sudden and undignified entrance, and was amused to see her friend blush again.

"I confess I was rather infatuated at first," Mary confessed.

"I thought as much. And no wonder, she is exceedingly pretty. Her hair is a glorious colour."

"If you met her, you would see that her beauty pales in comparison to her mind. Aunt Cecily and George evidently were of the same opinion. A very sensible pair, actually."

"Is she… I mean…" Charlotte couldn't think of a tactful way to ask if Edith was Mary's type. She recalled the nude drawing of the mysterious woman again, and compared the two in her mind's eye. Certainly they were both beautiful, with large expressive eyes and wild manes of hair. A far cry from her own smooth curls and plain face. The contentment she'd felt since the kiss began to ebb at the thought.

"Charlotte?" Mary was studying her, eyebrows furrowed. "What's wrong?"

"Nothing."

"You really ought to stop saying nothing when it is evidently something."

"Well, I…earlier, you said you wanted to kiss me again." Already, she could feel a hot flush creeping up her neck and spreading across her cheeks. "Surely you did not mean it." How could she have meant it, when Charlotte was nothing in comparison to these women?

Mary stared at her, lips slightly parted, confusion writ large across her face. "Why not? You kissed me and I kissed you back. I told you that I had nursed hopes that you might return my affections. Good grief, what deeper expression of interest do you need? A brass band?"

They stared at each in mutual incomprehension. "Oh." Charlotte bit her lip, a single tentative bud unfurling in her chest. *Could it really be?*

"May I kiss you now?" Mary's fingers touched Charlotte's

cheek, then slipped down to her chin, tilting it up. "I'm quite willing to prove my interest, if you'll let me. Though," she added hastily, "I'll happily wait until you're more comfortable with the idea."

"I confess you make me nervous," Charlotte said, and Mary began to withdraw her fingers but Charlotte caught them, kept them where they were. In the candlelight, alone, everything which had seemed so frightening and far off earlier that day now seemed entirely possible. "That is not a no. I am simply—" She swallowed. "Perhaps a little shy. Perhaps you might help me become less so."

Her heart beat a rapid tattoo, as Mary leaned in slowly, giving Charlotte time to back away.

Despite her nerves, she did not retreat. The second kiss was very unlike the first, which had been all fangs and claws and desperation. This one was the soft touch of a morning breeze, promising a beautiful day to come. Charlotte reached out blindly, her fingers finding the line of Mary's jaw, the soft flesh of her neck, the sharp angle of her collarbone. No one had ever handled her so gently before—her parents had been jovial, Lizzie friendly, Mr Collins keen but unwieldy. Mary's touch on her chin was barely there and yet something explosive crackled between them, veiled by sweetness.

Charlotte pulled back and studied Mary's face; it was flushed, her sparkling eyes still edged with concern for Charlotte's well-being—and oh, how that expression made her own heart swell in gratitude—and she wondered if she had been an utter fool all along not to see what was so obviously present.

Mary was a perfect gentlewoman for the rest of the evening. She made no secret of hiding that her eyes followed Charlotte around the room, but she made few overtures that had not already become part of their intimate friendship. If anything, she had pulled back a little, which made Charlotte's heart sink. Perhaps Mary had not enjoyed the second kiss as much as the first.

Perhaps neither had been up to the excellence she had expected. Perhaps Charlotte—who in fairness could not claim to be terribly skilled at such things—had been rather inept.

She had worried that conversation might be stilted now that there was something acknowledged between them, but in that respect Mary seemed just as she had before; just as witty, just as warm. "The salon will be held at Mrs Wilberforce's home, in two days' time. You will still accompany me, won't you?" Mary batted her eyelashes, making Charlotte giggle.

"Yes, of course. What ought I to expect?"

"Well, the topic of the moment is a new theory based on strata." Mary hesitated. "Do you know what strata are?"

"I confess I do not."

"Do not worry, I shall explain it to you. Here, give me your arm." Mary pushed the sleeve of Charlotte's dress back, exposing her bare forearm, and placed two warm fingers at the elbow joint. "They are natural layers of rock and sediment in the earth's crust. See, if we have a layer here," she drew a line across the soft flesh of Charlotte's arm, causing a slight shiver, "and then over time further sediments are deposited through various means—weather, water, and so on—then you will have a second layer on top of the first." She drew another imaginary line, an inch down. "And so on," another line, another shiver, "and so on. And therefore, when we examine these layers, we can use the thickness and the kinds of deposits made to determine the age and duration of that particular strata." Her fingers returned to Charlotte's elbow joint, and walked down the flesh until they stopped at her wrist. "The research into these layers gives us a more complete picture of the earth's history, or at least the parts of it currently above water. That is the short version of the explanation. Does it make sense?"

"Completely," Charlotte said, a little breathlessly, and when Mary sat back without kissing her, she found herself disappointed. "I... I ought to apologize," she blurted, her chest tight with trepidation.

Mary's eyes widened. "What on earth for?"

"I expect I'm no good at kissing."

Before Charlotte could add any explanation, or beg for mercy, Mary snorted. "I do not know who gave you that impression, but I have found quite the opposite to be true."

"So you did enjoy it?"

"Yes."

She frowned, not following the logic. "Then why do you not pursue me?"

"My dear Charlotte, I was concerned that I might be pursuing you too much already. This is all very new to you, and, well... I want you to feel comfortable. Besides, I too like to be pursued. Well," Mary corrected herself, "that depends on who is doing the pursuing, but in your case, rest assured that I am most receptive."

Charlotte turned the idea over in her mind. This was a fair point—the situation was very new to her, and she was not yet free of the guilt she felt about having such feelings in the first place. Still, the fear and shame had lessened every time they'd kissed, and she thought that with more kissing, it was entirely possible they too would fade. "Ah yes, I remember the young man at the ball who asked you to dance."

"It was not those silly boys I was thinking of, in all honesty." Mary sighed. "It was Mrs Tremaine."

Charlotte blinked, baffled. "Whatever do you mean?"

"I may as well tell you. When she first moved to town, over a year ago, she flirted with me incessantly," Mary admitted. "She would not take no for an answer, and became quite a nuisance. Turning up places she knew I would be, trying to visit the house every few days to catch me at home, alone. I imagine someone less stubborn might have simply given in and been made a conquest, though the more she pushed, the more determined I was to push back."

"But she is married," Charlotte protested, astonished that anyone could act in such a way.

"That was not my only reason for rejecting her advances, though it played a large part. Look, you must be careful around her, for your words will turn into skittering mice and she will be the hawk who catches the least fortunate one."

"She cannot be as bad as all that," Charlotte said, and was surprised at how serious Mary looked.

"She is all that and much more. Be on your guard."

"Gracious, I am well warned. Fear not, I shall be extremely careful around her."

Pitt brought in tea—how he always knew when tea was most wanted, Charlotte had no idea—and the conversation turned back to the previous meetings at the salon, who had attended, and what had been discussed there. As Mary talked, Charlotte watched her keenly; her lips, her fine dark eyes full of animation, her hands fluttering back and forth as she talked, like courting birds.

"What is it?" Mary asked. "I do hope I'm not boring you."

"Not at all." Charlotte swallowed hard. She had been brave before, she could be brave again. Besides, Mary had assured her that she would be receptive to advances.

Plucking up her courage, Charlotte leaned forward, fear and excitement thrilling through her in equal measures, and cupped Mary's face in trembling hands. Mary stilled, waiting, her lips slightly parted, eyes hooded. Kissing had generally been something that had been done to Charlotte, rather than something she sought, but this was different. She tilted her head and kissed Mary—not a tempestuous kiss like their first, or the second, more delicate one, but a soft, sweet kiss that spoke a kind of thanks.

When she drew back, Mary looked dazed and flushed. "What was that you were saying about being a poor kisser?"

"I do not recall," Charlotte murmured, sliding closer on the couch. Heady desire had overtaken her anxiety, clouding her thoughts. "Perhaps we ought to do it again, just to be certain."

Chapter Twenty

My dear Mrs Collins,
I hope you will not stay away long, for the weather here has been very fine for the last few days, and I have hit upon a wonderful scheme for your return—with a small party, we shall walk across to Primrose Hill and take a picnic. How wonderful does that sound? I am feeling well of late and must take the opportunity to indulge where I can, for soon enough the headaches will be upon me again. Mr Innes and Sir George have already agreed to attend and I decided that you would be the perfect companion to make up our foursome. Canterbury cannot be so fine in comparison to the glorious Kentish countryside, nor from the pleasant company of two handsome and most agreeable gentlemen. I know you will agree!
Your friend,
Anne de Bourgh

They spent the next couple of hours in a romantic haze, kissing endlessly, swinging from languid to vigorous, though neither Mary's hands or mouth wandered from their chaste positions. She was always careful to stop whenever things were becoming too heated, and although Charlotte longed for a little more, she was grateful for the brief breaks and nervous about what might come next. She'd participated in marital activities with Mr Collins, though her duty had been mainly to arrange herself appropriately during the act and offer plenty of praise afterwards. If her dream about Mary was anything to go by—and she hoped it was—then her participation here would be much more on equal footing.

While Mary poured tea, Charlotte winced at the recollection of her first few times in bed with Mr Collins; the graceless awkwardness of both parties, the lack of ardor on her part which she had tried to make up for by commending his efforts in a ladylike manner. It had all been so calculated, she saw in hindsight. The keenness with which she sought to prove that she was a good wife, worthy of being selected after all, sprung from her own insecurities. The deep discomfort she'd felt with his hands on her flesh, which she'd tried to cover by reassuring herself that most wives felt this way, that there was nothing wrong with her, that only husbands really enjoyed the marital act. She had known perfectly well that last fact wasn't true at all, had heard as much insinuated amongst married ladies of her acquaintance, but denial was a powerful tool, and the one she'd used most often to cull the ever-growing field of her anxieties.

Mary didn't bring up the subject of what might come afterwards, which made Charlotte wonder if she was perhaps not interested in taking matters further. However, she was too shy to ask for clarity, and too grateful for all that she was receiving already.

That evening, they said goodnight with chaste kisses, and Charlotte sat for a while in an armchair in front of the fire, staring into the flames. She'd spent so long convincing herself that her desires were wrong, that she ought to be ashamed for desiring her friend in such a perverse way, that allowing herself to enjoy these experiences now left her feeling strange and dizzy. To complicate matters, while it was one thing for well-off Great-Aunt Ethel to have a companion, and likewise for Mary, who had means at her disposal, it was quite another thing for Charlotte. She knew now that she could never marry again without much regret, though perhaps she would not have much choice in the matter. As long as her parents were alive, she would have a place at Lucas Lodge, but after they passed her brother, John, would inherit, and he already had a large family. Charlotte would merely be in the way, only useful as a sort of secondary mother to his brood. Her options, therefore, were limited. Her one hope was that Mary might want her to visit often, though she could not count on her friend's interest remaining steady forever. Hearts wavered and changed like the tides, and who was she to hope for something so wonderful as Mary's eternal devotion?

She sighed. That was the future; this was now. There was no point crying over what she could not change, and if she spent all her time in Canterbury moping, then what little time she had with Mary would be spoiled. Determined not to waste a single second more, Charlotte got ready for bed, and vowed to meet the new day with all the courage she possessed.

The next morning, Charlotte joined Mary in the dining room, and over a breakfast of fresh fruit and toast, they made a plan for the day. Mary insisted that she had been a dreadful hostess thus far due to the sheer mound of work heaped upon her, and had to remedy this immediately. "I did promise to make it up to you, did I not?" said she, arching an eyebrow, and Charlotte couldn't help blushing as she thought of all the ways in which Mary might do so.

Unfortunately, none of these licentious thoughts turned out to be part of Mary's plan, which encompassed first a carriage ride to Canterbury Cathedral, where Charlotte marvelled at the grand old building. She recalled a little history about the place, though her recollections were mainly the darker deeds which tended to stick in the mind, particularly the shocking murder of Thomas Becket inside the building itself in 1170. Mary provided the rest, leading Charlotte around the interior and pointing out where the monks had once done their sleeping, eating, and charity work. The stained-glass windows were particularly fine on such a bright day, and Charlotte lingered to admire the effect.

"I have heard it said that the northwest tower is dangerous and ought to be pulled down," Mary said, pointing at the tower in question. "Though it will take them an age to rebuild such a thing, and will cost an immense amount. I see why they are loath to do so."

"Whatever for? It is quite lovely."

"Some sort of structural damage." Mary shrugged. "I do not supposed it can be fixed, if there is talk of tearing it down entirely. And that over there is the medicinal herb garden."

The herb garden turned out to be exactly that, and after wandering through the cloister gardens, Charlotte declared that the place was most agreeable, if rather devoid of flowers. "Surely even monks must have enjoyed a bouquet from time to time," she added, picturing the poor men in their bare cells, with not even a single flower to ameliorate the spartan surroundings.

"A hard life, indeed." Mary nodded. "Now, I must ask, for it relates to our next activity—you are not fond of horse-racing, are you?"

"I confess I am not. It is too terrible when one falls, and must be put out of its misery."

"I'm glad to hear it. We may pass over that entirely, and move on to something that interests us both. What about a little shopping, and then a concert?"

Charlotte agreed that both sounded delightful, and so they returned to the carriage and drove through town to Mary's favourite dressmaker, Ashbrook's, where the employees were only too delighted to see them. After perusing several new bolts of cloth, including a dark blue the exact colour of a summer night sky, Mary insisted on having Charlotte fitted for a new dress. "No, please," Charlotte protested. "I could not possibly let you spend so much money on me."

"What is money for if not to help a friend?" Mary leaned in while the dressmaker bustled off to aid a new customer. "I'd like to buy you something that isn't black."

"I won't be able to wear it for months yet."

"Then it will be something to look forward to. How about this?" Mary held up a green silk which reminded Charlotte of a just-snipped stem.

Charlotte sighed. "If you must have your way—"

"Indeed, I must."

"Then…well…" She stroked the dark blue. "This would be lovely, especially with a little silver or gold sewn into it."

"Celestial," Mary remarked, and then lowered her voice even further. "You will look ravishing in it."

Charlotte blushed, but before she could think of a charming reply, the dressmaker bustled back over, and the next few minutes were taken up with measuring and marking. Once they had exited the shop, Charlotte insisted on paying Mary back in a small way by purchasing both tickets to a concert at a nearby guild hall. The music was delightful—an orchestra, accompanied by a young soprano—and though Charlotte did not know enough to know whether the girl was really good or not, it certainly sounded wonderful in the echoing space.

At home, before the drawing room door had quite closed, Charlotte had leaned in and tugged Mary flush against her, seeking her mouth for a passionate kiss which turned out to be a little harder than she had first intended. "I apologise," said she, when it was over. "I simply could not wait any longer."

"Please do not apologise for something so delightful," Mary murmured, and leaned in for another.

A soft knock sounded, and they extracted themselves from each other in just enough time before Pitt entered the room to announce that dinner was ready.

Miss Brodie had surpassed herself again, this time with fish, so beautifully cooked it flaked at the slightest pressure from Charlotte's fork, atop a bed of braised greens. Dessert was a raspberry trifle, light and creamy. Although the fare was excellent, Charlotte hardly tasted any of it. Nothing existed that was not Mary's eyes, Mary's mouth, Mary's hands, and she found herself relieved when the meal was over and they could retire into the drawing room together.

"Come," Mary said, and arranged herself on the couch so that Charlotte could comfortably lie in her arms. "Is this too much?"

"Not at all." She wanted to ask for more, but shyness again prevented her. It did not take long for them to become entangled, much like Charlotte's dream, only these kisses were sweet and short. It was all very pleasant, but immensely frustrating. Charlotte shifted position; winding her fingers into Mary's hair, she tugged experimentally. Mary gasped, her body arching towards Charlotte.

She froze, panic rising. "Did I hurt you?"

"No." Mary's cheeks were flushed with high colour, her eyes darker than ever before. She licked her lips once, twice, her chest heaving. "No, you did not hurt me."

Charlotte leaned in, tentatively, and pressed a gentle kiss to Mary's lips. "Then what is it?"

"I am... You make me..." Mary huffed. "Do you really not know what you do to me?"

"No, not at all." Charlotte stilled her face, made it politely blank. "Pray tell."

"You're a monster," Mary mumbled, burying her face in Charlotte's shoulder, eliciting a giggle. "Very well." She looked up into Charlotte's eyes, desire writ plain across her face in every line of strain. "Every touch of yours sets me alight. Every kiss is another coal on the fire, and I can only let it burn so long before it threatens to consume me entirely. There, that's pretty language to say something plain. Are you satisfied?"

Charlotte's heart was hammering so hard she was certain Mary would hear it. "Not in the slightest." She smiled, then bit her lip. "Then...may I ask..."

"Why I am holding back?" Mary sighed. "It is not from lack of desire that we have not gone to bed together. I thought I had made that clear. It is simply that I am, perhaps, slower than most to bare my body and soul in such a way. I do not take lovers casually, as some do. I hope that is acceptable."

"Of course." Charlotte blinked, surprised. The idea of taking a lover casually had never occurred to her, though she had expected Mary to be a little less formal in this regard. There was something she was missing in this explanation, she was certain—some obvious fact staring her in the face, but she could not quite work out what it was. "I'm happy to be with you in any respect."

"Give me time," Mary said, pressing another kiss to the corner of Charlotte's mouth, eliciting another smile. "I will endeavour to be worth it."

"I have no doubt that you will."

And yet, Charlotte thought, *time is a currency fast running out.* She was aware they had talked of her staying for a week or two, though Mary had said nothing beyond this and besides, even if invited to linger, Charlotte had responsibilities to attend to. She would have to return to the parsonage to oversee the packing of boxes for the journey back to Hertfordshire. She would have to say tearful goodbyes to Bessie and Mrs Waites, as well as Anne de Bourgh. She could put it off a little longer, perhaps another week, but at some point she would have to face the truth: her parents would be expecting her at Lucas Lodge, and she would have to once again don the guise of Mrs Collins, widow and burden, rather than Charlotte, free to kiss whomever she pleased and go wherever she liked with not a single thought given to the rules and expectations that governed polite society.

"What is it?" Mary murmured.

Charlotte shook off the thoughts and forced a smile. Mary must be as aware as she of their impending separation. There was no need to mar happy times with a reminder. "Nothing a good kiss cannot fix."

"Well then, come here."

Breathlessly, Charlotte acquiesced, and the next few minutes were spent exploring all the healing properties of a very good kiss.

"I have something to tell you," Mary murmured, catching her breath once they'd parted. "I hope you will not find this habit too strange, but once a week I have lunch downstairs with the servants."

Charlotte gaped at her. "Really?"

"Is that so odd?" Mary frowned, her tone defensive.

"Not at all," Charlotte hastened to reassure her. "In fact, I have spent many a pleasant hour in the kitchen with Mrs Waites."

"You do not think me queer?"

"I do, but not for this." Charlotte grinned at the way Mary's eyes rolled in amusement.

"The thing is…" She shifted uncomfortably on the couch. "Over the last year I have rather lost touch with some society friends. It is a long story, and I—well. Suffice to say that these weekly lunches were a tradition begun by Aunt Cecily and I have enjoyed continuing them in her absence. After all, the servants and I may be separated by class, but there is something deeper which binds us together. I find it cheering to have more people around who understand my particular situation, and I theirs. Does that make sense?"

"It makes the most perfect sense in the world," Charlotte declared.

"Would you care to join us tomorrow?"

She blushed with pleasure. "I would be delighted to."

Lunch began quietly, with each member of the party seated around the long kitchen table. Strips of pork belly, well-seasoned and flavourful with a crispy, crackling skin, were accompanied beautifully with buttered new potatoes liberally sprinkled with thyme. Though the meal was excellent, Charlotte worried that her presence was inhibiting the servants from being their usual selves. She needn't have worried. Before long, the footmen—Henry and Thomas—began to chatter excitedly about a dance they intended to attend, and begged Miss Brodie to join them on the excursion, since the young housemaid who was apparently their usual companion had gone home to visit her parents.

"I notice you have not invited me," Pitt said, passing a bowl of glistening peas along the table. Charlotte caught his quick glance at Miss Brodie, who looked uncomfortable.

"We do not invite you any longer because you never come," Henry said, tucking a lock of dark hair behind his ear. "Why, you are quite in your prime, sir, and any man in the place would surely—" Thomas elbowed him hard. "Ow! It was a compliment, do not jostle me so."

"I would rather not go out," Miss Brodie murmured, her voice barely audible. "But if Miss Bennet would not mind terribly, I wondered if my friend might visit for a few days? He has secured a little leave from Mrs…" she swallowed, "from my former place of employ."

"Ooh, Nancy, a special friend!" Henry cried, and earned himself another elbow in the ribs from Thomas. The two footmen descended into giggles.

Mary smiled. "Of course. I am glad that you have someone

dear to you." She mock-glared at the footmen and moved her chair away. "Tell me, boys, is your silliness contagious?"

They grinned, unabashed, and Henry dropped a quick kiss on Thomas' shoulder. The rest of the meal continued in much the same way, and Charlotte discovered that the servants had at their disposal immense pools of gossips, like great fungal networks, reaching across Canterbury and beyond. Indeed, even shy Miss Brodie seemed to possess a wealth of knowledge about all the nearby families, especially who among them employed a decent cook. Mary chimed in from time to time, looking more comfortable and relaxed than Charlotte had ever seen before. This was clearly a cosy, familial space that Mary had been unable to create while living with the Bennets. Here, she was among her people, and it suffused Charlotte with a warm pleasure to know that class boundaries were, at least in the privacy of this house, not so strictly observed.

Afterwards, once she and Mary returned to the drawing room, she said how pleasant and agreeable the atmosphere had been. Mary looked relieved.

"It is not that I do not have friends of my own rank," said she, as though preempting an argument that Charlotte had not actually made. "There is Miss Highbridge, of course, but though I treasure Delia greatly, she has her own life to lead and cannot spend every afternoon lunching with me. Besides, she too has a new beau." Mary smirked. "And I quite understand the desire to be sequestered away with the object of one's desire."

"Indeed, I quite understand the notion myself." Charlotte leaned in for a long, slow kiss, full of tender warmth. "How did Miss Brodie come to your aunt's employ? She does not seem the type to present herself at the door and make her case."

"Ah." The smile vanished from Mary's face. "Nancy—Miss Brodie—was working as a kitchen boy for a friend of Mrs Tremaine's, a Mrs Grendel, who espied her more feminine side and made one too many romantic overtures towards her. I have never known precisely what happened, nor do I wish to, but the result was that Nancy fled. The butler at the house, an old friend of Pitt's, asked him to do what he could, lest the poor girl be homeless. Pitt brought her here," she shrugged, "and that was that. Once Aunt Cecily had tasted her cooking, there was never any question of trying to find her another position."

Charlotte's jaw dropped. "Why, how terrible! And she is such a dear, sweet little thing. I cannot imagine her saying boo to a goose."

"The sweetest nestlings make for the quickest meals," Mary said darkly. "I've had them make it clear to the rest of Mrs Grendel's staff that should such a thing happen again, any one of them would be welcome here. I also warned Mrs Grendel herself, which went over about as well as you can imagine." She sighed. "Sometimes I would like to burn society down entirely. I know I cannot change anything myself, but if I can provide a small safe haven then perhaps I can claim to have at least improved the lives of a few."

"You are a noble and courageous knight," Charlotte said, unable to help a fond smile. "No wonder I have become quite besotted with you."

The cloud over Mary seemed to lift a little. "Is that so, fair maiden? Do you have any dragons you need slain?"

Her hands wound around Charlotte's waist as the fire crackled, and the next kiss scorched them both.

Chapter Twenty-One

Dearest daughter,
Of course, we understand very well that spending some time away
from the parsonage will do you good.

Mary Bennet always seemed a quiet, steady sort of girl.

Just remember that we are ready to receive you with open arms,
and one or both of us are quite prepared to travel down to Kent
to help you pack your belongings.
With fondest regards,
Mama and Papa

The next day passed in a blur of kissing, punctuated only by
breaks for meals, reading and correspondence, and a little playing upon the pianoforte. Charlotte found it difficult to sit even
an inch apart from Mary, so deep was her craving, and only the
raptures of Miss Brodie's cooking kept her from pulling Mary
into her lap at mealtimes.

Pitt had warmed to her too, now that it was obvious the relationship between Charlotte and Mary had changed; he watched
his mistress with far less anxiety than he had once done, and
more than once Charlotte had caught him looking at their
linked hands with a kind of wistful longing. *How hard it must*

be for him, she thought, *to have loved so deeply and lost such a sweet, fascinating man.* She would have liked to question him about Barton, but to open such a wound would no doubt be very painful.

When the clock struck ten that evening, Charlotte was astonished that the last hours had passed by so quickly. "Would you stay with me again?" she asked Mary. "I find I do not wish to let you go so soon."

"Of course. Would you prefer your room or mine?"

"Yours," Charlotte decided.

They prepared for bed in separate rooms before Charlotte tiptoed along the hallway, feeling like a forbidden lover in a Shakespearian play, and slipped in without knocking. They cuddled up together under the sheets, Charlotte marvelling once again at how hot Mary seemed to run—a wonderful contrast to her own cool hands and feet, which never seemed to warm much regardless of the season. She had hoped for at least a little kissing, and therefore was disappointed when Mary merely slung an arm over her waist and tucked her head under Charlotte's chin. *Time is ticking,* the voice in her head whispered. *In a few days you will have to leave her, and once you do, things will never be the same.*

All the more reason to enjoy things as they are now, she argued back, and though the voice fell silent, she did not feel entirely reassured.

The day of the salon dawned bright and sunny, though the humidity left Charlotte feeling unpleasantly clammy. Pitt had thrown open the windows in the drawing room, and the wonderful smell of mignonette had paled under the smell of the street below—the sour stench of chimney smoke from a hundred kitchens mixing with the sweet-bitter stink of horse manure.

"Summer will be upon us soon," she said aloud.

Mary looked up from her page, her quill slowing its scratching. "And yet you sound unhappy about it." She leaned over and pressed a kiss against Charlotte's shoulder. "Do you prefer winter? Snow outside and roaring fires?"

By winter, I will be a mere footnote in the book of her life, thought Charlotte. "No," she said, and forced a smile. "I much prefer spring, truth be told. Everything fresh and new, with little buds sprouting everywhere and darling lambs in the fields." She sighed. *Back when we first met. If I could only live these last few weeks all over again, I would stop being foolish far sooner.*

"Is something bothering you?"

Charlotte returned to the present to find Mary studying her, brow furrowed in concern. "I was just wishing that I had sooner realised my..." *My what?* she wondered. *My inclinations? My feelings?* "Everything, really."

"You poor dear." Mary reached for Charlotte's chin, tilted it up, her thumb swiping over her bottom lip. "Don't be too hard on yourself. We have lofty expectations impressed upon us from the moment we begin to walk and talk. It is not easy to break free from such things or to realise what truths lie hidden in our hearts."

"You make it look easy. You make it feel easy."

Mary's eyes glittered in the light. Though neither had moved a muscle, the air between them grew thick. "I'm glad you think so."

Charlotte bit her lip. "Please put your quill down, lest I ruin your dress."

Mary cast it aside without looking to see where it landed, and the stack of papers on her lap went the same way. A heartbeat later, their mouths met in a scorching kiss which seared Charlotte all the way down to her toes. She pushed Mary back on the couch, slotting her body into the gap between Mary's thighs. The kiss deepened, Mary's breath hitching as Charlotte pulled her closer, pressing them together so tightly that she could feel the thud of Mary's heart.

"If we continue down this path," Mary murmured, her voice

rough, "then I shall keep you in bed all day and we will never make it to the salon tonight. Have mercy, dear one. I am barely holding myself back as it is."

Charlotte couldn't help a whimper catching in her throat at the insinuation, her hips rolling forward once without her quite meaning to do so; Mary made a half-strangled noise under her, and then they were kissing again, harder than before, hands grabbing at each other with fierce abandon, and by the time they broke apart, both gasping for air, Charlotte was quite prepared to ignore that such a thing as a salon had ever existed, far less that they were obliged to attend one. However, Mary had been kind enough to take her to the ball at Mrs Cromley's, and now Charlotte had to act the part of the amiable husband in turn.

"Very well," she said, smiling, though she had never wanted to attend an event less than she did right now.

"Are you sure?"

Charlotte bent and kissed Mary, marvelling at how easy it felt to do so, how sweet and already familiar. "Of course. Anything for you."

Lest she tempt them both into a situation from which neither wished to retreat, Charlotte did her best to behave well in the hours that followed. She occupied her hands with the pianoforte while Mary wrote, playing soft lullabies and lively tunes, and even began to compose a little something of her own. It was hardly Bach, but it passed the time, and when she grew tired of that, Mary offered to lend her the key to the shared garden so that she could pick a bouquet.

"Not today, but perhaps I shall do tomorrow." Her hands were too restless for flower arranging, her mind still simmering with the heat which had blazed between them during their last kiss. It had been a while since she had picked any flowers, and a thought struck her as she closed the lid of the pianoforte. "Do you recall that when you returned from Meryton, I made a wreath for the table? White peonies and purple pansies?"

"You did. I thought it odd that you did not tell me what they meant, though I had supposed you were too amused by my mimicry of my mother to remember." Mary glanced up, a slow smile spreading over her face. "Was it a secret message?"

"Of sorts. Pansies signify a lover's thoughts unspoken, while the peonies represented new beginnings." She blushed. "And perhaps a certain bashfulness on the part of the giver."

"Why Charlotte Lucas, you utter romantic." Mary chewed the end of her quill. "And what flowers would you choose now? Would they differ?"

Fortunately, Charlotte was saved from having to produce any sort of coherent response by the entrance of Pitt, who announced that dinner was ready, and by the time the first course was served, Mary appeared to have forgotten she'd asked the question in the first place. Charlotte put it to the back of her mind, vowing to consider the matter later; such a weighty thing as the perfect bouquet could not be rushed.

After dinner, they travelled in the carriage to the Wilberforces' home, which was in the eastern part of the town, in quite the opposite direction they'd taken to attend the Cromleys' ball.

The Wilberforces owned a townhouse much like Mary's, though theirs was precisely in the middle of the row. The foyer was not quite as grand as Aunt Cecily's, and the walls were painted a deep scarlet which Charlotte knew had been all the rage a few years prior. The chandelier which lit the room was a beautiful specimen, all loops and curves supporting a set of flickering candles, while the staircase they passed was constructed of a fine dark wood, and the bustling maids had a plump, healthy look to them. The drawing room was a large one, though the presence of some twenty people made it feel rather crowded. Charlotte could not see a pianoforte, which was unusual, but a grand harp in the far corner suggested that this family's musical tastes tended towards something quieter.

She had expected to recognise the young woman from the nude drawing, but there was no trace of a dark mane amongst the women present. "Oh no," Mary muttered, as a blonde woman in a bright green gown made a beeline for them. She was attractive, in a way, with high cheekbones and pouting lips, but something about her reminded Charlotte horribly of Caroline Bingley, whose snobbery had almost caused Jane Bennet to lose a happy love match.

"Good evening, Miss Bennet. And who is this?" the woman asked, eyeing Charlotte as if she were something the kitchen cat had dragged in.

A muscle jumped in Mary's jaw—a sign of frustration, Charlotte knew by now—but her voice was calm. "This is Mrs Collins, a friend of mine from childhood. Mrs Collins, this is Mrs Tremaine."

"Indeed? And what branch of science are you pursuing, Mrs Collins?"

"Oh, I am not pursuing anything," Charlotte said, embarrassment warming her cheeks. "I am here merely to listen and learn."

Mrs Tremaine sniffed. "You do know, Miss Bennet, that these salons are for scientific discussions and not simply another event on the social calendar. I am sure there is very little here to interest those not interested in the advancement of science in all its glory."

"Mrs Collins is too modest about her myriad talents," Mary said, her dark eyes narrowing. "And besides, we were all beginners once." She hesitated only slightly before adding, "Some of us still are. Come, Charlotte, we must present ourselves to our hosts."

Leaving Mrs Tremaine glowering in their wake, they moved towards a large fireplace, encircled by three leather couches. Mary steered Charlotte towards the occupants of one couch. "You mistake me, sir," a lady in a large pink hat was saying to a grey-haired gentleman smoking a foul-smelling pipe. "I am not saying nobody can criticize him for producing what seemed like a sound theory ten years ago. I simply think that we ought to carefully consider whether the mark of a good scientist is one who proposes a theory, or one who discards a theory when it is proved wrong."

"And yet some who cling to their arguments and weather the storm of protest are found to have been correct long after the fact," said he, blowing a cloud of blue smoke. "There is something admirable about tenacity, is there not?"

"Not in the face of evidence to the contrary, no," the lady disagreed. "Oh! Here is Miss Bennet, whom I am sure will provide a sensible argument."

"You flatter me." Mary grinned. "There is something to be said for both sides, is there not? It is only hindsight which proves whether the endeavour has been worthwhile."

"You do not often play the diplomat," said the lady, peevishly. "I wish you had chosen another day to do so. And who is your friend?"

"I'm delighted to present Mrs Collins, who is visiting from Kent."

Charlotte smiled, and the next few minutes were taken up with introductions, which revealed that the man and woman were their hosts, Mr and Mrs Wilberforce. She was surprised to hear that this was the case, and wondered if they might be only related by marriage—a brother and sister-in-law, perhaps. "I know what you are thinking, but in fact they are married to each other," Mary murmured, leading Charlotte back across the room, "though one would never think it to hear them talk. I hear they argued all through their acquaintance, and their engagement, and the wedding too. And yet they are happy as lambs, twenty years later."

Charlotte glanced back to find the lady fussing over the gentleman's lapels while he tried to escape her attentions, though both were smiling at each other with good humour. "Love is certainly a mystery, is it not?"

Mary only smiled in response, for they had arrived in front of a gentleman with white hair, white whiskers, and piercing blue eyes which crinkled with pleasure at the sight of them; Charlotte liked him at once. Mary introduced the gentleman as Mr Mellor, then introduced Charlotte so warmly that she flushed with equal parts pleasure and embarrassment. "Miss Bennet is too kind," she said, "I am merely here to observe and educate myself a little."

"That is what we are all here for, Mrs Collins," said he, smiling. His jacket, beautifully cut to encompass his portly frame, was a striking bright blue that Charlotte had rarely seen on a man, emphasising his eyes to greatest effect. If she had to guess, she would think him no younger than five-and-fifty, though his exuberance was that of a much younger man.

"The foxgloves that enraptured you came from Mr Mellor's collection," Mary confessed. "I believe the faded reds were your favourite?"

"You recall perfectly," Charlotte agreed, smiling. "I must thank you, Mr Mellor, for granting the favour. I was very taken with them."

"You are very welcome, my dear! I was only too happy to help Miss Bennet with her request. She tells me that you are very fond of your garden back in Kent."

"I am, sir. Though I am not a botanist, merely a humble gardener."

"Well, then it seems we have more than one thing in common."

Charlotte blinked, not quite sure what was meant by such a statement, but before she could work out how best to answer, Mr Mellor turned to Mary. "And where is Miss Carlisle? Still in Austria?"

For a moment, Mary looked stricken at the question, but the next moment her face smoothed out entirely. "I believe so."

Ah, so her name is Miss Carlisle, Charlotte thought, jealousy stinging. *Miss Anne Carlisle, then, who sent Mary a drawing—either of herself or of someone else, but evidently designed to cause jealousy in the recipient—and whom Miss Highbridge thought important enough to mention in their conversation on the balcony at the ball.* "Whatever will Anne say?" Miss Highbridge had asked, and though Mary had replied that Anne's opinion had no bearing on her current situation, Charlotte was not so sure that this was the entire truth.

"In fact, Miss Carlisle is already on her way home from Austria." Mrs Tremaine had edged into the conversation. Her emerald necklace caught the light as she shifted from foot to foot, feigning astonishment, though her smile was snide. "Miss Bennet, I expected you to know such things."

"I confess it is news to me." Mary had paled, though her voice was still steady.

"Why, that surprises me a great deal, what with you two being such good friends and all," Mrs Tremaine clucked, shooting a sly glance at Charlotte before sashaying away.

Mr Mellor glanced at Mary, and the two exchanged arch looks. "If we were not in polite society," said he, "then I would have words for that lady which would set her hair ablaze."

"Hellfire cannot harm the devil," Mary muttered, causing Mr Mellor to snort. Charlotte brushed the back of Mary's hand with her own gloved one, in a vain attempt to give comfort, and was rewarded with a small smile. "I shall fetch us drinks while you two become better acquainted."

As Mary disappeared into the crowd, Mr Cromley appeared, mid-argument with a dapper gentleman in a red tailcoat. "My dear Monford," he cried. "You cannot still be holding to Werner when Hutton has made such a compelling argument."

The man in the red tailcoat shrugged. "As a chemist, I feel

bound to look at things a certain way. And it seems to me—
ah, Mellor! I have a bone to pick with you later."

Mr Mellor offered a slight bow. "Pick away, dear fellow, pick
away." He seemed relieved that the men had not stopped to talk,
but continued towards a long table at the back of the room,
which held bowls of fresh fruit and trays of biscuits. Charlotte
eyed the pistachio queen cakes and *millefeuille* with interest, and
vowed she would try at least one or two. "So," Mr Mellor said.
"You have a keen interest in flowers, do you?"

"I do indeed. I love flowers for their own sake, whether
fresh or dried, but I am particularly interested in their meanings. I have no doubt been boring Miss Bennet with all my
talk on the subject."

"Oh, I suspect Miss Bennet would listen to you for hours
upon any subject," said he, and winked. Panicked, Charlotte
flushed, but the gentleman lowered his voice and added, "Do
not worry, Mrs Collins. I am part of the same club. That is
why I have no heir, and why I have devoted much of my life
to creating vast, interesting collections. The flowers in particular have been splendid, and I have won many prizes for them.
Do you like roses?"

She felt rather light-headed. It felt strange to have a stranger
openly acknowledge some part of herself that had remained
hidden for so long. "Very much."

"She did not tell me anything," said he, seeing the anxiety
on Charlotte's face. "I merely guessed by your face when I mentioned Miss Carlisle that you and Miss Bennet might be…close.
Though I already had some idea when she specifically requested
flowers for you." He leaned in slightly, looking apologetic. "I
do hope I have not upset you by mentioning the lady."

"I am not…that is to say, that I have never met her." Charlotte forced a smile. "You are most astute, sir."

"Well, that reminds to be seen." He winked again. "You
must come to visit my estate and view my roses, Mrs Collins.

It is not too far from here. I shall insist that Miss Bennet bring you before you leave town."

"Oh, I—"

"Bring her where?" Mary asked, materializing at Charlotte's elbow and offering them each a glass of sherry

"To view my collection."

"Of course! We shall come whenever it is convenient for you. I say, have you seen Miss Highbridge anywhere?"

"I believe she sent her regards to the Wilberforces. A sudden head cold, though nothing serious."

"Poor thing," Charlotte said, feeling rather guilty. She'd been so busy suspecting Mary of being in love with Miss Highbridge that she hadn't spent as much time getting to know the girl. "Ought we to send her something? It is dreadful to be sick abed with nothing to entertain you."

"What a wonderful idea." Mary smiled at her, though she still looked pale. "I shall have Pitt arrange something tomorrow morning."

After a few sips of sherry, the warmth of the drink began to relax Charlotte's nerves; apart from Mrs Tremaine, no one seemed to mind at all that she was there, and visiting such a vast floral collection was an exciting prospect. However odd and anxiety-provoking it had been to be acknowledged by Mr Mellor, it had also been rather nice—like becoming a member of a secret society, existing in plain sight. They were soon joined by Mr Cromley and the gentleman in the blue tailcoat, who struck up a conversation about the latest theory of strata. Charlotte was glad that Mary had explained at least the basics to her, though she could not follow the more complicated references they made. Likewise, Mary seemed to be having trouble paying attention—she spoke when spoken to, but otherwise appeared distracted, her gaze wandering off into the distance.

"I say, Mellor," Mr Cromley said, "it's been a glorious season for my roses. Perhaps this is the year I finally best you, eh?"

"It might well be," Mr Mellor admitted. "I'm having trouble with some of the flowers, though I cannot for the life of me work out what to do about these confounded insects. They've already eaten their way through my pink lilies, which as you know I was breeding apart in the hope of—"

Mrs Tremaine had sidled into the group, a simpering smile plastered onto her face. Mr Mellor hesitated before continuing. "Anyway. The blasted creatures are everywhere, and my gardeners claim they've never seen anything like them. No idea where they came from, either. If I do not find a solution, then indeed, Cromley, you may have me beat this year."

"Then I shall beg everyone not to help you," Mr Cromley joked, raising a laugh.

"Have you tried poison?" Mrs Tremaine asked.

"Of course." He waved a hand dismissively. "Tried everything."

"Dill," Charlotte said, without thinking. All eyes turned to her.

Mr Mellor blinked. "What was that, Mrs Collins?"

She swallowed. "Those kinds of insects seem to love dill."

"We're not trying to feed the creatures," Mrs Tremaine smirked. "We're trying to eradicate them. That means *destroy*, you know."

Temper rising, Charlotte met Mrs Tremaine's eyes coolly. "That's the beauty of this approach. They love dill so much that they'll leave your other plants alone and congregate there." She smirked back. "That means *gather*, you know."

Mary choked on her sherry, hiding a splutter of laughter behind a hastily raised handkerchief.

"What's this?" Mr Mellor cried, his forehead furrowed with surprise. "Is it really that simple? Have I wasted half a fortune employing horticultural specialists who could not cure the problem, and never thought simply to move it elsewhere?"

Charlotte blushed. "It has worked many a time in the gardens

I have known. Some insects are staved off by the use of mint or basil, but some cannot be dissuaded by any means except death, and they often reproduce in numbers so great that extinguishing them entirely is a lengthy and time-consuming endeavour. In such cases, encouraging them to withdraw to a dill plant at least has the advantage of leaving your other flowers alone. You could use marigolds too, but those would take longer to grow."

"What an excellent military tactic. Draw the enemy to a particular point—a point which they believe to be most advantageous, then strike once they have gathered in numbers." Mr Mellor stroked his white whiskers, thinking the idea over. "Yes, I see how it might work. My, my. You ought to have been a military commander, Mrs Collins. The enemy would have been shaking in their boots after such a manoeuvre."

Charlotte laughed while Mrs Tremaine slunk away into the crowd, scowling. "I do not know about all that. It is a simple enough remedy, and one which ought to work, though I make no promises."

"Now I must insist that you come and visit my collection. If what you say works, then I shall be in your debt forever."

"Very well," said she, delighted by the invitation. "If it's not too much trouble, Miss Bennet?"

"Hmm?" Mary smiled, though there was still a crease between her eyebrows. "Not at all. We shall come two days hence, if it please you?"

Mr Mellor agreed that the date did please him, and so the matter was settled to everybody's satisfaction. By the time Mary had drained her glass, she was looking well again, chattering away as lively as ever, though Charlotte knew that there was something wrong. She just didn't know how to fix it.

Or perhaps she was the problem.

Chapter Twenty-Two

"You see," Mary said, in the carriage on the way home. "I did warn you about Mrs Tremaine."

"She certainly had her claws out tonight."

"It is nothing to do with you, really." Mary sighed. "She has taken it upon herself to be as unkind as possible to me and all my acquaintances, no matter who they are. Apart from Mr Mellor, whom she is afraid of."

"Oh. I had no idea." Alarm prickled between Charlotte's shoulder blades. "Do you think she suspects us of being more than friends?"

"Only because she suspects me of bedding every friend I dare spend time with."

"I am sorry that I did the same thing." Shame roiled in Charlotte's stomach. "I thought you were with Miss Highbridge, and then—"

"You are nothing like Mrs Tremaine," Mary said, her tone sharp. "In any case," her voice softened a little, "I am grateful that you attended the salon and, I must confess, deeply amused that you were the one to put her in her place. These meetings have meant a great deal to me in the past years, and lately she has been intolerable."

"Then it is I who is honoured." Charlotte leaned closer. "Would you like to stay with me tonight?"

"I'm afraid I have a bit of a headache." She waved a hand in the air. "All that smoke, you see. I do so hate the smell of pipe tobacco, but one cannot expect a gentleman to forgo pleasure in the safety of his own home."

"Of course." Charlotte bit her lip. *Is that really true*, she wondered, *or was it the mention of Anne Carlisle which has caused her to shut down?*

The rest of the carriage ride was silent, though they held hands the entire way home. Mary did at least kiss her goodnight in the hallway before returning to her room and closing the door without a backwards glance. Worry plagued Charlotte for the rest of the evening, though she could not precisely pinpoint the reason—she did not even know for certain that Miss Carlisle and Mary had had a former attachment, yet it seemed plain enough from the clues she had gathered. *Just how attached had Mary been?* The notion kept Charlotte awake until the small, hours of the morning; she tossed and turned interminably before finally falling into a broken, troubled sleep.

In the morning, Charlotte came to breakfast to find Mary scowling over a letter. "Good morning," said she, throwing the parchment aside with a vehemence that was quite unexpected. She did not look up at Charlotte, but instead stared at the plate of eggs in front of her, which lay untouched. "Did you sleep well?"

Pitt gave his mistress an odd look as he poured the tea. Nothing was obviously wrong, but a certain tension in the room made the hair on the back of Charlotte's neck prickle. "Yes, thank you. Though I missed you terribly last night. How's your head?"

"What?" Mary continued to stare into her eggs. "Oh, yes. Fine."

Pitt cleared his throat. "Would you like me to reheat your food, ma'am?"

"You needn't hover over me like a nursemaid," Mary

snapped. "If the eggs are cold, it is my own fault for leaving them so long, is it not?"

Pitt raised an eyebrow, his lips thinning. "Of course, ma'am."

Charlotte stared at Mary, perplexed, as Pitt marched out of the room. "What on earth is wrong?"

"Nothing."

"You once told me I ought not to say *nothing* when something evidently was wrong." She meant it to be teasing, but Mary only glowered at her.

"Anne wrote to me. Miss Carlisle, I mean." She sighed. "I cannot expect you to understand all the ways in which this news discomfits me. I had hoped Mrs Tremaine was merely needling me for sport last night, but..."

"I see." Charlotte buttered a piece of toast, though her appetite was gone. "You needn't tell me anything you would rather not share. I understand that Miss Carlisle," oh, and how that name tasted like ashes in her mouth, "was important to you once upon a time." *And evidently still is*, she thought.

She was rather hoping Mary would correct her, but no such correction came. Mary continued to glare at her eggs as if each one had personally affronted her. "She sent me a drawing of herself a few weeks ago. Someone else drew it, of course—it was not done in her hand, which is far less expert. She meant to make me jealous, for she thinks that by doing so she can pick me up again like a book whenever she returns to Canterbury."

Charlotte had always known this was coming, though she'd thought it would happen weeks or months from now, long after she was back in Meryton. She had already pictured the letter which began *Dear Charlotte* and ended *I hope you will understand*, and done her best to make peace with the idea. Their own brief romance of a few days could not compare to what had evidently been a complex relationship, to say nothing of the fact that Miss Carlisle had likely become well acquainted with Mary's body over their time together, while Charlotte still had no experience whatsoever. The notion stung like a wasp. Mary was kind and tender-hearted, and the idea of letting Charlotte down, however gently, was no doubt troubling her.

"I will leave you to your thoughts," Charlotte said, rising abruptly from the table. She could feel the prickle of oncoming tears at the back of her nose, and she would not make things harder for Mary by crying about the situation in front of her. "I do believe I have a book to finish reading."

She forced a chuckle, and fled the room before Mary could say another word.

Despite this, it was only an hour or so before Mary found Charlotte in the latter's bedroom. Charlotte had spent the better part of that hour weeping—better to get it all out now, and compose herself so as not to embarrass her hostess—and after splashing her face with cold water, was feeling thoroughly drained. She looked up when the door opened, the unopened book still lying in her lap.

"Am I bothering you?" Mary asked, hovering in the doorway.

"Of course not. Come in."

Mary crossed the room, but rather than seating herself in the opposite armchair, she leaned in for a kiss. Charlotte blanched, unable to help herself. It was too much to be expected to perform these familiar, sweet actions now that she knew she was only a placeholder until Miss Carlisle returned.

"Why do you pull away?" Mary frowned. "Surely now—I thought we had an understanding."

Charlotte rose, sidling past Mary. "Perhaps I ought to take a walk in the garden. Some fresh air would be lovely."

Mary glanced at the fully open windows, through which a gentle breeze blew, and back at Charlotte. One eyebrow arched in disbelief. "Indeed. If you give me a moment, I shall accompany you."

"There is no need," Charlotte said hastily, feeling tears prickle again. "I would not like to bother you."

"Good grief, what is going on?" Mary snapped. "First you run from breakfast, then you don't want to kiss me, then you avoid spending time with me."

"I should think it was obvious."

"You may think what you like, but that does not make it so. Pray, give me an explanation." Mary stepped closer, the familiar scent of violets flooding the air. "Why are you acting this way?"

"Because I want you," Charlotte cried, startling herself with the violence of her own temper. "I want you and I should not. Have you never thought what it must be like for me? To discover that there is a world with you in it, far less a world where you desire me even for a moment—me, plain old Charlotte Lucas, who was never anything to anyone—and then I discover that other women want you too and—" Her chest heaved, her lungs short of breath.

"You're jealous," Mary breathed, as if the idea had never occurred to her before. Her forehead wrinkled. "Dearest, I—"

Charlotte was tired of this charade. "Of course I am jealous! And you wouldn't take me to bed, so you needn't pretend I am not lacking in some way. I just wish you would have told me why, so I could have attempted to correct it, or at least—"

I wish I could have had you, she thought, her chest aching with unspoken words, *even once. I would have spent the rest of my life dreaming of that moment.*

"Please, stop. Please. Let me speak. I did not think—I mean, I hoped that…" Mary reached for Charlotte's hands, held them tightly. "That is to say, I am very fond of you, and I do not say such things lightly. My friends would tell you as much, were they here, though I am glad that they are not."

Though sweet, the words barely made an impact. Of course Mary had prior relationships. Of course she had experienced such things with other women. Had kissed them, had taken them to bed. Had felt bare womanflesh pressed against her. Had sought enjoyment and given pleasure. Knowing it was one thing, picturing quite another. Mary's mouth on Miss Carlisle's neck; Mary's hands unbuttoning Miss Carlisle's dress. The jealousy Charlotte felt now was hot and sickening and entirely new.

"Did you love her?" Each word dropped like a mossy stone into a fathomless well. She waited to hear the impact.

"I did, once."

Splash, Charlotte thought, nausea simmering in her stomach. *I ought to throw myself in too.*

"I suppose I should tell you a little about it, though I would rather not," Mary continued, guiding Charlotte onto the rug, where they sat side by side with their backs against the sturdy armchair. "In short, Anne and I were together for two years, though we broke things off several times. It was rather tempestuous, for we were ill-matched, and rather than see sense from the beginning, we kept trying to make the relationship work. She was charming and persuasive, but her word meant nothing." Her laugh was bitter. "After each fight, she would go off chasing any society lady she thought might be useful to her or elevate her rank in some way. Anne succeeded in bedding a couple of my friends, too, though I did not discover this until after we ended things for good. One I think she simply bedded for fun, and one I know she must have chosen to hurt me, for they often flirted together in front of me. She even tried to woo Delia Highbridge, though Delia would never have been interested even if Anne were the type of woman she found attractive."

"That is deplorable behavior indeed," said Charlotte, shocked beyond belief. "I cannot believe you would ever stand for such a thing."

"Behaviour I can only attribute to the weakness of love. And yet, I never felt as if I really knew her, or that she knew me. And worse, when Mrs Tremaine first came to town, Anne bedded her too, even though she and I were together. After I had broken things off with Anne for the last time, almost a year ago, Mrs Tremaine tried to pursue me, first by befriending me by using my perceived vulnerability, which was bad enough." She rolled her shoulders, evidently uncomfortable with the memory. "Then when I refused to succumb to her advances, she tried to persuade me that bedding her would be a great revenge on Anne. It was not a notion I cared for, and it was all rather a mess, in the end." Mary tried to smile, though it did not extend as far as her eyes. "So perhaps now you see why I have been rather reticent to go to bed. I have not taken a lover since."

"Of course." Charlotte's mind was in turmoil. Mary had been badly wounded and although it was something of a relief to discover that Charlotte was not the cause of her reticence, she felt terrible that Mary had been put through something so horrible by someone who purported to love her. "Please allow me to reassure you that your comfort is my foremost concern."

Impulsively, she wrapped her arms around Mary, who leaned in with a sigh. "We shall never do anything you are not certain of, and rest assured that I would wait as long as you wanted. Forever, if that were the case."

"You are too kind. I ought to be the one saying such things to you."

"I am not some blushing virgin," Charlotte reminded her. "I was married for four years. Though I do not pretend to know what I am doing in this particular instance, I am sure that if we ever reach that stage, you will be so kind as to instruct me in the subtle arts of lovemaking." She pressed a kiss to Mary's cheek. "I apologise for my behaviour. I was so jealous, I could hardly think straight."

Mary turned her head so that her lips were pressing against Charlotte's neck. Her breath was warm, tickling the sensitive spot under Charlotte's earlobe. "You have no reason to be, you know. Before you came along, I had sworn off love entirely."

Charlotte's heart sped up.

"And, without realising that there was any encouragement on your part," Mary continued, "I discovered my thoughts were dangerously full of your every look and word. I quite fell for you, Charlotte Lucas. I mean, I am falling."

"I believe you mean those things, I do. It is simply that..." She swallowed, then reached up and stroked Mary's hair, her hands trembling as Mary's lips pressed against soft flesh, kissing a trail down to her collarbone. "You know full well that even before my late husband, I had never been courted. And I had certainly never experienced the kind of passion that I... that we..." She tipped her head back, biting back a moan, then shifted so that she could gaze into Mary's eyes. "I suppose it is no secret that I think the world of you." Her cheeks flamed at the admission. "You're beautiful and brilliant and funny. You could have anybody you wanted."

So why me? she didn't add, though she dearly wanted to.

"I wish you could see in yourself what I see, for then you would understand why I adore you so completely. I have only been obstructing my own path forward, for fear of..." Mary's eyes were dark and thunderous, her fingers digging into Charlotte's hips in a way that was at once pleasurable and painful. "Perhaps we have been doing too much thinking and talking and worrying, and not nearly enough feeling. How do you suggest we remedy that?"

It was less a question than a suggestion, to which there could only be one answer. *Is this really happening?* Charlotte swallowed, her mouth suddenly dry. "Are you sure?"

"Yes," Mary said without hesitation. "Are you sure?"

"Yes."

"Then follow me."

In Mary's bedroom, shafts of sunlight peeked through the half-opened curtains, illuminating Charlotte's shaking hands as she unbuttoned Mary's dress, fumbling with excitement and nerves. Mary's hands were far more skilled, peeling the dress from Charlotte in moments, the petticoats soon following. Her mouth never stopped moving, kisses peppered over Charlotte's shoulders and collarbones, brushing the cusp of her ear as they tumbled backwards onto the bed. Words rushed out as if Mary had kept them in all this time; a swollen river finally bursting its banks. "You are so beautiful," she said, again and again. Charlotte blushed to hear such compliments, and yet Mary's eyes glittered so fiercely that she half fancied that Mary meant it, really found her pretty, saw something in her that the rest of the world had overlooked. "What do you like?"

Charlotte wasn't sure how to answer the question. Wasn't sure she could, really, not with her heart hammering so hard it ached and Mary's palm trailing over her bare hip, palming the underside of her breast. Mary's warm thigh pressed against her own. "I do not rightly know."

Mary paused, resting her forehead against Charlotte's, her breathing ragged. "Shall we find out together?"

"Yes, please."

Mary's fingers dipped down until they reached soft, slippery heat. A single moment of pressure and Charlotte was lost in the inferno, burning up, desperate for more, grabbing Mary tightly. Letting out an irrepressible, guttural groan, she buried her face in Mary's shoulder, smothered every inch of skin she could find with desperate, panting kisses while the fingers between her legs pressed and stroked and finally, achingly, entered her. She wriggled one hand free, desperate to touch Mary in turn, and was shocked and delighted to feel the same aching heat. Mary's moans undid her, breathing Charlotte's name over and over as Charlotte's fingers slid over soft flesh, discovering a new place to enter the world. "Inside," Mary begged. "Please."

Instead, Charlotte drew rough, shaky circles, never quite dipping where she was needed, until Mary groaned, her free hand digging into the sheets, clawing at the bed, her teeth grazing Charlotte's shoulder.

"Darling, please, I beg you," she gasped, and Charlotte marvelled that she had this power, this novel ability to reduce another person to such helpless, mewling gasps, and tried not to think of how the single word *darling* had sent a fresh wave of fire sweeping through her chest. "Don't tease me," Mary growled through gritted teeth. "I've wanted you for so long. Touch me. Take me."

No one had ever desired her before. Not like this, with a raw, urgent need. "Call me that again," she whispered, half bold, half afraid that Mary would make fun of her.

Those fine, dark eyes weren't laughing now. "Darling. Please."

Charlotte did as she was bid, her fingers pushing inside, and was rewarded with a long, shuddering sigh that was brighter and more melodious than any music she had ever heard. She clenched around Mary's fingers as they slid inside her again and again, the wonder of some familiar and previously banal action becoming something new, something that built inside her like water brought to a steady boil.

She clutched at Mary again, their mouths finding each other, as the strange feeling crested inside, building to a crescendo. In a single moment of lucidity at the top of the wave, time stood still. Charlotte opened her eyes and met Mary's. She knew she had been forever changed, that she would never, could never forget this, that the life she had been living prior had been little more than a shadow self comprised of grey shades. Bright colours exploded behind her eyelids as she squeezed them shut, a shiver rippling through her body. She cried out as a sharp feeling—a cousin of agony but much, much sweeter—shuddered through her, and she clung to Mary, clung and clung and never wanted to let go.

Chapter Twenty-Three

Afterwards, they lay entwined, Charlotte pressing hot-mouthed kisses to every piece of flesh she could find, unreasonably afraid that Mary would melt away, a grief-made phantom her imagination had produced in the aftermath of Mr Collins' death. How easy it had been to make love and be made love to in return. The urge to flee was sudden and strong, guilt winding colubrine through her belly. Perhaps she should never have known how glorious it would feel, for now that she did, the memories would plague her more when she returned to Meryton.

She bit her lip. "I hope I was not a disappointment."

Mary looked at her sharply, then tilted her head. "Do you regret it?"

"No! Never," Charlotte protested, "I just feel…odd. A little guilty, perhaps."

"About what?"

"That I…that we…" She paused, thinking the question over. In fact, she had no idea what she felt guilty for. "I do not know. It is a new thing for me to want something and then get it. I don't quite know what to do with myself." She smiled hesitantly. "That seems rather silly when said out loud, does it not?"

"I understand completely. It is a normal thing to think when one's entire world-view has been upended."

Mary gathered Charlotte to her without a moment's hesitation, and rained gentle kisses onto her cheeks and chin until Charlotte was as giggly as a schoolgirl. "Stop," she protested, still giggling. "You are tickling me."

Their eyes met. What Charlotte had thought was a dying fire was simply banked embers, roaring back into life. The next moment, their mouths met in a bruising kiss that tore a deep sound from her throat, one she hardly recognised or thought she'd been capable of making; something closer to a feral animal's snarl than a delicate, feminine moan of appreciation. Mary's hips bucked in response, and it was the most natural thing in the world for Charlotte to mimic the action, to let her own hips cant forward, bringing their bodies flush.

"Charlotte," Mary breathed. "I would like to touch you again."

She was ready for it. Had been ready since Mary's first sweet kiss, reassuring her that no matter how violent her inner turmoil, someone was there, ready to stand as anchor and hold her fast. "Please," she begged, and Mary obeyed.

The next few minutes—or were they hours? she could not tell—were lost to sweaty, rapturous entanglement. When they finally finished, Mary collapsing spent beside her, Charlotte was exhausted from the vigorous activity. The light outside had dimmed, the sunset shimmering a brilliant orange through the gaps in the curtains.

"Are you well?" The question was evidently meant sincerely, though Charlotte could not help laughing. "What?" Mary demanded. "What's so funny?"

It took long seconds before Charlotte could compose herself enough to get coherent words out. "I cannot remember a time I felt more well," she managed, before descending into laughter again.

She had expected, now the business was done, that Mary would leave, but Mary seemed content to stay where she was, embracing Charlotte and kissing every part of her she could reach. In turn, Charlotte couldn't get enough of Mary's kisses, trailing her fingers over the smooth, soft skin of stomach and hips, feeling muscles twitching under her ministrations. It was everything she'd dreamed and much, much more, and she felt quite love-drunk.

I shall allow myself the pleasure of being weak for a while. Just until I leave, she promised herself. *Then it will be over. She will find some other woman and probably never think of me again. It will hurt her far less than it will hurt me, and that is for the best.* She hated the thought, but it allowed her to sober up a little.

Mary rolled away and stretched languorously. "It is probably almost time for dinner. Could you eat?"

"Lord, yes," Charlotte agreed. "I am famished. I had no idea that making love could make one so hungry."

Dinner was white soup followed by a roast ham. Charlotte ate ravenously, as if it were her first meal after a long time ship-wrecked, and helped herself to warm rolls with extra butter. By the time they'd finished and the footmen had cleared the plates away, Charlotte heaved a long sigh of contentment.

"A package arrived this afternoon from Ashbrook's, ma'am," Pitt announced, wearing his politely blank expression.

"Oh, it must be our dresses. Please have one of the boys take them to Charlotte's room, Pitt, and we shall try them on later." Mary paused, watching the butler leave the room. "I ought to apologize for snapping at him this morning. He did not deserve it."

"Did you ask him this morning to send over something to Miss Highbridge?"

"What? Oh—no, I quite forgot. Thank you for reminding

me." Mary rolled her eyes. "I'm sorry I was in such a mood. I was entirely out of line."

"No apology necessary," Charlotte reminded her.

"Would you excuse me a moment?"

"Of course." Charlotte waited until Mary had exited the room before wandering upstairs, wine glass in hand. Dessert could wait—she was far too curious to see what the dress looked like.

A large, white box lay on one of the armchairs. Charlotte hesitated, wondering whether Mary would mind terribly if she peeked at the contents, and decided that even if Mary did, she was now certain she could charm her out of a scolding. Charlotte slit the seal and opened the box, which was full of carefully folded tissue paper. Peeling back a layer, she gasped; her dress lay on top, and the dark blue material had been exquisitely embroidered with a hundred tiny stars. No, they were not stars at all—Charlotte bent closer, examining the dress—they were lilies, a ghostly silver shade that made them look like glittering stars. White lilies, she guessed, meaning *being with you is heavenly*. How on earth had Mary known?

She lifted the dress out of the box and held it up. It was the most beautiful dress she'd ever seen, and her breath caught at the idea that she might actually wear this someday, might look as pretty as any lady at any society ball.

Charlotte unbuttoned her own dress, discarding it over the back of the nearest armchair. Slipping the new dress over her head, she eased into it, finding the buttons at the side, hidden under a thin flap of fabric she hadn't even noticed. She undid her hair and ran her fingers through it, letting it lie loose around her shoulders.

Footsteps on the stairs, light and quick, heralded her lover's arrival. Charlotte turned, anxious, wondering if she ought to have done something to her hair to make the ensemble appear more impressive, but there hadn't been time.

Mary stopped in the doorway, her mouth hanging open. "Good Lord," said she, after a moment. "Charlotte, you look magnificent."

She blushed. "You flatter me."

"With good reason." Mary's gaze travelled up and down, noting the full sleeves, the silver-edged hem, the way it clung to curves Charlotte had barely known she'd had. "You're a vision. Would you like to go somewhere wearing it?"

Charlotte blinked, surprised by the question. "I'm supposed to be in mourning, remember? Though I suppose that went out of the window the moment I started kissing you, it would not do to let down appearances in public. People would talk."

"You will not see anyone you know in the place I'm talking about," Mary promised. "Apart from Delia, that is. We could even dance together, and no one would blink an eye."

Does such a place really exist? Charlotte smiled. "I thought you did not dance."

"I did not say that I never danced. I said I was not a terribly good dancer, and unfortunately that is the truth."

"Perhaps I could teach you a waltz."

"You could certainly try, though I fear I am beyond all help." Mary looked unusually hesitant. "What ought I do?"

"Here, stand opposite me." Charlotte adjusted Mary until she was quite satisfied. "Now step back, and forth," she demonstrated, "and back, and turn."

"It is the turning I have a problem with," Mary complained. "And which direction ought I to be facing now?"

"Not me," Charlotte said, trying not to laugh. "In a group of four, you ought to now be looking at the partner who was on your right. Let us try it again." They practiced for a while, until Mary had grown used to the repetitive moments. "There," Charlotte said. "I'm rather proud of my pupil. You have improved greatly and are now fit to be seen at any dance you please."

"I'm quite sure that is a result of the quality of the teacher." Mary stepped closer, winding her arms around Charlotte's waist. "I would much prefer a dance that required only two people. Then I might gaze into your eyes and forget the rest of the world entirely."

Charlotte tilted her head to gain better access to Mary's neck, finding the spot which made her lover shiver with pleasure. "That does sound capital."

She could not keep her hands off Mary. She wanted always to be touching her, caressing her, kissing her, orbiting her as the moon did the Earth. However, her actions were not simply driven by lust. She had never felt such fire when Mr Collins had touched her, or kissed her. There had been eagerness on his end, and vigorous action on certain occasions, but the whole process had left her feeling empty. She knew she had been supposed to enjoy making her husband happy—and she had tried to—but Mr Collins had never really paid attention except to ask if he was hurting her, in the beginning. She'd never watched him across the room and wanted to pin him against a wall, nor felt his every glance fan a flame inside her. She had never felt as if she would drown if she did not get another mouthful of him.

And yet that was not all it was, with Mary. There was a blaze, certainly, but there was also tenderness, a delicate fragility that she had touched with wonder and had seen that same wonder reflected back in Mary's eyes.

"The way you look at me undoes me entirely, do you know that?" Mary smiled, her arms snaking around Charlotte's neck.

"I still find it hard to believe." Charlotte kissed her, softly, sweetly, still marvelling that there existed a spectrum of kisses she had never known about before, like discovering an entirely new language.

"You look exceedingly pretty in that dress, Charlotte Lucas," Mary murmured, "But I'd like to take it off now if I may."

"Please do." Her breath hitched. "I still cannot believe that you want me."

"Darling," Mary said, peppering a line of kisses down Charlotte's jaw, "I want you more than anyone I've ever known."

The words did something queer to her heart, making it feel as if a hand had grasped it and was squeezing tightly. Mary's eyes were half-drunk cups of fierce joy, her lips two blunted blades ready to slit Charlotte open from stem to stern. Flesh, hot under her palms. Jutting hips, pressing hard enough to bruise. Fingers exploring, creating bursts of rapture inside her body she hadn't known another person was capable of conjuring, far less maintaining.

They made love long into the night. Charlotte had never before known that she was capable of such passion, such desperate need. Every touch kindled a new flame, and the climaxes were so delicious that one had barely receded before she found herself desperate for another. If this was how women generally felt about men, then it was no wonder Lydia had run away with Mr Wickham. *Do not even dream of doing the same*, the little voice in her head warned, once Mary had slid into sleep, snuggled against Charlotte's side as if she had been born to fit there. *You have obligations to your family. They supported you even when it was thought you would never marry. You owe them a great debt, and you ought to repay it by not causing a scandal.*

Charlotte stared into the darkness, her head aching with the weight of unshed tears. She had no idea where she would find the strength to leave Mary, but she had better unearth it soon, for both of their sakes.

Chapter Twenty-Four

The day passed in a haze of lovemaking, and after a beautiful dinner of spiced lamb, they retired to the drawing room, where Charlotte begged Mary to play the pianoforte. Mary did so reluctantly at first, then warmed to her task, playing first a song which Charlotte recognised as being from Bach's *The Well-Tempered Clavier*, followed by a piece that Charlotte did not know.

"It is better that you do not know Haydn's original," Mary said, when Charlotte asked who the composer was, "for my rendition is so flawed and slow that it might as well be a different tune entirely. Come and show me your version of my piece, now—the one you improved upon in the parsonage."

Charlotte seated herself beside Mary, planting a kiss on her lover's cheek, and soon they were playing together in time. The room was candlelit, the curtains drawn, and with the rest of the house in silence, Charlotte felt once more like they might be the only two people left in the world.

"I find myself entirely fed up of reading and work. Shall we play cards instead tonight?" Mary suggested.

Charlotte agreed, closing the lid of the pianoforte, and they seated themselves at the small table in the corner, which had lain unused for the entire time Charlotte had been present. Mary spent the first hour teaching Charlotte to play piquet, which seemed rather complicated and required the memorization of many rules, though she picked it up as best she could. By the end of the hour, she had somehow managed to beat Mary twice.

"What say we make this a little more interesting?" Mary suggested.

"In what way?' Charlotte arranged her cards neatly in her hand, planning her next move.

"How about...if I win the next game, you will permit me to do whatever I want to you."

Charlotte stared across her cards, feeling a sudden urge to drop them and leap over the table. "And what if I win?"

Mary leaned back in her chair, smirking. "Then you may do whatever you want to me. Fair is fair, after all."

Charlotte was blessed with an excellent hand, and though she could see her path to triumph clearly, curiosity overwhelmed her desire to emerge as the victor. "Well, it seems you have bested me," she said, laying down her cards. "What now?"

Mary rose, offering her hand. "Come."

She led Charlotte back to the pianoforte without elaboration. *Are we going to play again?* Charlotte wondered, with a twinge of dismay, but her disappointment soon vanished when Mary pushed her against the lid, the wood hard and unyielding against her back, the pain of the pressure adding to the pleasure. Her gasp was cut off by Mary's mouth, meeting hers in a frantic, searing kiss. Mary pressed her body between Charlotte's legs, her hands frantic at the hem of the skirts lifting them up to the shin, the knee, fingers skimming over Charlotte's knees and then her thighs. Charlotte was on fire, writhing under Mary's touch, her body in ecstasy and Mary's fingers were stroking Charlotte's inner thigh, close to where the flame burned brightest and—

Mary's hands stilled.

"Please," Charlotte gasped, "don't stop."

"Do you trust me?"

"Of course."

"Then let me take the lead, darling. You'll like this." In the candlelight, Mary's smile was the curve of a scythe, ready to harvest all that had been sown. "I promise."

She dropped to her knees and licked a long, slow stripe up the inside of Charlotte's thigh. Charlotte was already quivering, with no idea of what might come next. "What—what are you doing?"

"I want to worship you. May I?"

Charlotte nodded, and Mary bent her head devoutly, her mouth level with a part of Charlotte that a mouth had never touched before. Mary could not possibly mean to kiss her there, could she?

She could.

She did.

Charlotte slapped a hand over her own mouth, quelling an undignified shriek as Mary's tongue worked its magic. The sounds turned to moans, spilling like candlelight, pooling in the ridges and furrows of her throat. Her other hand scrabbled uselessly at the smooth lid of the pianoforte, finding no purchase on the polished wood. She was babbling, she knew, though she hardly knew what she was saying in between gasps and groans, and before long she felt the ache rising, the crest of the now familiar wave building to a white-crested peak of sweet agony.

When she finished, her legs were shaking so badly she could barely stand. Mary caught her weight, and supported her over to the couch. "Good heavens," Charlotte whispered.

Mary held her close, stroking Charlotte's cheek with gentle fingers. "I confess I've wanted to do that since the first moment I saw you again. It has played no small role in my dreams."

They lay together on the couch. Mary seemed half drowsy with contentment, a look of satisfaction on her face, but Charlotte had no wish to be an ungenerous lover. "Shall I return the favour?" said she, dropping a quick kiss onto Mary's cheek.

Rarely had Mary looked so surprised. "Oh, not if you do not—I mean, not all women like to give as well as receive."

"I want to."

Mary hesitated, excitement flickering in her dark eyes. "Really?"

Charlotte tilted her head, puzzled by the back-and-forth. "Why, did your former lover not do so?"

"Well, no," Mary admitted. "Often things were based around her pleasure and not mine. I am afraid I rather felt like that was my purpose."

"I will not deny that your performance was magnificent," Charlotte said, sliding onto her knees and hooking her thumbs under Mary's skirts, "and that my own is likely to be the equivalent of a penny whistle played after the harmony of a full orchestra." Mary snorted, the slight nervousness fading. "But I am nothing if not fair, Mary Bennet. And I intend to give generously." She hiked the skirt up slowly, dragging her fingers over Mary's flesh, causing her lover to suck in air with a gasp. "Pray allow me to become as proficient as you."

"That might require a little practice." Mary's voice wasn't quite steady, and the hand grasping the couch cushion was pale-knuckled.

"One must apply oneself," Charlotte said, her lips twitching, as she pushed Mary's skirts back, revealing the treasure she desired, "in order to get what one wants. Is that not so?"

She bent her head as Mary had done and nuzzled the soft flesh there, trailing kisses. The motion really did feel like devotion, in a way—connecting with something holy and unreal, her body thrumming with energy that could not all be her own.

"Faster, darling," Mary gasped, her mouth open, her head thrown back in ecstasy. "Please. I cannot wait." Charlotte obeyed, and was rewarded with Mary's thighs twitching around her. "A little to the left, please," was all Mary managed between incoherent moans, before Charlotte felt fingers tightening in her hair to the point of almost-pain, and she gave an appreciative hum as her own muscles twinged in sympathetic response. The sound seemed to send Mary over the edge, shuddering against Charlotte's mouth, pressing a closed fist against her mouth to stifle a cry.

"Well," said she, after she had caught her breath. "Though I do not think you need much practice, I would be more than happy to oblige." The joke was covering something deeper, for Mary's eyes were bright. Charlotte wriggled onto the couch, tugging Mary closer, and was not surprised when a few tears spattered her bosom. "I'm sorry," Mary added, her voice muffled. "I don't know quite what has come over me. You were wonderful."

"I know what it is to feel overwhelmed," Charlotte reminded her. "Especially when one's deepest desires are finally acknowledged and reciprocated."

"I suppose you are right." Mary lifted her head, looking anxious. "Was it... I mean, did you enjoy it?"

Charlotte took Mary's hand and led it under her skirts, to where she pooled excitement. "What do you think? Is that confirmation enough?"

"Oh," she breathed, and began to move, but Charlotte stopped her.

"You have quite worn me out tonight," said she, smiling. In truth she felt as if she was capable of managing another round, but the memory of Mary's warm, broad tongue between her legs still lingered deliciously, and she did not want to forget the feeling so soon.

Mary pressed a kiss to Charlotte's lips and she tasted herself, sweet-sour, mingling with the intimate scent of Mary. Charlotte brushed tear tracks from Mary's cheek; her lover was gazing at her with adoration, radiating so brightly she wondered how she had ever missed such a thing in the first place. Love could begin in many ways, certainly—between Lizzie and Darcy it had been a seed of animosity, watered by mutual prejudice, which only blossomed into joy once both had gained a deeper understanding of the other's character. Between Jane and Bingley, it had been instant and sweet. Between her own parents, who had married young but with the full encouragement of both families, it had been kind and respectful; Charlotte could not remember either ever having raised their voices. Mr Collins had loved her in his own way, though without any real depth. She had tried to love him back, and succeeded with that same shallow effect, but she had never felt like this. Anne de Bourgh's friend Mr Innes had been handsome and his manners excellent, but nothing about him had ever sparked real interest in Charlotte's heart. Whereas, whenever she looked at Mary, she felt less like a wilted flower, than an entire garden in bloom.

After breakfast the next morning, Charlotte picked up her book again, which she had been putting off for some days now. Her reticence had to be overcome at some point, whether she liked it or not. While Mary puzzled over a diagram that looked more like an angry scribble than anything with coherent intent, Charlotte sighed and began the second-to-last chapter. The crew were back aboard the ship and had begun the return journey to England, though the captain had suggested a last stop at an island group a few miles east of their route. Barton was apparently looking forward to visiting this last place, which he had been assured held many marvels, though he had mentioned already a strange headache which would not stop even after a good sleep. Charlotte's fingers twitched around the jacket, but she took a deep breath and forced herself to keep reading.

The weather on-board had grown worse as they had headed up the African coast, back towards Portugal, and a strange, feverish sickness had spread through the crew. Barton complained of insects which had, unbeknownst to anyone aboard, buried their eggs in the hollow of wooden trinkets and gifts and had not revealed themselves for many miles. By the time they were discovered, many of the eggs had hatched, and the adults had eaten their way through several bags of grain. The captain, he'd written, had been inconsolable, blaming himself for the mistake, though the crew had been ordered plainly to check each new item brought on-board in case of this very event.

Though the captain, the ship's doctor, and Barton volunteered to go without rations to preserve larger portions for the crew, meals were still much smaller than they had been, resulting in high tempers and a worsening of the fever amongst the sickest men. Charlotte's eyes prickled with tears. *Poor man.* She laid the book aside. "I cannot bring myself to read the ending. I simply cannot do it, knowing what happens to him."

"All things must end," Mary said, glancing at her with sympathy. "Is that not what makes life so important? Without grief, anger, and fear, how would we appreciate the true delights of joy, gratitude, and security?"

"I suppose you are right." Still, she did not open the book again, and after a moment got up and wandered about the room.

"If you are looking for something else to amuse you, there is always the pianoforte."

"I can hardly look at one now without blushing," Charlotte pointed out. "Might I peruse your aunt's library?"

"Of course. Take whatever you like." Mary glanced up. "She has quite a lovely selection of poetry on the shelves behind her desk."

Charlotte meandered into Aunt Cecily's room, where she did indeed discover a shelf of interesting poetry, as well as several plants which had clearly been dead for some time—much longer than Aunt Cecily had been gone. "Your aunt is not a gifted gardener then?" she called through the open doorway.

"Oh, no. She claims it is not her fault, and insists that there is a particularly vengeful ghost in that room that hates flowers and causes them all to die. She may well have a point, for nothing brought into this room in the past year has lived to tell the tale." Mary appeared in the doorway, a streak of charcoal adorning her chin.

"That's odd," Charlotte said, stroking the crisp, dead leaves of what had probably once been a lovely begonia. She bent, examining the stalk, which was mottled and hollow, as if a hundred tiny bites had been taken out of it. "And they were never outside?"

"Not to my recollection. And it wasn't as if she didn't water them." Mary shrugged. "Very strange. Now, darling, speaking of flowers—I received a reminder from Mr Mellor. Shall we go tomorrow?"

Charlotte straightened, the dead plants forgotten, and followed Mary out of the room. "Oh, yes! I cannot wait to see his collection. If it is even half as wonderful as you say, then it will be more like one of the seven ancient wonders than any old country garden."

"I cannot wait to see what you think."

Chapter Twenty-Five

Dear Mama and Papa,
I am as well as can be and Mary is taking exceedingly good care
of me. Please do not think that I am not anxious to see you—
of course I am—but there will be time enough to catch up once I
return to Hertfordshire. Thank you for your offer of help, I shall
accept it gratefully, though I do wonder if it has anything at all
to do with John's promise to send the children to Lucas Lodge
for a long stay?
Your loving daughter,
Charlotte

Mid-morning, Charlotte and Mary climbed into the carriage
and set off for Amberhurst, Mr Mellor's grand estate. "He owns
a house in town, too," Mary informed her, "but when you see
Amberhurst, you will understand why he only leaves it for salon
meetings and business."

The ride took them west through Canterbury town, which
really was a very pretty place. The morning air was warm, hinting of the summer that was to come, reminding Charlotte that
she would have to leave soon. She rolled her shoulders, pushing the thought down. The closer her departure came, the less

she wanted to leave. To distract herself, she kept up a steady stream of questions about the surrounding buildings, which Mary was only too happy to answer. By the time they left the town proper, Charlotte could still see the great towers of Canterbury Cathedral in the distance, looming over the trees like a pale shepherd over a flock of green sheep.

For the next hour, the carriage rumbled along a road which passed over the Great Stour, the water gliding along in a stately, unhurried way. When they finally arrived at Amberhurst, Charlotte's excitement had grown almost uncontainable. She peered through the carriage window, craning to see if she could get a glimpse of the estate beyond, but her view was blocked by a high stone wall. Above the top of the wall, beech trees stood to attention at regular intervals, displaying beautiful green crowns. Birdsong rang out, and though Charlotte had never been particularly good at identifying their calls, even she recognised the questioning lilt of a blackbird, and the shrill, repetitive sound of a song thrush. "If flowers could sing," said she, turning to Mary, "which one do you think would make the prettiest music?"

Mary bit her lip, thinking the idea over. "I believe a rose would be able to hit the most pleasing notes, like an excellent tenor. What do you think?"

"Bluebells, perhaps. I imagine they would sound like a choir of sweet little children."

"I do so love your imagination," Mary said, and leaned in for a quick kiss. "Oh, we are almost at the gates now."

The large gates were made of black iron, each side wrought in the middle to form an *M*. "Is this his family estate or more lately bought?" Charlotte asked, as the carriage turned and began the long, tree-lined drive up to an unseen house.

"His family had it for at least a generation prior. His mother was quite the eccentric, though well-loved by everybody, and his father a very quiet man, though of course, I never met them. I believed they died in a boating accident some twenty years ago, and he had no brothers or sisters with whom to divide the family fortune."

When finally the horses rounded a bend, Charlotte let out a gasp. The house was magnificent on a par with Rosings—large and imposing, fronted by a large, stepped fountain, which reminded Charlotte very much of how a guest at the parsonage once described the fountain at Chatsworth House in Derbyshire. The flower-beds were neat but not overly pruned, offering bursts of bright colour to enhance the landscape. *Lady Catherine would never have permitted something so haphazard,* Charlotte thought to herself, *though really Rosings would benefit from a small amount of chaos instead of everything so uniform.*

The carriage slowed to a halt outside the pristine white steps leading up to the front door. The smell of stewing rhubarb drifted in the warm air. Though they'd had an excellent breakfast of eggs and fried kippers, Charlotte's stomach rumbled. As Mary descended, holding a hand out to assist Charlotte to the ground, a man dressed in a smart black coat emerged from the house. His shirt was so white it seemed to glow in the early afternoon sunlight. "Miss Bennet," he greeted Mary, and bowed. "Mrs Collins," adding another crisp bow. "May I escort you to the drawing room? Mr Mellor has been informed of your arrival and will join you shortly."

The butler led them into the house proper, and Charlotte did her best not to let her jaw drop. The foyer was painted a lurid shade of green, and several open doors revealed other rooms painted in equally shocking shades of reds, blues, and oranges. The drawing room was the kind of dark pink that probably only butchers saw on a daily basis, and while another gentleman might have tried to match the colour with pink furniture and upholstery, Mr Mellor had outfitted the sofas and armchairs in a most becoming teal.

The butler bowed, then disappeared. Charlotte stared around in amazement, hardly able to take in so much colour. A long side table against the opposite side of the room held several large vases of flowers. She was delighted to see that Mr Mellor understood that the purpose of such an arrangement was not to stuff every possible flower into a space, but to arrange them attractively in a way which allowed each their own space to breathe. White lilies and lavender looked enticing against the dark pink wall and smelled wonderful too. Mary settled herself on the teal sofa, seemingly content to let her lover wander around. "What do you think?" said she.

"It suits him so well," Charlotte said, laughing. "For he is such a cheerful man that of course his house must be painted in all the colours of a rainbow. One would never know it from the outside, however."

"And how does it compare to Rosings?"

Charlotte ambled towards the other end of the room, where the narrowest wall was adorned with small painted plates. Some depicted orange sunsets, glowing over yellow beaches, while others showed odd statues she thought might have been Greek. "Rosings is such a stuffy place. One can barely sneeze without feeling as if one is dishonouring some surly ancestor or other. This, on the other hand, feels very comfortable, as if someone actually lives here. The beauty on display is not simply for show, but to please the man who sees it every day."

"I completely agree," Mary said. "I have only been here a few times, but it is so refreshing to see a house made to fit its occupant perfectly, rather than the other way around."

Mr Mellor entered the room, beaming widely. Today he was dressed in a seaglass-green tailcoat over an ivory waistcoat and white cravat. "Mrs Collins! Miss Bennet! I am delighted to see you," he cried, throwing his arms wide. "Has no one brought you tea yet? I cannot abide an empty table."

"Your man only just left, sir," Mary said, amused, and sure enough, there was a clinking sound from the hallway and the butler soon entered bearing a tea tray, followed by several footmen though it caused not a little chaos and confusion when

Mr Mellor shooed all of them back into the hallway. "We cannot possibly sit in the drawing room, not when it is so beautiful outside. Take the trays to the terrace, please." Turning to Charlotte and Mary, he added, "Come, ladies. I am of the firm opinion that refreshments are much improved when there is an agreeable view to accompany them."

Back in the foyer, Charlotte spied a curio cabinet and could not help staring at the shelves, which were crammed with all kinds of objects. "Ah," Mr Mellor said, noting her interest. "Those are my favourite trinkets—well, almost all my favourites. I keep some in the glasshouses too, so they do not dry out."

Charlotte stepped closer, peering at a cluster of long-stemmed pipes sitting beside a long jawbone from a creature she could not identify. "That is one of my particular favourites," he added, pointing at the jawbone. "I would like to have a cabinet full of them someday."

"What sort of animal is it?"

"This one was a marine beast. I bought it from Cuvier and had it shipped from Paris last year, and he wanted a pretty penny for it, I don't mind telling you. There's a family in Lyme Regis who've been digging up similar things for a few years now, so I've sent one of my men over to have a look and see what might be purchased. The world is full of marvels, is it not?"

On the shelf above the jawbone, a box carved with long-legged birds was flanked by two large teeth, both as big as Charlotte's palm. She leaned closer and stared at the box. "In a book I am reading, the captain of a ship received something very like this as a gift from some islanders he traded with."

"I gave her Mr Barton's diary," Mary clarified, and Mr Mellor's eyes widened.

"Why, you are entirely correct. That is the very same box—I bought it at auction after the *Rositania* returned. The captain died, poor fellow, although he made it home in time to say his goodbyes, unlike poor Mr Barton."

"You knew him?"

"Not well." Mr Mellor sighed. "Not nearly as well as I would have liked to. Such a promising young man. Came to our salon meetings a few times prior to his departure on the *Rositania*. I'd hoped to hear all about his travels upon his return, and I—" He broke off, hesitating. "Adventures come with a high price, and most are forced to pay it. I wish I had travelled more in my youth, though perhaps if I had I would not be here today." Mr Mellor cleared his throat. "Come, let us step out of this gloom and into the sunshine."

He guided them through a hallway and down a narrow passage made of stone, which led onto the terrace. Charlotte, bringing up the rear of the party, was the last to step outside, blinking in the brightness of the day's sunshine. The grounds were impressive—an enormous, neat lawn bordered by flower-beds bursting with vivid scarlet, ivory, and black roses. Three glasshouses stood side by side on the right, a stone path leading to their doors. Gardeners in aprons and gloves bustled about, carrying trowels and mysterious bags. In the distance, far beyond the glasshouses, Charlotte could just make out several rows of low hedges. "Ah," Mr Mellor said, catching her gaze. "I am growing a maze, and intend to put some sort of treasure at the centre. A beautiful statue, perhaps, to make the journey through the labyrinth worthwhile. At the moment the hedges are only up to here—" he gestured halfway up his own thigh with a flat palm "—but so much of gardening is patience. Is that not so, Mrs Collins?"

"Indeed," Charlotte agreed, "that has been my experience, sir. It is not a pastime which lends itself to sudden excitement, but to careful and precise labour."

Mr Mellor smiled. "Speaking of precise labour—I had my gardeners plant dill, as you suggested at our last salon meeting. They were dubious about it, but I am delighted to report that your advice was correct and my poor flowers have already begun to recover."

"Oh!" said she, "I am terribly glad to hear it."

"See," said Mary, patting Charlotte's arm, "and you were worried that you might have nothing of value to contribute."

"Perish the thought, Mrs Collins." He ushered them towards a white table, shaded by a large parasol. "You have saved a fortune's worth of flowers and I am entirely in your debt."

Charlotte had been so taken by the view that she hadn't even noticed how pretty the terrace itself was—paved by stone slabs set in hexagonal patterns, bordered by raised beds of peonies in every possible shade.

"It is most beneficial for me, though I am afraid you have dealt a dreadful blow to young Mr Cromley's hopes of winning a prize this year," Mr Mellor added, grinning. Charlotte's smile grew uncertain. "Oh, do not feel too badly for him. I won't live forever, after all. Every dog hath his day, hmm?" He gestured for the butler to come forward and pour the tea, while they seated themselves at the table. "Now, may I interest you in a sugar biscuit? They're quite delightful."

Charlotte leaned forward while the butler poured tea. "May I be so bold as to ask a favour, sir?"

"Of course, my dear girl, anything you like."

"I'd like to see the insects."

Mary raised an eyebrow, her lips twitching. "Other women would have asked for jewels or dresses," Mr Mellor said with amusement, dunking a sugar biscuit in his tea. "And you ask for insects. My my, Mrs Collins, you are an interesting person. Miss Bennet told me as much, but even her praise failed to convey the true heights. Yes, of course you may examine the little beasts! I had planned to take you through the glasshouses anyway, for it is there that I keep my most exotic treasures."

"Have you sent any specimens away for examination?" Mary asked, taking another biscuit.

"Yes, to Mr Kirby and Mr Spence, who are writing a new book on entomology. I also sent a few to Mr Leach in London, though he has such a backlog that I expect it will take him weeks to get to my particular case now that he's moved onto crustaceans. Lovely man," turning to Charlotte, "and an excellent scientist, truly, but he works far too hard."

Since Charlotte had no idea who any of these people were, she settled for nodding politely and helping herself to another scone with jam. Mr Mellor had a wonderful way about him— whereas Mrs Tremaine had made Charlotte feel stupid and out of place at the salon meeting, Mr Mellor treated everyone with the same agreeable enthusiasm.

"How heavenly it must be to walk here every day!" she said, staring out at the view. "Gracious, I would never leave. One would have to prise me out like a mussel."

"I quite agree. That is why I spend as much time here as business permits, though it never seems to be enough. Every day brings a new joy at Amberhurst. Please do have as many biscuits as you like, Miss Bennet, for my cook will be quite ashamed of himself if we do not eat them all."

The ladies were perfectly happy to oblige this request, for the tea was lightly spiced and the sugar biscuits were a wonderful, sweet complement. "Well now," Mr Mellor added, once their cups and plates were empty. "Shall I give you a proper tour?"

"Yes, please." Charlotte smiled at him, delighted by the way his blue eyes twinkled.

He led them down the wide stone steps to the path below, and along to the right, past rhododendron bushes which grew much more ostentatiously than Lady Catherine would ever have allowed. A young man in rolled shirtsleeves, who wore a stained leather apron tied around his waist, waited in front of the first glasshouse's door. "Thank you, Henry," Mr Mellor said, and the young man pulled the door open. "After you, Mrs Collins."

Obligingly, Charlotte stepped inside and was transported into another world.

Chapter Twenty-Six

Charlotte had been in glasshouses before, though her memories had left her unprepared for the tidal wave of humidity which swallowed her whole. The heat felt like a physical presence, squeezing her from all sides, but she had to admit the effect was rather pleasant once one got over the initial shock. She fanned her face with her hand, creating only a draught of warm air against her cheek, and wished that she was wearing fewer layers, propriety be damned.

Orange trees lined one side of the building, their branches heavy with almost-ripe fruit, while lemon trees lined the other. The air was sweet with the smell of citrus flesh, yet bitter with the scent of its peel, and Charlotte breathed in the heady aroma with a sigh of contentment.

"I'm partial to the entire family, I admit," Mr Mellor said, wandering deeper into the glasshouse. Henry stood quietly by the door, looking perfectly content to wait until he was given his next order. "We grow pineapples here too, see? Though I'm afraid I cannot give you a taste today, for they are not yet ripe."

Charlotte had never tasted pineapple, though she'd heard it adorned the tables of those in the finest circles of society, and was intrigued by the strange, scaly fruit and its spiky crown of leaves. After admiring the lemons, already a stark yellow with only a touch of green, they stepped back out into the sunshine, which felt rather cool after the heat of the glasshouse, and strolled along the path until they came to the second glasshouse. "Now," Mr Mellor said, while Henry opened the door. "This is where I keep my tropical plants. We had to dispose of some which were too badly damaged to be of use to anybody, but we saved a great deal thanks to you, Mrs Collins."

Charlotte could smell the dill before she even stepped over the threshold, and sure enough, planted between each row of flowers were slender green stalks, each branching into heads of several fronds. She had always thought that dill looked a little like a sea of waving arms, eager to be noticed, but these had been eaten back until they were only elbows. Here and there, a shiny insect crawled over the pots. The flowers themselves were exquisite: slender orange and white orchids, pink hibiscus, and beautiful red camellias. There were violets, too, though not at all like the violets Charlotte was used to—their petals curved so that each flower resembled a small bowl. The air was distinctly floral in here, in stark contrast to the first glasshouse, though this too was pleasing.

"Now, Henry." Mr Mellor gestured the young man forward. "Could you fetch us one of those blasted insects? A dead one, ideally."

Henry dispatched an insect quickly and handed it to Charlotte, who flipped it belly-up in her palm. The shell was an odd, iridescent black, while the body proper was matte black. The six legs were uniform, the head small compared to the body, the wings neatly compact. "I've never seen anything like it," she said at last.

"May I?" Mary took it from her and studied it closely, before shaking her head, evidently coming to the same conclusion. She handed it back to Henry before turning to Mr Mellor. "I do hope one of the gentlemen you mentioned can shed some light on this case."

"As do I." He sighed. "As you can see, the dill has been most effective in keeping them from the flowers, but I confess the entire situation puzzles me. Where did they come from? And why, when we have gone to such pains to rid ourselves of them—for I even had a crew helping me to handpick the damn things off the flowers at one point—are they still appearing? It is like some terrible sort of magic."

Catching a glimpse of another wooden cabinet in the corner, Charlotte gestured towards it. "You keep curios in here too?" *Unusual,* she thought. Most people kept such valued objects in a drawing room or library, where they could be admired by visitors, though probably most visitors to Amberhurst ended up in the glasshouse sooner or later.

"Indeed. Of course, the humidity limits what I can store in here. No books or preserved specimens, lest they grow mould. I mostly keep rocks in that one, though you might be interested in the object on the second lowest shelf."

The item turned out to be a wooden statue of an old man with a long beard that trailed all the way down to his bare feet. Charlotte hummed thoughtfully. "This might be an odd question, but was this one of Mr Barton's possessions, by any chance?"

Mr Mellor gave her an odd look. "It was, but how could you possibly know that?"

Charlotte straightened, frowning. "In his diary, Mr Barton talked of a lingering headache and a fever that spread through the crew. He even gave up his rations so the working men could eat a little better."

"A kindness which probably killed him," Mr Mellor said. "What a shame that good intentions so often lead to terrible outcomes."

"I agree, sir."

"But how does that relate to the statue?" he asked.

"Well, Mr Barton also made note of the fact that the return journey on the ship was troubled by a plague of insects which ate their way through the stores of food, causing the shortened rations in the first place." She bit her lip, thinking it over. "It was odd, since the captain had ordered everything checked carefully for any mites or pests, to stop that very thing from happening."

Mary studied Charlotte, her eyes alight with interest. "Go on, darling."

"Well," Charlotte said, turning her attention back to the cabinet. "It's possible that…well, let me see." She reached out and ran her fingers over the wood, noting every bump and whorl. There was no hole that she could see, and the glass remained intact on the front. "Hmm. Help me turn this, would you?"

Mr Mellor and Mary put their shoulders to the cabinet and in moments had spun it enough so that the back was exposed.

"There," Charlotte said, pointing to a small hole in the wood. She bent closer, and saw that the edges of the hole were ragged—surely not made by any tool, but by the hungry jaws of a thousand newly-hatched insects desperate for freedom.

"No wonder we had no idea where they were coming from!" he exclaimed. "Good gracious!"

"And now would you mind unlocking the cabinet, sir?" Mr Mellor produced a set of keys and unlocked it without question, watching Charlotte with renewed interest. "Now we shall see," she said, pulling the door open and reaching for Barton's statue.

The statue was much lighter than she had expected, feeling almost entirely hollow. She handed it to Mr Mellor, who exclaimed in surprise. "Why this was much heavier when I purchased it. Henry!" he called, "Bring an axe, my dear boy."

Henry soon located an axe, and Mr Mellor laid the statue on the floor. A single well-placed swing sliced the wood clean in twain, and there inside were traces of larvae which had not lived to see freedom.

"An unexpected Trojan horse," Mary suggested. "Though the previous owner would not have intended anything of the sort." She smiled at Charlotte, adoration writ large over her face. "You have an extraordinary ability to see what nobody else can."

"I rather thought that was your talent, Miss Bennet," Charlotte teased, and was rewarded with an arched eyebrow and a twitch of the lips that promised sweet retribution later.

"Your instincts have proven to be correct once again, Mrs Collins." Mr Mellor shook his head admiringly. "I really don't know how I am to repay you."

"Perhaps, if it is not too much trouble, I could visit again before I return to Kent?" Charlotte suggested.

"Mrs Collins, I am quite of a mind to never let you leave at all. In fact…well… I do not wish to offend you with assumptions, my dear, but I believe I understand a little of what your circumstances must be now that your husband is dead, and I would be delighted to offer you a place to live here at Amberhurst, as well as a sizable wage, in return for your expertise and care."

A job, Charlotte thought, stunned. *Money. Freedom.*

Shame.

"Oh, sir, that is very kind of you, but I could not possibly take advantage of your, um—" she stumbled, not quite sure what to call it "—your generous nature."

"Charlotte," Mary said, giving her a reproachful look, "perhaps you might like to walk around the rest of the gardens?"

The butler had appeared from nowhere, and without actually moving a muscle, appeared to communicate with Mr Mellor. "Please excuse me for a moment, ladies. Miss Bennet, you know the path well enough by now—please show Mrs Collins around."

"You mustn't be so modest, darling," Mary said, as soon as Mr Mellor was out of sight. "Come, I shall show you the prize-winning roses that are the bane of Mr Cromley's existence."

Charlotte made a noncommittal sound, and was relieved when Mary began to ramble about the various kinds of lichen which had lately been discovered in America. This amused them until they arrived at the rosebushes, which were indeed the wonder they had been purported to be. They spent long minutes exclaiming over each shade, from scarlet to palest ivory; Charlotte had never seen such velvety petals, nor smelled such a strong scent from any rose she herself had grown. She made a mental note to question Mr Mellor on his gardeners' choice of fertilizer, and whether they added something like bone meal, for she had heard this encouraged growth.

She stopped to pick a tiny bouquet of cornflowers at the end of the garden. Giddiness overtook her and, laughing, she presented Mary with the bundle. "In return for the gift of holly you gave me once," she teased. "Pray tell me what these mean, if you know."

"You think to test me with something so easy," Mary replied congenially. "Even I know that oftentimes young suitors wear them, and if the flower fades quickly, it is taken as a sign that their love is unrequited." Her gaze found Charlotte's and held it. High colour flooded her cheeks, though they had not exerted themselves on the walk. "What say you to that?"

Charlotte's hands trembled. She was aware of every leaf rustling around them, every shrill chirp from the branches above. "And what if the flower did not fade?" she asked, heart hammering in her chest, scarcely believing her own boldness and terrified of the answer.

Mary grabbed Charlotte's hand and drew her into the shelter of a great oak. "Do you think we can be seen from here?" Her voice was low, conspiratorial.

"No," Charlotte said, puzzled, her pulse quickening. "Why should it—"

Mary stepped closer, touching the underside of Charlotte's chin with two gloved fingers. A desperate thirst, unquenched. "I am not one for speeches," she murmured. "But know that nothing need fade. If you feel even half what I—Oh, Charlotte. Only say the word, and I am yours, indefinitely."

She could not get enough breath in her lungs to answer anything more than a nod. Not a heartbeat passed before Mary kissed her; not gentle, after all, but a firm, encompassing embrace that stole the last remaining air from Charlotte's body. She sagged, limp, knees buckling under the onslaught of passion. She returned the embrace clumsily, fingers wending into the hair at the nape of Mary's neck, and oh, the sweet agony of being truly craved, truly perceived, truly loved was enough to pierce Charlotte's heart in a thousand places, sending shafts of light into its most secret chambers.

A shout in the distance startled them from their embrace and they pulled apart, staring at each other.

"What lovely flowers," Mary said, adjusting her gloves as if nothing had happened. The puffiness of her lips and the flash in her dark eyes were the only signs that something had taken place. "Shall we return to the house and say farewell to our host?"

Charlotte stammered an agreement—somehow the days of prior kissing and lovemaking had done nothing to prepare her for this—and followed Mary as quietly as a well-heeled dog. They said a fond farewell to Mr Mellor, who was clearly reluctant to let them go, though Charlotte could not meet Mary's eye without blushing.

"You have not grown shy now, have you?" Mary asked, once they were alone in the carriage. "Did I go too far, darling?"

"No, not at all," Charlotte said, blushing even harder. She had felt already like she was falling in love, and had done her best not to think about it. Now, avoidance was an impossibility. Her affection had grown immensely, and her desire for Mary was more than a passing fancy. Every kiss, every glance, every heartbeat confirmed her fate. "It is simply—"

"No need to explain," Mary interrupted. "I understand. We have all the time in the world, and I do not want you to think I am rushing you."

Charlotte opened her mouth to correct this statement, then closed it. Of course Mary believed that her love was indefinite, but once Charlotte was out of sight and out of mind, she would surely feel differently. It would be churlish to point this out, for Mary remained stubbornly insistent on seeing the rosy side of everything. Charlotte smiled, rather than spoil the moment, and they held hands all the way back to Canterbury.

Chapter Twenty-Seven

In the foyer of Mary's home, they removed their coats and gloves, handing them over to Pitt. Charlotte followed Mary into the drawing room, wondering idly what Miss Brodie was planning to make for dinner, and whether they had time to sneak off and make love beforehand. She closed the door behind her, and took her place on the couch next to Mary. Leaning in for a sweet kiss, Charlotte felt now-familiar sparks of desire crackling between them.

"My dear, I have—" Mary said, pulling away and smoothing her dress over her knees. "I want to ask you something."

Her stomach dropped. "What is it?"

"You needn't look so afraid, darling." Mary gathered Charlotte into her arms and held her close. "I merely wanted to ask if you might consider staying here? With me?"

Relief bloomed low in her gut. "Yes, I could stay a bit longer, though I must return to Kent by the end of next week. Lady Catherine will expect me to be packed upon her return."

"No, I do not mean an extension of your visit. I mean, would you like to move here for a while? Several months, perhaps? You could send your things here rather than home to Lucas

Lodge. I'm sure your parents wouldn't mind one whit, and of course they'd be welcome here too."

"Oh, I..." Charlotte blinked. "I couldn't trespass on your time in such a way. What would Cecily say?"

"I will write to her, but I cannot see that she would have a problem with it. I am in love with you, and she will be glad I am happy."

Charlotte stared at her blankly. She could not have possibly heard correctly. "Pardon, I did not quite... You're in love with me?"

"Yes. Why, what did you think I meant in the garden?" Mary arched an eyebrow, her expression quizzical. "I told you I would be yours, indefinitely. How else could one interpret such a thing? If you were a man, I would marry you in an instant."

A strange sensation thrilled through Charlotte; something bubbly and joyful, undercut by a feeling of foreboding. "You would?"

"Of course."

Mary had said it so lightly that perhaps it was only intended as a jest. "I would marry you too," she said, and meant it. "If only things were different."

Now it was Mary's turn to pause, studying her. "Why do you say it like that?"

The atmosphere had thickened. Charlotte pulled back and stood, feeling suddenly graceless and awkward. "Well, it is the truth, is it not? We could never marry."

"I hadn't realised that was such a problem."

Charlotte's jaw dropped. "Do you not think it one?"

"Not really, no." Mary looked hurt. "I believe we could keep house as well as any couple, married or not."

"And what would I tell my family?" She turned and paced towards the window, not knowing what else to do.

"Tell them what you like."

She turned back, biting her lip. "It would not be the truth."

"That would be your choice." Mary's smile was grim. "Are you saying this changes nothing?"

"No, of course not. It changes everything, for me. But in the larger world, there are expectations of me that I cannot—"

"And do not you think there are expectations on me, too? Pressures to marry, snide comments, occasional suitors looking to inherit Cecily's favourite niece's fortune?"

"Money makes a lot of problems go away," Charlotte pointed out.

"Hence why I am encouraging you to accept Mr Mellor's offer. You would not need to worry about landing a husband, and you would have money and freedom to do as you pleased and go where you liked. It is a great opportunity to be independent, Charlotte. Please do think it over carefully."

Surprised that Mary was genuinely suggesting she consider the offer, Charlotte continued to pace the room. For Mary, who had felt so chafed by the confines of polite society in England, the opportunity no doubt seemed like a chance to become a pioneer of sorts. Yet it was neither Mary's opportunity nor name at stake, and she could not expect to live her own desires vicariously through Charlotte. "You cannot be serious. Whatever would my family say?"

Mary shrugged, as if the answer were simple. "Do not tell them, then."

She stared, astounded. "I cannot lie to them."

"Cannot, or will not?"

"It is much the same thing."

"Curse your insistence on absolute honesty." Mary sighed. "Well, so what? If it provided you with a good living, then what would be the matter? Women of our station sometimes become governesses, do they not?"

"Under extreme pressure or after some terrible catastrophe, yes."

"And do you not consider your current circumstances to fall under that category?"

"Well, I—"

"And here you would be earning far more than working as a governess."

"But I would still be earning," Charlotte insisted. The idea of taking a job at such an advanced age—a position which entailed real responsibility, never mind opening doors into the dreams she had considered impossible—was overwhelming. "I have never worked before, and it would be...you must surely see that it is out of the question."

"I see nothing of the sort. Besides, it would also mean that we could be together in a slightly more public setting."

Panic rose like a tide, turning Charlotte's stomach into a mass of roiling green waves. It was quite one thing to love in secret, amongst people who had similar persuasions, and quite another to upend her life by confessing something unacceptable in her usual circles. *What would I tell my parents? What would I tell Lizzie?* The idea of everyone back home gossiping about her was a source of immense distress. "It is simply not conceivable."

Mary threw up her hands. "And what is the alternative? Go back to Hertfordshire and live off your parents' charity until they die, and then be at the mercy of other family? Or marry a husband you neither want nor love, and force yourself to endure a lifetime of unhappiness? You made that choice once already."

Charlotte flinched, her steps slowing. "It was not as bad as you may think it."

"You cannot expect me to believe that," Mary scoffed. "You had no real control, no friends, and no dreams. What little spark had ever been in you, life in Kent had crushed out. *He* had crushed it out."

This echoed Charlotte's own thoughts far too closely for comfort. She felt a sudden urge to defend Mr Collins; one ought not to speak ill of the dead, after all. "That is unkind. He was neither a bad man nor a bad husband."

"And for that I am glad," Mary retorted, "but you were not happy."

"Happiness isn't everything."

"Well, it ought to be." She took a deep breath. "It would be the easiest thing in the world to call a lawyer. I could give you all the trappings of marriage in the legal sense, even if the church would not recognise it."

Mary seemed to have a reasonable answer for everything. Charlotte cast about desperately for another line of argument, her hands clenching into fists before uncurling into flat planes of panic. "And what should happen if you grow tired of me?"

"I would never grow tired of you."

"You cannot know that for certain."

Mary frowned, apparently surprised by the question. Her cheeks flushed an angry red as she rose to face Charlotte. "You married Collins without knowing as much. Are you suggesting I am less loyal than he?"

"No, I—" She swallowed hard. "But he had limited options, and you are evidently much in demand."

"So you think me inconstant?" Mary's eyes were blazing now. "After all that we have been through? All that I have shared with you? All that I have confessed?"

Charlotte wanted desperately to make this argument stop, but every word seemed to throw more oil on the fire. "That is not what I meant. It is merely that—"

"Then whatever did you mean? You do not want to be reliant upon me, but you do not want to create your own fortune. What alternative is there? Look, I love you and I wish for your happiness but—"

"Love does not change the world."

"It has changed my world," Mary argued. "And I would

contend that it has changed you too, these past weeks. You cannot deny it."

"Of course it has, but—" Charlotte hesitated, her fingers running through her hair, smoothing that which she really wished to ruffle into a state reflecting the tumult inside her. "But however I myself may feel, I must do my duty to my family." The excuse sounded weak even to her own ears, though it was the truth.

"Then what was all of this? Did our time together mean nothing?" Mary was only a few feet away, but the distance between them had never felt greater. "You have been offered a way out, Charlotte. An opportunity to leave your old life behind and remake it anew in a way that suits you. You do not have to hide any more, darling."

"I will always be hiding, one way or another."

Mary stared at her, jaw working furiously. "I cannot understand you."

"You understand me perfectly. You just do not agree."

"So what was this for you? Merely some sort of game? A fling?" she demanded, her eyes filling with tears. "We are talking of my heart, darling. I gave it to you fully."

"It was never a game." Charlotte crossed the chasm between them and tried to take Mary's hands, but Mary shook her off angrily. "I simply cannot be so selfish as to let my feelings control my decisions. You said yourself that you would never do what Lydia did, that you would protect your family and keep them safe. I must do the same. You must see that!"

"I only meant not to flaunt a scandalous relationship in such a way as would draw suspicion and scandal. You knew perfectly well that I did not mean—" Mary stopped, her lips pressed into pale lines. "You led me to believe that... I thought... Do not you love me, Charlotte?" Her tone was desperate, her voice raw.

Charlotte opened her mouth, then closed it again. Mary had once said that the day Charlotte told a lie would be the day the world ended; she'd been right, in a way. The world they had created had to be destroyed for Mary to thrive. Charlotte was an overgrown tree cutting off the sunlight of a beautiful flower; if Mary would not chop her down, she must take the axe to her own trunk. Fear gripped Charlotte, wrapping icy fingers around her heart. She had no money and no prospects, and certainly could not accept a paid position of employment, which solved only one problem but created several more. Mary would find a better match in time, someone prepared to take risks, to fling caution to the wind in the grand pursuit of love.

"I cannot do what you ask of me," she said, at last. "I had thought you understood that. And if that means that I cannot give you what you need, then so be it."

She hadn't meant to say it like that—she'd meant to say that she understood, that if Mary had a bar Charlotte could not clear then it was for the best that they end the affair, no matter how it pained her to do so—but the words impacted Mary as if she had struck a physical blow.

"If that is your decision, so be it. I am sorry to have misunderstood you so badly, and I apologize for any offense given." Mary drew herself up straight, lip trembling, cheeks now pale as bone. "I shall have the servants pack your bags forthwith, Mrs Collins."

And with that, she swept from the room, leaving Charlotte alone and aching.

Chapter Twenty-Eight

Over the last few days, Charlotte had wondered where she would find the strength to leave Mary. She had pictured tearful, bittersweet goodbyes and at the very least, a couple of months of letters with which to console her poor broken heart. She had never pictured herself on a coach back to Kent with no such goodbye, and no hope of a single letter in her future.

The coach ride seemed twice as long without Mary; Charlotte wished to be home as quickly as possible, and had therefore immediately exchanged one coach for another upon disembarking, though this second one took a circuitous route. She had made a start at a letter to Mr Mellor, turning his offer down with the most sincere thanks she could muster, though the bumpy road and the spattering of hot tears upon the parchment left her words almost indecipherable. Folding the attempt up, Charlotte alternated between weeping and staring out of the window at the approaching dawn, her heart a clenched fist. She blew her nose hard and forced herself to take calming breaths, and by the time she arrived back in Kent, the small cottages and hamlets becoming familiar, she was sure she'd managed to erase the obvious traces of her grief. All she had to do was pretend to be fine for a few minutes, and then she could retreat to the safety of her bedroom and cry her heart out in peace.

The coach stopped outside the village tavern, and Charlotte alighted, blinking in the golden sunshine of the afternoon. Her bag was not particularly cumbersome, though she felt as if her body was encased in stone; heavy, dull, sinking into an endless quagmire. After downing a quick cup of water to quench her thirst, she marched through the village as fast as she could in such a state, trying not to draw attention. To her surprise, a familiar voice rang out from the doorway of the butcher's shop. "Mrs Collins!" exclaimed Bessie. "Why, we did not expect you back so soon. If you would wait a moment, I will walk with you back to the parsonage." She turned back into the store. "Let me have a bit of pork as well."

Charlotte grimaced. She was ill-prepared for a meeting, for she had not decided what she was going to say regarding her early arrival. Bessie joined her, swinging a basket full of parcels. "Mrs Waites mentioned that the butcher's son has been courting you," she said, casting about for something that might occupy the maid's mind.

"We are betrothed, ma'am." Bessie gave a toothy, delighted smile. "He asked me just after you left and I said aye."

Bessie was only too happy to tell the whole romantic story, which kept her occupied all the way back to the parsonage. Charlotte offered the appropriate expressions of delight and joy, and though her heart wasn't in it, Bessie didn't seem to notice. "Well, I am exceedingly pleased for you," said she. "Mrs Waites tells me that he is a very hard-working young man. Does this mean you will be leaving my employ?"

"Oh," Bessie shot her a worried glance as they neared the garden gate. "Yes, ma'am. I mean, not yours as such, for I am happy to stay on until you leave, but after that I'll work with William in the shop."

"I thought as much." Charlotte held the gate open for Bessie, then closed it behind her. The flowers looked brighter than they had when she'd left only two weeks prior, though it felt like a lifetime ago. *My darling garden,* she thought, gritting her teeth against a fresh wave of grief, *I will have to leave you too.* "Do not worry, I will simply tell Lady Catherine that the next parson will require a new maid."

Bessie trotted down the hallway and Charlotte followed, dropping her bag outside her bedroom door on the way. In the kitchen, Mrs Waites was rolling out dough, the smell of rosewater lingering in the air. "Oh, good," said the cook, "I was wondering if you were going to—" Her eyes widened. "Mrs Collins! Whatever brought you back so early?"

"I'm sorry," Charlotte said, swallowing hard against the prickle of tears. "I didn't have time to send a note."

"Hmm." Mrs Waites studied her, frowning. "Bessie, leave those things here. I've made three pies for the poor, if you wouldn't mind taking them back to the village. She needn't come back until dinner," now addressing Charlotte, "for all her work is done and whatever is left, I can handle."

Bessie didn't need telling twice, and after being loaded up with the pies, she hared out of the room. A moment later, Charlotte heard the front door close. "Now you can tell me what's wrong," Mrs Waites said, gesturing to a chair.

"What makes you think anything is wrong?" she said, half-heartedly, sinking into the chair. "Apart from my imminent departure."

The cook raised an eyebrow. "Have a biscuit." She pushed a tray of golden brown biscuits towards Charlotte, who took one. The taste was rosewater, as she'd expected, and while the biscuit had a satisfying crunch, the inside was chewy and delicious.

"What's wrong, ma'am?" the cook prompted. Her eyes were soft with concern, and the sympathetic look was almost more than Charlotte could bear.

"It is…complicated." She reached for another biscuit. She hadn't been able to force down any food on the journey, and though she had no real appetite, the biscuits were delicious.

"Most things are." Mrs Waites picked up her rolling pin again and began to work. Her hands moved quickly, but her eyes were trained on Charlotte. "And how fares Miss Bennet?"

Charlotte flinched. She had expected the question but the feelings she had been repressing for the last few hours roared back, hitting her with all the force of a hammer. "She is very well," she managed, before a lump welled up in her throat. "That is... I mean—"

"Your husband was a good man, Mrs Collins." The cook sighed. "A kind man, though not without his faults, as you well know. And yet in four years the only times I've seen you so animated and lively were those occasions when either of the Miss Bennets was around, and lately, the latter made you smile far more."

Shock fizzed through Charlotte's veins. She put the rest of the biscuit down.

"Do not be angry with me, please," Mrs Waites added quickly, seeing her expression. "If I have missed the target, I do apologise."

"You have hit it squarely," Charlotte admitted, after a moment's hesitation. She was too tired to concoct any sort of lie, nor could she easily evade the insinuation. "I hadn't realised I was so transparent."

The cook took a deep breath and lowered her voice, though they were the only two in the house. "On your first day, you asked me to always be honest with you, and I've never had reason to do otherwise in all these years. It isn't my place to speak on your life or what choices you may feel compelled to make in future, but...it was nice to see you truly happy for once. That's all. And when Miss Bennet asked me for the rum cake recipe, well." She shrugged. "She cares for you a great deal. An unusual girl, but a kind one. What I'm saying is, not all flowers thrive in the sunshine, ma'am. Some need the shade to flourish. Do you understand?"

The silence between them dragged on. The rolling pin went back and forth, back and forth, until Charlotte began to feel slightly seasick. Tears blurred her vision. "I did try to be a good wife," she admitted. "I had hoped if I tried hard enough, I would be."

"You were not simply good, you were perfect," Mrs Waites declared. "Nobody ever had a bad word to say about you, least of all Mr Collins."

"But I never loved him, and now I am in love with someone else only months after his death." She sniffed, and rummaged in her pocket for a handkerchief. "Does that not make me callous? Heartless?"

"It makes you human." Mrs Waites smiled. "Go on, finish your biscuit. Now, in the spirit of honesty, for you did ask me to—"

"How can I forget when you remind me so frequently?" Charlotte muttered, a trifle sulkily.

"Perhaps you could tell me a little of what transpired, and I can try to help you untangle the knot."

Charlotte heaved a reluctant sigh, then a second, before offering a condensed version of the tale. "And so, you see," she complained, "Miss Bennet put me in an impossible position. I could never let it be known that I had accepted a job, for society would judge my family harshly. I also do not wish to lie to my parents, though I admit I do not want to live with them again."

The silence lengthened. "I'm afraid that I must side with Miss Bennet."

"But the pressures upon me!" Charlotte spluttered, rising to her feet and wringing her hands. "My parents, and the circles they move in, to say nothing of the wider—"

"I've always liked you, ma'am." Mrs Waites' mouth was set in a hard line. "You were kind to a fault, always anxious to please and be pleased in turn. But you don't have half the sense

I thought you did, if you'd throw away your own true happiness for the perceived happiness of others."

Charlotte gaped at her, outraged. "You must see that it would be impossible for me to accept a paid position."

"I see nothing of the sort. Difficult, certainly. Impossible? No."

"Well, I—" She cleared her throat. "Semantics do not change facts, Mrs Waites."

The cook arched an eyebrow. "The trouble with your class, ma'am, is that they are so concerned with doing what is perceived as right, that they do not consider who set the standard in the first place, nor why."

Charlotte opened her mouth, thought better of it, and closed it again. "I will concede that I have been perhaps a little too honour-bound in my thinking, but I maintain that is no bad thing. However you argue it, you must agree that my duty is to my parents, to protect them from any harm as they have protected me throughout my life." She bit back tears of shame. "They accepted my limitations and did not pressure me to marry, when most other parents thought of little else. I love them dearly, and the thought of being another kind of disappointment to them is more than I can bear."

This was the truth, which she had never shied from, though she had never stated it so boldly before. Mrs Waites came around the table and folded Charlotte into her arms, letting Charlotte drop great rivulets of tears onto the cook's apron.

"There, there," Mrs Waites murmured, and eventually Charlotte quietened, wiping her streaming nose on her sleeve. "My husband is long dead and I'll not meet him again in this life," the cook went on, catching and holding Charlotte's gaze with a new intensity, "but I've been given a second chance at love and I intend to grab it with both hands. Do you know what I would give to have one more moment with my David? If your young lady died tonight, perish the thought, what would you regret? Saying something, or not saying it? What would you do with a second chance?" Mrs Waites clucked in disapproval. "And don't tell me there's nothing you'd do differently. I wasn't born yesterday, ma'am."

The retort died on Charlotte's tongue. She pictured Mary, cold and dead, lying pale against the silken inlay of a casket. Grief bubbled in her chest, threatening to submerge her. "Oh," she gasped, and leaned against the table. Her knees were weak, unable to support her weight. "I do believe I have made a terrible mistake."

"Mistakes can be undone, ma'am. Death cannot be."

Charlotte sank back into the chair and pressed two fingers to her temple, which had begun to throb. "How did you get to be so wise?"

"It's all the salt, ma'am," Mrs Waites said, her lips twitching. "It has preserved my sagacity for many a long year. And while I cannot speak for all families, for some do hold to different values and traditions, I know that if you were my daughter I would want only your health and happiness. Remember I talked of my son, James?"

"Yes, but I do not see what he has to do with—" Charlotte blinked, the memory of their previous conversation seen through an entirely new light. "Wait, are you saying... And his friend whom you spoke of, were they... Oh, good Lord." She buried her face in her hands. "You must have thought me so ignorant of the world."

"A little naivety is not a bad thing, Mrs Collins. Perhaps before you make a hasty decision, you might speak with your family. Ask for their blessing. Surely it is worth a try."

Charlotte blinked. She had never considered this an option. "Do not you think they would disown me?"

"Lord and Lady Lucas? Never," Mrs Waites scoffed. "They are sweet people, and they have raised a sweet daughter. You might think a little higher of them than that. They may not understand, but I am certain that they will at least try to. Look, ma'am, I've found that happiness lives in many places, not just the land of love. It's an old saying worth thinking about. Though if it be the land of love, well...that is not never a bad thing, ma'am, no matter what anyone says."

"Does happiness live in the grocer's shop?" Charlotte muttered, unable to help herself from teasing, and was rewarded with a blush and a splutter.

"Out! Out of my kitchen!" Mrs Waites ordered, though she was laughing, and Charlotte couldn't help a small smile of her own.

In her bedroom, she lay face down on the sheets while hot tears leaked down her cheeks, her chest tight with a deep blue grief that refused to release its stranglehold. She loved Mary, of course she did—that had never been in question. Everything had gone so wrong, so quickly, that Charlotte had acted like a wounded animal in a trap, struggling to get free at any cost. It wasn't as if she actually wanted to go back to Hertfordshire and live as she once had, filling her weeks with dull visits, occasional balls, and the ever-present expectation that she ought to pursue every available bachelor within reach. Quite the opposite, in fact; now that she knew that more options were available to her, it would be nigh impossible to ignore those open doors.

She could never feel about anyone the way she felt about Mary, rendering any marriage no better than a prison sentence. Nor could she spend the rest of her life pottering around in a single garden, knowing she had turned down the chance to work on the most incredible collection she had ever seen, and to spend every day surrounded by more happiness than she had known in all her first thirty years of life combined. If there was a path to joy, its only route lay through the valley of truth. Was she brave enough to journey there? Was the risk worth the reward?

It would have to be, Charlotte decided.

Chapter Twenty-Nine

My dear Maria,

I have long wondered how to answer your last letter. I am surprised that you think so little of my tolerance for difference in others, however, I understand that given to whom I was married, you may have had a particular preconception of my attitude on the subject. In truth, I hardly knew the subject existed, far less that people were open about it. Armed with this new knowledge, it may surprise you, therefore, that I have had similar inclinations all my life.

~~Lately, I have been~~

~~My feelings on the matter~~

I hope this does not change the way you see me or love me. Your answer led me to believe that would not be the case, but even so I cannot help but worry. Having lived so long with these thoughts hidden in the darkness of my heart, it is proving extremely difficult to drag them into the light.

Whatever kindness you can offer will be extremely appreciated. And please do not breathe a word of this to anyone yet.

Your loving sister,

Charlotte

It had taken Charlotte eight attempts to write a letter which managed to both invite her parents to Hunsford and give them enough of an idea why she was asking so that, if they found the idea intolerable, they could all avoid a scene. In the end, she was still not sure she had managed it, but she could do no better; passing the letters to Bessie, she sank back into her chair, exhausted. Regret was a blistering ache which throbbed scarlet in her chest. She ought not to have rejected the idea outright. She ought to have listened to Mary, and made Mary listen to her in turn. *How different things could have been, if I were not so afraid of everything all the time,* she thought, filled with self-loathing. *Cowardly little mouse, always running, always hiding.*

It was time to show her true self, at least a little.

She got up from her chair and wandered into the parlor. The windows had been pushed open, letting the musty air out and replacing it with the fresh scent of flowers, bathed in golden sunshine. Charlotte leaned on the windowsill and breathed deeply, allowing the air to revive her. Even if she managed to get her parents to approve of her new position as head gardener for Mr Mellor—and that was no certain thing—then she could not hope for additional felicity. It would be better, in fact, if she did not mention Mary much at all, and focused on Mr Mellor; no matter how much she desperately missed Mary, or ached to hear her voice again, or yearned to read even a single word which would give her hope that Mary did not loathe her entirely. *It is sensible to take one thing at a time,* she told herself.

And what if she is finished with you entirely? the little voice in her head suggested. *You wounded her deeply. She asked if you loved her and you did not even answer. No wonder she threw you out. What makes you think she would ever take you back, even as a friend?*

Charlotte had no answer for that. All she could do was wait and worry and weep.

Anne de Bourgh sent a breakfast invitation over from Rosings around six on the clock, despite the fact that Charlotte had only returned that afternoon. The very last thing she wanted was to spend time with company who would want some account of her time in Canterbury, as well as details of her future plans, but one did not simply turn down a de Bourgh. "Tell your mistress I will gladly come tomorrow," she said to the footman, who bowed and trotted away down the garden path. "How on earth does she know these things?" she muttered, and closed the door.

Bessie returned to the parsonage around five to assist with dinner. At Mrs Waites' request, the maid had also brought boxes with which Charlotte could begin packing up her possessions. It was a thoughtful and practical gesture, though Charlotte wished she did not have the reminder of her departure. She wanted to be alone, to sit in her garden and soak up all that had once been before she had to deal with everything that would come afterwards. Change was a complicated thing; one could not live in a constant state of tumult, but needed time to adjust to every new stage of life. She had barely become a widow before Mary's arrival, and then she'd had something entirely new to occupy her. Vowing to pack at a later date, she spent the rest of the day sitting in the garden, doing nothing more taxing than watching the flowers and letting her tears wet the grass where they fell.

Charlotte awoke the next morning, still exhausted, still prone to spontaneous fits of weeping. She washed and dressed in black, remembering the beautiful blue dress that Mary had bought for her, and which she would now never see again. *Might Mary wear it herself?* she wondered. *Might she have it tailored to fit some new woman, who would be less of a coward?* The awful thought plagued her all morning, and lingered while she walked over to Rosings. The short journey seemed longer than usual, and Charlotte found it hard to take comfort in the beauty of her surroundings. Not even wild daisies growing in the lane gave her the usual frisson of pleasure, nor the pretty flower-beds in full bloom. The world still turned, still rolled headlong into summer, no matter how much she wished it to stop spinning.

Anne de Bourgh greeted her with more joy than Charlotte had expected, and she did her best to match her host's exuberance. "I am so glad you are back," said Anne, beaming as she led Charlotte into the sunroom, where a lovely spread had been laid on the low table. A silver teapot steamed next to a pile of scones, jams, and an inviting array of biscuits. "Mr Innes is away on business, but he mentioned to me that he would be back in town in three or four weeks. I do think he has designs on you, my dear Mrs Collins. What say you to that?"

She hadn't even sat down and already she was being plagued with talk of marriage. It would never end, unless she put a stop to it in a manner which brooked no argument. "Miss de Bourgh," said she, choosing her words very carefully, while the footman poured their tea. Bergamot drifted through the air, undercutting the fresh smell of the scones and the tart scent of the strawberry jam. "Please know that I am exceedingly grateful to you and your mother for all the great kindnesses you bestowed upon me and my late husband. But I must confess to you that it would be impossible for me to marry again. I simply cannot."

"Cannot?" cried Anne. "Whyever not?"

It was one thing to admit her desires to her sister, a trusted confidante, and quite another to even hint at them to Anne. Charlotte sighed. Some white lies were necessary to preserve her standing in society, and if a single carefully chosen lie snipped the rope of marriage from winding its way around her neck again, then snip she must. "You see, I was so very fond of my husband. I wish to keep the memories of Mr Collins fresh in my mind. He was—" she clasped her hands together, hoping that God would not strike her down for such a weaselly sentiment, even if it was technically the truth "—the only man for me."

"Oh!" Anne's eyes filled with tears. "How romantic! Why, Mrs Collins, I had not known your river ran so deep. I ought to have noticed it sooner." She spread a scone with clotted cream and jam, then studied Charlotte, frowning. "But you did like Mr Innes, did you not? He liked you very well indeed."

"He is a fine gentleman," Charlotte admitted. "Everything one might hope for in a match. But even so, I could never bring myself to marry him. I don't suppose that will make a great deal of sense to other people, but..."

Anne picked her cup up and sipped. She made a face, evidently finding it still too hot to drink. "Perhaps you forget that my mother never remarried."

"Oh." Charlotte's eyes widened. She had indeed forgotten. "Yes, of course."

"Indeed. Other people thought that my father took a great risk, leaving it all to my mother." Anne stared down into her teacup. "They told him she would likely marry again, for whoever heard of such a lady remaining unwed with so great an estate? And yet, he knew her better than anyone in the world. I cannot say what passed between them, for it was so private, but it was love and what's more, it was respect. Though my mother can be overbearing at times, she believes in standing by one's beliefs, even if others may try to sway you from it with their expectations of what a lady ought to do. The only thing a lady ought to do, in her opinion, is fix her eye upon her intended target, and take it. If you do not wish to marry again, Mrs Collins, then let no one persuade you otherwise."

They passed the remainder of the time together discussing all the gossip Charlotte had missed while she was gone, and when she returned home from Rosings, her footsteps were a little lighter. One barrier was removed, but it remained to be seen whether the second obstacle would be quite as easy.

Chapter Thirty

Dearest daughter,
By the time you receive this letter, we will be on our way and
should arrive on Thursday morn.
It is so unfortunate that we cannot accommodate your brother's
whims nor his children; so, so unfortunate.
Life is full of little prisons and little escapes, is it not?
With fondest regards,
Mama and Papa

The letter was short, revealing nothing of their mood or intentions, though it was signed in the usual way with love. Attempting to decode it for hidden meanings revealed none, bar their usual mild humour, and only served to increase Charlotte's anxiety, so she threw herself into preparations for their arrival in a desperate attempt to distract herself. Mrs Waites permitted Charlotte to hover around the kitchen, tasting dishes and putting together a menu—usually, this was the cook's domain and Charlotte would never dare interfere, but she suspected that Mrs Waites was being extra patient with her and took full advantage. Bessie scrubbed every surface until it gleamed, and polished the silverware until the dining room looked like the treasure trove of an ancient king. Charlotte put together a wreath for the table; white, delicate lily of the valley for *humility*, blazing blue azalea for *temperance*, and regal, poised magnolia, for *the love of nature*. She almost added thistles, for defiance, but the memory of the thistle embroidery on Mary's dress stopped her short. Besides, she did not know yet whether she would need to be defiant or not.

Lord and Lady Lucas arrived in short order, and though they spent the first hour in the parlor watching Charlotte with worried eyes, as any parents might with a recently-widowed child, their anxiety lessened with every minute until they seemed quite comfortable. "I admit I was a little concerned when you did not want to come home immediately," her mother admitted, "but everyone grieves in their own way. I thought perhaps you felt most comfortable here in the home you shared with Mr Collins."

"Yes, I did," Charlotte confirmed. "But I also visited Canterbury for a couple of weeks with Miss Mary Bennet. I only returned a few days ago."

"Miss Mary Bennet?" her father repeated, looking slightly puzzled. "Why, I thought Miss Elizabeth Bennet—I mean, Mrs Darcy—was your particular friend."

Charlotte told them about Lizzie's son, assuring them that the illness wasn't serious, and how this had resulted in Mary visiting instead. She was thankfully saved from having to explain more about Mary—which she did not think she could do without breaking down into tears again—by Bessie's appearance in the doorway, announcing that dinner was ready. Mrs Waites cooked a wonderful dinner for her parents—a starter of Scotch broth, a roast chicken surrounded by honeyed carrots and parsnips for the main, and a slice of her infamous rum cake for dessert, liberally covered with thick cream. All the dishes were praised to the highest degree, and Charlotte sent a silent prayer of thanks towards the kitchen, for those with full bellies were more inclined to be agreeable.

"Now," her mother said, fixing her with a stern eye, "perhaps you'll tell us why you invited us here. Your letter made it plain that there was something afoot, though I could not tell what, and you have been careful not to mention it."

"Well," said Charlotte, laying down her spoon. She swallowed. "The thing is... I have been offered a position."

Lord Lucas paused, his spoon halfway to his mouth. "What do you mean?"

"In Canterbury I was introduced to a wonderful gentleman called Mr Mellor, who has the finest collection of flowers in all of England. He has won many prizes for them, and..." *Do not ramble*, she reminded herself. *Keep to the point.* "After he discovered that I am very fond of my own garden, he invited us to view the collection." She bit back the bitter memory of Mary confessing her love under an oak tree, kissing Charlotte like her whole heart was in it. "It was everything I expected it to be and more."

Lady Lucas raised an eyebrow. "And the position?"

"Well, I came up with a successful solution for an insect problem, which none of his gardeners had managed to solve." She took a deep breath. This was it. "And so he offered me a job. As head gardener."

A look passed between Lord Lucas and his wife that Charlotte could not decipher. "What sort of a gentleman is he?" her father asked, his tone measured.

"Oh, he is most agreeable, I am sure you would like him very much. The estate is very large, and he has no wife or living family, though Mr Mellor is too, uh," she licked her lips, "busy to consider producing an heir at this time. I would not call him lonely, though. He loves flowers, just as I do."

Lady Lucas chewed her mouthful before responding. "I have

heard the name before. You say he has won several competitions for his flowers?"

"Yes, Mama. Many years running."

"And you want to...work for a living?" her father added, looking politely bewildered.

"Yes."

"Well, I—" He caught his wife's eye, and again something passed between them. "You have always been a sensible woman, Charlotte, and you have never asked us for anything. If this is something you want, then we shall try to support it. Though I do not like the idea of you living somewhere with a man we have never met. Is he... Is he..."

"What your father is trying to ask," Lady Lucas interrupted, "is whether the man intends you to be his wife. Sometimes men, even elderly men, lure a young lady in with a promise of—"

Charlotte could not help snorting. "No, Mama. He is an established bachelor with no interest in me beyond my ability to maintain his flower-beds. I am quite certain of it. Look." She leaned forward, using her most earnest tone. "It took me seven-and-twenty years to find a first husband, and I am not likely to find another any sooner. I do not wish to be a burden on you both, nor do I wish to be a burden on John when he inherits Lucas Lodge. This way, I may save my money and have a little independence. It is a radical notion, to be sure," she added hastily, "but a sound one considering my circumstances."

Lord Lucas shrugged and reached for his wine. "I would not be opposed, though I find it strange. What say you, my dear?"

Lady Lucas studied Charlotte. "You are quite sure this is what you want? You would not mind doing labour?"

"I worked in our gardens all the time at home," Charlotte reminded her. "I have always been happiest around flowers."

"Well... I would like to meet this Mr Mellor first," her

mother said. "Upon that condition, I may give my approval of the scheme."

Charlotte blinked. She had been expecting much more of a fight. Surely it could not be this easy. "You do?"

"You put forth a persuasive argument." Her father smiled. "We would love to have you at home, of course, and had expected that—but no matter. I must say I never expected you to go this particular route. Still, if it makes you happy, then who are we to stand in your way?"

"What will you tell people?" This was what Charlotte had been most afraid of, and the point she was sure her parents had forgotten. "What if word gets around?"

"People will gossip. People always do. But sooner or later they will begin talking of something else." Her father smiled, loading his spoon with another large chunk of rum cake. "Do not worry so about other people, Charlotte. It is what you want that signifies."

She could not stop the tears, though this time, they were tears of happiness and relief. Her parents got up and hugged her tightly, one on each side, encasing her in the warmth and comfort that she had feared might be lost to her forever.

After some discussion, Lady Lucas agreed to travel on to Canterbury with Charlotte, while her father would journey back to Meryton after he had, in his own words, "sampled the entirety of your Mrs Waites' wonderful cooking."

"That being said," Lady Lucas glanced at Charlotte, "I would like us to be able to enjoy a few days together as a family first, especially since you may not be returning home with us after all."

Charlotte agreed readily, and after she had dashed off a letter to Mr Mellor, the next few days were very happy ones. Her parents provided a wonderful distraction during the day, which was exactly what she needed to keep her mind off Mary, though at night grief and anxiety wound into a heavy ball which lay in the pit of her stomach. She never would have considered the job offer were it not for Mary, but Mary was not the only reason she wanted to accept it. Charlotte's words to her parents had been spoken from the heart, though they hadn't been an impassioned plea so much as a practical suggestion. All the things Mary had pointed out during their last dreadful conversation had been perfectly true, though Charlotte had been unwilling to admit it in the heat of the moment, and they formed the basis for her new goal.

Soon enough Charlotte and her mother were kissing Lord Lucas goodbye and promising to write all their news immediately. Lady Lucas had written to a family friend, who had offered a place for them to stay in Canterbury—though it was, Charlotte was glad to hear, far away from Mary's home. She did not want to see her former lover until she had quite worked out what to say. Far better to put it in a letter where her words could be neat, ordered, and rational. Besides, she had to focus on the meeting with Mr Mellor first, for if that did not go well, then the rest of her plans would crumble to dust.

Returning to Canterbury felt rather overwhelming. She could hardly sit still in the coach, wondering if every woman on the street was Mary, her heart jumping with dread and hope every time she saw dark hair snaking out from under a bonnet. Upon arrival at the Palmer-Parkers', Charlotte discovered that Mr Mellor had already written with an enthusiastic invitation to come whenever they pleased, and she wrote back to set a date for two days hence. Now that they were in town, all her attempts to write a heartfelt letter to Mary proved worse than the last, and she was forced to give up lest her nerves consume her entirely. The Palmer-Parkers—a wife, a husband, and two young sons—were perfectly lovely and almost always out on social calls, which suited Charlotte and Lady Lucas very well. Mother and daughter took advantage of their freedom to indulge in a performance of Bach by a talented string quartet, and did a little shopping in the town proper, though Mary was never far from Charlotte's thoughts.

On the carriage ride to Amberhurst, Charlotte was plagued by memories of her first journey there, of hearing birdsong in the trees while Mary's warm fingers pressed her own. She talked rather a little too much to make up for it, and pressed her mother for even the slightest detail of Meryton gossip which had not already been picked over like a carcass left in the sun.

She watched her mother's face carefully as the carriage rumbled up the driveway of Amberhurst, and when the house came into view, Lady Lucas looked suitably impressed. Mr Mellor was waiting for them on the front steps, wearing a red tailcoat that made him look like a particular rotund, merry robin, and was effusive in his delight. He was proud but not vain about his estate, charming without being obsequious. The tour through the house itself was a little more extensive than on Charlotte's previous visit, and the waterfall, the house, the glasshouses were all admired and praised to the highest degree.

Over an extravagant lunch, Mr Mellor told the story of Charlotte's detective work, while she modestly chimed in here and there. By the end of the tale, Lady Lucas looked agog.

"Well, Mama?" Charlotte said. "What say you?"

"I think I would quite like to live at Amberhurst myself," Lady Lucas said, smiling fondly at her eldest daughter. "I see precisely what appeals to you, and I believe you would be happy here. I must say, I had no idea you had such an aptitude for solving mysteries."

"Neither did I." Charlotte blushed. "Though I suspect I could only do so if they were plant related."

"I'm more than happy to have my lawyer draft some kind of agreement, Lady Lucas," Mr Mellor suggested, "if that would make your family feel more secure. Mrs Collins will have every comfort money can buy, and all I ask in return is her care and dedication to the flowers which I adore with all my heart."

"And—" Lady Lucas leaned forward. "I hope the question is not a forward one, but…what if you should marry? A wife might not like your female gardener."

"Marriage is not to my taste, I'm afraid," Mr Mellor said. "I'm certain I wouldn't like it one whit. And at my time of life, I am quite content to live as I am."

A well-muscled footman trotted by, and Mr Mellor's eyes followed him. Lady Lucas raised an eyebrow. Charlotte braced herself for some sort of outburst, but her mother only smiled. "Then I believe the matter is settled."

Charlotte breathed a sigh of relief. She had been prepared to accept regardless, but hearing that her parents approved— nay, supported the idea—was a great weight off her shoulders.

Chapter Thirty-One

Dear Mary,
~~I am so sorry.~~
~~Cannot you understand what a predicament~~
~~I must apologise heartily for my~~
~~I know you did not understand my reasoning, but I felt obliged to~~
I miss you.
Charlotte

Now that one obstacle was out of the way, Charlotte knew she'd have to face the much more complicated matter of how to address Mary. Writing countless letters hadn't provided the clear answers she required, so she was finally forced to acknowledge that she ought to visit. If she could only persuade Mary to give her a moment, a single chance to apologise from the bottom of her heart, perhaps she could begin to undo some of the damage she had wrought previously.

That morning, Lady Lucas decided to pay a call to another family friend who lived around the corner, but Charlotte begged off, claiming a mild headache. After her mother had left the house on foot, Charlotte slipped out and used the Palmer-Parkers' carriage to travel across town to Mary's house.

It took her a long moment to pluck up the courage even to step out of the carriage and walk up the steps, and longer still to knock on the door.

Pitt answered, and his face told everything Charlotte had been afraid of. "Good morning, Mrs Collins," he said, stiffly, not moving to let her inside. "May I help you?"

"Who's that, Pitt?" a woman called.

Charlotte froze. Had Mary moved on so soon?

"It is a—" his lip curled with distaste "—a friend of Miss Bennet's, Mrs Langley."

Charlotte had entirely forgotten that Aunt Cecily was supposed to be returning home. "Oh, I—"

"Let me see." Aunt Cecily appeared in the doorway, and Pitt moved aside. She was dressed in a simple ivory gown, trimmed with ivory lace, the buttons polished to such a shine that Charlotte could see twenty tiny versions of herself reflected in them; each one looked terrified.

"Pardon me. I ought not to have come," Charlotte said, backing away hastily.

"No, don't think you're getting away so easily. Come in, girl, and let me have a look at you," Aunt Cecily commanded. Charlotte had no choice but to obey, her mouth dry. In the foyer, a tall man and a red-haired woman hovered outside the door to the drawing room—this must be her husband, George, and their lover, Edith.

"Hmm," Aunt Cecily added, eyeing Charlotte with disdain. "So you're the chit who's broken my Mary's heart."

"Um..." said Charlotte, wishing she were dead.

"Cecily," Edith scolded.

Mr Langley rolled his eyes. "And they tell me that the English are well-mannered."

"When we mean to be, certainly. And when we intend to get our point across, I believe we're as blunt as the French. You'll stay for tea."

"Oh I really couldn't—" Charlotte began, but Cecily had already swept into the drawing room.

She followed, feeling only slightly better after Edith and Mr Langley shot her sympathetic glances.

Pitt served tea with his usual civility, though Charlotte had the distinct impression that he would very much like to pour the contents of the pot over her head. Cecily lounged on the couch, Mr Langley beside her, while Edith wandered about the room, apparently unable to sit still. Charlotte sat opposite, twitching. She had made love in this very room, on this very couch. She had found joy in this house and lost it here too. Tears prickled her eyes but she focused on the cup in front of her, determined not to weep.

"So?" Cecily asked. "What have you to say for yourself? It is an audacious move indeed to turn up here after what you did."

"I never meant to hurt her."

"If that is true, then why did you? And why have you not written since?"

"She threw me out," Charlotte pointed out. "And I tried, but I... I could not find the words."

"An apology would have been a good start," Cecily snapped.

She deserved that. "Yes, it would have. Though I hardly think I could ever apologise enough. And besides, I could not be sure that anything I wrote would actually be read." The idea of Mary recognising her handwriting, and throwing a letter into the fire without so much as opening it was a painful one. "I came to say that I will be accepting the position Mr Mellor offered me, and will therefore be living at Amberhurst, if Mary would like to visit me there."

"You ought to ask her yourself."

"I was trying to," Charlotte muttered, and for the first time Aunt Cecily's lips twitched in amusement.

"Hmm. Well, far be it from me to interfere. If you should come again this time tomorrow, I believe you will find her here.

Though I cannot say with any certainty that you will find her open to any apology you care to give."

"I understand." Charlotte rose. "Thank you for the tea. It was nice to meet you all." She forced a smile. "I have heard so much about you."

"Before you go—" Cecily gestured to the butler, whose expression had melted into something far less mutinous. "Please fetch the box, Pitt."

Charlotte frowned. *What box?* The question was answered quickly enough when Pitt vanished and returned with a large white box Charlotte immediately recognised as the dress Mary had bought her.

"I believe this is yours," Aunt Cecily said. "No, no—" when Charlotte tried to protest. "I know my niece, and she is not unkind. She wanted you to have it and take it you shall."

"Thank you," she said, and meant it.

Pitt led her back into the foyer, but before he opened the front door, he hesitated. "I cannot pretend to understand what happened, nor is it my place, ma'am. But I do think you ought to finish this," he said, pressing Barton's diary into her hands.

"Oh, I cannot possibly—"

"I strongly suggest that you do, ma'am. We cannot move on from a situation until we accept that things are what they are, not the way we wish them to be." His eyes were bright with unshed tears. "I would give anything to have one more moment with Simon. And if that is not the way you feel about Miss Bennet, then—" He studied her. "Though we both know that it is, do we not?"

Charlotte nodded. "I swear I would not be so foolish a second time."

"I'm glad to hear it." He opened the door and bowed as she exited.

Back in her room at the Parker-Palmers', Charlotte put the box in the wardrobe and closed the door, without so much as a peek. She could have asked Cecily whether Mary had insisted on this gift, or whether it had been a casual suggestion, though she did not think Cecily would have told her which. Instead, she opened Barton's book and began to read the final chapter. Barton was failing, his words becoming more stilted, the sentences less coherent. Still, his mind shone through in glimpses. He wrote of his great love for the natural world, and his sinking feeling that he would never live to see his dear homeland again, nor his beloved P. *In amor speramus*, he had written, and though Charlotte's Latin was rather poor, mainly gleaned from the lectures and readings her late husband had given, even she could understand this sentiment: *in love we trust.*

She got up and paced about the room. That was it, ended. Mr Barton lived no more. And yet…

In love we trust.

Charlotte crossed the room and took the box from the wardrobe. Setting it on the bed, she lifted the lid. There was a drawing of a violet inside, and the words *I know what this means. Do you?* scrawled underneath.

Faithfulness, she thought, a spark of hope igniting in her chest. It was possible that she still had a chance with Mary, if only she could find the right words.

Charlotte sat at the desk and pulled out a fresh sheet of parchment. All the words which had been lodged inside her flowed onto the page in a stream of incoherent thoughts, followed by a trickle of tears which smudged the ink. She wiped her face, blew her nose, and began again. She told Mary everything in her heart; how afraid she'd been, how shamed. How stupid she had been. How in love she had been. How in love she still was. How the thought of never telling Mary exactly how she felt, of never getting a chance to confess her innermost desires, was worse than death. She'd thought she was protecting Mary, that Mary would move on and find someone new, someone better than Charlotte, without all her foibles and anxieties, someone clever and brilliant and beautiful, to match Mary.

And then I had sense knocked into me, several times, she wrote. *I was wrong. I was so wrong. Please forgive me. Please allow me to tell you how deeply I adore you, every day, with every flower that means such a thing. I will lay bouquets at your feet so that they will never touch common ground again.*

She hadn't known she possessed such poetic sensibilities, but the letter hadn't been written to impress; this was her heart, slashed open on the page. She could only hope now that Mary would see it for what it was.

Exhausted, Charlotte leaned back in her chair. The afternoon sunshine had warmed the room, and she felt rather drowsy after expending so much effort on the day. She wandered downstairs to find the house empty of everyone but servants. Uncertain when her mother would return, Charlotte donned her bonnet and set out for a nearby café. A nice cup of tea in a pleasant location would provide a change of pace. The Parker-Palmers were very nice people, and their house was lovely, but what little tea they drank always tasted of soap.

After ordering a pot of tea and rejoicing that it did not smell or taste at all like something one might use in a bathtub, Charlotte sat at a small table adjacent to the window and stared out at the street. Her hands trembled with possibility and terror in equal measures; it might be her heart slashed open on the page, but that was no assurance that it would be enough to appease Mary. She was just wondering whether she ought to rewrite it to add something else, when a blonde woman with sharp cheekbones stepped inside, accompanied by a friend. *Oh no,* Charlotte thought, the moment Mrs Tremaine locked eyes with her.

"Why, Mrs, uh, Chalmers," Mrs Tremaine piped, while her friend moved towards the counter to order. "How lovely to see you."

Charlotte didn't bother to correct her; the name had been

mistaken on purpose. "Mrs Trendley," she said with a broad smile. "How are you?"

Mrs Tremaine's left eye twitched, her smile slipping for a moment. "Whatever are you doing here?"

She stared down at her teapot and cup; the table was otherwise empty. "Writing letters, of course."

"I—" Mrs Tremaine frowned. "Indeed."

Feeling guilty for being so rude, though it was terribly entertaining, Charlotte cast about for something polite to say. "I don't suppose you've seen our mutual friend lately, have you?"

"You're not staying with her?" Mrs Tremaine's eyes narrowed.

Charlotte gritted her teeth. *You must be careful around her,* Mary had said, *for your words will turn into skittering mice and she will be the hawk who catches the least fortunate one.*

"Now that you mention it," Mrs Tremaine added, "I did see her recently in the company of Miss Carlisle, who has recently returned from Austria." She sighed ostentatiously. "Such a dashing figure, Miss Carlisle. There is no one in London as fashionable as she, nor as cultured. What a great pity you have not had the chance to make her acquaintance yet."

Charlotte's stomach dropped through her shoes. "Indeed."

"Have a pleasant day, Mrs Coolidge." Mrs Tremaine smirked, and spun on her heel, joining her friend at the counter where they began to giggle.

Charlotte forced herself to finish the remainder of her tea before leaving in order to prove that Mrs Tremaine had not managed to get under her skin, though of course the blasted woman had done exactly that. She returned to the Palmer-Parkers' to find the family returned, but not her mother. Making an excuse to return to her room, Charlotte read and re-read the letter to Mary. When she was done, she paced the room, eventually halting before the fire. She stared into the flames, her heart aching all over again. Was it unfair to send such a letter? Mary deserved happiness and yet, in return for her love and kindness, Charlotte had broken her heart, had let fear override her decisions. What right had she to ask for another chance? On the other hand, perhaps this was just another wrong turn down a road so already full of them. Even now, the fear of yet another rejection might be pulling on the reins of her soul, guiding her into a future more lonely than the past she had left behind.

She rubbed her eyes, feeling suddenly exhausted. No, she would not send it. Mary deserved better. She took out the letter and held it over the flames, but could not bring herself to drop it. Tears welled up as she tucked it back into her pocket.

It would serve as a constant reminder of all her past mistakes.

Chapter Thirty-Two

After promising that they would write frequently, Charlotte and her mother shared a tearful goodbye. "I am very proud of you, darling," her mother sniffled. "I do not say that enough."

"Oh, Mama, I do not believe I had really done anything to earn it before now."

"Nonsense," Lady Lucas said, and pulled her into another tight embrace. "Now, I shall have to run before I miss my coach. I will arrange to have all your things packed and sent down to Amberhurst at the earliest possible convenience."

After her mother left—carrying a letter of sincerest thanks to Mrs Waites and a promise that Charlotte would visit the very next time she passed through Kent—Mr Mellor's own carriage arrived to collect Charlotte. Upon her arrival at Amberhurst, Mr Mellor showed her a variety of rooms from which she could take her pick. Charlotte selected a pretty room on the south side of the house, which guaranteed the most sunlight, and additionally overlooked the glasshouses and lawn below. "I did not ask about Miss Bennet in front of your mama, of course," said he. "Are you and she…"

Charlotte shook her head.

"Ah. I'm sorry to hear that." He patted her on the shoulder. "The course of true love never did run smooth, eh?"

Though Mr Mellor did his best to make her feel at home, the moment she was left alone Charlotte could not help drifting off frequently into awful daydreams of Mary and Anne Carlisle together. Perhaps Mary's heart had been broken so badly that she had run straight back into the arms of a philanderer; if so, Charlotte blamed herself even more.

Her possessions arrived two days later, and unpacking everything proved a welcome distraction, as did her work in the glasshouse. Under Henry's supervision, Charlotte learned how best to maintain the exotic fruits and plants, for each one required some different kind of attention. At night, she borrowed books from Mr Mellor's library on the subject of hothouse flowers and frequently fell asleep in one of the room's large, winged armchairs. It gave her no small amount of pride to do a good job, to say nothing of the physical exertion of working with her hands all day, which left her too exhausted to dream.

The days passed. The blisters on her hands became hard-won callouses, and she could soon identify every flower by scent alone, as well as recite the soil type and quantity of sun it required to thrive. At last, she felt as if she was contributing something, that she was no longer a burden on anybody, but a free, independent person all her own. The first wage she received was twice as much as she'd expected, but Mr Mellor refused to negotiate down, and laughed off her every attempt.

One morning, while Charlotte pored over a book at the breakfast table and idly spooned porridge into her mouth, Mr Mellor slid a batch of papers across the table. "I had my lawyer draft a new will," said he.

"Oh?" Charlotte flipped the page, wondering whether she might experiment with fertiliser to see whether she could increase the size or speed of blooms. It was entirely possible that—

"I'd like to name you as my heir. What say you?"

Her spoon hit the bowl with a clatter. She stared up at him, her mouth hanging open.

"Come now, do not leave an old man waiting for an answer," said he, his blue eyes crinkled in amusement.

"I do not know what to say, sir," Charlotte gasped, putting a hand to her chest. "Why, you hardly know me."

"That response is precisely why I want you as an heir, Mrs Collins. Anyone more mercenary would have agreed without a single protest." He smiled, genuine affection writ large over his face. "You are a kind soul with a keen mind and an eye for problem solving. I believe you will take excellent care of the estate. And though your heart was recently broken, you have not allowed that grief to shatter your spirit. I have watched you, day after day, toiling away in pursuit of a beautiful bloom with tireless enthusiasm. Besides, you understand that a flower is a temporary thing, do you not? The passage of time can never be slowed or stopped. All things must die eventually, and so shall I. At the very least, I wish to pass knowing that my beloved garden will be in safe hands, not packaged up and sold to the highest bidder, or to some high-born idiot who will tear everything down to make way for his or her latest fancy."

Charlotte took his hand and squeezed it between her own. "I am so grateful, sir, for the opportunity to work in your garden. It is a reward in itself."

"A sweet sentiment, Mrs Collins," said he, smiling, and reaching for the quill. "But a needlessly penurious one."

She could not bear to hear that name anymore. "Please, call me Charlotte."

"Very well, Charlotte. And in turn, you may call me Maxwell. Care to add your name?" He offered her the quill.

She hesitated, feeling as if it were all some fabulous dream, before signing the papers.

"Incidentally, I am attending a ball tomorrow night in Canterbury," Mr Mellor continued, "and I would like you to pick a wide variety of flowers for it. I would also like you to accompany me."

Charlotte hesitated. She couldn't very well say no now, though the absolute last place she wanted to be was at a ball, surrounded by crowds of people.

"I insist," he added. "It will be for your own good, my dear girl, I promise you that."

The following afternoon, Charlotte stood in front of her wardrobe, frowning. The dress Mary had purchased for her still lay in the box, unworn. Her mourning period was not yet over, but she was already sick of black. With an aching heart, she slipped into the dress and buttoned it up, recalling with a pang the tender way that Mary had once taken the garment off her. She sighed. No, she could not possibly wear this dress—not now. Not until she'd spoken to Mary and set things right between them.

A soft knock at the door startled her. "Yes?"

A maid entered, carrying a dress over one arm. "Mr Mellor sends his regards, ma'am, and asks that you wear this tonight."

Charlotte took the dress and stared at it while the maid bobbed a curtsey and scuttled out. At first glance she had thought it black, but in fact it was an extremely dark green silk. Someone had carefully embroidered tiny red tulips around the sleeves and neckline, which made the garment look less foreboding. *A declaration of love,* Charlotte thought, frowning. *But to whom is this declaration made?* With no one to answer, she sighed, and put the dress on. It fit her perfectly, and the effect in the looking-glass was stunning.

"Aha!" Mr Mellor cried, when she descended the stairs. "You look the very picture of beauty, Charlotte."

"I thank you, sir." She blushed. "How did you know my measurements? And why red tulips?"

"I have my secrets," said he, tapping his nose with one finger, "and you have yours. Come now, the carriage awaits!"

★ ★ ★

The ball was an elegant affair indeed, taking place on an estate about half the size of Amberhurst, just outside Canterbury town proper. The sun had only just set, the last orange gasps highlighting the underneath of fluffy clouds. Inside the ball, candles illuminated cheerful countenances as dancers spun to a lively jig. The air was full of floral scents, and when Charlotte saw the flowers she had so carefully picked arranged about the rooms, a thrill of pride warmed her heart. She had just turned to Mr Mellor to say as much, when she caught a glimpse of Delia Highbridge.

Charlotte's heart stuttered. Where Miss Highbridge was, Mary was sure to be. "Excuse me a moment, sir," she said to Mr Mellor, and sidled through the crowd until she was within touching distance of Miss Highbridge. "Good evening."

"Oh! Good evening, Mrs Collins." Her tone was not as frosty as Charlotte had expected, but it definitely held a glacial chill.

"I wondered if you knew where I might find—" Charlotte began.

"Delia." Mary's voice came from behind Charlotte. "Perhaps we might move outside for a moment? It is a little crowded in here."

Charlotte could hardly bear to look at Mary, and the scent of warm violets in the air fairly took her breath away. Realisation struck her. The red tulips on her dress—Mr Mellor's message must be to encourage her to speak her piece. He must have known Mary would be in attendance. She bit her lip. *Now or never.* "May I speak with you for a moment in private, Miss Bennet?"

"I do not think that wise."

Charlotte forced herself to look up. Mary's eyes were red-rimmed, her cheeks pale and gaunt. "Please," she murmured, her voice full of raw need. "Please, let me have a moment of your time."

Mary sighed. "Very well." She led Charlotte into a side passage and into a large room fronted by even larger curtains, which swept the floor regally.

In other circumstances Charlotte would have taken the time to appreciate the scarlet walls, the potted plants in the corner, and the portraits of the hosts above the unlit fireplace, but all distractions must be set aside until her task had been achieved. Even the long tables against the wall, which held a range of her most elegant bouquets intended for the host's luncheon on the following day, could give her no reprieve.

"I cannot imagine what you need to say to me," said Mary, half-closing the door and heading towards the window. Her voice was steady, though her hands were trembling.

Charlotte pulled the letter from her pocket. Mary backed away even further. "Do not worry, I won't read it to you," Charlotte said hastily. "I simply beg a chance to explain why I made such a stupid and terrible mis—"

A man's voice sounded in the corridor outside. "This way, you say? Are you quite sure?" The voice was familiar, but there was no time to think about that now. Charlotte turned, ready to shoo whomever it was out instantly, and came face to face with Mr Innes. *Of all the people*, Charlotte thought in despair. *Poor man, he has the worst timing.*

"Ah, Mrs Collins!" said he, emerging through the doorway. "I thought it was you. I did not expect to see you until my return to Kent, so this is a very pleasant surprise."

"Um," said Charlotte, glancing back over her shoulder. Mary had vanished, though a twitch of the curtain fabric gave her position away. "Good evening, Mr Innes. If you'll give me just a moment, I really need to speak to—"

"Actually, Mrs Collins," he said, and stepped closer, "I have a question to ask, and I hope you will give me a favourable response."

Oh no. This cannot be happening here and now. Charlotte cast about wildly, wondering what she could possibly do to stop this from happening. Mr Innes smiled down at her. He smelled of wood smoke and pine needles; a winter scene, cold but not unpleasant. "I would like to become much better acquainted with you."

"Any friend of the de Bourghs is a friend of mine," she offered blandly, watching his smile fade a little.

"You are most gracious," he said, hesitating. "Yet I must confess I was hoping for a deeper intimacy. Perhaps I could call upon you in Hertfordshire?"

I need to get him out now, before he ruins my last chance with Mary. She pitched her tone carefully. Grateful, but not encouraging. "I am flattered, sir, but you must recall that I am recently widowed."

"Yes, of course." He looked flustered, as if he had not expected such resistance. "I had not thought—but of course. Do you think that you might ever be able to find a place in your heart for me? I am willing to wait as long as need be."

Charlotte took a deep breath and turned slightly towards the window. *Courage, now, if I ever possessed it.* "You did not know my husband, Mr Innes, so allow me to share something with you. He was a clever man and a wonderful speaker, yet he listened to all I had to say. He sought to understand himself, and to find the beauty in the world's darkest places. He was the kind of man who noticed a single lonely flower in a vast meadow of far more beautiful blooms. I—" She flushed, heart hammering. These words were like bricks, obstructing the obvious path of her future, yet at the same time building a new, unexpected road. "Though the time we spent together was comparatively short, I do not think anyone could ever compare to him. I intend to remain loyal for the rest of my life."

A tiny gasp, quickly stifled, came from the general vicinity of the curtains.

"I understand," Mr Innes said, a little flushed himself. "I confess myself disappointed, but the way you talk about him makes me sorry I did not meet him myself. I would have liked to better myself by his example."

"We all may do so." Charlotte smiled, her vision blurry.

He bowed deeply. "Then I shall take my leave. Good day, Mrs Collins."

No sooner had the door closed behind him than Mary appeared, her gloves crushed in clenched fists. She opened her mouth to speak, but Charlotte interrupted. "A wise woman once told me that she preferred to see a flower in full bloom shivering in the breeze, rather than a lifeless bloom pressed in a book."

Mary swallowed. "I did, but—"

"What do you say, darling? Is it time I planted myself outside? Or is the season already past?" A heartbeat of silence passed, their eyes locked on each other, and Mary did not offer a response. Charlotte's heart hammered even faster. "I heard you were lately seen with Miss Carlisle," she added. "I hope you did not—at least I hope that I did not push you to—" She drew a deep breath. "If you assure me that you're happy and that she has changed her deviant ways, then I will gladly step aside."

"Who told you that?" Mary demanded.

"Mrs Tremaine," Charlotte admitted ruefully. "Else I would have come back the next day, like your aunt told me to."

"Your mistake was believing anything that awful woman said." She swallowed. "I told you the truth of what Anne did to me last year, and I thought it would have been evident that I would never agree to partner with her again. She tried to accost me upon her return from Austria, and I told her as much. We were never out together—not like that."

Relief flooded Charlotte. She could never have forgiven herself had she pushed Mary back into the arms of someone who did not care a single fig for fidelity. *Perhaps there is still a chance.* She held up the letter again, and this time Mary did not flinch.

"You cannot imagine how many of these I wrote and did not send, for none of them contained even a tenth of my true feelings. I turned up at your house and your aunt gave me a very hard time indeed, though nowhere near as hard as I deserved. Mary, if I believed that another woman could ever make you happier than I, I would not be here now." She took a deep breath. "And yet I have still not said anything to you worth hearing. I see now that my mistake was trying to use English, when I ought to have been using the language I speak best." She turned her back on Mary, and strode to the longest table. "A red tulip," said she, plucking one, "for I wish you to believe my declaration of love. A handful of forget-me-nots, to represent all the memories we've shared." She added the flowers. Mary's eyes had begun to fill with tears again, and Charlotte's own lip was wobbling. "I would add fern if it were here," her voice quavered, "for all the shelter you gave me, to say nothing of the confidence you instilled in a pathetic wallflower."

"Charlotte—"

"I am not finished," she said, smiling. "I must add violets, for the perfume that bewitched me from the start, and to signify my faithfulness in turn, should you wish it. I was foolish, and I did not see all the opportunities life had gifted me. I am so, so sorry I hurt you. Can you ever forgive me?"

She presented the bouquet and Mary accepted it, her cheeks glistening. "I can," Mary said, her voice wavering. "Could you ever love me?"

Charlotte pressed her forehead against Mary's, her breath ragged. "Darling, I never stopped."

"I told you once that I was yours, indefinitely," said she, "and I meant it."

"I know you did." She sighed. "I am only sorry that I did not start forever sooner."

The bouquet slipped from Mary's grasp as their lips met. The kiss was long and sweet, promising of more to come. The scent of violet drifted through the air, mixing with the smell of apple blossoms. "I prefer you to all others," Charlotte murmured, smiling. "Hmm. I did not include those in my selection for this evening. Was this your doing?"

"No," Mr Mellor said from the doorway, making them both jump in surprise. "It was mine. Though I confess it was prompted by your love of meanings, Charlotte." He turned and threw a backwards glance over his shoulder, grinning. "I'll watch the door while you two young fools sort yourselves out."

Charlotte buried her face in Mary's neck, holding the woman she loved close. "I love you," she breathed. "I have loved you since your knee first touched mine, since you drew me with such exquisiteness, since you went out of your way to find flowers you knew would enchant me. I should have said all this far sooner."

"How I have longed to hear you say those words." Mary's breath caught, her voice hitching, her arms tightening around Charlotte's waist. "I love you too."

Charlotte knew that the path ahead would not be easy, but happiness was never a smooth road. The important thing was that she was finally where she belonged; planted firmly, ready to bloom.

Epilogue

Charlotte dibbled a hole in the warm soil to the depth of two inches, marking the size with her thumb, then dropped a single seed into it. Filling up the hole again, she wetted the soil carefully, and sat back to admire her efforts. It had taken the best part of an hour to seed four rows, and she still had to examine a wilting orchid and oversee the pruning of Mr Mellor's new topiary. Wiping her forehead with the back of her hand, she felt pride bloom in her chest. No matter how hard she worked, or how long the days, the fruits of her labour were there at every turn. The roses had won their usual prizes, and the citrus trees were producing even more luscious bounties than usual. Mr Mellor was delighted with her work, and Charlotte's growing confidence had allowed him to hand over more and more responsibilities.

She exited the hothouse, sighing in relief at the breeze which cooled her sweaty skin, and caught sight of a familiar figure in the distance, sitting at the white table on the terrace. Waving, she trudged up the path and ascended the steps, arriving even sweatier than she had been minutes before. Upon seeing Charlotte, a handsome servant poured a second cup of tea and pulled out her chair.

Mary lowered her teacup, arching an eyebrow. "Hello, darling. Hard at work?"

Charlotte grinned. "Always. Thank you, William."

She was still not quite used to having so much fortune at her disposal, though she had used it to gift her family in small ways—an exquisitely beautiful new dress for her sister Maria and four violins for the remainder of her brother John's children. Two horses, well-muscled and even-tempered, had been sent to her parents as a thank you for all that they had done for her. Mary's gift had taken her more time and thought. "I have something for you," Charlotte announced, nodding to William, who trotted off in search of it.

"What a coincidence, for I have a gift for you too." Mary leaned over and pressed a kiss to Charlotte's damp cheek. "And whenever you have a moment, I'd like to lick every inch of you clean. You may consider that a second present, if you like."

Charlotte swallowed, momentarily speechless, and was saved from having to make any coherent reply by William's return. The servant hovered in the doorway behind Mary, and Charlotte indicated that he should stay there for the moment. "Your gift first, then." She squinted, but Mary was holding no package, nor was there anything on the table or ground around her.

"Henry took it from me when I first arrived," Mary clarified. "I am certain you will love it. They call it a tulip tree."

Charlotte frowned. "A tulip...tree?"

"Indeed. When it has grown, the leaves will be a wonderful, buttery yellow. Once you have eaten something, for they tell me you have had nothing since breakfast, we can visit it. Aunt Cecily said it was quite the sight once mature. Not only has she forgiven you entirely, but I suspect she might actually be rather fond of you. She does not send entire trees back across the Atlantic for just anyone, you know."

"Is that so?" Charlotte's lips twitched. "I am glad indeed. I think I would rather face a thousand furious Lady Catherines than one mildly annoyed Aunt Cecily."

"You are a very sensible woman, Charlotte Lucas. I have always thought so." Mary picked up her teacup again, shooting Charlotte a lascivious look over the rim. Her fine, dark eyes made Charlotte feel as if she were being undressed in the midday sun, which was not an unwelcome idea. "And I bring with me an invitation to a special kind of dance next month, which will be attended only by our sort of people from all classes. It was really Delia's doing, though my idea," said she. "What a lark it will be to have a ball all to ourselves. You must show me those dance steps again, lest I embarrass myself in front of our sistren."

A lark it might be, but Charlotte saw the seriousness of the matter underneath. To have a space to call their own was a rare thing, not easily obtained, and the driving motivation— to bring people together, to connect when so often the shame and secrecy kept people apart—brought tears to her eyes. She reached for Mary's hand and grasped it tightly. "What a wonderful idea."

Mary blinked back her own tears. "Yes, well. Perhaps it will become a regular thing, who knows? Now, you were saying something about a gift?"

Charlotte beckoned William forward. The young man carried the pot to the table and placed it carefully, turning it so that the black petals caught the light. The stem was narrow and pale, the petals themselves rounded with the look, if not the temperament, of a pansy. "This is something Mr Mellor—I mean, Maxwell—lately imported from China. A delicate specimen, though under the right conditions and with a little attention, it will flourish wonderfully. Do you know what it means that it is new to England?"

Mary looked blank before realisation dawned. "Why," cried she, "that means it has no significance yet. It is a blank slate, as yet unlabeled, at least to us. Do you mean to assign some tender desire to it?"

"Ought it be a sweet, coy flower? Or a passionate declaration?"

"Perhaps it could be a message of optimism?" Mary suggested. "Or a desire for change?"

Charlotte nodded, understanding at once. *"Dum spiro spero,"* she murmured. "While I breathe, I hope."

William sidled back into the house while Mary dragged her chair around the table, landing next to Charlotte's, and pulled her close, pressing tender kisses all over her face. "Now that we are happy and settled, perhaps it is time we examine what might be done for others who are less fortunate."

"You know," Charlotte leaned in, feeling her heart flutter in that familiar way, "it is that kind of nobility of spirit which makes me fall in love with you all over again."

Words faded until there was nothing left but the breeze, the sky, and the sweet, faint scent of faithful violets.

★ ★ ★ ★ ★